THE DIVINE THRONE OF MAHARANI MEERAMANI

Meenakshi Verma

Invincible Publishers

First published in India in 2017 by Invincible Publishers

ISBN: 978-93-86148-77-3

The author does not support child marriage, dowry system, caste system and sati system. It has been mentioned in the book in the form of a story, only to explain the complexities of the situation that arise because of the societal demands.

Invincible Publishers

G - 120, Sushant Lok III, Sector 57, Gurgaon-122002

Opposite Kasturba Ashram, Radaur Distt Yamuna Nagar, Haryana- 135133
Digitally Printed at Replika Press Pvt. Ltd.

Dedication

My book is dedicated to all those great human beings, who have the courage to raise their voice against the evil customs and rituals of society.

Contents

Acknowledgment

I am thankful to God, whose devotion made me sensitive and because of which the qualities of writing awakened in me.

I am grateful to the youngest sister of my father, my aunt, Kanta Singh, who gave me full support in writing my book, only because of her I have been able to complete this book within 24 days. She took all my responsibilities on her shoulders so that I could devote maximum time to my book. My aunt has given me selfless love like a mother, which I will never be able to repay. She has been like an elder sister and a best friend to me.

I am an honest daughter of an honest father and I always thank God for that. I always feel proud of my father Shri Raghubir Singh for his gentleness, politeness and soft-hearted personality. The qualities of attachment to literature and social work have reflected in me from my mother, Kamlesh Singh. I grew up like a princess, whose wishes were fulfilled well before they were even spoken off.

I am thankful to my husband Sanjay Verma, who took some time out of his busy schedule and helped me in the publication of my book. He taught me lessons of the bitter truth that life entails and which made me realise about my hidden talents. "Never to give up in life and Never to stop until you attain your goal," I have learnt this too from him.

My only daughter, Devangi, encouraged me and helped me

in achieving my dreams. Though she is a teenager now, but she is very intelligent to handle the situations with her calm and polite nature. I am also grateful for the love of my little niece Shivika.

I am thankful to all those people too, who have always criticized me, and have always taken advantage of my simplicity. If such people had not come in my life, then I probably would never have known the good people.

In the end, I am thankful to all those people whose love, faith, prayer, blessings and cooperation have always been with me.

I'm grateful to Invincible Publishing House and it's owner Ajay Setia. His cooperative and understanding nature has boosted my self-confidence as an upcoming author. He has really worked very hard to make my dream come true. I always thought it was very difficult to publish more than writing a book, but Ajay and his efficient team are a boon for new or upcoming writers.

I am thankful to Cheena and Bhavna for helping me in good translation and editing, and also to Sneha for final designing of my book and logo.

Many thanks for Mr. Shanmugaewel Velu for the beautiful cover page design, he is an awesome painter. Every painting he makes seems to be telling its own story.

Chapter 1:
Jairajgarh: The Grand Empire of Rajputana

The dawn set on "Jairajgarh", the grand empire of Rajputana, with loud drumming sound. People started coming out of their houses while trying to listen to the announcement, wondering what is it that the Maharana wants to proclaim this early in the morning and what is the message he has sent.

The moment the royal messengers of the king saw the residents of Jairajgarh coming closer, they signaled the drummers to stop drumming and began reciting the message of the king – "Listen! Listen! Listen! All the residents of Jairajgarh, our king, Maharana Ranjeet Dev Pratap Singh, has commanded us that all the residents of Jairajgarh be informed that the Maharana will set out for his victory parade at the crack of the dawn tomorrow. The people of Jairajgarh are hereby alerted that they should remain ready to deal with the emergency war-like situation. Having made the announcement, the messenger signaled the drummer to restart drumming, so that those who didn't hear could come and listen to the message.

The news cast a gloom over the whole Jairajgarh empire. People started talking amongst each other after listening to the announcement.

"O! One more war!," said a local.

"The good times had just set in and we had got some time to spend with our families. Now, once again we will have to burn ourselves in the war zone," said the other.

"But, it is only recently that the Maharana had announced that he desires some rest now and there shall be no war. Then, what happened now?" another wondered.

"Why does the Maharana want another war?" asked another local, "He has already conquered most of the parts of the Rajputana, and the ones that are left belong to either his family or friends. So, now who does he want to outfight in the war?"

"O brother!" added an old man, "Just one of these days, a rumor was making the rounds that the festivities around the marriage of the prince, Samar Dev, would begin soon and, now, we hear that the Maharana is getting set to take out the army for war."

"Uncle, Maharana has restrained from war for a long time now and he must be getting bored. So, instead of commanding to take out the procession for marriage, he is commanding the warriors to take out the procession for war," said a middle-aged man.

"After Maharani Meeramani Devi had claimed the 'Maharani throne', there were many religious activities happening in the state; we thought this would imply prevailing of happiness and peace," added an elderly woman, "But the affinity for war in Maharana seems to be reigniting now."

"You are right, Aunty!" spoke another dweller, "Maharani Meeramani Devi is, indeed, an avatar of Goddess. She has brought up prince Samar Dev with all her heart and soul. Just wait and see, prince Samar Dev will not be as harsh as our Maharana; he anyway talks about peace."

"Didn't you see, during his swearing-in ceremony for the post of Prince, Maharani Meeramani had urged him to take an additional oath that his sword will only rise to establish peace. He will only engage in a war to protect his empire, not to satiate his desire for wars," stated another local.

"You're right!" added one more person, "But I don't think our Maharana liked this thing coming from Maharani Meeramani. That's why he had commanded our Maharani that all the oaths taken by prince Samar Dev will be strictly as per the customs of Jairajgarh and not as per the beliefs of Maharani Meeramani Devi."

"That is true," everyone responded in chorus.

"Alright, brothers, let us go to our houses. We have to set out for the war zone tomorrow. Nobody knows when we will be able to spend time with our families next," sighed a person while dispersing.

"Nobody can say when we will be able to meet each other," spoke another while moving away, "After all, who can predict what's written in the destiny. Let's caress our children a little more."

"And let us also seek blessings from our ageing parents. Nobody can say if we will return from the war zone or not," expressed a young person from the crowd.

In this way, everyone walked back to their homes while exchanging their thoughts.

Jairajgarh was an extremely powerful and prosperous grand empire in the whole Rajputana. It was blessed by the best of the nature's blessings. Half of the security of the state was being taken care of by the nature.

On one side of the state, Jairajgarh, there were gigantic hills of smooth rocks. The rocks were so slippery that nobody could set his foot on them. If anyone tried to climb the hills, he would either slip to his death or would injure himself very badly. Therefore, the risk of any animal or enemy encroaching from here was minimal. This first border of the state was completely secured.

The second frontier of Jairajgarh was a dense forest beginning from the foothills. The forest was so dense that there was no trace of sunlight. It would feel as dark as night. The forest was inhabited by deadly animals. The forest was terrorized by the attacks of lions and cheetahs that any person would think twice before going there even during the daytime. However, only the family and friends of the royal family of Jairajgarh would visit the forest for hunting. After some 5-10 kilometers from beginning of the forests, were the private camps of the royal family which were completely fenced by thorn bushes. After the bushes, there was a very deep trench. If at all any animal was able to make through the thorns, he would die of falling in the trench. The greenery of Jairajgarh could well give way to cold breeze, but never to its enemy.

The third boundary was right behind the royal palace. There was a lake, "Sapta-Sangama". It was called so because seven lakes would meet here. It is in this lake that the members of the royal family would enjoy boating. Due to the dense forests and the lake, the palace was always replete with pure and cold breeze. The starting point of these lakes was somewhere in the forest, but it was not possible to locate it due to inaccessibility of the forests. Nobody till now has been able to return from the forest once entered. That's why the princes and the kings of Jairajgarh used to hunt only close to their camps.

The fourth way to reach Jairajgarh was a rocky way, which was used by everyone to make an entry to the state. That is the reason why a major segment of the army used to remain at this border because all other ways were well secured by the nature.

The weather here was very cold during winters and very hot during summers and because it was surrounded by forests and lake, it used to rain a lot during monsoons. In totality, Jairajgarh was a very prosperous and happy state.

The family deity of Jairajgarh was Chandika Devi, who had slaughtered Mahishasur, and had eight arms and was bejeweled with the arms and ammunition. Although, there were several temples of the goddess in the kingdom, but the biggest was behind the palace, at the banks of the lake, Sapta-Sangama, where only the members from the royal family could worship. It was a custom to offer only coconuts and red scarves, but the heads of some dangerous enemies, who were defeated and killed in wars, were also offered in the holy feet of the goddess. However, sacrificing was barred in the temple now.

Only the king and the Maharani could use the chariots or buggies pulled by 8 horses. Besides, only both of them could use any elephant for a ride. The prince, other queens and the rest of the members of the royal family used to ride on chariots or buggies pulled by 6 horses. The important ministers, like the chief ministers, the chief of the army and other prominent members of the court used chariots or buggies pulled by 4 horses. Apart from this, based on the positions in the army, the various rides available were chariots pulled by 2 horses, soldiers riding single horse and the walking army.

The king of Jairajgarh was called as "Maharana". Only the queen who would give birth to a son first would claim the title of "Maharani" or the "Empress". The first son of the Maharana would claim the royal throne and his mother would get all the rights of an empress.

There was a Maharani court inside the royal court, where the Maharani would sit inside the veils and would solve the problems related to women. The Maharani was supposed to solve issues or crimes with women involved in them. Although, the Maharani had the last word in the decisions, but only the king could intervene any time. The mother of the second son of the king, or any queen especially preferred by him, used to play the role of the prime minister in the Maharani court and took charge of all the responsibilities of the Maharani in her absence. It was mandatory for every queen of Maharana to contribute in the royal tasks.

The queens of Jairajgarh were well-read in Vedas and were also familiar with politics. If at all the king would marry any uneducated girl, he would make her stay with the learned female gurus, so that she could seek knowledge. All queens would stay in veil, but also ride horses. All this was a part of the royal work and all these rules were brought into practice for one reason that if a king loses to death in a war, the queens are capable enough to train the prince to be able to claim the throne and be a worthy emperor.

There was a custom prevalent in Jairajgarh, named Jauhar. There was a separate rule that on account of the death of Maharana, only the Maharani was safe of the tradition of Jauhar, and all the rest of the queens would mandatorily follow this custom. That was another reason why there was a serious competition amongst all the queens to become a Maharani and all the queens desired to deliver the first boy of the king, so that they could lead a respectable life.

The current emperor of the great grand empire Jairajgarh is Maharana Ranjeet Dev Pratap Singh, who is the eldest son of the previous Maharana, Surya Dev Pratap Singh, and is aged above 50 years. Although, the king had three wives, only two remain now as his first wife, Queen Vaishali, had died of drowning in the lake, Sapta-Sangama. He had no children with his first queen. The second wife, Queen Ambika, was three-four years younger to King Ranjeet and had a love marriage with him. The king has 17-year old son, Samar Dev, with Queen Ambika. Samar Dev is also the current prince of the empire. The third wife, Queen Meeramani, is although half the age of Maharana, but is so beautiful and intelligent that the Maharana can't help, but surrender in front of her. This is the reason why despite having not bore the first son of the king, she is still the Maharani of the empire. With Maharani Meeramani, Maharaja Ranjeet Singh has twin kids - a prince, Rudra Dev Pratap Singh, and a princess, Amritamani, - who are around 11 years old. There is zero animosity of being co-wives between Queen Ambika and Maharani Meeramani, and Maharana Ranjeet Singh loathed this.

Chapter 2:
The Death News of Prince Samar Dev Pratap Singh

The current emperor, Maharana Ranjeet Dev Pratap Singh, was walking anxiously in the palace of the grand empire, Jairajgarh. He had commanded the army chief, Akroor Singh, and, now, nobody could prevent the murder as the army chief always delivered as directed. He had promised to the Maharana that if ever he fails to deliver on his promise to Maharana, he would decapitate himself on his own. That's why the only person who Maharana Ranjeet Pratap Singh used to trust completely was the army chief, Akroor Singh. Even in the war zone, no enemy could reach the Maharana in the presence of Akroor Singh. There have been a lot of wars in which Akroor Singh had risked his life in order to save the life of the king and a lot of wars which the king had won not because of his politics, but because of Akroor Singh's power. Akroor Singh is not only the army chief, but also his best friend.

Nobody could solve the labyrinth laid down by the army chief, Akroor Singh. In the war zone, he would lay down such a labyrinth around the king that nobody would be able to reach anywhere close to him. Each warrior of the squads of the Akroor Singh's army could well handle ten warriors from the enemy's side. They were all adept in sword art, throwing spears or using disc weapon and that's the reason why Maharana Ranjeet Dev Pratap

Singh had to never face defeat in wars. He was so addicted to winning in every field, be it war zone or relationships; his politics used to work in each sphere. He didn't like objections or protests against his decisions. It was only his third wife, Meeramani, who used to fight and get her say approved. The Maharana also used to forgive her, considering her young age and her intellect, which was always a matter of awe for him.

The next day at the break of the dawn, Maharana sought good wishes from both his wives, the eldest, Queen Ambika, and the youngest, Maharani Meeramani, by getting *tilak* (paste of sandalwood) smeared on his forehead.

Queen Ambika asked him, "Maharana *ji*! Have you sent Prince Samar somewhere; he is nowhere to be seen since yesterday?"

The king became *ji*ttery having faced such an unexpected question; upon thinking something, he said, "The night before the last, I got informed that some enemies have encroached our forests; so, I had immediately sent him to have a war with them."

"What?" the eldest, Queen Ambika, widely opened her kohled eyes while expressing her shock. She said, "You sent that child for his first war and you didn't even bother to inform us!" the anger now clearly reflecting on her clear complexion.

"We don't feel it is important to keep you cognizant of the secret government tasks," retorted Maharana, while ignoring her wrath.

"What did you say? You don't feel it is important to inform us!" tears now rolling down her cheeks, she continued, "He is our son, Maharana *ji* and I am his mother; you don't feel it's important for a mother to know the whereabouts of her son. To this date, you need to get *tilak* (paste of sandalwood) smeared on your forehead in order to seek good wishes from us before you set out for any war, but our son went for his first war and you didn't feel it was important for his mother to bless him by singing *aarti (prayers)* for him or wishing him good luck by smearing *tilak*? What was the hurry that you snatched this right from us and from him?"

"Ambika!" the Maharana roared, "Stop whining! You've *ji*nxed the air right before my departure for the war. Foolish woman! the Maharana yelled, "If you feel troubled by giving us your good wishes for any war, then there's no need for this sham." Having said this, he snatched the *aarti (prayers)* tray from Ambika's hands and threw it aside.

"We win wars because of our courage and power, not because of the religious activities you do. Worshipping God day and night doesn't make him descend to Earth to help us win wars," Maharana turned a blind eye towards Maharani Meeramani while saying the last sentence as he knew that she is an ardent follower of Lord Shiva and she believed that nothing happens without his consent. She used to worship Lord for every small or big thing happening in life and used to completely trust him and her devotion.

Maharana stopped and turned around to ask Meeramani, "Didn't he meet you before leaving?"

Maharani Meeramani raised her voice to question him back, "When it was your command that he doesn't meet anyone before leaving, then who here has the audacity to disobey you?"

"Hmm," Maharana hummed loudly and asked Meeramani, "Where is our son, prince Rudradev?"

"He's sleeping in his room," Meeramani replied blatantly, "Do you want to meet him as well before leaving?"

"No, it's OK," Maharana now lowered his voice while speaking, "Just take care of him. He is a precious possession of our empire. What about our daughter, princess Amritamani?"

"She is also sleeping in Ambika *jiji's* (elder sister) room," Meeramani maintained a callous tone, "Anything else?"

"Why are you talking to me like this? Have I said anything to you to deserve such a treatment from you?" Maharana Ranjeet asked softly.

"Leave it, Maharana *ji*. You won't understand all this. You just prepare yourself for the war; aren't you getting late now?" Meeramani answered bluntly.

Maharana Ranjeet became sad. The more he wanted to love Meeramani, the more she used to ridicule him. This used to hurt him.

"Oh! No matter how I talk to people, in which tone I converse, I don't know how Meeramani gets affected by it. I always talk sweetly with her, but she always irks me by talking harshly,"

Maharana was questioning himself, "What is it that I have not given to Meeramani. She has not even given the first son to the empire; even then I made her sit on the Maharani's throne. I haven't loved any female more than I love her. There was no temple of Lord Shiva in our empire, yet I built one for her happiness's sake. I have lived on all my promises, but she doesn't understand my love." Ranjeet Singh blabbered, "I don't know what example these co-wives want to set in the world by loving each other like sisters. Let them go to hell; these women anyway don't have brains. They anyway take love for granted." Maharana Ranjeet exited while looking back on his soliloquy.

After his exit, Ambika said to Meeramani, "Did you see, Meera? How Maharana *ji* is expressing his anger. He's angry all the time. He doesn't leave any chance of offending anyone and we've been getting offended by him all our lives. Why did he marry us if we are such big fools? We didn't take any marriage proposition to him; it was he who came to us. He doesn't have any respect for females; instead, they are only objects of pleasure for him. Re! Where was I wrong? He sent such a young child for war and didn't feel it was important to inform his mother. Did he inform you about this?" Queen Ambika asked while wiping her tears.

"No, Ambika *jiji*, he didn't inform me, too. He's anyway keeping a lot of secrets from me these days," replied Meeramani.

"O Lord!" Queen Ambika prayed with folded hands, "My child is only 17 years old; please protect him."

"Let it be Ambika *jiji*, don't worry too much. Lord Shiva will do good to all. Don't think too much about Maharana *ji*'s words. You know he doesn't approve of straightforwardness. Everyone has to face the consequences of their evil deeds; his time is also not that far," Meeramani smiled slightly while concluding.

Queen Ambika also couldn't help, but smile at Meeramani's words.

* * *

Right at the exit of the palace, Akroor Singh bowed down before the king to express his greetings. A shiver ran down the spine of Maharana Ranjeet Singh having seen him and he thought that the work he had assigned him is done.

The army chief was able to understand the reaction of the king and, therefore, he went ahead and supported the king in order to stand. He politely said, "Welcome, Maharana *ji*! The army is all set for the departure for the war."

The Maharana boarded the chariot pulled by 8 horses and while commanding the departure of the army, also commanded that the bugle to mark the beginning of the journey for war be blown.

The army chief had begun getting the war bugle blown and this was a sign for the military to commence the war journey.

Maharana Ranjeet was continuously getting teary eyed and he was cautiously wiping his tears off.

They hadn't even reached the state territory yet that the chief of the army of Prince Samar Dev Pratap Singh, Sushant Singh, anxiously came riding on a horse. He was the son of Akroor Singh and had set out for the forest-war with the prince.

The army chief, Akroor Singh, came close to the Maharana and asked, "Maharana *ji*, the chief of the army of Prince Samar, Sushant Singh, wants to meet you and says there's an emergency."

Maharana Ranjeet Singh could feel his heart sinking, yet he permitted him in a stable voice.

The army chief of Prince Samar Dev, Sushant Singh, greeted the Maharana and said, "Not just my tongue, but also my heart is burning while giving this message to you that today's dawn was exceptionally dark. Prince Samar got into a war with the jungle intruders last night and a result of which, he killed all the intruders of the enemy. However, he moved a little too far from the forest while outfighting them and there he got attacked by a pack of lions. He got killed as a result of this attack. We could only hear his shrieks, but couldn't get his body. The grand empire Jairajgarh has lost its prince today." Saying this, Sushant Singh fell on his knees and further lowered himself to the ground.

Maharana lost control on his senses. His army chief, Akroor Singh, supported him. He could barely voice the command, "Stop the army!!! Stop the army!!!" and he rested his grieved head on the shoulder of Akroor Singh.

Akroor Singh instructed the military to return and they

acted accordingly.

* * *

The entire Jairajgarh was struck with grief. Everybody was shaken by the news of an untimely death of Prince Samar Dev Pratap Singh. They couldn't even see him for the last time.

Queen Ambika was losing consciousness by the extreme grief of losing her only son. While she was being attended by a group of government doctors, this news was not letting her open her eyes.

Maharana Ranjeet Singh had locked himself up in his personal room. Everyone was instructed that the Maharana will come out of the room himself and nobody should disturb him. After all, he was a father too, besides a Maharana, and this father was completely immersed in grief of the untimely death of his young son.

In the entire royalty, it was only Maharani Meeramani, who was acting with serenity and was quiet all the time. She was explaining a lot of things to her children, Prince Rudra Dev Pratap Singh, and Princess Amritamani, and they were also trying to understand the situation. In the end, both the kids assured her that all her orders will be followed and she breathed a sigh of relief.

It was two days ago when Maharana Ranjeet Singh had commanded Prince Samar Dev to go to the forest for a war. Prince Samar Dev had obeyed his orders and had set out to the jungle with an army squad because the Maharana had received a piece of information that some intruders had entered the forest and were setting their camps there. If it was about hunting, Prince Samar Dev would never have agreed to even the strictest orders of his father because he didn't like killing innocent animals. But here the matter was related to the enemies and no Rajput could sit silently having heard a challenge from an enemy and how dare they tried to enter the state through forests; it was crucial to stop them. Maharana also mentioned that although this was a duty of the army chief, Akroor Singh, but he was far away and couldn't be called as he was guarding some other frontier of the state. Maharana Ranjeet Singh also said that since he was already impressed by his war skills, this was the first opportunity for Prince Samar to prove his credibility because Maharana wanted to test him if he's ready to be taken to the warzone or not.

Maharana Ranjeet Singh had planned to arrange a meeting of Samar Dev with Sukanya Devi, the daughter of the king of Garudgarh, Satya Rajsingh, after a few days in the forests, right where they had their hunting camps. Samar Dev wouldn't get ready for the marriage and, thus, both the friends had thought if he would meet the princess, then he would definitely fall for her beauty and would agree for marriage. Maharana Ranjeet Singh had given a word to his friend that he would get his son married to his friend's daughter and, thus, he had already fixed the marriage. His sole intention was to get Prince Samar Dev fall for the princess, as she was no less than an angel, a celestial nymph or Urvashi and Samar was not like a Vishwamitra (a sage) to not get impressed by her. However, before Samar could meet her, the news of his demise had come.

The grand empire Jairajgarh, which was filled with ecstasy on hearing the news of Prince Samar Dev's marriage, was all grief-stricken.

Maharana Ranjeet Singh was all alone in these testing times, because Queen Ambika had been unconscious and Maharani Meeramani was too busy in handling the governmental tasks in the absence of the Maharana. Yet, Maharana was getting irked by the behavior of Meeramani, as neither did she cry nor did she say anything to anyone. Samar was more affectionate with Meeramani than Ambika, as she was the one who had gotten everything, like his bringing up and education, done under her direct supervision; then, why doesn't she cry on the demise of his dear son; otherwise, she loved him a lot.

Then, it occurred to the Maharana that this might be a part of political scheme of the Maharani. Even an enemy would cry looking at the seriousness of the situation, but she looks patient. No woman could bear all that patience which she's showing she has. Nobody knows if she wants her own son, Rudra Dev, to claim the throne and her love for Samar was mere a showoff. Queen Ambika is too docile to understand politics and Meeramani is totally opposite to her. She's an expert in war tactics, politics and Chanakya policies, but she can't be doubted as well, as she is an ardent follower of Lord Shiva and her reverence for the Lord is so high that she doesn't step back in abstaining from anything for it. She has a significant role to play in making the grand empire Jairajgarh happy and prosperous. Her greatness in keeping the family together and breeding healthy relationships between co-wives is unmatchable. Prince Samar was a result of her penance. She gave Queen Ambika a chance to become a mother first over her and she loved Prince Samar more than herself. Then, why she doesn't cry over his death? It might be a possibility that she cries in isolation as she is also the Maharani of the empire and grieving like a normal ladies doesn't suit her. She is courageous and brave and is known for her allegiance and dutiful attitude, though. Maharana was lost deep in his thoughts.

On the other hand, the residents of Jairajgarh were not able to believe that an army, which never got defeated before, couldn't save the prince. The army chief of the prince's army, Sushant Singh, had conveyed to them that the moment the prince heard some noises from the forest in the middle of the night, he set out in the forest all alone saying he's leaving and the army should follow him. While following that intruder, Prince Samar ran his horse too fast and Sushant Singh kept raising an alarm that there might a risk of lions ahead and requested Prince Samar not to proceed any further, but he didn't listen and continued moving further. Later, he could only hear Prince Samar's shrieks.

No matter what had happened, the fact was that the grand empire Jairajgarh had lost its young prince, who was only 17 years old, forever.

On the other side, Maharana had restricted himself to a dark room, as if he didn't want to face himself in the light. Today, the words from his father, Maharana Surya Dev Pratap Singh, were echoing in his mind, "This is the gruesome side of politics. Here, virtue and sin walk hand-in-hand together and most of the times, it is the sin which wins in pride. The politics in relationships is the most dangerous amongst all, as here, even if you win, you still end up losing big. Relations are only formed by love and are respected with love. The relations, whom you fabricate with politics, only leave you alone in the end. This great throne of Maharana represents supreme power and if you won't use this power with justice and law, then it will overpower you to lead to some devastating misuse. "Only time will tell what and which politics this throne of Maharana will teach you."

Tears started rolling down Maharana's cheeks and his entire childhood starting flashing in front of him.

Chapter 3:
The History of Maharana Ranjeet Dev Pratap Singh

Maharana Surya Dev Pratap Singh was the father of Ranjeet Singh. He was the then Maharana of Jairajgarh and had two wives. His first wife was Queen Manorama Devi and the second wife was Maharani Kesar Devi.

Although Kesar Devi was the second wife of the Maharana, but the first son to claim the throne of the Maharana, Prince Ranjeet Dev Pratap Singh, was born from her womb. Therefore, according to the customs of Jairajgarh, since she was the prince's mother, she got the throne of Maharani. Later on, she gave birth to two more kids - a daughter, Neelima, and the youngest son, Manjeet Dev Pratap Singh.

The name of the first wife of Maharana Surya Dev Pratap Singh was Manorama Devi. His son, Jagjeet Dev Pratap Singh was born one year after the birth of Ranjeet Singh and, thus, she could not claim the throne of Maharani and she regretted this. She always used to traduce her son, Jagjeet, against Ranjeet Singh, and was always plotting against his mother, Kesar Devi, but hadn't been successful in her endeavors till now. Queen Manorama Devi had even told her son, Jagjeet Dev Pratap Singh, that they won't be able to get any rights till the time Ranjeet Singh and his mother are alive; that's why, both of them were always busy plotting games. Even

Manorama had three children after Jagjeet, all three were daughters, Rukma, Padma and Shobhna.

So, in total, Maharana Surya Dev Pratap Singh had two wives and seven children from them. Both the wives were always busy in pulling each other down and the same was also true with their kids. His family was not a family, but two groups. One belonged to Maharani Kesar Devi and her kids and the other to Queen Manorama and hers. Both the groups were always busy making plans to trouble the other and, therefore, there was no unity in the family and where there's no unity, there can never be peace. The grand empire Jairajgarh of Maharana Surya Dev Pratap Singh, was happy and prosperous but his own family was shattered and divided. The plotting and clashes happening every day had broken Maharana Surya Dev Pratap Singh from inside. For the sake of peace, he had divided his palace into two parts, one for Maharani Kesar Devi, and her kids, and the other for Queen Manorama Devi and her kids, yet he was not able to develop peace among the family. Being a father, Maharana Surya Dev Pratap Singh used to love all his children equally.

Shamsher Singh was the army chief of Maharana Surya Dev Pratap Singh and he was also his dear friend. He used to discuss the state as well as the family problems with him. The ancestors of Shamsher Singh had been serving Maharana as army chiefs. This was nowhere a tradition of the grand empire Jairajgarh to have an army chief from Shamsher Singh's family, but the sons of his family had such a great expertise in war tactics and dedication towards Jairajgarh, that whenever there was a selection for the army chief, only his family in the entire Jairajgarh used to bag this opportunity and that, too, on the basis of merit. He used to create such labyrinths in the war zone that nobody from the enemy side was able to get through them and he had designed such a labyrinth for the security of the Maharana , that nobody even dared to even enter it. That's why the army chief from Shamsher Singh's family had made sure that Maharana remained untouched in the war zone. Even the territory security plan of the army chief had been so alert and agile that no enemy or intruder had been able to enter the boundary of the empire in its entire history. That's also the reason why everyone used to blindly trust the dedication of their family and used to prefer Shamsher Singh's family as the first choice for the army chief.

The son of the army chief, Shamsher Singh, Akroor Singh, was also around the same age as that of Prince Ranjeet Singh. That's why Shamsher Singh was training both of them equal in war skills. He was training Prince Ranjeet Singh for the throne and his son for the position of the army chief. The same age and the same training had made Akroor Singh and Ranjeet Singh as fast friends as their fathers or even more, just like brothers. Akroor Singh was ever ready to sacrifice his life for Prince Ranjeet Singh. He used to understand even the slightest of gesture of Ranjeet.

There was a gurukul (seminary) in the outskirts of the empire Jairajgarh, whose headmaster was 'Acharya Chaturanand'. He was adept in teaching Chanakya policies, politics and the Veda policies and that's why a lot of children from various empires and clans used to come to him for gaining knowledge. Although a lot of children were staying there, there was no such need for Prince Ranjeet Singh, his stepbrother, Jagjeet Singh, and Akroor Singh, since the gurukul (seminary) was situated just outside the boundaries of Jairajgarh and, thus, it wasn't a trouble for them to go there every morning and return in the evening. The army chief, Shamsher Singh, used to drop them under his supervision. The younger brother of Ranjeet Singh, Manjeet Dev Pratap Singh, was still breast-fed and, thus, couldn't be sent along. Ranjeet Singh met another prince there, Prince Neelkant. He was the son of the king of Ballabhgarh. Ballabhgarh was quite far from there; thus, he used to stay in the gurukul (seminary) to study. He became a close friend of Ranjeet Singh. Neelkant was fast in learning war tactics and the knowledge imparted and he was also a simple and soft-hearted person. Whatever was in his mind was reflected on his tongue. Although he was learning politics here, he was never clever by nature and was especially clear in his relations with friends. His courteous behavior had made him a dear student of Acharya Chaturanand.

On the contrary, Prince Ranjeet Singh and Akroor Singh, both were extremely clever and notorious. Ranjeet was proud of being a prince of the grand empire since childhood and, therefore, was only used to giving orders. The person who would agree to him would be a friend and the one who would disagree would be a foe; this was clear in his mind. He only loved himself winning. He was used to winning by using various methods, be it advice, money, punishment or diplomacy and Akroor used to always support him.

Prince Neelkant was able to understand that Ranjeet Singh does not have a great rapport with his stepbrother, Jagjeet, and both were always busy in putting the other down. Neelkant had seen through his own experiences that it was tough to make Ranjeet understand, while Jagjeet Singh used to agree things he tried to make him understand being friends. Gradually, Neelkant started liking being friends with Jagjeet Singh more, but since he had become friends first with Ranjeet, he didn't want to hurt him by telling this to him. He always used to think that he will make both of them understand being friends and would unite the two brothers forever.

Once, when he reached the gurukul, he got to know that the acharya has fallen and hurt himself badly and, thus, a holiday for five days had been declared. Ranjeet Singh invited Neelkant to spend the time off in Jairajgarh. Neelkant sought the permission from the gurukul (seminary) and accompanied him to Jairajgarh.

Children were strictly asked to keep off the jungles of Jairajgarh; however, Ranjeet Singh and his friend, Akroor, had traced a secret way of reaching there. That way was along the smooth hills beside the Sapta-Sangama lake behind the forest and used to go till where the camps for the royals were set up. There was a little danger of wild animals on that way, but there was a danger of venomous and horrendous pythons. Ranjeet Singh and Akroor Singh had a clear idea on which pits would have black, venomous cobras and which direction would have more of pythons. They both used to play around with the snakes and, sometimes, also used to kill them. They used to put a long stem of a tree inside a pit and 3-4 snakes used to curl that up; they used to immediately pull the stem out and used to leave the snakes on the ground. The moment the snakes used to run hither-thither, they used to hit them with the same stem. The snakes used to get scared and, thus, used to spread their fangs in order to avert the danger. They both used to fight with the snakes and used to cut their fangs off. They used to enjoy the sight of the snakes quivering in pain. They used to enjoy playing such cruel games and Ranjeet was used to such games since childhood. That's why he used to believe in crushing the head of every person, who tried to raise it in front of him. At times, he used to put the snakes in his leather bag and hand them over to the snake charmers and they used to wonder from where these boys get such exotic species of snakes. They had also learned the art of sucking out the venom from the snake from these snake charmers.

They both used to play several other heinous games apart from this. They used to catch mice, dip them in colors and place them on the roof of their palace, calling out for eagles and vultures to take the live mice away. They used to relish the sight of a mouse quivering in pain. Seeing someone quiver in pain showcased their cruel mentality and was a means of entertainment for them.

When Neelkant had come to Jairajgarh, they both took him to the jungle to play the same games. When they both showed him the risky as well as cruel games, he got scared and, also, was appalled seeing the helpless animals getting killed. While the two boys were enjoying the same, Neelkant pitied their cruel mentality. Neelkant had understood that their friendship was going to be perilous. That's why Neelkant started distancing himself from the two. He had understood that it's better to be neither friends nor foes with such people. He not only started spending more time with Jagjeet Singh, but had also warned him to stay alert of the activities of the two boys.

* * *

Time flew and, slowly, all the boys were turning into young men, leaving their childhood behind. Their education at gurukul had almost come to an end and thus, everyone was getting ready to go back. Prince Ranjeet Dev Pratap Singh had turned 18 and had turned into an attractive, young man who could become a heartbeat of any beautiful girl. His looks and personality were so magnetic that every girl used to get attracted towards him; however, he had not been interested in any of the girls and hadn't even thought about marriage yet. He was a little above 6 feet, had curly black hair and black moustache. His strong stature used to certify him as a great warrior. He was getting better in politics and war tactics. The army chief, Shamsher Singh, who was his teacher in war tactics used to fret standing in front of him. Shamsher Singh had understood that no warrior could stand easily before Ranjeet. He was also aware of nuances of the war tactics. His father, Surya Dev Pratap Singh, was happy and satisfied seeing his bringing up.

Surya Dev Pratap Singh was himself teaching the war tactics to his younger son Jagjeet Singh, fearing the clash between the stepbrothers. Prince Jagjeet Singh was one year younger to Ranjeet and had turned into an attractive man too. He used to share a lot of similarities with Ranjeet. Even he was adept in a lot of skills and seeing this, Surya Dev Pratap Singh had decided to make Ranjeet Singh as the king and Jagjeet Singh as the prince.

Akroor Singh had a dusky complexion and had a stature similar to that of a warrior. He used to look tough through his looks, which were inadvertently inherited through his father. His father, Shamsher Singh, had made him understand that an army chief shouldn't look calm, but very tough and serious so that he could already shake the confidence of the enemy through his looks. Shamsher Singh had passed on all his qualities to Akroor, because he knew that he would be the next army chief. In fact, Akroor was an exact copy of his father.

The prince of Ballabhgarh, Neelkant, was also getting ready to leave for his home. He had also grown up into an attractive man, but he had pleasing looks than tough. He was a dear student of Acharya Chaturanand, because he used to contemplate every idea with a cool mind and didn't lose his cool in emergency situations. Anger never used to control his mind. He stood first class in politics and tactics in his gurukul(seminary) because of these qualities. Acharya Chaturanand had even made Ranjeet Singh and Jagjeet Singh understand to keep their anger under control. Though Jagjeet Singh had agreed a bit, Ranjeet Singh was just not ready to listen to him, as according to him, anger was a symbol of pride and respect.

Sometime back, Ranjeet Singh had a terrible feud with his stepbrother, Jagjeet Singh, settled later by their father, Surya Dev Pratap Singh. Their father had a set of rule that the younger brother would touch the feet of the elder brother while seeking apology. This behavior of his father had hurt Jagjeet Singh deeply and he told the entire incident to Neelkant as a friend. Seeing his friend upset, he asked Jagjeet Singh to come to Ballabhgarh along with him; this would give him a break from Ranjeet Singh and would also give a nice time off. When Ranjeet got to hear about this, he got very angry with Neelkant. He told Neelkant that he had brought him along to his empire, but now, when the time had come, he invited only Jagjeet to go to his palace. Now,they were not kids anymore; Neelkant knew that Ranjeet is going to be the next Maharana and he would be the next king of Ballabhgarh; that's why, he didn't want to spoil his relations with Ranjeet because Ballabhgarh was relatively smaller in comparison with grand and powerful Jairajgarh and, secondly, Ranjeet Singh was proud and assumptive. He used to breed enmity against people rather quickly for his ego used to get hurt too soon. Ranjeet Singh used to like people who did constant bootlicking over those who were straightforward. That's why Neelkant invited Ranjeet, too, to come along with him. He didn't want to take Akroor Singh along and his father, Shamsher Singh, only solved this problem for them. Shamsher Singh was teaching them the art of sketching labyrinth and, thus, didn't allow him to go.

Neelkant was happy and thought that in the absence of Akroor Singh, he would make both the brothers understand that they should live together with peace and love. He wanted to make them understand that they won't be able to face the enemies if they would continue to fight among themselves.

When the day to set out for Ballabhgarh came, Jagjeet Singh didn't quite agree to go along with Ranjeet Singh. Neelkant tried to persuade him to come along, but he didn't agree and that's why Neelkant had to go with Ranjeet Singh only.

Chapter 4: Ambika, The Princess of Ballabhgarh

The empire of Ballabhgarh was a well-established state of Rajputana. Its then king was Krishnakant and he had only one wife, Jamuna Devi. They had two kids, the elder son who had turned 18, Neelkant, and a daughter, Princess Ambika, who was just 14 years old now.

Prince Neelkant was serious by nature. He was quite and calm since childhood and he had an unwavering faith in God. He was a responsible son, who was rightly aware of his responsibilities. He used to love his younger sister, Ambika, more than his own life and he had only lookout in his life that was to get his sister married in a house where she is loved and cared after. He couldn't stand seeing his sister upset.

Being the youngest in the house, Princess Ambika was an apple of the eye of everyone. Her father and brother used to love her the most. Although she was just 14 but her long height and a fuller body made her appear beautiful and youthful. Her big eyes and her fair complexion used to attract anyone in the very first look; the mischief reflected in her eyes used to certify her as impish. She had become overtly spoilt and extrovert due to all the love showered on her. She was just not familiar with patience. The entire atmosphere of the palace used to remain cheerful and active because of her notoriety and playfulness.

The dusk was setting in when Neelkant reached his empire, Ballabhgarh, along with his friend, Prince Ranjeet Singh. The mother of Prince Neelkant, Queen Jamuna Devi, came to the main gate of the palace to welcome Neelkant and his friend, Ranjeet, by greeting them with *aarti (prayers)*. Suddenly, Princess Ambika came running and jumping in joy and hugged his brother, Neelkant.

Prince Ranjeet Singh was amazed to look at Ambika. "How beautiful she is, just like a nymph!" thought Ranjeet while staring at her without batting an eyelid. He had never seen such a beautiful girl before. Everybody noticed Ranjeet staring at Ambika. Prince Neelkant didn't appreciate him staring at his sister like that; however, his mother, Queen Jamuna Devi, was happy inside as she knew that he is the premeditated successor of the great empire Jairajgarh.

Neelkant scolded his sister gently, "You've now grownup Ambika, but when you shall become intelligent?" Neelkant introduced her to Ranjeet, "Friend, this is my younger sister, Princess Ambika," and while gestured her to greet him. He said, "He's my friend, Prince Ranjeet Singh, he's also like a brother to you."

Ambika retorted, "I don't have any brother apart from you, Neelkant bhai*ji*. Our mother anyway tell me that if I would keep on making every boy brother, then who would I marry?" She started laughing loudly having completed her remark.

The maids standing along also started laughing along with her making the entire atmosphere pleasant. Prince Ranjeet Singh was amazed and impressed looking at her frankness and child-like nature. He had liked her childishness from the first look. The sisters in our kingdom do not joke around like this or probably, they aren't allowed to, thought Ranjeet. His all the three stepsisters, Rukma, Padma and Shobhna, had gotten married, but his own younger sister, Neelima, was not married as yet as she was just 14. Ranjeet had like Ambika from the first sight and he was getting interested in marrying her. He had thought this in his mind that after reaching home, he shall talk to his mother to get his younger sister, Neelima, married to Neelkant, and bring Ambika home as her daughter-in-law.

Prince Ranjeet Singh was welcomed warmly in Ballabhgarh.

King Krishnakant and Queen Jamuna Devi were taking care of him very well and Ranjeet was enjoying all the love he was being showered with. He had decided that he will definitely get his sister married to Neelkant. He was getting overwhelmed thinking how Neelkant would take good care of his sister, keeping in view his house, his family and his behavior towards everyone.

Having left Prince Ranjeet Singh in his bedroom, Prince Neelkant furthered to his mother Jamuna Devi. His father, Krishnakant, was also present there and both of them were busy in a deep conversation. Seeing their son, Neelkant, coming, they both said, "Come, son! We were about to call you. We were talking something serious and wanted you to listen."

"First, you listen to me," resented Neelkant, "Teach some manners to Ambika. She has grownup now, yet she behaves like a kid. She doesn't even know who she should face and who all she shouldn't. She was jumping around like a child in front of my friend. Does she have any shame or honor like other girls?"

"Was Prince Ranjeet Singh complaining?" asked Krishnakant.

"No, why would he complain? It was she who was jumping around… he was looking at her as if…" Neelkant left his words unsaid, hesitating to complete.

"Then, what we are thinking is right," Jamuna Devi said, "Your friend, Ranjeet Singh, likes our daughter, Ambika."

"If this is true, just try to judge what's there in his mind, Neelkant," continued Krishnakant, "This alliance would be very nice, if they approach us with the proposal. Anyway, Prince Ranjeet Singh is the successor of the throne of the great empire Jairajgarh. Our Ambika will rule there."

Before Neelkant could add anything, his mother, Jamuna Devi said, "Prince Ranjeet Singh is such a handsome gentleman. This couple would look good together."

"And this alliance with Jairajgarh would open the floodgates of good fortune for us," chuckled Krishnakant.

"Stop it, you guys! Pushing Ambika into a well would be a better task to do than this," vented Neelkant out.

"What!" Both his parents exclaimed in shock, "Why are you saying like this? What happened?" asked Jamuna Devi.

To answer both of them, Neelkant familiarized them with the history of Jairajgarh and the nature of Ranjeet Singh and, also, his likes-dislikes. After telling everything, he said, "Don't worry, I will look for an alliance for Ambika and will get her married to a great boy and into a very good family, where she is loved and respected."

"Alright, son, you know it better; as you wish," Krishnakant concluded.

There, in his bedroom, Prince Ranjeet Singh was taking turns on his bed. Princess Ambika had deep resided in his mind. He wanted her at any cost and he had decided that he will make her his own.

Two days had passed and he couldn't see Ambika anywhere. It seemed as if her family had hidden her somewhere. Ranjeet was getting anxious to see her and this was visible to Neelkant, but he had strictly ordered his mother to ask Ambika to play elsewhere till his friend, Ranjeet, was there and to not face him at all.

* * *

One day, when Ranjeet Singh was sleeping in his bedroom, Neelkant woke him up and said, "Friend, the army chief Shamsher Singh *ji*, of your empire Jairajgarh, has come along with the army to take you back home."

Ranjeet could see Neelkant worried. He asked him, "Why? What happened?"

"Only he can tell what has happened. I have been ordered to inform you to take a shower and get ready to leave," Shamsher Singh *ji* was telling us that it's an emergency situation and that's why, they had to come like this to pick you up," Neelkant narrated.

Prince Ranjeet Singh got ready soon and went to the guestroom where everyone was seated. Even Ambika was there as a courtesy to bid everyone adieu.

The army chief Shamsher Singh, greeted the Prince Ranjeet Singh.

"What emergency situation has risen Shamsher Singh *ji*? Is everything alright in our empire? I hope no one has made the first move for a war,"Ranjeet Singh asked anxiously.

“In the entire Rajputana, nobody’s arms have got that much of power to even think of attacking Jairajgarh or nobody’s eyes has the audacity to give a side look to our empire. We are sufficient to handle that,” Shamsher Singh roared with pride, “I have come on the orders of Maharana Surya Dev Pratap Singh; he will explain the rest of the situation to you. I have had our snacks and I will now get the army ready to go back. Meanwhile, please have your snacks,” Shamsher Singh said and joined his hands seeking a permission to leave.

Out of courtesy, even King Krishnakant and Prince Neelkant accompanied Shamsher Singh out of the dining room, while Queen Jamuna Devi and Princess Ambika served him food.

After having his breakfast, Prince Ranjeet Singh sighed while looking at Princess Ambika. Ambika smiled in response and this furthered his love for her. Ranjeet Singh took his leave from Queen Jamuna Devi and exited the room. After coming out, he also bade adieu to King Krishnakant and Prince Neelkant and left for Jairajgarh along with Shamsher Singh.

Chapter 5:
The Revenge of Prince Ranjeet Dev Pratap Singh

Prince Ranjeet Singh, while on his way back on his chariot, was wondering what emergency situation would have raised that his father had to call him up like this. He thought it must have been something serious, otherwise his father would never have sent Shamsher Singh. He would have sent either Akroor Singh or anyone, but sending Shamsher Singh implies there must be a big trouble. He was running out of patience, although he didn't have any, and ordered to stop the chariot.

The moment the convoy stopped, Shamsher Singh came to Ranjeet Singh and asked, "What happened, Prince? Is everything alright; why did you ask to stop all of a sudden?"

"Shamsher Uncle, please tell me what emergency situation has occurred in Jairajgarh? I cannot be patient anymore. Please tell me right now," Ranjeet Singh asked impatiently. If not related to the royal tasks, the kids of Shamsher Singh and Surya Dev Pratap Singh used to address them as 'Uncle' keeping in view the friendship of their fathers.

"I had thought of apprising you of the situation once we would reach close to the boundary of Jairajgarh," said Shamsher Singh in a low tone, "But now that you are asking it for the sake of personal relations, I may have to tell you the truth. However,

I'd request you to be patient. The way is too long and you won't be able to stand the grief. That's why I don't think it's right to tell you anything now."

"Don't talk in riddles, Uncle; tell me the truth," Ranjeet Singh insisted.

"Ranjeet, my son, you will have to listen to this with great strength. Your sister Neelima and your younger brother Manjeet Dev Pratap Singh, are no more and even your mother Maharani Kesar Devi, is fighting for her life," Shamsher Singh said while getting emotional.

Ranjeet Singh let out a loud shriek of pain and grief. "This can't be true! This can't happen with me! How did this happen; you, Akroor Singh and my father being there, how did this happen? How did this happen, Uncle, answer me!" tears were rolling down the cheeks of Ranjeet Singh.

"I cannot understand how this happened," said Shamsher Singh in a heavy voice, "Investigations are on; may be this is some enemy's conspiracy. Everyone was sleeping in their rooms at night after the dinner. When we woke up in the morning, we saw your sister and younger brother fallen to the ground and their bodies had turned blue. Blood and froth was oozing from their mouths. It was quite apparent that they had been poisoned. Similar case was true with your mother. She was lying right in the middle of the door of the bedroom and only she had a little life left in her. However, she is critical right now and is fighting for life. Since Princess Neelima and Prince Manjeet Dev Pratap Singh had already passed away, they had to be cremated for their bodies couldn't be held for long."

"All this is done by Jagjeet Singh and his mother," Ranjeet Singh said while crying uncontrollably, "That's why that sinner didn't want to come with me and stayed back so that he could finish this task in my absence because he couldn't have even touched my brother, sister and mother in my presence. This is the time those sinners and evildoers have chosen...I won't leave them; I will kill them."

"Be patient, Prince!" Shamsher Singh asked while trying to control his emotions, "Your father has ordered to investigate. If your stepmother and stepbrother are involved in this conspiracy, your father will punish them. Be patient; justice will prevail. A decision taken in haste often spoils a lot of other things. Then, there's no way left other than repenting. That's why, I am requesting you being your elder to be patient; your father will definitely punish the culprits."

"*Arre*! What punishment would father give to them; he is a puppet himself in their hands. He is too meek to punish them. Only my sword can punish them now," uttered Ranjeet while crying.

Shamsher Singh said in a stern tone while interrupting him, "You're getting emotional, Prince, but you must control your words. You are talking about Maharana Surya Dev Pratap Singh. He's not only your father, but also the king of the great empire Jairajgarh. I, being his servant, can't hear a word against him. If you hadn't been his son then...," Shamsher Singh left his speech unsaid and continued, "Now, please allow us to depart. We would get late in reaching Jairajgarh."

Prince Ranjeet Singh gestured the convoy to proceed and everyone furthered towards Jairajgarh.

* * *

When the convoy of Ranjeet Singh entered the boundary of Jairajgarh, they noticed the entire kingdom to be unusually silent. The entire state was stricken with grief. The moment the chariot of Ranjeet Singh stopped at the entrance of the palace, he sprinted inside to his mother, Kesar Devi's bedroom. A team of royal doctors were operating upon her while she was lying unconscious on the bed. Her body appeared blue-black. Maharana Surya Dev Pratap Singh, along with Queen Manorama Devi, and Jagjeet Dev Pratap Singh and other family members, was sitting beside her. Ranjeet Singh noticed the mother-son duo with great attention and yelled at them, "Get out, everyone! Leave my mother alone!" Maharana Surya Dev Pratap Singh assumed that the mental state of Ranjeet is not so well and, thus, he gestured Queen Manorama Devi and Jagjeet to leave the room, to which they agreed.

After both of them left the room, Maharana Surya Dev Pratap Singh hugged Ranjeet. Ranjeet started crying uncontrollably in his embrace. Maharana Surya Dev said, "Don't worry; whosoever has done this conspiracy will not be saved; no matter who that person is."

After some time, Maharani Kesar Devi slowly opened her eyes. Ranjeet Singh was seated beside her. She was not in a position to speak. When he brought his ear close to her, he could only hear her broken words, "Ksha… Ma…(forgive)," before she finally stood still and her soul rested in peace.

Ranjeet Singh started crying like babies; his father hugged him to console him. When Queen Manorama Devi placed her hand over his head, Ranjeet got irritated and said, "Never touch me." and went outside the room while staring at Jagjeet Singh. Once out, he unleashed his horse and rode on it towards the forest.

It was getting dark in the night and nobody knew where Ranjeet Singh had gone. Maharana Surya Dev Pratap Singh called Akroor Singh and asked him, "You must know where Ranjeet is, for you are his best friend. Go and get him back here."

Akroor Singh immediately agreed to obey his orders.

Akroor Singh reached Sapta-Sangama Lake while looking for Ranjeet. He saw there that Ranjeet is laying on a soft rock and tears are flowing endlessly from his eyes. Sternness was being reflected from his face. Akroor Singh went close to him and hugged him and both the friends kept crying for a long time.

When he finally stopped crying, Ranjeet said to Akroor, "Friend, I want to take revenge."

Akroor Singh replied, "Once we get to know who that person is, we will give him an even worse death."

"Who else would that be; that Jagjeet Singh and his mother have done everything. They have taken a benefit of me not being here. Jagjeet Singh didn't come with us despite Neelkant insisting him because he had already planned this conspiracy," Ranjeet said gravely.

Akroor Singh came back, "Don't worry, friend, your friend is still alive. I will give a result you desire to see to this mother and son. But for now, let's go back; I had promised Maharana that I will come back with you. Besides, we also have to cremate Mother Kesar Devi. For the sake of our friendship, stand up and come with me; Maharana *ji* must be looking for us."

Ranjeet Singh stood up immediately when it was about their friendship and got ready to leave.

* * *

Maharani Kesar Devi had been cremated right now and silence prevailed in the entire kingdom. Nobody knew why Queen Manorama Devi was crying uncontrollably. The onlookers were not able to understand how she always had an enmity with her co-wife and, now, she was crying nonstop. Even Jagjeet Singh was deeply grieved, but it all was appearing drama to Ranjeet Singh.

It was growing darker and Ranjeet was unable to sleep due to anxiety when his servant informed him about the arrival of Maharana Surya Dev Pratap Singh. Having heard the news of the arrival of his father, Ranjeet Singh stood up and started wondering what is it that his father had come to his room, that too this late in the night.

Maharana entered his room and told clearly, "I want to talk about something important with you, Ranjeet."

Ranjeet Singh bowed before his father and offered him a place to sit.

"Ranjeet," Maharana said without creating any drama, "I have been broken way more on hearing the news of the deaths of my wife and two children than what you have been on hearing about your mother, brother and sister. Our grief is the same; thus, try to understand what I want to say to understand my pain. I know who you are doubting for the murders of your mother, brother and sister, but I have got the entire investigations done and these two don't have any role in this, because the day you had left for Ballabhgarh, the same evening even Manorama Devi had left for her maternal home, Amargarh, and had taken Jagjeet along for his cousin was unwell. That's why Jagjeet couldn't accompany you for he had to take his mother to his maternal grandmother's house. Moreover, since it was late in the evening, I had sent Shamsher Singh along with a unit of army to fight any unknown danger. Shamsher Singh was along with them all this while, from the time they went to the time they came back here.

Surya Dev Pratap Singh continued, "The day this incident happened, I had gone for a boating with your mother, Kesar, and we had returned late in the night. Since it was quite late in the night, she went to check on the kids whether they had slept or not and didn't return at all. I thought that she must have slept with the kids and, hence, I, too, went to sleep. In the morning, when servants informed me that Maharani was lying at the door of the bedroom and both the kids were lying on the floor, I ran to see them."

Surya Dev started crying while reiterating the incident; he continued, "When I reached there, the servants had already picked them from the floor and made all three of them lie on the bed. There, I saw both the kids dead and Kesar counting her breaths."

Surya Dev furthered, "If you think their food was poisoned, all four of us had our dinner together that night. If they were poisoned, then even I would have consumed it; then, why am I not dead? I had sent an informer to inform Shamsher Singh about the same and he further informed Queen Manorama and Jagjeet. Then, they both had returned along with Shamsher, a day before you came back. I had asked Shamsher to pick you from Ballabhgarh after they were back here. I have conducted the investigations on the micro level because this is after all related to my queen and my children, but I have not been able to investigate why and how this happened."

Prince Ranjeet Singh was listening to his father with utmost seriousness.

Maharana Surya Dev took a deep breath and said, "You will be the successor of the throne after me and, hence, keep in mind to never commit any injustice with anyone in a haste that you don't even get time for repentance. You have to do justice leaving your anger aside. If you still are convinced that your stepmother and stepbrother have done this, get me some evidence… one evidence, and I assure you that I will get both of them decapitated by you, through your sword. I will give you this fortune of punishing them yourself. However, if you don't have any evidence, I cannot punish them without any reason. Even Manorama is my wife and Jagjeet is my son too, and I can't do injustice to my children. If Jagjeet, too, comes to me complaining about you, I just don't take any action by buying his words. Similarly, I cannot punish them on the basis of your words or suspicion. For a father, all his children are equal, Ranjeet, and you would understand this when you would become a father yourself."

Surya Dev looked at Ranjeet to see the effect of his words on him and he noticed no change in the expressions of Ranjeet.

Surya Dev continued, "You will have to promise me one thing, Ranjeet. If you'd find any evidence against them, you would first show that to me and then, they are your convicts and you could punish them the way you wish to. However, you wouldn't even touch them without any evidence. You should swear by me, Ranjeet; promise me."

Surya Dev ordered Ranjeet to obey by his words and Ranjeet Singh had to promise his father that he wouldn't harm them.

Maharana Surya Dev was now satisfied having made Ranjeet promise to him. Although Ranjeet had promised to his father, his blood was still boiling and his sword was still thirsting to drink the blood of his stepmother as well as stepbrother. However, he had to stand silent because of his father and he wasn't able to find any evidence against them anyway.

This politics of his father had fueled the fire of revenge burning inside him. He was now looking for a way in which he could get both of them killed, without taking the onus on himself. This way, he would be able to keep the words of his father and, also, quench his thirst for revenge.

* * *

Ten months had already passed to this incident. Prince Ranjeet Singh used to stay lost in thoughts and, also, was becoming serious. His father, Surya Dev, was not appreciating seeing him like this. He wanted Ranjeet to forget this incident as soon as possible and get over it; he wanted him to start leading a normal life once again. That's why he got him married to Princess Vaishali, the cousin sister of the King of Mewar. Princess Vaishali was a wise and simple girl. Maharana Surya Dev had an old friendship with the royalty of Mewar and he had already committed to get Ranjeet Singh married with Vaishali. Ranjeet wasn't mentally ready for the marriage, but he had to keep his father's words. Dusky and serious Vaishali hadn't appealed to Ranjeet Singh much, as he had already given the space in his mind and heart to Princess Ambika. Surya Dev had thought that wise Vaishali would be able to impress Ranjeet, and he would eventually leave the feeling of revenge having being lost in the pleasures of a married life. Surya Dev had contemplated that Ranjeet would forget all the old things and would start his life afresh; he had even thought that after his child is born, he would hand over the throne to Ranjeet, and he would completely forget that incident having handling his married life and the state tasks. However, thinking this was the biggest mistake of Surya Dev's life.

After their marriage, Ranjeet never went close to Vaishali; they even didn't have their honeymoon night yet. Having known this, Surya Dev asked Vaishali to try to impress and please Ranjeet as he was just not able to move out of that incident. But, poor Vaishali, she could only do something if she met Ranjeet and Ranjeet didn't even use to pass by her room; he was only concerned about his revenge.

Then, a day came when Ranjeet could finally think of an idea. He plotted the entire plan along with his friend or his personal army chief, Akroor Singh.

In those days, the nephew Prince Khushaal Singh of Queen Manorama Devi had come to spend his vacations in Jairajgarh and Ranjeet Singh had provoked this cousin of Jagjeet Singh by saying that the people who cannot hunt should not call themselves as men. This angered Khushaal Singh and he persuaded Jagjeet to go for hunting with him. Jagjeet Singh sought the permission to hunt from his father and Surya Dev asked an army contingent to accompany both of them, so that they could enjoy hunting.

After a day had passed since Jagjeet had left for hunting, Ranjeet Singh invited his father, Surya Dev, to his room to play chess; he also insisted that he needed to take his suggestions on a few governmental tasks. Surya Dev thought that Ranjeet had now started to turn normal and, thus, he accepted his request.

The moment Surya Dev reached Ranjeet's room, that moment even Shamsher Singh came in and requested Surya Dev to grant a leave to Akroor Singh along with him, provided Ranjeet Singh doesn't have any important work to do that day. Shamsher wanted both himself and his son to have food together at their home. Maharana Surya Dev granted a leave to Akroor Singh, too.

On this hand, the game between the father Surya Dev, and his son Ranjeet Singh, had begun and on the other hand, Akroor Singh had a little food and, then, went to his room to sleep, letting his father know that since they had gotten a leave after so many days, he wanted to sleep and that nobody should disturb him. At midnight, Akroor Singh changed his avatar and went outside his bedroom from the window carrying a dagger in his hand. He directly reached the bank of the Sapta-Sangama lake, from where there was a way leading to the forest. Having reached there, he reminisced their childhood when he and Ranjeet Singh used to go into the forest by the same way, hiding from everyone. These two even used to reach the backyards of the camps. There were no guards there, since no enemy could reach there because that way used to cross the insides of the Jairajgarh and enemies had nothing to do inside the territory. The way was short, but it had a lot of pits there and it was rocky, too, but Akroor Singh was familiar with its way and, thus, he knew where there was a pit and where there was any danger.

Akroor Singh lit a firelight he had brought along with himself and broke apart a long stem from a tree. He stopped by a pit, where he knew there were a lot of black, venomous cobras. He opened the mouth of a huge leather bag and placed it right outside the pit. Then, he inserted the stem he broke from the tree inside. Soon, four to five snakes encircled the stem. He immediately took the stem out from the pit and put the snakes inside his bag. One-by-one, all of the snakes settled inside the bag. He closed the mouth of the bag right away and took it along with the stick.

From there, Akroor Singh reached the place where the royal camps were set up. He went to the backyard of the camps. He fairly knew where the camps of the princes were and, thus, he straight away crawled to that place. If he had wanted, he could have released the snakes into the camp, but he had a principle to complete the work and, therefore, he wanted to be sure that the venomous snakes have reached the bed of the prince Jagjeet Singh. Inside the camp, both, Khushaal Singh and Jagjeet Singh, were fast asleep. Ranjeet Singh had no personal enmity with Khushaal Singh and, thus, following the orders of Ranjeet Singh, he released all the snakes on the bed of

Jagjeet Singh. Following this, he moved his way back from where he had to come to his room and went to sleep.

The next day, Akroor Singh reported at work to Prince Ranjeet Singh at his stipulated time. Ranjeet Singh gestured to Akroor Singh through his eyes.

Akroor Singh answered to Ranjeet Singh, "Prince, obeying your orders is more important for me than my life. If ever I would be unsuccessful in doing that, I would behead myself right in front of you with your sword and would place my head at your feet.

Prince Ranjeet Singh got emotional and hugged Akroor Singh.

The next morning, the sad news had engulfed the state that the younger prince, Jagjeet Singh, and his cousin, Khushaal Singh, were stung by venomous snakes and they were found dead on their beds. Maharana Surya Dev and Queen Manorama Devi were not able to get out of this grief. Manorama Devi kept insisted while crying that this has been done by Ranjeet Singh, but Maharana Surya Dev didn't hear any of her words. Manorama Devi was unable to get over the grief of losing her son and one day, even she committed suicide having consumed poison.

The entire family of Maharana Surya Dev had gradually finished. Both of his queens and three out of seven children had died. There were three daughters surviving, but all of them were married. Maharana Surya Dev, his son, Ranjeet Singh, and his daughter-in-law, Vaishali, who couldn't get close to Ranjeet, that's all he had to count in his royal family.

Chapter 6:
The Truth behind the Deaths of Maharani Kesar Devi and her two children

Maharana Surya Dev had been broken from inside on the deaths of his two queens, two sons and a young daughter and the way they died had completely made him oblivious to the worldly affairs. He had turned sick and was losing interest in managing the state. That's why he consulted the government advisors and handed over the throne to Prince Ranjeet Singh and gave a new Maharana to the grand empire Jairajgarh – "Maharana Ranjeet Dev Pratap Singh".

After the coronation of Ranjeet Singh, Surya Dev called him to his room one night . While making a gesture towards him to sit, Surya Dev asked him without any formality, "Do you know which substance intoxicates the most?"

"No, father," replied Ranjeet Singh softly.

Father Surya Dev looked deeply at Ranjeet and said, "The most intoxicating substance is power, the desire to own the throne is intoxicating; the power to rule over everyone is intoxicating. When the whole world starts bowing before you, you start forgetting yourself. The intoxication of power rides on a man's head that he forgets that he is challenging the power of God. He starts crushing and trampling over everyone and starts imposing his decisions on others; this is the time when he doesn't realize that he has made his pride his God. When a person makes his pride as his God, it should be understood that he has challenged God for a war. Now, if the war is with God, humans can never win. Gradually, he starts losing all his relations in the mania of pride and, in the end, is left empty-handed. This is the day of not his physical death, but the death of his soul. So, in order to make sure that you never have a war with God, it is important to keep your pride under control. Otherwise, everything will be destroyed and ended and you'd be left empty-handed. Surya Dev took a deep breath and continued, "Make the Royal throne as the "Divine throne" and rule it as per the ethics. If you live according to the ethics, your acts will be pure and when your acts will be pure, God's blessings will always be with you. Did you understand anything, Maharana Ranjeet Dev Pratap Singh?" asked Surya Dev in a serious tone.

"Yes, father. I will always remember this," Ranjeet Singh answered sternly.

"Hmm..." Surya Dev made a loud humming sound and continued, "Now, your mother, Kesar Devi, has expired and so have your stepmother and stepbrother. So, I want to tell you a truth of my life. Listen carefully."

Ranjeet Singh sat alert.

Surya Dev said, "I had defeated and killed the father and brothers of Kesar in a war. If I had any brains then, I would have known that we can also forgive our enemies; there isn't any need of killing them. Even then, I did so out of my pride. When our army units reached the empire of Kesar Devi, all the ladies of the empire had already consumed poison. Kesar, too, wanted to consume poison, but the ring in which she had filled the poison was a little loose and, thus, had fallen off from her finger. She was busy looking for it. The moment she found the ring, our army chief Shamsher Singh caught hold of her and didn't let her consume the poison. He tied her up with chains and brought her to me. I fell for the beauty of Kesar and forcibly married her. She didn't want to marry the murderer of her father and brothers, but I was so blind in my pride and zeal that I didn't want to hear a word, that too from a woman. She surrendered in front of my obstinacy then and this was the biggest mistake of my life. I could only realize my mistake much later. If you would respect women, their desires, their esteem and honor in your life and home, then she would take up the avatar of Lakshmi and Annapurna (The Goddesses of prosperity); she would commit herself to her husband and family and get ready to take up any danger or challenge herself. Even God stays happy with her penance and blesses the house where she stays and where she is respected.

On the contrary, if anyone tries to force her into something or disrespects her wishes, she takes the avatar of a Chandi or Kali (the Goddesses of destruction). When she takes this avatar, she only causes destruction. Even Lord Shiva couldn't stand in front of the avatar of Goddess Kali, then where do we men stand. The whole world bows before her powers. A woman is never weak, Ranjeet, she is a storehouse of superpowers. When she realizes the powers hidden inside her, she never gets scared of the physical power of a man, as even we men can't face her then. Every woman has been born with spiritual and mental powers and that's why there's no sage capable of standing before a woman. She even has the powers to make the throne of God tremble. When a woman comes to her husband's house after marriage, then if her husband doesn't respect her or derogates her, every moment, she heaves such sighs from inside which don't let his house flourish or prosper. Just like us, men, who love and can't stand a word against our house, parents or siblings, these women, too, love their house, parents and siblings dearly and can't stand a word against them. If you'd respect her maternal relations, even she will respect your relatives and would do so even more to you, her ideal husband. However, we, men, commit the biggest mistake by holding a lot of expectations from women that they have come to our houses as slaves and we, then, start torturing them physically and mentally. This is the same mistake you are doing with your wife, Vaishali."

Surya Dev took a deep breath and continued, "When I had brought your mother, Kesar Devi, to this palace after marriage, then my elder queen, Manorama Devi, was pregnant of seven months. Queen Kesar Devi plotted a conspiracy to take a revenge on me for the murder of his father and brother by trying to kill Manorama and her child. She poisoned her food. Although the doctors could save Manorama, they couldn't save the child. When I am sitting on the throne of Maharana, I have to be familiar with everything happening around. I got to know that Queen Kesar Devi was the culprit, but I couldn't punish her as she was already pregnant with you in her womb. She gave birth to you and took over the position of Maharani, which could have been of Manorama. One day, when I was qu*Aree*ling with your mother over something, then I said in a fit of anger that she was the murderer and she took the revenge of the deaths of her brothers and father by killing my unborn child and taking over the position of Maharani. Manorama overheard everything and she was enraged to take revenge. I tried to make her understand, but that was of no use. Even she wanted to kill your mother and all her children, but I never let that happen," Surya Dev wiped tears from his eyes.

Ranjeet Singh started getting hyper on his father being silent and he was, now, eagerly waiting to listen to the rest of the story.

Surya Dev read the face of Ranjeet and continued, "When you had gone to Ballabhgarh with your friend, Neelkant, an incident happened which melted the hearts of these two ladies. Due to your younger sister Neelima's fault, your younger brother Manjeet, fell into Sapta-Sangama Lake while playing and Neelima started shouting for help. Before anyone could come for help, Jagjeet, having taken the permission from Manorama, jumped into the lake. Your mother, Kesar, saw the big-heartedness of Manorama and fell on her feet to seek apology. Even Manorama forgave her and hugged her. May be, both of them were now familiar with the pain of losing a child and they had understood that they won't be able to save a thing or a person by fighting with their family members. If a family will conspire against the other, then how would they deal with the external enemies?

"Why didn't you tell this to me earlier?" Ranjeet was now shaking with fear.

"Because you were not ready to listen to anyone, despite everyone trying to explain to you." Surya Dev answered loudly, "You should not drown yourself in your pride to an extent that you don't hear anyone who wants to talk to you or tell you something and start making assumptions. If anyone wants to tell you something, will he have to chain you first to make you understand his side of the story? There's no bigger criminal than a person who passes judgments based on half knowledge. If anyone wants to become a judge, he should prepare to listen to both the sides before passing his judgment, so that the criminal doesn't walk free and the innocent doesn't get punished. You would only commit a sin by punishing the innocent."

"But, father, if you want to say that Queen Manorama Devi and her son were not responsible for the deaths of my mother, brother and sister, then who was the culprit? Who wanted to murder them and why? Who could have been benefitted by their deaths? Why did anyone conspire against them?" Tears were now flowing from the eyes of Ranjeet.

"It wasn't a mistake, but an accident," Surya Dev admitted, "I didn't know this earlier, but now I do. I have assumed based on the information I got. This is only a half truth."

Ranjeet Singh said anxiously, "I cannot wait to get more information about the accident or murder of my mother and siblings and I am tired of thinking. Please tell me the entire truth, father."

Surya Dev furthered, "I had already told you that by the time I reached there, the servants had already made all of them lie on the beds. I saw that both my kids were dead and my wife was counting her last breaths. That time, I was so lost that I couldn't notice in which bedroom they were found lying. I thought it was their bedroom. However, when I asked the servants, they told me that it was your bedroom, Ranjeet. It was your bedroom, where your siblings were lying on the floor and your mother was lying at the gate. The next day after their deaths, the gardeners of the royal garden and the guards had caught and killed some terribly venomous snakes. That time, I was lost in the grief that I didn't pay attention to them and, anyway, it was not an important thing as per them. I have not reached the end of the investigations yet, but I am assuming that the kids would be playing in your room and the snakes would already have been there and stung them. When your mother would have reached there, she couldn't have been able to see the snakes in dark and would have gotten stung, too."

The face of Maharana Ranjeet had turned pale and his body was shivering. When Surya Dev saw him like that, he offered him a glass of water. After some time, Ranjeet got normal.

Seeing him getting normal, Surya Dev said, "But before I could let you know anything, you got Jagjeet murdered, along with his innocent cousin, Khushaal, who was the only successor of their empire."

Surya Dev got overwhelmed and couldn't hold back his tears, "The day Manorama had consumed poison, she had told me that if she wouldn't kill herself, she would kill you."

"She told me that she could still forgive you for the murder of her son, but could never forgive you for the murder of the only successor of her brother's empire, Khushaal,"said Surya Dev.

"She said this and gulped the poison right in front of me; while dying, she cursed you that even you would face the pain of losing a child. I don't know what I have done to Lord Shiva that he has sent all the venom-holders here to destroy my family," Surya Dev said while crying.

Ranjeet Singh anxiously held the hand of his father and both sat in silence for some time.

Then, Surya Dev forced his hand free and said, "That's why I wanted to tell you that this feeling of revenge breaks a family and destroys everything. Your mothers had forgiven each other. For the sake of peace, they had agreed that Jagjeet Singh will work in the command under you and would give you, your due respect. But, you superseded me in this game of politics, Ranjeet. You got your innocent brother killed."

"We can never run away from our deeds, Ranjeet," Surya Dev said with a heavy heart, "Everyone has to reap what he sows. Everyone has to face the consequences of all their mistakes, be it intentional or unintentional. You'd never be able to get free from the murders of your brother and stepmother. I had planted a seed dipped in the venom of my pride and a plant grew from it, which has converted into a venomous tree. That venomous tree is you, Ranjeet. I have honestly told you all the mistakes of my life, so that you don't repeat them. When you would have children, you would understand that all children are equal before a father. However, I cannot blame you anymore, as these are all my sins and I will have to face the punishments."

Surya Dev said harshly, ,"This is the gruesome side of politics. Here, virtue and sin walk hand-in-hand together and most of the times, it is the sin which wins in pride. The politics in relationships is the most dangerous amongst all, as here, even if you win, you still end up losing big. Relations are only formed by love and get respected with love. The relations, whom you fabricate with politics, only leave you alone in the end. This great throne of Maharana represents supreme power and if you won't use this power with justice and law, then it will overpower you to lead to some devastating misuse."

Surya Dev was now feeling tired, "Only time will tell what and which politics this throne of Maharana will teach you." But I am now tired of this politics of revenge. That's why, I want to go to Kashi to seek atonement for my mistakes and die there. I have heard that atoning there frees you of all your sins. I want to go this week only; so, get all the preparations done. Now, go, Ranjeet, and leave me alone."

Maharana Ranjeet Singh was sitting perplexed on hearing the truth behind the deaths of his stepmother and stepbrother. Then, Ranjeet Dev bowed before his father and left his room with a heavy heart, but the words of his father were still echoing in his mind, "This is the gruesome side of politics. Here, virtue and sin walk hand-in-hand together, and most of the times, it is the sin which wins in pride......it is the sin which wins in pride."

Walking on his travelator, he reached his room where his mother and siblings had expired and started looking for something. At last, he found what he was looking for and it's safely kept in his drawer, the thing that he had completely forgotten about, but it was empty now. That thing was a leather bag in which he had brought four venomous snakes to take to Ballabhgarh and kill Jagjeet on the way. However, Jagjeet refused to go at the last moment and he must have forgotten about keeping the bag there and left for Ballabhgarh. Maybe, his siblings would have come to his room while playing and would have opened his leather bag and freed the snakes. In turn, the snakes would have stung them. When the snakes would have gotten out of the room, it must have been difficult to catch them and the similar thing would have happened with his mother. His mother and siblings faced the consequences of his bad deeds, thought Ranjeet and started crying loudly.

Till now, Ranjeet had not regretted murdering Jagjeet, but now he was repeatedly slamming his head cursing himself for murdering innocent Jagjeet.

"I am the murderer of my mother and siblings; no, those snakes were. I will kill all the snakes and end their existence. I won't let them live; they don't have any right to live," thought Ranjeet and rode his horse towards the forest carrying a lot of oil with him. There, he put all the oil into the snake pits and lit them. All the innocent snakes were burning to death and Ranjeet was feeling satisfied thinking he has taken the revenge on the murderers of his family members.

However, he was a big fool. He was unable to understand any of the teachings or the depth of the preaching of his father. His own family had fallen and died in the pit he had dug for Jagjeet Singh. His family had reaped the consequences of his bad karma. Instead of repenting, he had filled himself with pride as if the snakes had dared to enter his house. He had brought the reason of the death of their family along with him and, now, by killing the snakes, he had increased his bad karma manifolds. His mind had started to work in the opposite way; instead of understanding his father, he had started loathing him. He had started to think that if his father had not married his mother forcibly, none of these things would have happened and instead of learning from his mistakes, he had begun to hold his father as the culprit. He thought that if his mother had given birth to their first son, he shouldn't have had children with his stepmother, Manorama.

He stood up in rage and said to himself, "Father, I wouldn't ever repeat your mistakes; I would never give birth to my stepchildren. I would only have children with a girl who would deserve to be the Maharani. I would marry as many women I would want to and would also consummate my marriage, but would have children with only one woman so that the fight of stepchildren could be averted."

Father Surya Dev was correct in assuming that Ranjeet had become a venomous tree and would only reap venom and no fruits now. He didn't claim the throne with ethics, but had blamed God for all his faults. He didn't look at his faults, but instead looked at how God had done injustice to him and, therefore, resolved to never worship God again. He had made his pride his God; now, nobody could avert his fateful fate. This was a characteristic of the low and extremely cheap mentality of a person that he would never thank God for the good happening in his life and would always blame him for the bad.

Surya Dev had left for Kashi and there was no one to educate Ranjeet on morals and ethics. He had started fighting with the neighboring states to win over them. The army chief Shamsher Singh, was getting worried as Ranjeet had put the friendships established by Surya Dev with the neighboring states on stake. Ranjeet denied them to be his own friendships and put forward his thoughts of expanding his empire. At last, one day Shamsher Singh admitted that he was now too old to handle the position of an army chief and proposed to him to hire a new chief. Ranjeet immediately made Akroor Singh as the new army chief. Shamsher Singh didn't appreciate this decision of Ranjeet as he didn't want his son to work with Ranjeet, but little did he know that Akroor was as good as Ranjeet's shadow and didn't agree to his father's desire. After some time, under the leadership of Akroor Singh, Ranjeet Singh took over all the neighboring states.

Chapter 7:
The Shiromani Palace of Kashi and the Marriage Proposal For Princess Ambika

Maharana Ranjeet was once lying on the terrace of his palace along with Akroor Singh and was chatting with him like friends.

Suddenly, Akroor asked a question to Ranjeet, "I wanted to ask a question to you, but I'm scared if you'd feel bad."

"What are you saying, friend?" Maharana Ranjeet lovingly said, "You've been my friend since childhood. There's nothing any secret about me that you don't know. Ask without any hesitation."

"It's personal; that's why I am hesitating," Akroor Singh said.

"I've never hidden anything from you. It's only you who knows everything about me. Ask what is there on your mind," Ranjeet persuaded Akroor.

"From the time you have been married to Queen Vaishali , you have never entered her room. The entire empire is talking about this that if this continues, how would the empire get its new prince. Friend, please tell me if there's any problem," Akroor Singh asked tenderly.

"Yes my friend, there is a problem and a big one and there are various reasons behind it. Now that you've asked this today, I will certainly let this weight off my chest. The first reason is that I don't like her much. Father Maharaja got me forcibly married to her. However, the bigger reason is that I don't want to have children with her. I won't ever repeat the mistakes of my father. I would never be a father to stepchildren. I would only have children with the lady, who would deserve the throne of Maharani. I would marry as many women as I'd want to and would also consummate my marriages, but have kids with only one lady so that there is no qu*Aree*l among the children. And, now my problem is what if I approach a lady and she gets pregnant? Suggest a solution, if you have any, to this problem," Ranjeet Singh explained.

"There may or may not be any solution to this problem," Akroor Singh suggested, "I know a big, royal doctor who can treat any disease. But for this, I'd have to go to Kashi."

"Ok, go, but keep in mind that this is also a matter of the esteem of my empire and, therefore, should stay between me and you," Ranjeet Singh said with seriousness.

Akroor Singh replied, "Do you even need to mention this? All your secrets are locked in my heart. Now, one could take my life , but not your secrets."

Ranjeet hugged Akroor and asked him, "Who is this doctor? Tell me in detail."

Akroor Singh responded, "There's a famous palace in Kashi by the name of Shiromani Palace. The extremely efficient royal doctors of Kashi Empire live there. The name of the current chief doctor is 'Shiromani Pandit Gangeshwar Nath Shastri'. He has two sons; the elder one is Someshwar Nath Shastri, who is married and has three children and lives in the palace of the king of Kashi as he is the king's personal doctor. The younger son is Rameshwar Nath Shastri, who is also married and has one son. Apart from this, he has two daughters who are married..."

"Leave their personal lives and come to the point, Akroor," Ranjeet Singh said while interrupting him.

"O friend! You never know if you'd find a solution to your problem here; that's why I was telling you all this," Akroor Singh furthered, "The truth is that 'Shiromani' is a rank bestowed upon their family and is being used by the sons of their family since ages. Some ancestor from the Shastri family was a great intellectual pandit and the royal physician, the king had gifted the palace to them and had also honored them with the rank, 'Shiromani'. Each son of the Shastri family is not only an efficient doctor, but also an expert in Vedas and astrology. The backyard of their big palace has been made into a private clinic, where they see the patients, and oversee the process of preparation of medicines from herbs. They have employed a lot of people, who get paid every month by the Shiromani family. The great salary keeps the employees and the entire family happy and content and there's no scarcity of money or food. They could detect the disease just by seeing one's pulse and had also inherited the knowledge of herbs. The Shiromani family is well-known in entire Kashi; even people from far-off places go there to get treated for their incurable diseases. By the grace of Lord Vishwanath, no patient has ever returned from them without being treated and, thus, it was imperative for the education of the eldest son of the Shastri family to begin since childhood as it was him, who would eventually take the place of the chief doctor. They were handling this job pretty well since generations and their contribution in the field of medicine was invaluable."

"Hmm..." Ranjeet hummed loudly.

"One more thing, the empire of Kashi is the maternal place of your dear friend, Neelkant. It's his mother's birthplace," Akroor added.

"And also of Princess Ambika," Ranjeet Singh chirped.

"Princess Ambika?" Akroor Singh asked in suspicion, "Now, what is this story?"

Ranjeet Singh told Akroor the entire story of how he met Ambika and fell in love with her at the first sight and how we was desperate to make her his own.

"So, you want your child to be born from Princess Ambika?" Akroor Singh teased Ranjeet.

Ranjeet Singh smiled in affirmation.

"Then, I'll have to leave for Kashi tomorrow only," Akroor Singh said while smiling.

Ranjeet Singh enquired, "How do you know so much about the Shiromani family and palace?"

"My younger sister, Sushma, has gotten married in a town near Kashi. Last year when I went there to get her, I got to visit Kashi along with my brother-in-law. His father was ill and we went there to get medicine for him. Their mansion resembled some palace and that's when I enquired about the history of the palace. Then, my brother-in-law told me that there's no disease that they can't treat," Akroor Singh explained.

"Then, our work has been simplified. If they have a medicine which could prevent a girl from getting pregnant until I want, then, ask Sushma and her husband to get it. Our empire's name shouldn't be made open and even you stay away from there. Give them as much of wealth as they demand. I'd pay four times the price of each medicine, but they should keep this to themselves," Ranjeet commanded.

"Alright, I'll leave for Kashi tomorrow; please send your proposal for marriage with Princess Ambika," Akroor teased him playfully.

"I don't trust anyone but you. Why don't you take the proposal there once you are back from Kashi and talk to Neelkant yourself? After all, he is my friend. He should talk to his parents," Ranjeet suggested.

"Even this is correct. I'll come back soon with both the good news," Akroor Singh jumped joyfully.

The next day, the army chief, Akroor Singh, set out with a small army unit to meet his sister, Sushma, in Kashi.

* * *

Firstly, Akroor Singh changed his avatar and met Shiromani Pandit Gangeshwar Nath Shastri in his Shiromani palace. He introduced himself as a wealthy businessman, who was there to take medicine for his daughter. He said that he had already gotten his daughter, who was just 12 years old, married. Since she was too young right now, he didn't want her to become a mother; that's why he was not sending her to in-laws' place. However, now her in-laws were pressurizing him to send his daughter else they would get their son married to someone else. He was in trouble and wanted to know if Shiromani had any medicine which could prevent a girl from getting pregnant until she wants.

The great Shiromani Pandit Gangeshwar Nath Shastri was puzzled as he had never heard of this problem before. He thought that usually childless mothers used to come to him for medicines to conceive. However, this person was also correct as his daughter was too young right now and she would be vilified for life if she gets dumped by her in-laws. Then, what she would do. He thought he would definitely make some medicine for this, and the wealthy person was also willing to pay four times the price of the medicine. Shiromani Pandit Gangeshwar Nath Shastri weighed everything and agreed to make the medicine.

Shiromani Pandit Gangeshwar Nath Shastri sought a time of three days to make the medicine for six months and also agreed to send the medicines every six months. The girl had to take one sachet of medicine with warm milk every day. When she wanted to conceive, she should leave taking the medicine and within four to six months, the ill-effect of the medicine would wash away and she'd be able to conceive.

Akroor didn't tell anything to his sister to ensure she doesn't tell anything to his parents. He took his brother-in-law into confidence and bribed him with a lot of money to send him the medicines from Shiromani mansion after every six months, but didn't disclose the reason to him either. He made his brother-in-law, Heeranand, meet Shiromani Pandit Gangeshwar, but didn't tell him that these medicines were meant for the king of Jairajgarh, Maharana Ranjeet Dev Pratap Singh.

Having taken the medicines from Kashi, Akroor left for Ballabhgarh. There, he gave the confidential message by Maharana Ranjeet Singh to Neelkant.

The moment King Krishnakant received the message that the army chief of Jairajgarh had arrived, he wondered what issue had risen that the army chief had to come himself. He asked Prince Neelkant to check what the matter was. Even Neelkant was a bit anxious as he didn't like Akroor Singh much anyway. He was wondering why he had turned up without any prior information.

Neelkant, along with a few soldiers, went outside his palace to welcome Akroor Singh.

Akroor Singh bowed before him and asked, "How are you, friend?"

Neelkant responded to his greetings and asked, "How are you, Akroor? Without any information, is everything alright?"

Akroor Singh said, "*Aree*! Will you ask all the questions here only? A friend has come to meet the other friend; why are you so surprised? Also, friend Ranjeet Singh has sent a message for you."

Neelkant was relaxed having listened to Akroor Singh. He said, "You are always welcome, friend!"

Neelkant made Akroor stay in the guest house and went to make arrangements for his snacks. He also informed his father that Akroor has come as a friend and, thus, even Krishnakant was relieved. From the time Ranjeet Singh had claimed the throne of Jairajgarh, he had conquered so many neighboring states in just one-two years that going anywhere along with his army was, indeed, a bad news for any king or state.

The next day, Akroor Singh had to leave for Jairajgarh. Therefore, he informed Neelkant that he wanted to talk to him after dinner if he had time, for he had to leave the next morning.

After dinner, Neelkant asked Akroor, "What is the important work?"

Then Akroor told him everything about Ranjeet Singh's feelings and said that Ranjeet wanted to marry his sister, Princess Ambika. After consulting with his family, he could send his message to Jairajgarh so that they could come with a wedding procession.

Neelkant was taken aback; he got himself together and said, "We would have accepted this offer and would have also considered ourselves very lucky, but Ranjeet Singh is a little late in sending this proposal as we have already fixed the marriage of Princess Ambika with the prince of Kaushambipur."

"Kaushambipur!" Akroor said in shock, "I have come here to propose to make your sister the queen of the great empire Jairajgarh and you have fixed her marriage in that small state, Kaushambipur! Nevertheless, this is our mistake that we were late in sending you the proposal. It's not your fault; but if you want, you can talk to y father once. I am sure he would want to make your sister the qu of Jairajgarh than the wife of the prince of Kaushambipur."

"Akroor Singh..." Prince Neelkant said in a stern vo "Rajputs don't budge from their promise. We have promised th and now, Princess Ambika will only go to Kaushambipur. I apolo for not calling friends on her engagement, but you are invited, al with Maharana Ranjeet Singh, to the wedding. I would person come over to invite you." Neelkant lowered his tone now.

Akroor Singh was now silent as he could feel the harshn in Neelkant's voice and could also understand its underly meaning. He thought now only Maharana Ranjeet would take final decision.

The next day, Akroor Singh had set out from Ballabhg towards Jairajgarh.

Later, King Krishnakant came to the bedroom of Neelk and asked, "*Aree*! Why did Akroor leave so early and why dic come?"

Neelkant told his father about the marriage prop Akroor Singh had put forward and also about his answer.

King Krishnakant got anxious listening to him and s "You didn't do right, you should have at least spoken to me o Whatever I have heard about Maharana Ranjeet, I can conclud is very arrogant; this would not yield good consequences. If a we had to refuse to him, I would have done it very tactfully, but spoiled everything so early in your childhood."

"Don't worry father. Akroor Singh had come as a fri and I have made him understand like a friend. If it was not ab friendship, I would have definitely told you. If Ranjeet Singh wo consider me a friend, he would also understand this. He anyway a wife already; how would he make my sister Maharani? You alre know about the bad conditions of his step-relatives. Therefor can't get my sister married into a family where I know she will sad."

"I wish whatever you are saying is right," said K Krishnakant anxiously.

Neelkant assured, "Don't worry, father. Everything will

alright."

However, King Krishnakant was not able to feel content looking at his prior experiences.

Chapter 8:
Maharana Ranjeet Dev Pratap Singh and Queen Vaishali

Akroor Singh had reached Jairajgarh and before he went to his home, he went to meet Maharana Ranjeet Singh. Maharana was happy on the success of his Kashi journey. However, he got angry the moment he got to know about what happened in Ballabhgarh.

"How dare Neelkant refuse us," roared Maharana.

Akroor Singh explained, "Why do you worry? Anyway, Princess Ambika will get married next year and one year is quite a big span of time. I assure you that Princess Ambika will only become the Maharani of Jairajgarh. If you had allowed me earlier, I would have brought her with me here."

"You are not my friend but a brother Akroor," Ranjeet Singh chirped, "Listen, I have a plan in my mind. Kaushambipur is such a small empire that acquiring over it would be such a shame. Therefore, you take my sword there and convey my message to them to either have a war with us or agree to serve under us. I am sure they wouldn't want to have a war with us because that would lead to their states getting devastated. When Kaushambipur would be under us, would Neelkant still want his sister to get married to my servant?" Ranjeet Singh smiled wickedly while stating the last statement.

"Your plan is very good, Maharana, but I don't understand why don't you just have a war with them and kill them?" Akroor

Singh asked.

"Have I not told you everything about what my father Maharaja had told me about the history of our royal empire? That's why, I don't want Ambika to come to us with malice in her heart. After all she is a woman too. Moreover, I don't want to make her mine forcibly. I want her to love me because I, too, love her," Maharana Ranjeet explained.

"Don't worry about Kaushambipur, I will take care of it," Akroor Singh replied, "But what if Neelkant still doesn't agree?"

"Then… You'd take my message yourself asking them what is it that Ballabhgarh wants – war or relationship? You'd either get *tilak* done on my sword by King Krishnakant or Ballabhgarh would decide to fight the war. I will forgive Neelkant for being our friend, but King Krishnakant is not a child to not understand that building relations with Jairajgarh is beneficial for them; after all, who would he marry his daughter to if his empire would cease to exist?" Ranjeet Singh roared.

"This is great, Maharana!" Akroor Singh said happily, "I want to request you for one more thing. Shiromani Pandit Gangeshwar Nath Shastri has taken full responsibility of his medicine that till the time a woman would have it, she can't get pregnant. I want to tell you that the entire state is talking bad about you and Queen Vaishali. I don't want the progeny to lose trust in you and you to face the insult. Therefore, before Queen Ambika comes to this palace, please give Queen Vaishali her right to be your wife. After all, even she is a woman. What if she starts conspiring against you in anger? Then, people wouldn't talk about it if you don't have a child. You can say that your first wife is infertile and that's why you are bringing your second wife. Considering herself as infertile, even Queen Vaishali won't dare to raise her head. You have children with whosoever you want to and Queen Vaishali won't be able to accuse you of not letting her claim the throne of the Maharani. You would always have the upper hand."

"Wow, Akroor Singh! You are becoming sharper in politics," Ranjeet said while laughing, "But how did your thoughts become so fine in the context of women?"

Akroor Singh, too, laughed and said, "Your maids talk to

ours and our maids exaggerate those matters to my mother. The other day, my mother was talking to my father that Maharana Ranjeet is doing great injustice with Queen Vaishali and my father should try and explain to you as she cries all the time. Everybody is sympathizing with Queen Vaishali; so, it is imperative for you to be alert."

"You are absolutely right, Akroor," Maharana Ranjeet continued with sincerity, "I, too, feel pity for her. She should get the rights of a wife. Once Ambika comes, I am not sure if I will even see her. Now, explain the procedure of the medicine to me and leave for now."

Akroor Singh explained the procedure of taking the medicine to Mahrana Ranjeet and took his leave.

Maharana Ranjeet sent an informer to the palace of Queen Vaishali in order to inform her that Maharana *ji* will be taking her for boating that night. He also urged her to meet him by the Sapta-Sangama lake all dressed up. When Queen Vaishali got this message, she couldn't believe her ears.

The maids help Vaishali dress up like a bride. Even if she had a dusky complexion, the personality of Queen Vaishali was extremely attractive. She had long, black hair and her kohled eyes increased her beauty manifolds. She had no dearth of beauty inside, but Maharana Ranjeet had never even looked at her, so how he would have known. Before he could even see her, he was already enchanted by Queen Ambika. Queen Vaishali had a slim and tall body. She had a melodious voice and she always spoke politely.

The maids of Queen Vaishali were helping her dress up for Maharana. She was wearing a red-colored Lehnga (Indian skirt) and blouse, which were adorned by a green-colored border. The colors were greatly complementing her complexion. Even Vaishali was unable to take her eyes off herself, when she was finally bejeweled with exquisite stones and jewelleries. The maids let her hair open so that Maharana falls for her beauty and their hard work doesn't go in vain.

Maharana Ranjeet was waiting for her by the Sapta-Sangama Lake. When he saw Queen Vaishali coming from the front, he was amazed. Her long, black hair waved along with the blowing wind and she tried to tame her tresses along with her chunari. When she reached close to Maharana and touched his feet to convey her greetings, only then he could come out of his thoughts. Seeing Maharana staring at her without a blink made Queen Vaishali blush. When even the maids started laughing, Maharana felt embarrassed. He gestured the maids to leave.

Maharana Ranjeet stretched his arm in front of Vaishali and she held his hand immediately and entered the boat. Their royal boat was quite big; it had a small room right at the centre, furnished with comfortable cushions and pillows. A lot of other facilities, too, were made available for the inhabitants of the royal palace. He sat, resting himself on a pillow and gestured Vaishali to sit, too. The boat was floating on the lake and the hair of Queen Vaishali still seemed to romance with the blowing wind. Maharana Ranjeet was enjoying her beauty, while Vaishali sat looking down, blushing.

Maharana Ranjeet broke the ice to start the conversation with her. He said, "Vaishali, I haven't been able to come close to you from the time you have married me and come to this house. I know you must have felt bad, but I was helpless."

Queen Vaishali admitted, "Maharana *ji*, I definitely felt bad; however, I knew that the circumstances you were going through were not easy to face. I am sure, in those situations, it was not easy for you to form a new relation."

Maharana Ranjeet hadn't expected such a reply from her; he, instead, had expected her to start cribbing, nagging and crying. He had thought of females like that only and hearing this reply from her left him stunned.

"You don't have any complaints?" Maharana Ranjeet asked Vaishali in astonishment.

"I would have had complaints if you had not come to me for my entire life, but you thought of me quite soon. I am indebted to you for this," Vaishali said while smiling.

"Father Maharaja was right, you are quite intelligent," Maharana smiled.

"What else have you heard about me?" Vaishali asked and grinned.

Her smile was endearing and Maharana Ranjeet was hooked

to her pearl-white teeth. He thought that beauty had nothing to do with the complexion. Father Maharaja was correct in saying that her beauty and qualities were quite attractive, but I was blind in my revenge that I didn't even look at her. Suddenly, Vaishali wrapped her chunari (long scarf) around herself as if trying to warm herself in the cold.

"I think you are feeling cold. Let me get something warm for you. I have got special saffron-almond milk prepared for you. I'll ask a maid to get it for you," Ranjeet suggested.

Queen Vaishali was astonished looking at this side of the personality of the Maharana Ranjeet as she had heard something else about his personality and behavior.

When maid brought just one glass of milk along, Vaishali asked Ranjeet, "Won't you drink, too?"

"No, I don't like drinking milk. I only prefer *somras (alcohol)*," Maharana smiled, "But I got this prepared especially for you and you'd have to drink it no matter what."

"Why is it necessary for me?" Vaishali questioned.

"Because my mother used to say that every woman should consume almond milk at night. This way, she becomes a mother sooner," Maharana answered.

Vaishali giggled having heard Maharana's answer, "Are you in a hurry to have a son?"

Maharana replied in a serious tone, "Yes, I am in a hurry. I want the Jairajgarh empire to get its prince soon."

Vaishali now got sober and said, "I'd try my level best to keep up the respect of your wish."

"Then, promise me that even if I am not here, you would have this almond milk every night," Maharana persisted.

"You're so good. You've so much of love for your wife and you take such a good care of her. I have never heard of any husband taking care of his wife in such a way. I am so lucky to have you," Vaishali said this and touched Maharana's feet and he responded with a hug.

"You've not promised me yet," Maharana Ranjeet smiled looking at her.

"Maharana *ji*, a promise is such a small thing, even then I am promising you," Vaishali answered in a flood of emotions, "My life is for you and if you'd give me a poison with love, I would keep the respect of your command."

"If I'd give you poison in real some day, would you have it without any issues?" Ranjeet asked mischievously.

"Yes, Maharana *ji*, I would have every poison from your hand," Queen Vaishali said emotionally in a determined tone.

"You don't even know me yet; then, how do you trust me that much?" Maharana was taken aback.

"Maharana *ji*, I only know love. I love you and that's why I would not ask for anything in return. Love only knows giving and trusting and I completely trust you," Vaishali answered.

"What are your other interests? You can share those with me," Maharana Ranjeet asked.

"You can share your interests with me, Maharana *ji*; I will mould myself according to those," Queen Vaishali answered with love.

"I liked you, Vaishali. From this day, I would spend all my nights with you. I enjoyed talking to you even more. You are welcome to my bedroom from this moment and this day," Maharana Ranjeet expressed himself.

"I am very lucky to get you as my husband," Vaishali said in immense happiness and Maharana Ranjeet engulfed her in his embrace.

Queen Vaishali had committed herself entirely to the love of Maharana Ranjeet Singh and even Maharana Ranjeet liked her, but was also not budging from playing his political games. He continued to give the medicine to prevent her from becoming a mother and poor Queen Vaishali continued consuming it considering it her husband's love. She increased her meditations and prayers and also started fasting as she wanted to fulfill the wish of her husband as soon as possible and give him the prince of the empire. She was totally oblivious to the political games played by Maharana Ranjeet.

On the other hand, when Akroor Singh reached Kaushambipur and delivered the message conveyed by Ranjeet Singh, the rulers of Kaushambipur were, indeed, scared looking at the size of their army as compared to Jairajgarh's and readily agreed to surrender to them. Following this, Maharana Ranjeet Singh kept waiting for Neelkant to personally come to him with the proposal, but that never happened and his waiting period kept extending.

One day, he got to know that Neelkant is preparing to take Ambika's proposal elsewhere and his blood came to a boil. He sent Akroor Singh with his sword, instructing him to either come back with it adorned with the sandalwood *tilak* and the marriage date if King Krishnakant approves of the relationship or with it tainted with his blood, if he doesn't.

The army chief, Akroor Singh, set out with his entire regiment to Ballabhgarh.

Chapter 9: The Marriage of Maharana Ranjeet Dev Pratap Singh and Princess Ambika

King Krishnakant was busy in some discussions with his courtiers when one of the soldiers came running to him and said, "Namaste, Maharaja! The army of Jairajgarh has surrounded Ballabhgarh from all the four directions and the chief of their army, Akroor Singh, is asking for your permission to meet you."

"What!" King Krishnakant yelled in astonishment and asked the soldier, "Do they want a war with us?" The soldier replied, "I don't know, Maharaja, but he has asked to meet you in the imperial court only."

"Alright, bring him inside with all the due respect," King Krishnakant ordered him.

"What are you saying, Father Maharaja?" Neelkant asked in bewilderment, "Don't you know why the army of Jairajgarh has come? Have you forgotten the pride in the attitude of Maharana Ranjeet Singh? Just allow us to have the war; why are you calling him inside the court with respect?"

"You just stay silent, Neelkant," King Krishnakant ordered strictly, "Till the time I am talking, you will remain silent. We can discuss this later in our personal room. Don't forget he has not come to Ballabhgarh as your friend. This is a discussion of the royal court and it needs to be resolved as per the court policies. You would only keep your temper under control. Moreover, don't forget I am still the king; you must obey the role of a prince."

"I am sorry, Father Maharaja," Neelkant took his seat.

The army chief of Jairajgarh entered along with two guards and an informer, who could read out the message of Maharana Ranjeet Singh.

"May King Krishnakant accept the greetings of the army chief of the great empire Jairajgarh," Akroor Singh said politely, "Our Maharana has sent his sword along with his message. If you'd allow, we would read out his message."

"Permission granted!" King Krishnakant ordered.

Akroor Singh, then, gestured the informer to read the message and he began,

"May the king of Ballabhgarh, Krishnakant, accept the greetings from Maharana Ranjeet Dev Pratap Singh of Jairajgarh.

The great empire Jairajgarh is progressing aggressively towards expanding its empire and the revered sword of our ancestors has now been taken out of its cover. Even you are a Rajput and would be understanding its implication that if the sword of a Rajput comes out of its cover, it either asks for red vermilion *tilak* or red blood. It can't now lower the esteem of the great empire Jairajgarh by entering its cover back without the *tilak*.

If you accept the relationship proposal from Jairajgarh, then adorn the revered sword of our ancestors with the sandalwood *tilak* and accept my proposal of my marriage with your daughter, Princess Ambika.

If your answer is in negative, then allow the swords of Ballabhgarh to talk with the swords of the grand empire Jairajgarh and the swords would decide.

I hope your decision would be in favor of the progeny of Ballabhgarh.

The Maharana of the great empire Jairajgarh,

Maharana Ranjeet Dev Pratap Singh"

The message led to Neelkant, the chief minister, the army chief, all reaching out for their swords, but King Krishnakant said after a minute of silence, "O Royal Priest! Bring the tray adorned with vermillion, *tilak* and fix the marriage of Princess Ambika."

"Father Maharaja, what did you just say!" Neelkant thought to himself in aghast.

Akroor Singh looked at Neelkant in anticipation and said to King Krishnakant, "O King Krishnakant! Congratulations for building relations with the great empire Jairajgarh."

"Congratulations to you, too, Akroor Singh," Krishnakant said while spreading *tilak* on the sword.

"You are welcome, now, Akroor Singh *ji*," Krishnakant said while gesturing to his chief minister, "You are now in the place of in-laws of Maharana; so, please allow us to serve you and the army of Jairajgarh. Mr Minister, arrange for the snacks for the relatives of Ballabhgarh."

"As you say, Maharaja!" the chief minister said politely while bowing before him and requested Akroor Singh to come along.

Akroor Singh said to Neelkant, "Congratulations to you too, friend, are you not happy? You have not exchanged any pleasantries yet."

"Congratulations to you, Akroor Singh," Neelkant said in a stern voice, "Also let Maharana Ranjeet Singh know that we would only be relatives and not friends."

"Sure, Prince Neelkant," Akroor Singh said with bitterness in his voice and went outside along with the chief minister.

King Krishnakant was sitting along with his wife in his personal chamber and was briefing her on the entire incident when Neelkant entered the room and said to his father, "Father Maharaja, what did you do? Had I not told you everything about Ranjeet earlier? Then, why did you spread *tilak* on his sword? You could have also permitted us for the war."

"Don't be foolish, Neelkant," King Krishnakant roared in

anger, "Don't you know there's no army or state comparable with the great empire Jairajgarh? Would we have been able to even stand in the war zone? You cannot think a thing in politics; how come you stood first in this subject? If I would have allowed for war, not only yours, but the head of every inhabitant of Ballabhgarh would have been lying in the war zone and even then, they would have taken Ambika along. We are Rajputs and are not scared of getting decapitated in the warzone, but even that wouldn't have helped Princess Ambika in averting this marriage. She was destined to be the queen of Jairajgarh. If that's how it has been planned; then her maternal place might as well be safe and secure. Why her maternal place be devastated? Answer me, Neelkant."

Neelkant had no answer. He knew whatever his father was saying was the bitter truth.

"Your father is right, Neelkant," Queen Jamuna Devi furthered, "You never know if she is destined to be the Maharani of Jairajgarh as the first wife of Maharana hasn't mothered any baby yet; so, you never know if all this is in the destiny of our Ambika. We had already liked him, but you were always against him and it's not necessary that Ambika would stay happy where you would get her fixed. We won't be able to utter even a word if you would get her married elsewhere. After all, your sister is going to be the queen of such a grand empire of Rajputana; bid her adieu by being her good brother. This decision is in favor of everyone, son," Queen Jamuna Devi said in a heavy voice.

"Get rid of this enmity, Neelkant. We are very happy with this relation," King Krishnakant said while letting out a deep breath, "At least I would be able to see my daughter becoming the queen of such a grand empire of Rajputana and secondly, I would see my son sitting on the royal throne of Ballabhgarh. May both my children stay happy; what else would I ever ask for and I assure you, Neelkant, Ambika would be very happy in Jairajgarh and would also become the Maharani. Now, go and see if all the guests are comfortable; let us also sit with the royal priest to decide an appropriate time for the wedding of Ambika," said Krishnakant and progressed towards his court.

Queen Jamuna, too, stood up and said, "Let me also share

this good news with Ambika." She left the chamber leaving Neelkant alone.

The auspicious date for the marriage was just twenty days away; that's why, King Krishnakant bade Akroor Singh adieu with a lot of goodies and paraphernalia marking good omen.

Akroor Singh had already sent an informer back to Jairajgarh to share the update with Maharana. Maharana Ranjeet was, as usual, very happy with another achievement of Akroor Singh. The moment he received the news of Akroor's arrival, he asked Akroor to meet him in his personal chamber instead of the court.

"You are really my brother, Akroor!" Maharana Ranjeet said in excitement and asked him to tell him everything in detail.

Akroor Singh put all the auspicious paraphernalia he had brought along and reiterated the entire series of events to him.

"Akroor Singh," Maharana said gladly, "I am very happy after a long time. I even liked Queen Vaishali a lot. It was you who motivated me to go near her and it's you who has fixed my marriage with Princess Ambika. Now, I even got my love. I am deeply indebted to you. Now, I would see which of these queens deserve to be a Maharani. Today, I am happy and content and you are the one who is responsible for this, my brother!"

"I am happy to see you happy, my friend," Akroor Singh replied cheerfully.

That night, when Maharana reached the room of Queen Vaishali, the news of his second marriage had already reached her. She fell on his knees and started crying, "What crime have I committed that you are giving me such pain? We have not even completed one year together and you have already left me; why?"

Maharana Ranjeet Singh helped her stand up, hugged and said, "Why are you thinking like this and where is the pain in this matter? All your rights are secured. I am not leaving you. Your position would stay intact, Vaishali, even after the arrival of the new queen. Moreover, you know that a king has to do political marriages and there's nothing wrong in this also."

"But what was the need of a political marriage right now?" Queen Vaishali asked while crying.

"Stop spreading this bane, Vaishali. I was so happy today that I got my love and you have spoiled my mood by crying and creating this mess," Maharana Ranjeet said getting annoyed.

"Your love… so, Princess Ambika is your love?" Vaishali asked in wonder.

"Yes, Vaishali, I love Ambika a lot," said Ranjeet and explained everything to her.

The matter ended there. After hearing everything, Queen Vaishali said with a faded smile, "You are getting your love. Congratulations to you for this, Maharana *ji*. What are your orders for me now?" Queen Vaishali asked in a serious tone.

"There's just one order for you. Continue keeping me happy the way you have been doing. I am not able to resist myself from talking to you, Vaishali," said Maharana and pulled her into his embrace and Queen Vaishali kept getting deeper into her pain.

Queen Vaishali had broken from inside. She had understood that Maharana only considers her an object of pleasure and doesn't love her. She was badly hurt having realized this. Till the day he left to bring his new bride, Princess Ambika, to the palace, he continued coming to the bedroom of Queen Vaishali daily. Although Maharana Ranjeet had thought that he is giving her rights to her, but this right seemed sheer insult to Queen Vaishali. Her heart was broken because of this self-centered behavior of Maharana. She realized she was just serving to the physical desires of Maharana in the name of rights.

Maharana was all set to take his wedding procession to Ballabhgarh and, then, he came to the room of Queen Vaishali to meet her. Maharana said to Vaishali, "Bid me adieu happily while doing my *tilak* (holy sandalwood paste). I have nobody else, but you to share this happiness with."

Queen Vaishali got up like an electronic doll and did the *tilak* for Maharana. Maharana urged her to smile and be happy. However, Vaishali was not able to consider herself more than a puppet. She was deep in pain and the happiness of Maharana was worsening it further.

Maharana Ranjeet had set out and Queen Vaishali was lying on the cold floor of her room. A maid came and asked her for food or lightening up her room, but she didn't respond. She kept crying day and night. In the morning, she fell ill and she only had the maids to serve her. She didn't have her parents in her maternal place. Her father had expired in a war and her mother had died along with the last rites of her father as *sati*. She had only one person to call her own, Maharana Surya Dev Pratap Singh, who had loved her like a father and also understood her pain, but even he wasn't there now. She had no one to call her own in the whole wide world to pacify her or understand her pain. Not getting any pleasure from her husband would have been better for her. Had Maharana never come close to her, she would have still considered that he was never really hers. There was no pain bigger than a known person turning a stranger.

"Why are men so harsh and self-centered? Would they ever be able to bear a similar pain?" she thought.

There in Ballabhgarh, the marriage of 17-year-old Princess Ambika had successfully completed with the 21-year-old Maharana Ranjeet and they were all preparing to go back to Jairajgarh.

Queen Jamuna took Ambika to her room and explained to her, "Listen, Ambika, now you are going to your in-laws' place; so, carefully listen to me. There, always keep your husband tamed. Make sure he doesn't go to your co-wife, else it will be your defeat. Keep this clear in your mind that you have to take over the throne of Maharani and for this, you would have to give birth to a son first. If you are able to do this, then Maharana would be your slave for life. Just make sure that your co-wife doesn't become mother first and that Maharana never goes to her. What purpose would your beauty serve otherwise?

"What are you teaching her, mother?" Neelkant entered the room laughing and said, "Would you give all your lessons to your daughter or would you save some for your soon-to-come daughter-in-law also?"

"Son, the lessons for a daughter and a daughter-in-law are different. You men won't understand this," Queen Jamuna explained.

Neelkant furthered, "Now, take Ambika along. Everyone outside is waiting to leave."

The princess of Ballabhgarh was now the queen of Jairajgarh. Maharana Ranjeet was able to get her along and had already set out for Jairajgarh.

When they reached Jairajgarh, Maharana Ranjeet noticed Queen Vaishali to be missing among the women present at the main gate to welcome them. Upon enquiring, the maids told him that she was badly ill.

Maharana Ranjeet heard this and shouted, "She is just ill and hasn't died yet. Ask her to come here and welcome the new bride. Hearing this, Queen Ambika became happy thinking that Maharana doesn't consider her co-wife important. It was good for her as she wouldn't have to put in as much of efforts as her mother had mentioned.

The moment Queen Ambika saw Vaishali, she smiled with pride and thought, "Oh! She is Queen Vaishali! She is dusky and slim and doesn't stand anywhere in front of me. Maharana *ji* was after me because she doesn't deserve him. Anyway, while I am here, Maharana *ji* can never be hers."

Queen Vaishali had turned red and pale because of the high fever and Maharana felt pity for her after looking at her condition. He realized she was, indeed, unwell. He had thought her to be acting to express her displeasure on arrival of new Queen Ambika.

Queen Vaishali prayed and did *tilak* for both of them with extreme difficulty. She further welcomed the new bride and said, "Come, sister. You are welcome to the royal palace."

Queen Ambika walked with pride, looking at the entire palace through her veil. Everybody was getting mesmerized looking at her beauty and was constantly staring at her. May be, they had never seen such a pretty queen before. Queen Ambika was extremely proud of her beauty, for she knew that beautiful women could easily tame men.

Queen Vaishali was barely able to stand and, thus, she bowed before Maharana and asked, "Are there any other orders for me, Maharana *ji*?"

Maharana Ranjeet answered politely, "No, Vaishali. I didn't know you are this ill, otherwise I wouldn't have bothered you to come here. Queen Ambika would have come to your room to meet you. Come, let me drop you to your room."

"No, Maharana *ji*, please don't bother," Queen Vaishali

responded in a low voice, "I know the way back to my room; I will go on my own." She moved to her room along with the maids.

"Janki Devi," Maharana called one of his special maid servants and asked her, "Are you giving the almond milk to Queen Vaishali?"

"Yes, Maharana *ji*, I make it every day myself and give it to her. However, she has not been keeping well since last three days, hence the chief physician has stopped giving the milk to her and that's why I haven't made any for her," Janki Devi replied.

"Alright, start giving her the milk once she is cured. It is very important for her health. Now, give the same milk to my new queen, Ambika, also. Don't show any carelessness in this. Have you understood?" Maharana Ranjeet commanded the maid.

Janki Devi replied, "Yes, Maharana *ji*. As you wish."

Maharana took his new bride, Ambika, to his room, where it was his honeymoon night with her.

Chapter 10:
The Untimely Death of Queen Vaishali

Maharana Ranjeet was under the complete spell of the beauty of Queen Ambika; in fact, she had taken over his mind through her beauty. She didn't allow Maharana to go close to Queen Vaishali and if ever he attempted to, she persuaded him by either fighting or not talking to him. If ever Maharana Ranjeet used to go to the room of Queen Vaishali to ask how she was doing and if Ambika used to get to know about this, she used to create hue and cry about it. She disliked them meeting. She always used to fear Vaishali mothering the son of Maharana Ranjeet first and snatching away Maharana from her. That's why she used to always stay miffed with Vaishali and used to consider her authority over Maharana. She was turning aggressive, too, out of her insecurities.

After the arrival of Queen Ambika, Queen Vaishali fell deeper into the dig of loneliness and sorrow and Ambika used to enjoy seeing her in pain. She used to take pride in the fact that she rules over the heart of Maharana and her co-wife feels jealous of this. Queen Vaishali was already of a serious nature and, now, was slowly turning into an introvert. She never used to complain or call Maharana Ranjeet. Gradually, even the youthful Maharana was also turning to a more mature man. However, Ambika was still not mature and her child-like behavior used to create fresh problems for him every day. Queen Vaishali was tolerant but, like all other qualities, even tolerance knows some limit and this limit got exceeded one day.

One night, Maharana Ranjeet was coming back from boating with Queen Ambika when a shadow came from behind the tree. It was Queen Vaishali, who bowed before Maharana and said, "Namaste, Maharana *ji*! I want to talk something really important with you personally."

Queen Ambika was peeved seeing her. She retorted, "Why personally; why don't you talk here in front of me? After all, I am his wife."

Queen Vaishali said with seriousness, "You should stay in your limits, Queen Ambika. May be you are forgetting that I am, too, his wife and Maharana *ji*, I am asking you again, I want to talk to you personally. If you want me to continue in front of your second wife, may be it will be tough for you to make her understand later. So, please decide for yourself what you want to do." Vaishali said in a stern voice.

Maharana Ranjeet had never seen this side of her and, thus, he instructed Ambika to go to her room assuring her that he will join her there later.

Ambika looked furiously at Vaishali and furthered to her room. However, she hid herself behind the tree in dark and attempted at overhearing their conversation.

"Tell me, Queen Vaishali, what is that important thing you wanted to talk with me?" Maharana asked.

"Maharana *ji*, please come into the moonlight. I want to clearly see your face," Queen Vaishali requested.

Maharana Ranjeet thought to himself that may be she would nag and complain that he hasn't visited her after the coming of Queen Ambika and would throw her tantrums to please him; it also occurred to him that it had, indeed, been quite some time since he had visited Vaishali in her room. Thinking this, he took Vaishali into his embrace and asked her if she wanted him to spend that night with her.

"It has been quite some time we'd spent time together. It's all my fault; I have done great injustice to you after the coming of

Queen Ambika," Maharana Ranjeet said lovingly.

"That's not required, Maharana *ji*. I have come to express my condolences over the death of one of your special maids, Janki Devi," Vaishali said in a rather harsh tone.

"What are you saying? Just two days back, I'd met her and she was fine. What happened to her?" he wondered.

"The pot of her bad karma had filled to the brim, Maharana *ji*," Vaishali didn't try to sugarcoat her words.

"What do you want to say, Queen Vaishali?" Maharana Ranjeet said angrily, "I don't have time to solve your riddles. Speak clearly."

"You won't be able to hear it clearly, Maharana *ji*, because those who don't have pure acts can't even hear pure truths," Vaishali retorted.

Maharana's face went pale. He still asked her, "What do you want to say?"

"I mean, Maharana *ji*, that the truth behind the saffron-almond milk, which you have been giving me since so many years obeying your late mother has been disclosed to me by maid Janki before her death and I am not a fool like your other queen," Vaishali said rhetorically.

Maharana Ranjeet was now standing stunned and didn't utter a word.

Queen Vaishali was now furious. She yelled, "Maharana *ji*, the entire world calls woman as 'triyacharitra' (dubious character). They befool men and use them, but what name should be given to men like you who befool innocent women and throw them in a corner to die when your self-interest has been satiated. When you had brought Queen Ambika, I used to cry missing your love, but now I loathe you. Why did you do this to me? What wrong had I done to you? For a very long time, I kept cursing God and myself that I was not able to give a prince to this empire; I had started thinking that I was infertile, and you? You continued playing this disgusting game with me. Aren't you even a bit scared of God? The Goddess Mahishasurmardini, who is worshipped by your empire, and who is also your family God, aren't you ashamed of yourself when you stand in front of her with your hands folded? Doesn't your conscience blame you? You are not a human being, shame on you! Did you hear, Maharana *ji*? Shame on you!" Queen Vaishali said while crying.

"Yes, I am not a human being," Maharana Ranjeet said heatedly, "I am a beast. Is that what you want to say?" He held Queen Vaishali by her neck and roared, "You have invoked my beast avatar by raising your voice in front of me. I cannot stand a woman either raising her head or voice in front of me. And listen to me clearly, Vaishali," Maharana now pulled her hair, "I would give the fortune of mothering my child to whosoever I'd want and that Maharani would claim the throne, too. This entire empire is mine. You hadn't brought this empire in dowry. If it was not for my father, I would have never married you. Have you ever looked at yourself in the mirror? You are not even worth standing beside me. Neither I love you, nor would I have a child with you, no matter what. I won't ever repeat the mistakes of my father maharaja. I won't allow the birth of any stepchildren. I would only consummate women and only those who fulfill my expectations. The woman I love would only be the mother of my son and no one else. You are a queen, and you should better live like one. Don't dream about becoming a Maharani and don't you even try to ride on my nerves, because if I'd deal with this, you won't be able to even die as per your wish. Did you get it,Queen Vaishali Devi?"

The moment Maharana let go of her neck, she fell on the ground and started crying profusely. She said, "If this is the respect a woman gets in your palace, then I don't have any right to live here. It'd be better if you'd rather kill me. At least, I won't be dying every day like this."

Maharana Ranjeet laughed on this and said, "This is also correct; I should kill you. Are you not even capable of dying on your own?"

Queen Vaishali was crying out of the increasing grief and insult and she started wailing, "O Lord! If I have ever done anything good, please kill me this moment. I cannot stand more insult of the feminism."

Maharana Ranjeet started slapping hard on her face and roared on her face, "Don't insult me any further by shouting like this and don't even try to create a scene in front of the servants. If you want to die, then do that in your room. Don't create a drama here for the servants and the entire empire to see. If you don't leave this moment, I would get you thrown in your maternal place, understood?"

Maharana Ranjeet walked inside the palace with extreme pride of having shown his beast side to Vaishali. Even Queen Ambika, who was hidden behind an adjacent tree, was scared out of her wits and was standing holding her breath so that Maharana doesn't see her and show this beast avatar of him to her, too.

Queen Vaishali was crying uncontrollably lying by the lake. Ambika felt pity for her and wondered if she should stand by her in this moment of grief when Queen Vaishali stood up with a jerk. It seemed as if she had lost control on herself. Tears were not stopping from her eyes and pain could be seen reflecting on her face. Her chunari (long scarf) was sliding along and her long hair was let open. She reached by the Sapta-Sangama Lake and shouted, "Hey Mother Chandika! Hey Mother Mahishasurmardini, seeing the insult of your powers and avatars in this empire, I am not even able to breathe here. Send one of your avatars to end this loathsome game of this beast. If I have ever done anything good at your pious feet, this egotistical man should never get loved by any woman and he should not be able to touch my dead body by his tainted hands. With this wish, I sacrifice my life at your pious feet. Jai Mahishasurmardini!" saying this, Queen Vaishali jumped in the Sapta-Sangama Lake.

Queen Ambika was witnessing everything standing behind the tree. Suddenly, two guards standing for the security ran towards the lake shouting, "Queen Vaishali has fallen into the lake!" Two divers, too, jumped into the water to save her, but Goddess Mahishasurmardini had already listened to her prayers; maybe that's why the divers couldn't find her dead body. They could only come out with her chunari (long scarf). All the servants of the palace started gathering around the lake. When the news reached to Maharana Ranjeet, he got worried and ran to the lake. Taking this opportunity, even Queen Ambika came out from the ambush and joined the crowd and later, stood by Maharana Ranjeet. Maharana had never thought that Vaishali would commit suicide. Even his soul was shaken that very moment.

Queen Ambika had witnessed everything and had clearly heard every word said, yet she was not able to tell this to Maharana. She considered being silent as the better option. She was trembling in fear and Maharana instructed her to go to her room, to which she agreed. Queen Ambika was extremely scared of Maharana Ranjeet and she was terribly missing her maternal home. However, she was not able to understand the meaning of the conversation happened between Maharana and Vaishali.

Prince Neelkant had come from Ballabhgarh to share his condolences over the death of Queen Vaishali. Ambika had told the entire truth to his brother and she wanted to go back to her maternal home. Neelkant was shocked listening to her. He asked for the permission of Maharana to take her sister to her maternal place for some time, but Maharana denied him to take her then.

Neelkant shared the truth behind the death of Queen Vaishali with her father, Krishnakant, and mother, Jamuna, but even they denied getting Ambika home without the permission of Maharana Ranjeet. Although they started crying, but said, "It's her destiny now. We can't become a subject of insult by bringing our daughter back home after her marriage. It's a shameful thing for a father if his married daughter comes back. She should now live and die there."

A few days later, Jamuna Devi came to Jairajgarh to meet Ambika and she tried to explain to her that it happened for good that her co-wife was no more. She asked her to forget the past and begin a new life with Maharana and try to mother a son as soon as possible in order to seize the throne of Maharani.

Maharana Ranjeet was deeply shaken by the death of Queen Vaishali. Although he never loved her but he was deeply affected by her sudden demise. He had always considered it the fortune of the ladies to get insulted by their husbands and there was nothing to feel so bad to commit suicide. He was sad for her death, but he was still not able to see his own mistake anywhere in this. He wondered she was a serious and intelligent woman, then how come she turned so weak in that moment that she considered dying easier than living.

Maharana Ranjeet had inadvertently started taking the blame on himself. In these moments, he desired the sympathy from Queen Ambika, but she was really happy because of all this and she didn't even make an attempt to hide her happiness. She was happy as her mother had explained to her that the biggest obstacle from her path had been removed now. After the demise of Queen Vaishali, Maharana Ranjeet had started to dislike the impishness of Ambika and he had started to prefer spending time in either war zone or forests over spending time with her. He had started distancing himself from Ambika.

Time took its turn and the fate of Queen Vaishali had now become the fate of Queen Ambika. Maharana Ranjeet didn't return for years and used to stay in the war zones. He didn't even want a child with her, as he didn't like her much now and that's why, his special maid, *Gulabo*, used to give her the same almond milk every night with the added medicine which prevented her from getting pregnant.

Years had passed. Maharana had crossed the age of 30 years and even Queen Ambika was now 27-28 years old, but hadn't been lucky to be a mother. In all these years, there had been no difference in her looks or youth. She was, in fact, getting prettier every day. Although Maharana Ranjeet was still under the spell of her beauty, he didn't prefer talking to her as he found her talks more childish and foolish than wise and he didn't want her to mother his child. In this case, he always used to miss Queen Vaishali.

There in Ballabhgarh, Neelkant had gotten married and was, now, a father of two children. King Krishnakant had died in the war zone, during a war, and his wife, Jamuna Devi, had burned herself along her husband's pyre as *sati*. The coronation of King Neelkant had been done and he was busy in minding his married life and the state.

Chapter 11: Meeramani, The Princess of Sambhalgarh

Maharana Ranjeet had taken over a major part of Rajputana and, now, his army was progressing towards another state, Sambhalgarh. The army of the great empire Jairajgarh, under the leadership of the army chief, Akroor Singh, had already surrounded Sambhalgarh, and had also set up their camps. Akroor Singh, having received the permission of Ranjeet Singh, had already set out for the court of Sambhalgarh.

Sambhalgarh was a small empire, with its ruling king being 'King Surat Singh', who had two wives. He had two children from his first wife, Uma Devi, – a daughter, Princess Meeramani, who was around 16 years old and a son, Prince Virat Singh, who was around 11. His first wife had died shortly after the delivery of their son, Virat. The second wife of Surat Singh was the younger sister of Uma, Sheetla Devi. He had one son from her, Prince Somesh, who was around 7 years old.

Princess Meeramani was an ardent follower of Lord Shiva. Her father, Surat Singh, had declared to his wife, Uma Devi, that he would have a second marriage if she wouldn't give him a prince soon. Uma Devi used to worship earnestly asking for a son. Her pain reached Meeramani, too, and even she joined her mother in worshipping Lord Shiva. She was not even 5 when she had already started fasting for the entire spring for Lord Shiva as even she wanted a lovely brother. Lord Shiva couldn't overlook the prayers of his young follower and gave her a younger brother, Virat, before the next season of spring. However, when Virat was not even one, his mother, Uma Devi, had passed away. King Surat Singh had got a successor to his throne and the empire had got its prince, but Meeramani and Virat had lost their mother, who could love them and care for them.

Meeramani knew the reason behind her mother's death. According to the traditions, Uma Devi delivered her son, Virat, at her maternal place. The elder brother of Uma Devi had come to drop her to her in-laws' place in Sambhalgarh, along with Virat, who was 3 months old then. Then, their younger sister, Sheetla Devi, who was just 15 years old, had also come along with them. Meeramani was enjoying the company of her aunt, Sheetla, who was taking a good care of Virat, too. Uma Devi had requested her to stay at Sambhalgarh for some time, after which she could go back. However, Sheetla and King Surat Singh had developed illegitimate relationship. When Uma Devi got to know about this, she insisted to send Sheetla Devi back, but Surat Singh didn't agree to this. Had Surat Singh married Sheetla Devi otherwise, she would have still accepted her as kings generally had several marriages, but she was not able to accept their cheating. She called her brother and briefed him on the entire incident. Her brother was furious hearing everything and he scolded Sheetla and urged her to return with him. However, Surat Singh insulted him and didn't send Sheetla back. All this was turning bad for Uma. Her brother had declared that if Sheetla wouldn't accompany him back then, they would consider her as dead and would break all relations with Sambhalgarh. Uma Devi was deeply disturbed because of this, as both her maternal as well as in-laws' houses were destroyed. She was hurt because of this and, also, because Sheetla and Surat Singh had started residing in the same room without marriage. Both of them had put every other relation on stake and, thus, Uma Devi had committed suicide.

Sheetla Devi became the new mother to Meeramani and Virat and wife to Surat Singh, but she was quite young and inexperienced to be a mother to motherless children. She could only be the lover of

Surat Singh and not the mother of the children. However, 5-6 years old Meeramani became the mother of her brother, Virat, and started caring for him with great affection. Young Virat had even started calling her "*jiji* ma"(elder sister who cares like mother) as she had become more than a sister for him. They got everything in the royal palace except for the love of their parents. Meeramani had become a mother-figure for everyone, for she was so used to mothering his brother, Virat, from a very young age.

Despite belonging to 'Kshatriya' (ruler warriors) clan, Meeramani never ate non-vegetarian food. She loved animals and birds alike. By the age of 16, she was an expert in war tactics and fighting with sword. She always thought that like the trident of Lord Shiva was used only to kill the sinners, even her sword would only be raised to kill the sinners. She was teaching the same to Virat also, but Surat Singh used to dislike this. However, he stayed silent considering he was anyway not able to give them his love and their stepmother wasn't doing anything, too. He thought he would make Virat understand his ways when Meeramani would leave the palace after her marriage. After all, Virat had to be the king of the empire.

Apart from Virat, the only person whom Meermani considered as her own was their chief maid, Malini.

The story behind Malini goes like – when Virat was born in his maternal place, they had liked this maid, Malini, who was a child widow of 14 years. Her mother-in-law used to physically torture her. Young Meeramani had great sympathy for her and she insisted her to be with them. Then, their mother, Uma, had in a way purchased her. She had given huge amount of money to the mother-in-law of Malini, so that she could live with Meeramani and even her life could be bettered. Since Malini's mother-in-law was a greedy woman, she readily agreed to leave Malini with Meeramani. Malini was very happy to join them and took great care of Meeramani and Virat. When Uma Devi had committed suicide, she had urged her to be with Meermani and Virat and never leave them. Meeramani shared all her secrets with only her and even Malini was familiar with each thread of her mind. She loved both Meeramani and Virat more than her life.

Meeramani had turned 16 and the talks of her beauty and

war expertise had started to spread in the entire Rajputana. When their royal minister, Jagat Singh, used to teach Prince Virat Singh on politics, state work and Chanakya-policies, even Meeramani and Malini used to be present there. That's why Meermani was adept at politics more than Virat. Her skills and beauty were developing at the age of 16. The chief maid, Malini, was also getting adept at fencing, especially being taught to her by Surat Singh for the protection of both the children.

Meeramani was extremely fair and clearly looked wise. She looked innocent, but her eyes reflected seriousness and confidence. Her beauty could challenge that of a nymph, but she stayed simple like saints. Once, she had gone to Kashi with her mother, where one of the saints had made her wear a Rudraksh beaded string in her neck and this had remained with her ever since. Meeramani loved her string and used to wear it all the time, like a mangalsutra. Later, Uma Devi had got the beads strung in a golden wire and had also placed a small locket depicting Lord Shiva. Meeramani wasn't fond of jewellery, but loved her string. Her personality was so attractive that anyone looking at her and talking to her would stay enchanted. Her voice was charming and her being wise added value to it. Her thoughts were revolutionary and she never took anything easy. If she believed in whatever she did, she remained strong on her thoughts, no matter what everyone said. She was courageous and strong-minded. However, she was not obstinate; she used to think through things and believe in them. She was self-confident and knew its difference from pride. She was kind-hearted, but never forgave cheaters easily.

On the boundary of Sambhalgarh, there was an old Lord Shiva temple, where Meeramani had great trust. She used to find solace there. She bettered the temple, which was in a shamble, and looking at her faith, even Surat Singh had arranged for a priest there. Whenever Meeramani was in stress or sorrow, she used to go to the temple and meditate for hours. She believed whenever she sat there and meditated, Lord Shiva filled her mind with the solutions to her problems and she always used to return with the answers to her prayers.

Everybody knew that Princess Meeramani was an ardent

follower of Lord Shiva; they were not surprised when Meeramani went to the temple to worship at any point in the day. They knew that there was no fixed time for her to worship and she went to the temple whenever she wished to. She used to go to the temple when she was happy, sad or worried any time in the day. The entire Sambhalgarh believed that throughout Rajputana, a Saint 'Meerabai' was an ardent follower of Lord Krishna, and one 'Meeramani' was an ardent follower of Lord Shiva.

One morning, Meeramani was going to the temple along with her chief maid Malini, when the army chief of Jairajgarh, Akroor Singh, was entering the royal palace with the message from Maharana Ranjeet Pratap Singh. Akroor Singh had read out the message by Maharana asking King Surat Singh to either surrender to them or be ready for a war the next morning as their army had surrounded them already. King Surat Singh wasn't able to understand what should be done, as their army couldn't have stood before the vast army of Jairajgarh. Therefore, he asked for time till the evening as he wanted to discuss this internally with this council of ministers. He said there was an old Shiva temple at the boundary of Sambhalgarh, where he went with his family every Monday to worship and mentioned that he would share their decision after their prayers.

Akroor Singh set out to the camp carrying the message of King Surat Singh of Sambhalgarh and shared the message with Ranjeet Singh upon reaching there.

The king of Sambhalgarh, Surat Singh, after discussing with his council of ministers arrived on the decision that it was better for them to surrender in order to avoid mass destruction and bloodshed. He had clearly understood that their fistful of soldiers couldn't stand in front of the vast army of Jairajgarh. In the evening, he sent out the message to the royal family that no one would accompany him to the Shiva temple that evening, but before this news could reach every member of the family, Meeramani had already left for the temple for her customary preparations for the prayers.

King Surat Singh got worried on knowing this and quickly said to his defense services chief, "Get the army ready; the enemies have set up their camps there. I am afraid she might get caught by them."

When Meeramani reached the temple, she saw the camps set up by the soldiers of Jairajgarh. She said to Malini, "What is the army of enemy doing here? The war has neither begun yet nor has it ended. Then, how come they have entered our boundary? Malini, get hold of your sword, also." Meeramani held her sword in one hand, while the tray of prayer paraphernalia in the other and stepped down from the chariot. Her soldiers started following her with their arms.

Maharana Ranjeet was progressing towards the temple from his camp when he saw a royal chariot stopping by the temple and two women getting out of it carrying swords. Maharana asked his charioteer to race as he wanted to see what was happening.

"As you wish," said the charioteer.

In the courtyard of the Shiva temple, Akroor Singh was briefing the soldiers to tighten the security around Maharana Ranjeet Singh as he was soon going to meet the king of Sambhalgarh, King Surat Singh. Suddenly, he saw a chariot from the royal palace stopping by and a nymph-like girl stepping out of it, accompanied by her maid and some soldiers.

"Alert!" said one of the soldiers of Sambhalgarh, "The princess of Sambhalgarh has come here to offer her prayers and she wants to know what is the enemy army doing inside the boundary of Sambhalgarh?"

Akroor Singh had lost his senses looking at Meeramani's beauty. He was constantly staring at her. Meeramani gestured Malini and she placed her sword on the chest of Akroor and that's when he could be brought back to his senses. He removed the sword placed on his chest and said while looking at Meeramani, "Princess, your father has invited us here to meet him and have a discussion. Even our Maharana Ranjeet Singh would be reaching here any time soon."

That moment, Maharana reached there and was surprised looking at Meeramani. In the crimson color of dusk, Meermani was dazzling in her orange attire. She had a distinct charm on her face, akin to the Goddess Durga. Maharana's mouth was left open upon looking at her.

Akroor Singh bowed before Maharana Ranjeet and said politely, "Maharana *ji*, she is the princess of Sambhalgarh and she has come here to offer her prayers."

Maharana Ranjeet looked at the Meeramani and said politely, "It seems as if Sambhalgarh doesn't practice the customs of veils."

Princess Meeramani was enraged hearing this. She said, "Only places where men are uncultured, practice of veils are followed there. Every man in Sambhalgarh knows how to stay in his limits and who he should look down before. However, I think there's no ruler to put a bridle on the men of Jairajgarh.

Before Akroor Singh could answer her, Maharana Ranjeet gestured him to abstain. Suddenly, the chariot of King Surat Singh arrived and he was accompanied by his senior army men on their horses. The army unit took Princess Meeramani into their security.

"Meera, I didn't expect such impishness from you. You knew since morning that our empire has been surrounded by the enemy and still you came to the temple without informing anyone," Surat Singh said to Meeramani.

"I apologize, Father Maharaja, but I hadn't ever taken anyone's permission before coming to the temple and you hadn't given me any such instruction before," Meeramani bowed before him respectfully and explained.

"Then the matter was different, my daughter. Hurry up; go inside the temple and wait for me to come there once you are finished with offering your prayers," King Surat Singh got irked.

Meeramani went inside the temple and Akroor Singh introduced the king of Sambhalgarh with the Maharana of Jairajgarh. Both greeted each other formally and sat outside the temple to discuss.

"What have you decided, King Surat Singh *ji*?" asked Maharana Ranjeet Singh.

"We are in a dilemma, Maharana *ji*," King Surat Singh said with his folded hands, "You have just met my daughter, Meeramani. My son, Virat Singh, who is the Prince of our empire, considers her as his mother and obeys all her orders. I have discussed with my council of ministers and have arrived on a consensus that we don't want any bloodshed and, hence, we don't have any problem in working under your reign, but..."

"But what, King Surat Singh *ji*?" asked Maharana Ranjeet.

"I apologize, Maharana *ji*, but my daughter, Meeramani, and my son, Virat Singh, have told us that if we would surrender before you, they would kill themselves having consumed poison," Surat Singh said hesitatingly.

"What!" Maharana Ranjeet asked in shock.

"Yes, Maharana *ji*, Meeramani says that dying in freedom is better than living in slavery or under dependency. She is not afraid of anyone or anything. She expresses her disbelief to me openly. I am her father and I am helpless and I doubt if anyone in the entire Sambhalgarh would have any answer to her questions. I listen and agree to her. If she would command a war in the state assembly, then every child in Sambhalgarh would happily decapitate himself in her honor," Surat Singh explained.

"I've never seen such a revolutionary side of a woman. You've brought up your daughter differently, King Surat Singh *ji*," Maharana Ranjeet commented rhetorically.

"You are right, Maharana *ji*, but it's all my fault. Her mother had passed away in her childhood and..."King Surat Singh explained the entire story of Meeramani's childhood. "Now, please tell me what should I do? That's why I have come to request you for one more day. If I am able to explain to my children in one day, then it's ok; otherwise, we would meet you in the war zone. Then, whatever would be the will of Lord Shiva will happen."

"Hmmm..." Maharana Ranjeet took a deep breath and said while smiling, "Would your daughter marry according to your will, or would she have her say in that, too?"

"You're misunderstanding Maharana *ji*, my daughter has revolutionary thoughts, but is extremely cultured. Everyone bows before her because she always talks sense. Sin and iniquity are miles apart from her and, thus, she is always fearless. Now, please allow me to take your leave, Maharana *ji*, my informer would come to you with our message by evening tomorrow." Surat Singh stopped for a minute and continued, "Till the time we don't decide for a peaceful union or a war, could you please have your army stay outside our boundaries because my obstinate daughter wouldn't stop coming to the temple. No matter what anyone does, this is one area of her devotion where she doesn't listen to anyone. She would come tomorrow, too, and the days after, too, till she is alive. So, I'd request you, that your army should be staying in their limits and not cross our boundary."

"I promise you, King Surat Singh *ji*, no one from my army would enter your boundary till any decision is made. Have your heard, Akroor Singh *ji*?" Maharana Ranjeet declared.

"Yes, Maharana *ji*! As you wish, " Akroor Singh bowed and replied.

"King Surat Singh *ji*, I would like to make a request to you. I liked this Shiva temple a lot and I found solace here. I am experiencing a happiness that I never had before. If you allow, can I offer my prayers here?" Maharana Ranjeet Singh asked.

"Sure!" King Surat Singh said respectfully, "God's temple is open to all; why do you have to seek permission to enter a temple? You can pray here any time."

"Thank you so much!" Maharana Ranjeet folded his hands and replied.

Suddenly, a sound of a conch shell echoed in the silence of the evening. King Surat Singh said, "Maharana *ji*, it is the time for evening prayers. If you'd allow me, I want to attend the prayers. If you wish, you could also join us."

Maharana Ranjeet said to Akroor Singh, "We would leave from here after the Lord Shiva prayers."

"As you say," Akroor Singh left to inform the army men.

Maharana Ranjeet entered the temple with Surat Singh. Inside the Shiva temple, Maharana Ranjeet was left amazed looking at the Princess Meeramani singing the prayers for Lord Shiva. The light spread from the fire from camphor and incense sticks had lit up the face of Meeramani. She was lost in her prayers and resembled a goddess. Maharana had lost all his senses looking at her that moment.

After the prayers, Raja Surat Singh greeted Maharana Ranjeet Dev Pratap Singh with his daughter Meeramani and left for his palace.

Maharana Ranjeet sat on a platform outside the temple. His army chief, Akroor Singh, then came to him and asked, "Maharana *ji*, is there any problem? Are you not well? Let's go to the camp so that you could take rest."

Maharana Ranjeet said in a low voice, "Let me sit here, Akroor. Ask the army to move back to the camps, but you could stay here if you want. I want to talk something important."

Akroor Singh asked a few important army men to stay back and the rest of them to move back to the camps. He sat beside Maharana Ranjeet and smiled, "I feel there wouldn't be any war."

Maharana Ranjeet asked surprisingly, "Will King Surat Singh surrender to us?"

Akroor Singh asked, "First you have to tell me from whom you want to listen to an answer – the army chief or your friend?"

"Both," Maharana Ranjeet answered.

Akroor Singh said, "The first answer is from your army chief – King Surat Singh would only ask for a war and the second answer is from your friend – even then the war won't happen because you wouldn't fight."

Maharana Ranjeet was now confused. He asked, "What do you mean, Akroor, that King Surat Singh would opt for a war and I am a coward, who would show his back and not fight?"

Akroor Singh started laughing and said, "Maharana *ji*, special relatives don't fight. You would only marry and won't be able to fight. Now, I think I'd have to take another message with your sword to the court of Sambhalgarh tomorrow."

Maharana Ranjeet, too, laughed and said, "Not right now, Akroor. I want to hear the message Surat Singh would send tomorrow evening and I would deliver whatever message I'd wish to in the warzone the day after tomorrow. Let's go to the camp now. The air of Sambhalgarh is too intoxicating; I can barely sit here."

Even Akroor Singh couldn't help, but laugh at what Maharana Ranjeet just said.

Chapter 12:
The Marriage of Princess Meeramani

Maharana Ranjeet couldn't sleep the entire night, for he was turning in bed thinking about Meeramani. He was vying to make her his own. He was hoping for King Surat Singh to send the proposal for their marriage himself so that even they are not left bereft of their self-respect. The next second, he was thinking one could not trust that arrogant girl who could just say that she would consume poison if was forced to marry the enemy. Her father had no control over her. He felt he will have to handle the things himself or else that girl would spoil her own and his life by consuming poison. He was remembering King Surat Singh mentioning that she visited the temple daily. He thought of reaching the temple early morning so that he could tweak the message to be received from Surat Singh. He jerked out of his bed and left the camp on his horse before the sunrise not knowing when Meeramani would come there.

It had been quite some time for Maharana Ranjeet to be sitting outside the temple. The sun had risen and it was only turning hotter by the day. No priest had come to open the gates of the temple and even Meeramani hadn't come for the prayers. Maharana Ranjeet was getting anxious sitting there when his army chief, Akroor Singh, came there looking for him.

Akroor Singh said, "I knew you would be here, but you

should have at least told me. I wouldn't have been worried for you."

Maharana Ranjeet didn't pay heed to what Akroor Singh was saying and said, "Akroor, why hasn't she come as yet."

Akroor Singh said, "Maharana *ji*, she would be here any moment, as when I was coming here, I had seen her chariot coming here." Before Akroor Singh could complete, a chariot stopped outside the temple.

"So what are you doing here now? Leave!" Maharana Ranjeet said while smiling at him.

"I will guard outside the temple so that your deep conversation with her isn't interrupted," Akroor Singh smiled too.

Princess Meeramani entered the temple wearing simple monk-like white blouse and skirt; she was still looking like a nymph. She got surprised looking at Maharana Ranjeet sitting outside the temple and said, "What are you doing here? This is not a warzone."

"Does Sambhalgarh not follow the custom of greeting beside that of veils?" Maharana Ranjeet asked Meeramani while smiling.

Meeramani smiled hearing a question in reply to her question. "I am sorry; please accept my greetings. You didn't answer me," Meeramani said while opening the gates of the temple.

"Here's the answer to your question," Maharana Ranjeet said while furthering towards her, "The reason why I have come here is the same as that of yours, to worship Lord Shiva."

Meeramani smiled listening to his answer and further asked, "Maharana *ji*, tell me one thing, is there a Shiva temple in your empire, too?"

"No, not even one," Maharana Ranjeet replied in a hurry, "Our family goddess is Chandika, who is Mahishasurmardini. We have only her temples in all our empire. There's not a single Shiva temple. Why do you ask?"

"Maharana *ji*, you become a big sinner if you lie standing inside a temple. Don't you even know this?" Meeramani asked by laughing.

Maharana Ranjeet was a little embarrassed listening to Meeramani. He asked, "How can you say that I am lying? I am telling you the truth. There isn't a single Shiva temple in our empire.

What's there to lie in this?"

"There isn't a single Shiva temple in your empire; this is the truth you are telling. So, you mustn't have even worshipped Lord Shiva in your entire life. How did you turn into one of his ardent followers that you came to sit outside the temple so early in the morning. What's this if not a lie? Now, tell me the truth, what's that important thing which didn't let you sleep last night and made you wait for me outside the temple so early in the morning?".

Maharana Ranjeet was shocked. He said, "Are you like a God that you get to know about every subject and thing?"

Meeramani started giggling hearing his reply and Maharana Ranjeet was hooked to her divine, beautiful face. Then Meeramani said seriously, "Yesterday, my father maharaja was praising you a lot that you are not as he had heard about you. Even I think you are not what you look like. First answer me, why were you waiting for me here and what do you want to say?"

Maharana Ranjeet was completely trapped in her attractive personality. He was getting even more enchanted listening to her. Taking inspiration from the straight-forwardness and straight talks of Meeramani, even Ranjeet asked his question clearly, "Princess Meeramani, I am interested in getting married to you. Will you marry me?"

Princess Meeramani looked closely at Maharana Ranjeet for the first time. This 30-year-old Maharana was a little over 6 feet in height and had long, curly hair. His black, curled up moustaches were complementing well his fair complexion. His muscular body was certifying him as a warrior. He was an extremely attractive man, who could win over any woman. The red *tilak* on his forehead was looking extremely elegant. Maharana Ranjeet looked at Meeramani expecting an answer.

Princess Meeramani neither blushed nor reddened like ordinary girls upon hearing the proposal for marriage. She turned even more serious and questioned Maharana, "Are you interested in a war or a marriage, speak clearly. If I refuse to marry you, then you would go for a war. In that case, you are anyway looking for a war."

"If you'd agree for the marriage, why would I still fight? Then, your empire would be our relative," Maharana answered clearly.

"And, why do you want to marry me?" Meeramani asked.

"Because I fell in love with you at the first sight," Maharana Ranjeet said politely and lovingly.

"Firstly, Maharana *ji*, anybody could get carried away looking at beauty and might feel like seizing her or taking her into his charge and this feeling couldn't necessarily be called as love. Love is like a seed, which gets burst in one's soul and then sprouts into a plant. Later, it becomes a tree when nurtured with sacrifice and loyalty. So, you surely don't love me."

Maharana Ranjeet was left flabbergasted hearing Meeramani.

"Such a young girl with such great knowledge. Even I am fading before her intellect and knowledge. I can't get defeated by her; I would achieve her at any cost." Maharana Ranjeet thought to himself. He asked, "What do you want? How should I prove my love and what should I sacrifice to marry you?"

"Because I doubt that you don't love me, I would challenge you on this basis. If you'd fulfill all my challenges, then this marriage would be possible, otherwise not. Whatever that will happen later, will happen. I would accept the desire of Lord Shiva."

Maharana Ranjeet answered, "I promise you that I will fulfill all your challenges except for the one that till the time I don't give the great empire Jairajgarh a successor, I cannot die. Except for this, you can ask for anything. And, don't think that I am scared to die. Rajputs carry their life on their swords. That's why, when my empire would get its successor, I would happily offer you my life. Now, you shouldn't have any problem."

Maharana Ranjeet said while getting anxious, "A lot of lives from Jairajgarh as well as Sambhalgarh would be saved as a result of this marriage."

Meeramani smiled after listening to Maharana Ranjeet and said, "I am indebted to you for agreeing to all my challenges without even listening to them, but now you have promised me and being a Rajput, you cannot budge from them. So, listen Maharana *ji*, my first condition is that I'd promised my mother on her deathbed that I would not leave Sambhalgarh till the time I won't make my brother,

Virat, worthy of the throne. You would have to help me in this task."

"I completely accept this," Maharana Ranjeet said, "There's a huge Gurukul (seminary) close to our empire. Even I have gained all my education there. We could send Virat there and Acharya Ghananand, the son of Acharya Chaturanand, would teach him properly. I have solved your this problem. Now, what's your second problem?"

"My second condition is that I can't live without worshipping Lord Shiva and as you have told me, there isn't a single Shiva temple in your empire. I want you to construct such a Shiva temple in your empire that even an atheist is compelled to fold his hands upon entering it. I should be able to bid adieu from Sambhalgarh only after that and only then I'll enter your empire. And as you know, honeymoon for a girl doesn't happen at her maternal place, so we'll consummate our marriage only after entering your empire," Meeramani explained.

"I accept this, but I would marry you now and would take you only after the construction of Shiva temple. Further, I would only establish any relation with you after worshipping our family goddess Chandika and the rudrabhishek(special prayers of Lord Shiva) of Lord Shiva," Maharana Ranjeet said in a determined tone.

"Before I tell you my third condition, I want to know how many queens do you already have and what are their names?" Meeramani asked.

Maharana Ranjeet answered, "The name of my first wife was Vaishali. She had an untimely death by drowning in a lake in our empire. The name of my second wife is Ambika, who is still my queen, but I don't have any children with her.

Princess Meeramani said, "So, my third and last condition is that you either do love marriages or political marriages, you would give equal rights to all your wives. You wouldn't even make them feel the pain of loneliness."

"I didn't understand," Maharana Ranjeet got confused and asked, "I can fully understand your concern if you want to secure your own rights, but I didn't understand why you want to give equal rights to all my wives? I cannot love everyone equally. Then, how can I give equal rights to them?"

Meeramani answered, "My rights would begin when I'd enter your empire. I am talking about giving equal rights to all your wives. As you have told me, your first wife has passed away, but your second wife is experiencing the pain of loneliness. Tomorrow, when you would be bored of me and you would marry someone else, then I would experience the same pain of loneliness. God has made me a female and, thus, I am acquainted with all her pains. A woman can share everything except for the love of her husband and this is the most unfortunate thing that she still has to go through. So, Maharana *ji*, I want you to promise that you would treat all your wives equally and love them equally. If you would love your children and wives equally, they wouldn't ever conspire against each other and wouldn't ever dread step-relations. If all your wives would stay like sisters, then even your stepchildren would stay like brothers-sisters and not like step-relatives. An empire stays strong if the family relations are strong. Before I bid adieu to Sambhalgarh, I want you to give Queen Ambika her share of love and rights. I want you to be accompanied by Queen Ambika when you come here to take me. I want to come like her younger sister and not like her co-wife. You never know, Maharana *ji*, your love would fill her up with so much life that the successor to your empire would have arrived before I reach there. You never know if Lord Shiva would bless you for the construction of the temple before I reach there."

Maharana Ranjeet was surprised looking at this side of feminism. It was true that age had nothing to do with knowledge. She didn't seem to be normal girl for the knowledge she possessed. God must have made her for some bigger task.

"Meeramani, you don't look like a normal girl. You are really an avatar of some goddess. I would be blessed to have you as my wife. I have always seen women getting jealous of other women; I have never seen this side of you in any women. I want to make one more promise to you that if I would get the successor to my throne from you, I won't marry anyone else. You are not my first life-partner, but pray to God that you be my last and also that you become the mother of my child. I accept all your conditions. Now, you should not have any problem in marrying me."

Meeramani said, "Alright, Maharana *ji*, before an informer

from my father reaches you with a message for war, please send the proposal for my marriage with all the customs in the royal court of my father. When they would ask me, I would say yes, but please don't discuss anything about my conditions with my father; I would tell him myself. You can just tell him that we have discussed and decided that you would take me after the construction of Lord Shiva temple. Now, I request you to leave as I am also getting late for my prayers and even you should take rest in your camp."

"Before leaving, can you tell me how did you get to know that I haven't slept the entire night and have been waiting for you since early morning?" Maharana asked in curiosity.

Meeramani answered while smiling, "Your eyes are telling that you haven't slept the entire night and the priest of this temple had told me about you sitting here since early morning. He had come here to collect some of his belongings as after fixing of the war, he found it apt to move somewhere else. However, he saw you and sneaked furtively from here and told me about the same when I was leaving the palace."

Maharana Ranjeet laughed after hearing this and bowed before God to leave.

When Maharana Ranjeet left the temple, he was smiling and Akroor Singh understood having looked at him that his task is done. Akroor Singh said, "Congratulations for your new marriage, Maharana *ji*." and Ranjeet Singh hugged him in response.

Akroor Singh once again approached the royal palace of Sambhalgarh, but this time he was only carrying the proposal for marriage along with trays carrying all the auspicious paraphernalia. King Surat Singh happily accepted the proposal as Princess Meeramani had already briefed him on the entire incident that happened outside the temple.

King Surat Singh anyway wanted Meeramani to marry in a bigger empire. This was his political thinking as even he wanted to safeguard his boundaries through this marriage and increase his powers. When the marriage proposal came from the great empire Jairajgarh, he didn't even think for once that Maharana was aged 30-32 years and his daughter was just 16 and readily agreed for the marriage as he knew the powers of Jairajgarh. The Jairajgarh was a developed empire and no other empire in Rajputana was bigger than it or no other ruler could stand in front of Maharana Ranjeet Singh. Even if he had married twice before, he had no successor to his throne as yet. King Surat Singh thought that may be his daughter could be fortunate to mother Maharana's first child and claim the throne of Maharani.

The warriors of Jairajgarh were sent back and Maharana Ranjeet was left with his army chief and a few other special soldiers. He had also sent an informer to inform Jairajgarh about his new marriage.

The wedding procession for Princess Meeramani had left the war camps and had reached the royal palace of Sambhalgarh, where it was warmly welcomed by King Surat Singh and both his sons, Virat Singh and Somesh Singh, along with a few special ministers and soldiers. The marriage of Meeramani and Ranjeet had completed and all the members of procession were made to stay in 'Rang Palace'. This palace was made of glass and all the entertainment proceedings used to happen here. Women were restricted to enter this palace, but the dance girls could enter.

If a girl was not bade adieu from her father's place, then it was a shame for the father and if the bride didn't reach her in-laws' place, then it was a shame for the groom's side. Therefore, the senior priests from both sides arrived on a consensus that Queen Meeramani would go till the boundary of the empire of Jairajgarh with both his brothers, Virat Singh and Somesh Singh, and a few soldiers. She would be welcomed like a new bride on the boundaries of Maharana Ranjeet's empire. Queen Ambika would herself welcome Queen Meeramani from the in-laws' side. After completed some rituals of her in-laws side, she would return to her maternal place, Sambhalgarh with both her brothers and she would be able to spend as much time there. The priests from both the sides believed that in this way, both the sides, father and husband, would be saved from getting tainted. The bride was bade adieu from her father's place and was welcomed in her new house, too, and most importantly, the respect of the promise was maintained. An informer was sent to inform Queen Ambika and the chief minister, Shambhoo Singh, to make the appropriate arrangements at the border.

The next day before dawn, the preparations for the adieu of Meeramani had begun and King Surat Singh had readied a lot of boxes with diamonds and gold along with a lot of horses and elephants to give away in dowry. Maharana Ranjeet had arrived at their doorstep with all his procession and everyone was now waiting for the new bride, Meeramani.

Suddenly, a conch shell was blown in order to announce her arrival. Women were singing pious songs and King Surat Singh and Queen Sheetla Devi were leading the procession. They were followed by Meeramani, who had covered her face in a long veil and was accompanied by her brothers, Virat Singh and Somesh Singh, who had metaphorically covered her head with their swords. This implied that till the times the brothers were alive, they would stay ready for the security of their sister.

King Surat Singh applied *tilak* on the forehead of Maharana Ranjeet and Queen Sheetla sang prayers for him. Then, Prince Virat and Prince Somesh, put their swords at the feet of Maharana Ranjeet and touched his feet. They both, then, stood up and handed over the hand of their sister in the hand of Maharana Ranjeet and stepped back. This implied that their sister's husband was sacred to them and they wouldn't ever raise their arms on him and would also guard him alongside with their sister.

Then, Maharana Ranjeet took his sword out of its cover and put it over the head of Queen Meeramani while holding her hand. This implied that till the time Maharana Ranjeet was alive, his wife was under his custody and nobody could put an evil eye on her. Both, Maharana Ranjeet and Queen Meeramani, bowed before Sambhalgarh and all its inhabitants and started marching towards the chariot. The chariot of Maharana had eight horses and was followed by another chariot with 4 horses. This was for the new bride Queen of Jairajgarh and was decorated beautifully with cushions made of silk, so that the new bride doesn't face any discomfort while travelling. Maharana Ranjeet claimed his comfortable throne on the chariot, which was covered by an umbrella to protect him from rain and sun. The charioteer had taken the charge of the lead rope of the horses and was waiting for a signal from the army chief.

The army chief, Akroor Singh, gestured the warriors to take their positions and, thus, all the soldiers, riding horses or elephants, spread around the king and the queen to protect them from all the sides. Akroor Singh inspected the entire security cover and upon his satisfaction, reached close to Maharana Ranjeet and asked him politely, "Maharana *ji*, we are now ready for the movement. What are your next orders for me?"

"Let's begin the departure," Maharana Ranjeet announced.

The army chief, Akroor Singh, moved to the front and announced, "Blow the conch shell; we have been commanded to start moving. Receiving the orders, the royal priests started blowing the conch shells, which echoed in the entire atmosphere. This was an indication that the time for the departure of the new bride had arrived.

The procession towards Jairajgarh began. It was led by a regiment of warriors led by Akroor Singh, who was adept in dealing with all sorts of dangers. He was followed by warriors on horses, carrying spears. They were then followed by the 8-horse chariot of Maharana Ranjeet and further by 4-horse chariot of the Queen Meeramani. One unit was guarding on the right and the other on the left of Maharana and the Queen, protecting them from both the sides. They were followed by special servants of both the king as well as the queen. They, in turn, were followed by warriors on elephants and further by warriors on horses. This was the army of Jairajgarh.

The huge army of Sambhalgarh, under the leadership of their chief, Ajeet Singh, was following the army of Jairajgarh and they were guarding Prince Virat and Prince Somesh. The processions of the armies of both the empires were progressing quickly towards Jairajgarh.

Chapter 13:
The Sorrow of Queen Ambika

Queen Ambika was already informed about the arrival of Maharana Ranjeet Singh along with his new wife, Queen Meeramani.

Maharana Ranjeet had promised Meeramani that he would bring Meeramani only after the construction of the Lord Shiva temple in the grand empire Jairajgarh and Queen Ambika was required to reach the state border without any delay and supervise all the preparations.

Tears welled up in the eyes of Ambika upon receiving the message. "What sort of an injustice is this? When I had come to the empire as a new bride, he had been kind to Queen Vaishali by not pressurizing her too much for my welcome. What obstinacy is this that Maharana *ji* wants me to welcome my co-wife on the state borders and supervise the preparations, too? I have heard that the new queen is beautiful and worthy, that's how she would have enchanted Maharana *ji*; otherwise how a harsh person like Maharana could promise her to take her only after the construction of the Lord Shiva temple. I could not fathom Maharana *ji* giving respect to females. Maybe, her youth and beauty has cast a spell over Maharana *ji*. Anyway, the spell would be over soon and, then, even she would cry day and night, like me, for Maharana and Maharana, having being bored of her, would bring a new queen...The bee would be around the flower till the time it bears juice, thought Ambika, and wiped her tears. After all, it was Maharana's orders and she had to obey them.

Queen Ambika reached the border and noticed a station-like scene there. Camps were set and the chef had started preparing sweets. The chief minister, Shambhoo Dev Singh, was overseeing the entire preparations.

When Queen Ambika reached there, Shambhoo Singh bowed and informed her, "Queen Sa (Her majesty), the camps have been set. The chefs are doing their work and are preparing all the favorite dishes of Maharana *ji*. Would you want to see if everything is going as per Maharana *ji*'s orders? The bedroom for the Maharana *ji* and the queen has been set up. The procession of Maharana *ji* would reach here before dusk and the bedroom of Maharana *ji* and the queen has been decorated with flowers. The arrangements for stay for her brothers and the soldiers have been made in the camps at the back.

Queen Ambika was listening to Shambhoo Singh while inspecting everything. She didn't want to hear any complaints from Maharana or pass a message that she was not happy upon the arrival of the new queen. That's why she was doing her job well. She went to the bedroom decorated for Meeramani and Maharana. It smelled of fresh flowers. She asked her chief maid, Kaushika, to keep the tray for prayers there. "The new queen would be tired after a long journey and that's why I want that they be allowed to take rest after we offer prayers for Maharana *ji* and her," she said. She also asked Kaushika to place a silver pot full of cold saffron-almond milk there.

Kaushika replied in affirmation and left the camp.

Queen Ambika started inspecting the room closely, so that she doesn't give any reason to complain to the new queen.

"Anyway, Maharana Ranjeet didn't have any space for me in his heart, then why complain? I am nothing in his eyes and after the arrival of the new queen I won't even exist for him. My days of reign are over and hers are going to begin. I am like a piece of junk for him, which will lie in the corner and watch the lovemaking of Maharana *ji* and his new queen. It's true, when I had come here, the position of

Queen Vaishali was like that of mine; I hadn't understood her pain then. Today, I am at her place. The way I hadn't understood her pain yesterday and snatched her husband from her, today mine has been snatched away. These are the days for the new queen to have a good time with Maharana *ji* and my time to sulk and die."

Queen Ambika started remembering how she used to enjoy the sight of Queen Vaishali sulking and being drowned in pain. She used to take pride that she rules Maharana's heart and her co-wife cries out of jealousy; one day when Queen Vaishali had committed suicide after drowning herself in the lake, she was happy thinking she now got rid of her co-wife, but when Maharana started avoiding her, only then she could relate her pain to Queen Vaishali. When she got to know about the new marriage of Maharana, she got poison arranged for herself through her maid, Kaushika, thinking that she would live only till she would be able to tolerate. Otherwise, she would end her life the way Queen Vaishali did. Queen Ambika started crying thinking about this and started hiccupping. She was wondering how she should ask Maharana about her fault that he left her. She tried her best to keep Maharana happy, but the things which earlier made him happy now irked him.

Queen Ambika also sought an apology from the soul of Queen Vaishali, "Forgive me, Vaishali *jiji*, if I had considered you a sister and not a co-wife, I could have at least cried today resting my head on your shoulder. Today, our pains are similar. Please don't curse me, but forgive me." Queen Ambika's kohl was flowing along with her eyes.

Suddenly, there was an announcement by Shambhoo Singh that Maharana Ranjeet Singh along with his wife and the entire procession were only a few seconds away and the welcome tune should be ready to be played.

The chief maid, Kaushika, entered the room of Queen Ambika and said, "Queen sa (Her majesty), the announcement for the arrival of Maharana *ji* has been made and the tray for prayer is ready; what are your next orders for me?" Queen Ambika's makeup had gone haywire because of crying. "Queen sa, what happened; are you alright?" Kaushika got worried and sat at Ambika's feet.

Queen Ambika said in a low voice, "Give me some water to

drink, Kaushika."

Kaushika got up and gave her saffron water in a silver glass.

Queen Ambika had cold water, gathered herself and said, "Kaushika, the tears of pain that you have seen; this thing should remain inside this room."

"As you say, Queen sa, but please control yourself. The life of women is only for sacrifice. We have to give happiness while enduring pain. Let me reinstate your makeup; the new queen shouldn't see you like this," Kaushika said.

Queen Ambika hugged Kaushika and said, "You're right. No matter a queen or a maid, we all are women after all. May be we look different from outside, but we all are hollow from inside. Our heart is a victim of one kind of pain. Applying makeup outside would make me appear fine from the outside, but on the inside, nothing would be able to repair the damage." Ambika wiped her tears and stood up to get ready.

The procession of Maharana Ranjeet had reached the border of Jairajgarh. The sound of conch shell was echoing in the silent evening. The servants started singing pious songs. When Maharana Ranjeet helped her new queen, Meeramani, step down from the chariot, everybody present started cheering for them. Flowers and rosewater was being sprinkled on them while they walked from the chariot to their camp. Maharana Ranjeet and Queen Meeramani stopped at the entrance of the camp and Queen Ambika did *tilak* of Maharana Ranjeet and his new Queen Meeramani and sang prayers for them. She even touched Maharana's feet and congratulated him for his new wedding. When Queen Ambika asked them to come inside, Queen Meeramani bowed at her feet. Everybody present there, was surprised that a co-wife enjoyed a parallel status with her co-wife, then why was she touching the feet of Queen Ambika.

Even Maharana Ranjeet Singh was surprised. He said, "Meeramani, she is my second wife, Ambika."

Queen Meeramani answered in a low voice, "I understood, Maharana *ji*, that's why I have touched the feet of my elder sister." Queen Ambika helped her stand and said, "You're welcome to the grand empire Jairajgarh, Queen Meeramani. Maharana Ranjeet and Meeramani entered the camp. Maharana Ranjeet was happy seeing the decoration of the camp and even Queen Meeramani was appreciating the view.

The maid, Kaushika, brought drinks for everyone in silverware.

Queen Ambika said to Meeramani, "You must be tired. Have something to drink. Please take rest. I shall meet you later. Meanwhile, I will check the arrangements outside." She was about to step outside when Meeramani said, "*Jiji*, please have drinks with us." Before Queen Ambika could say anything, Maharana Ranjeet said, "Kaushika, serve the drinks to Ambika, too. After this, I want some lone time with both my queens."

"As you say Maharana *ji*," Kaushika bowed before them. Ambika was compelled to sit with them. Kaushika made arrangements for their drinks and stepped outside the camp leaving Maharana Ranjeet with both his wives.

Queen Meeramani looked at Ambika through her veil. Even she was so beautiful, but sorrow had faded her beauty a bit. The tears behind her kohled eyes were not hidden from Meeramani. Queen Ambika sat there like an idol.

Queen Meeramani got up quietly and poured some fruit juice in a glass and offered it to Queen Ambika.

Queen Ambika looked at Meeramani and wondered, "*Uff*! So much of beauty, such a bright face, that's why Maharana *ji* has fallen for her; even God would fall for such beauty. Queen Ambika said, "*Arre*! You're new here, why do you bother? This is going to be my work. These are your days to reign till the time a new queen comes."

The sarcasm of Queen Ambika couldn't be hidden from Maharana Ranjeet. Even Meeramani had understood, but she had expected this from her.

Meeramani answered politely, "*Jiji*, you are elder to me in age as well as status. This will always be my work." Ambika didn't answer her and held the glass from her. She thought that maybe she was showing her 'triyacharitra'(dubious character) before Maharana *ji* and she would treat her like a maid later. Meeramani handed a glass to Maharana Ranjeet and picked one for herself. All three of them sat quietly and drank their soft drinks.

* * *

It was getting dark and everybody had their dinner and had gone to sleep as they were tired after the long journey. Even Queen Ambika had left Maharana Ranjeet and Meeramani in their camp and returned to hers; however, she was unable to sleep.

Maharana Ranjeet and Meeramani were sitting quietly in their camp. Meeramani broke the silence and said, "Maharana *ji*, have you ever seen this side of *jiji*; had I not told you the same about women? Her pain was reflecting on her face; didn't you notice?"

"Yes, I saw it," Maharana Ranjeet took a deep breath and said, "But she didn't have any right to make a comment sarcastically."

"She has all the rights, Maharana *ji*, and it is the right of a husband to relieve his wife of all the pains instead of showing his objection. You should go to her right now. I know she must be getting restless and only you can relieve her of this pain. Go and explain to her that I want to stay as her younger sister and not as a co-wife. Tomorrow if a similar thing happens, then I expect the same behavior from you what I am asking you to do right now," Queen Meeramani said.

"But Meeramani, you would leave from here tomorrow morning. I don't know when the construction of the temple would be over and when I would be able to see you next. There are several nights to explain to her; is it necessary to do this tonight? Even you are my wife too; don't I have any responsibilities towards you?" Maharana Ranjeet explained.

"You are right, Maharana *ji*, but I am alright and would come back after the construction of the temple. However, she is your wife from before and she is in pain right now. Tomorrow will be too late as she needs you now. Then, it's you who has given her this grief and pain; so, it's your responsibility to relieve her of them. Please go, Maharana *ji*, before we are only left with repentance. Explain to her that your love has been distributed, but is not over for her. Clarify to her so that she could consider me as her sister. Make her believe that you would never leave her alone. You should better support her before she gets completely shattered from inside. Today, your wife needs you. When you would have needed her, she would have supported you with all her means; then, won't you support her today as a responsible husband? You must go, Maharana *ji*. You might not understand this being a man, as men generally are harsh. If you haven't been able to understand my emotion, then at least fulfill them. Even God cannot understand the emotions of a woman and call her 'triyacharitra'(dubious character), but this is not true," Meeramani was getting emotional now.

"You have made this subject very serious," Maharana Ranjeet said seriously.

"Yes, This subject is very serious, Maharana *ji*," Meeramani replied.

"Speak clearly what you want to say, Meeramani," Maharana Ranjeet was getting anxious.

Meeramani replied, "This pain belongs to women, a pain, which men can never understand. As you would know even my father had married two women, one my mother, Uma Devi, and second after her death, my aunt, Sheetla Devi. The entire world knows only this truth, but there's another which only I know."

"Which truth?" Maharana asked in surprise.

"The truth behind my mother's death," Meeramani took a deep breath. "When my mother was worshipping Lord Shiva asking for the successor of the throne, my father and aunt were having a love affair. My father had left my mother bereft of love. She was deeply affected because of this. Although she was prettier than my aunt, the feeling that her husband had chosen her sister over her had distressed her. She was dying from inside each day and she had no desire left within her to live. That's why she had killed herself shortly after the birth of Virat by consuming poison," Meeramani started crying while narrating her life story.

"If my father had handled things a little more wisely and hadn't left my mother bereft of love, my mother would have been alive today and we wouldn't have to spend our life like orphans. I wouldn't have had to take the responsibilities of a mother at such a tender age. Such incidents happening in childhood make or break us. Although it is common for kings to marry many women, but they don't think about treating their wives equally."

"But, what's wrong in this? Most of the marriages are political and queens already know this. Besides, it cannot be possible to love everyone equally. I had told this to you earlier as well," Maharana Ranjeet stated.

"There are no relations in politics and love, Maharana *ji*. I know love relations are from heart, but there are certain needs of a woman; after all, even she has come after marrying you. Just like a king has needs beyond his royal work, he has family life, even a woman has needs. A king has many marriages, but this doesn't end his responsibilities towards the women he marries. If she only stays as the queen of the state and stays bereft of her husband's love, then it's an insult of her feminism. This is a right of every wife to question her husband. There are a certain rights of a wife fixed in scriptures which are applicable to even Gods, then even she could demand her rights from her husband," Meeramani stopped for a moment to catch up on her breath and continued, "Then, how can a man leave his family after becoming the king? If he cannot give equal love and respect to his wives, then it's a shame on his manliness. Even the scriptures won't allow him for many marriages. I have seen my mother burning in the fire of separation. She was not against his second marriage, but if a husband forgets his wife like a piece of junk after the arrival of his new wife, then how would that woman of flesh and blood feel? Scriptures regard her as goddess, but men only consider them as an object of pleasure. He only gives importance to the woman he loves and only loves the children she mothers. Then, why does a man like this need to marry at all? Why does he even have political marriages if he keeps the woman bereft of her rights?"

Maharana Ranjeet was sitting in surprise. He had never imagined such an avatar of a woman. He was sure she was an avatar of some goddess.

"She might be an avatar of Chandi," Maharana Ranjeet thought. He was surprised listening to the views of his new bride. She was so young, yet full of revolutionary thoughts.

Meeramani continued again, "Men have either political marriages or love marriages, but why do they write loneliness in the destiny of the women; why don't they understand this pain of women. Why are men like this, Maharana *ji*? They ditch a woman who doesn't ever get tired of sacrificing for him." Meeramani started crying.

Maharana Ranjeet stood up and hugged her.

"Please hurry up and leave now, Maharana *ji*," Meeramani requested.

Maharana Ranjeet said, "Alright! I will meet you in the morning," and left the camp to move towards Ambika's room.

Seeing him leave his camp so late in the night, the guards approached him and asked if he needed anything.

"There are no issues. Go and do you work. I am going to Queen Ambika's camp," he replied.

The guards moved back to their positions.

Chapter 14: The Reunion of Maharana Ranjeet Singh and Queen Ambika

When Maharana Ranjeet was furthering towards Queen Ambika's camp, he saw the chief maid, Kaushika, outside the camp. She bowed before Maharana when he asked her, "It's quite late in the night; what are you doing here?"

Kaushika said, "I apologize, Maharana *ji*, but I can't disclose this to you."

"What did you say? Maharana Ranjeet yelled. If I am asking you something, then being our maid, you must answer me. How dare you not do that! Are you not even concerned for your life anymore? Tell me before I turn even rougher,"

Kaushika stretched her hand before him and answered, "The matter is I have stolen this from Queen Ambika's room and I am going to throw this away."

Maharana Ranjeet saw the open hand of Kaushika and a small silver box in it. Maharana asked her what it was and why she had stolen it to throw it away. He further asked her to answer him clearly.

Kaushika replied, "Maharana *ji*, Queen Ambika had asked me to get poison for her as she was completely shattered from inside, but I had given her saffron mixed with dried neem leaves calling it as poison because I didn't want bad for her and disobeying her is beyond my area of authority. When the news of your marriage reached Jairajgarh, she decided to kill herself and had even consumed poison having mixed it in milk, but nothing happened to her as it wasn't really poison. This made her doubt me and she arranged for this poison from somewhere and hid it. She was going to consume it today as after watching the new queen, she has started to believe that even her fate is going to be like that of Queen Vaishali. That's why I am going to throw it away and I have told her that I am going to bring warm milk for her."

Maharana Ranjeet was shaken from inside. He wondered, "If Meeramani hadn't alerted me at the right time and hadn't persuaded me to go to Ambika, I would have lost Ambika the way I'd lost Vaishali."

Maharana Ranjeet took control of his emotions and said, "Kaushika, what you have done for the queen of this empire is appreciable. This empire would be indebted to you forever. I wish some maid like you was present with Queen Vaishali so even she would have been alive today." Maharana said while taking a deep breath.

"Sorry, Maharana *ji*," the tone of Kaushika's voice rose a bit, but came back to normal, "Queens don't need good maids, but good husbands." Kaushika now looked down for she didn't know what Maharana would say.

But contrary to his belief, Maharana Ranjeet said, "You are right, Kaushika. Go and bring warm milk for Queen Ambika. I would take it myself. And listen, this matter or our conversation shouldn't reach anyone else. I need some lone time with Ambika. So, quickly go and bring the milk. I am waiting for you here."

Kaushika agreed and almost ran to bring the milk.

Maharana Ranjeet reached the camp of Ambika and found everything haywire. She herself was looking disturbed. Her *chunari* (long scarf) was lying somewhere; she had no jewellery on her body and all of it was lying on the floor. All her hair was let open. The moment she heard some movement, she assumed Kaushika had come. She roared, "Where have you died, Kaushika; does it take this long to bring milk? I am unable to find my silver box, the one I had kept in the red silk cloth while moving from the palace. I need it right now. Find it fast for me, otherwise no one would be worse than me."

"Is this the box you are talking about, Ambika?" Maharana opened his fist towards Ambika. Queen Ambika was shocked looking at Maharana as if she had seen some ghost. "Maharana *ji*, why are you here now? It was your honeymoon night, then what are you doing here?" Queen Ambika started crying.

Maharana Ranjeet took a deep breath and said, "If not here, then where else should I be?" He then took her into his embrace. Queen Ambika started sobbing like kids in his embrace. Even Maharana got a little emotional and held her even tighter. She kept crying for a long time and he kept rubbing through her hairs. When she was relieved a bit, he filled the silver glass of water and fed her water himself. Ambika sipped water from the glass and also sprinkled some cold water on her face. Her face and eyes had turned red because of crying.

Meeramani was right that I shouldn't have run away from Ambika, but explained to her. Meeramani had unintentionally made Ranjeet Singh feel guilty. He wouldn't be able to love Ambika because he had consummated his marriage with her. The meaning of love was explained to him by Meeramani and he was content after getting her in his life. He was now feeling complete.

Queen Ambika had now stopped crying and she had also gathered herself. "Maharana *ji*, how come you are here?" she asked.

"To atone for my mistakes," Maharana Ranjeet answered.

"Atone for which mistake?" She asked.

"Atonement for not obeying my responsibilities as a husband, turning away from them and making my wife reach this stage," Maharana Ranjeet now got emotional.

Ambika was surprised looking at this side of Maharana. She said, "I am not able to understand you today. You've come today after marrying someone; today is your honeymoon night and you are sitting in my room, when you had quit even looking at me. Anyway, you have already consummated me, so there's nothing new left. Besides, the beauty and youth of your new queen Meeramani is at its peak. Then, why have you left her and are sitting with me; it's not that you love me so much. Don't waste time and come to the point what's that need that dragged you to my room?" Ambika asked in clear words.

Maharana Ranjeet was surprised looking at her. The girl, who he had considered extrovert earlier, was talking clearly to him today. It's true, a man judges another person based on his perception. When he disliked Ambika, her being straight-forward appeared as her assertiveness, but when he is looking at her emotionally, she was appearing as clear and pure. No adornment, she was saying what she was feeling, just like a kid who doesn't know politics.

"If you want to know the truth, then listen," Maharana Ranjeet reiterated the entire conversation he had with Meeramani. Ambika was listening to him in surprise while he repeated Meeramani's words.

After listening to everything, Ambika said, "She cannot be an ordinary woman. She must be some avatar of a goddess. Her feelings and thoughts could invoke anyone. Such patience and wisdom at such a tender age! Maharana *ji*, you must have done great deeds that you got her as your wife. I am not even worth the dust at her feet. I won't be sad even if I am appointed as her maid." Ambika got emotional while saying this.

"Ambika, you are not her maid, but elder sister. She hasn't got love from her parents, but you have got it enough. If you really want to give something to her, accept her as your younger sister and give her all the love of an elder sister. Even she wants the same." Maharana Ranjeet stated.

"Maharana *ji*, this Rajputani Ambika promises you that Meeramani would be my younger sister all my life. I would love her like a mother, which she hasn't seen since her childhood. I would never consider her as my co-wife. She has done a great favor on me by returning my husband to me, that's why I commit my life for her. If she hadn't sent you now, I would have been dead; so, I am alive because of her. She has the first rights on my life and I would keep up the respect of all her wishes," Ambika elaborated.

"Let's go, Maharana *ji*, let's go to meet her," Queen Ambika was about to get up.

"Not right now, Ambika. Let her take complete rest. She has come after a long journey. Meet her tomorrow."

"You are right, Maharana *ji*, I had to gift her something for our first meeting. I had prepared a box of jewelry, but had forgotten to give it to her. Tomorrow, I would give her clothes and jewelry from her in-laws' place and would dress up her by myself," Ambika said.

"What should I do with this silver box?" Maharana Ranjeet asked while smiling.

"Give it to your enemies," Ambika started laughing like kids and Maharana hugged her right then.

The next morning, Queen Ambika sent Kaushika to the camp of Queen Meeramani with some wedding clothes and jewelleries.

Queen Meeramani accepted the greetings from Kaushika. She asked her to come inside and what she had got.

"All this has been brought as per the instructions of Queen Ambika and she would soon be here to meet you. I don't know anything beyond this," Kaushika answered.

"Alright. You may leave now," Meeramani ordered.

"As you say," Kaushika said and exited the camp.

After some time, Queen Meeramani got the information that Queen Ambika was coming. Queen Meeramani set her veil right.

Queen Ambika entered the camp and instructed Kaushika that no one should enter the camp as she wanted a lone time with Meeramani.

"As you say," said Kaushika and exited.

As soon as Kaushika exited, Queen Ambika sat with her hands folded in front of Queen Meeramani.

Meeramani said, "*Arre jiji*! What are you doing? Don't do such a disaster; else I would go to hell. I am too young to you." Meeramani picked Ambika up.

Queen Ambika smiled and said, "Meeramani, you are very good and I am saying this from my heart. I don't know how to sugar-coat my words. Whatever is there on my mind is there on my tongue. I like to talk straight-forward and that's why Maharana *ji* calls me an extrovert."

"But this is your quality, Ambika *jiji*. The people who talk clearly are not shrewd," Meeramani said.

"Meeramani, why and how are you so good? By sending Maharana *ji* to me last night, you have given me a new life. Otherwise, yester night would've been my last night. I feel guilty of myself by listening to your great thoughts. If I had even one quality like yours, Queen Vaishali would have been alive today. I am alive because of you and, thus, I have promised myself and Maharana *ji* that you'd have the primary right on my life. You have made me proud by letting me be your elder sister, otherwise I don't even deserve to be your maid," Queen Ambika took Meeramani's hand in hers.

"It's Ok, *jiji*," Meeramani lovingly brushed, "If a female won't share the pain of a female, then who else would? Men are harsh from birth; they wouldn't understand the sensitive emotions of a woman. I am happy that Lord Shiva has blessed me with this house and an elder sister like you."

"Meeramani, these jewelries and clothes are a gift for our first meeting. I would help you get ready today," Queen Ambika hugged Queen Meeramani.

Queen Meeramani was leaving for Sambhalgarh and Maharana Ranjeet and Queen Ambika bid her adieu with a heavy heart. Meeramani had started crying.

Queen Ambika said to Meeramani, "I am still not done with our meeting. We sisters should spend more time together."

This time, Virat answered instead of Meeramani, "Ambika *jiji*, the way Meeramani is our sister, even you are our sister. If Maharana *ji* allows, even you could come with us and let us serve you."

Queen Ambika hugged Virat and Meeramani and said, "I am very happy to get one more maternal place and siblings. I have to get the construction of the Lord Shiva temple completed soon so that I could have you with me forever and you could come to your empire, Jairajgarh, forever. I promise you that I would come to meet you when the construction of the temple would be about to get over. Then, Maharana *ji* would come to take both of us together and we sisters shall stay together forever. We both would have two maternal places and we won't ever go to our maternal place alone."

"As you say, *jiji*, I will wait for you," Meeramani wiped her tears.

Virat said to Meeramani, "*Jiji Ma*, we have a long journey to cover. We should start now. Let us take permission from Maharana *ji*."

Queen Ambika said, "Virat brother, please come along with me; Meeramani, please wait, I will send Maharana *ji* here." She left along with Virat.

After some time, Maharana Ranjeet entered the camp of Meeramani and she touched his feet. He hugged her and said, "Meeramani, you have made me your servant in just a few weeks. I am a fan of not just your beauty, but also your intelligence. Now, I won't be able to spend a second without you. I would call the craftsmen from the nearby states and would get the temple work done as early as possible. After that, I would come to bring you home and would not take any further promises which would keep us away."

"Maharana *ji*, I would wait for your call and don't forget to bring Ambika *jiji* along." Meeramani touched his feet and exited the camp where Virat was waiting for her along with the entire procession.

Queen Meeramani bid adieu to Jairajgarh and all its inhabitants and returned to her maternal place, Sambhalgarh. Maharana Ranjeet and Queen Ambika returned to their empire and started the work of Lord Shiva temple construction.

Chapter 15:
The Construction of Lord Shiva Temple in the Grand Empire Jairajgarh

The construction of the Shiva temple got completed in five years. Maharana Ranjeet had got everything done under his supervision. He had got the Lord Shiva temple constructed close to the temple of their family Goddess, Chandika Devi, adjacent to the Sapta-Sangama Lake. He had called together some of the best craftsmen from his state as well as the adjacent states and he had told them to not worry about the money, but construct a Shiva temple, which makes Meeramani feel as if she had visited Kailash to see Lord Shiva and his family.

According to his promise, he had to construct such a temple which would compel even an atheist to become a follower of Lord Shiva. He had let his entire treasures open for the construction and he wanted to gift this temple to Meeramani for their marriage.

Although it had taken a lot of time for the temple construction, the temple had turned out to be extremely beautiful beyond everybody's expectations. It seems as if the craftsmen had put their own lives into thc idols. The intricate carvings on doors were done with gold and silver. On the left of the temple door was a huge idol of Veerbhadra, which is the most powerful Maharudra and which were brought to life by Lord Shiva himself by one of his tresses. On the right side of the door was the god of snakes. From the outside, the temple seemed as if it was the royal palace of Lord Shiva and without the permission from the royal guards, no one would be able to enter his temple or the royal palace.

From the inside, it seemed as if Lord Shiva was sitting with his family in Mount Kailash, as the hills behind the idols didn't seem to be made of marble, but of snow. The entire temple walls were adorned by carvings of Lord Shiva. All the idols of Shiva family were made of white marble; even the lake was made of white marble, but the Shiva linga was made of black marble and it was a five-directional Shiva linga. The snake surrounding the Shiva linga looked real. Everything in the temple, except for the Shiva linga, and the snakes, was made of white marble.

When entered from the entrance, one could first see Lord Nandi. Lord Nandi was present in the avatar of a bull and it was the vehicle of Lord Shiva. Lord Shiva had blessed Lord Nandi after looking at his devotion that he could see Lord Shiva all the time and that's why, his idol was always placed in front of Lord Shiva. Their idols face each other. Scriptures even say that if one said all his wishes or problems in the ears of Lord Nandi, they reached directly to Lord Shiva's ears.

The entire Shiva family was made to sit on a throne made of white marble. The white idol of Lord Shiva was adorned by a black snake flaring its neck and hood. In place of the third eye of Lord Shiva, an extremely rare and exquisite gem was fixed. When the light from the lamp would fall on the third eye, it would appear as if the third eye of Lord Shiva has opened and is emitting light. His neck was adorned by a 1008-bead Rudraksh string, which was beaded by the royal jeweller, who used to make jewelleries for the royal palace, under the direct supervision of Maharana Ranjeet. In the lap of Lord Shiva was Lord Kartikeya, who was the first son of Mother Ganga (whose pure water flows from the tresses of Lord Shiva) and Lord Shiva.

On the left side of Lord Shiva was Mother Parvati; the left side is the place for wife only according to the Hindu scriptures. The jewellery adorned on Mother Parvati was made of Rudraksh, gold and rare stones. In the lap of Mother Parvati, Lord Ganesha was made to sit. According to Hindu scriptures, Lord Ganesha is always worshipped first and is the remover of obstacles.

Around the marble throne, on which the Shiva family was seated, there was a lake circling them and this was continuing from the one end of the faux mountains to the other. In the same pool, a huge Shiva linga was fixed, which was black in color. A water string was coming out from the tresses of Lord Shiva, just like Mother Ganga, and was directly falling on the Shiva linga.

Along with the temple, they had also got a huge hall constructed near the temple. One way to the hall was through the temple and the second got open at the bank of Sapta-Sangama Lake. Maharana Ranjeet had got this constructed in order to arrange for a comfortable stay of the saints present at the time of Rudraabhishek (special prayers of Lord Shiva). Later on, Queen Meeramani could use the hall the way she wished to.

Maharana Ranjeet had really worked hard in order to fulfill his promise to his wife Queen Meeramani.

After the construction of the temple, Maharana Ranjeet had got it locked as he didn't want anyone else to see or move inside the temple before Meeramani. He wanted only Queen Meeramani to worship and offer her prayers first. He wanted all the first tasks of the temple to be done by Queen Meeramani.

He had even asked Queen Ambika to refrain from entering the temple. Queen Ambika used to feel jealous of the deeds of Maharana Ranjeet, but when she used to think about Meeramani, her heart used to well up with love.

After the construction of the Shiva temple, Maharana Ranjeet had called the royal priests to fish out an appropriate date for the return of Queen Meeramani. The royal priests, after calculating the movement of the stars, said that there was no auspicious date for the next 3-4 months. Maharana Ranjeet got upset listening to this.

Suddenly, Queen Ambika asked the royal priests if she could go for a stay to Sambhalgarh.

The royal priests said that there was no problem in her going there, but Maharana Ranjeet shouldn't go now to take Queen Meeramani back from her maternal place.

It was decided that Queen Ambika would first go to her maternal place, Ballabhgarh, for two months, and would further go to Sambhalgarh with her brother, Neelkant, and would stay there till Maharana would come to take them. Maharana Ranjeet would come to take both his queens after the spring was over and would do Rudraabhishek (special prayers of Lord Shiva) along with both his queens.

Maharana Ranjeet sent a message of arrival of Queen Ambika to both Ballabhgarh and Sambhalgarh and Queen Ambika starting preparing for her departure.

Chapter 16:
The Arrival of Shiromani Pandit Rameshwar Nath Shastri in Ballabhgarh

King Neelkant was briefing his courtiers that he would be travelling for next one week to Sambhalgarh with his sister. He had to set out after two days and, therefore, he was discussing with his army chief to make necessary preparations. Suddenly, one of the courtiers came to him to inform that one of his friends, Shiromani Pandit Rameshwar Nath Shastri from Kashi, had arrived and wanted to meet him.

Hearing this, King Neelkant got very happy and said that his friend had come to meet him from Kashi. Inform my queen, Padmavati, and sister, Ambika, and take him respectfully to the guestroom inside the palace. I'd finish this work and meet him there.

"As you say," said the courtier and exited the palace.

King Neelkant had gotten married when he was still a prince and his father, King Krishnakant, was alive. Now, he was a father to three children. His wife's name was Padmavati and he had two sons and one daughter. The royal palace of Kashi was the maternal place of Neelkant and Ambika; their mother, Jamuna Devi, was the daughter of that family. In fact, the birthplace of both Ambika as well as Neelkant was Kashi, as at that time children were born at their maternal places. The current king of Kashi was Shantanu Dev, who was the eldest son of the brother of Late Jamuna Devi. Although Jamuna Devi had passed away, Neelkant was still attached to his maternal place. Shiromani Pandit Rameshwar Nath Shastri was the younger son of the current chief doctor of Kashi.

"Shiromani" was a title bestowed upon their family. Some ancestor of the Shastri family was a great Priest and Ayurveda doctor in the royal palace of the king of Kashi and this palace was given to them as a gift along with the title, "SHIROMANI"(Highly knowledgeable brains). Each son of the Shastri family was not just a doctor, but were also expert in Vedas and astrology. The backyard of their big palace has been made into a clinic, where they see the patients, and oversee the process of preparation of medicines from herbs. They have employed a lot of people, who get paid every month by the Shiromani family. The great salary keeps the employees' entire family happy and content and there's no scarcity of money or food. They could detect the disease just by seeing one's pulse and had also inherited the knowledge of herbs. The Shiromani family was well-known in entire Kashi; even people from far-off places used to visit them to get treated for their incurable diseases. By the grace of Lord Vishwanath, no patient has ever returned from them without getting treated and, thus, it was imperative for the education of the eldest son of the Shastri family to begin since childhood as it was him, who would eventually take the place of the chief doctor. They were handling this job pretty well since generations and their contribution in the field of herbal medicine was invaluable."

King Neelkant and Pandit Rameshwar Shastri were of around the same age and were friends since childhood and used to love each other like brothers. Even Ambika had been tying a Rakhi on the wrist of Rameshwar and even he used to consider her as his real sister. The friendly relations of Neelkant with Shiromani palace had now become familial relations.

King Neelkant quickly wrapped up all his work and rapidly progressed towards the guest room, for he knew that without meeting him, his friend wouldn't have any food. King Krishnakant had got two guest house constructed during his lifetime. One was huge hall, a little far from the palace, where all the formal guests used to stay and the other inside the palace, where family and close relatives used to stay.

While progressing towards the guestroom, Neelkant was wondering the reason behind Rameshwar's visit without any prior information, maybe he'd have some important task or maybe he would have thought of getting Rakhi tied by Ambika as raksha bandhan was approaching and Ambika had been sending him 'Rakhi' after her marriage. Her husband Maharana Ranjeet didn't allow her frequent visits to her maternal home. Since the time Ambika had gotten married to Ranjeet, their relations have been merely formal and since the time Ambika had told him the truth behind the death of Queen Vaishali, he had stopped visiting Jairajgarh. He had started loathing Maharana Ranjeet and although he was always concerned for his sister, he never visited her. Ambika never conceded anything from her brother. When he got to know that Maharana Ranjeet had a third marriage with a young princess of Sambhalgarh, he got even more concerned for his sister and started to hate Maharana Ranjeet. Neelkant had conveyed a message to his sister that now their father King Krishnakant was not alive, so were his principles has too gone with him, and she could stay with fully respect at his brother's place for as long as she was alive. However, Ambika hadn't accepted this as she loved Maharana Ranjeet and after coming of Meeramani, she was even more content. Ambika had told everything about Meeramani to him and, thus, he was eager to meet a woman whose thoughts were so bright at such a young age. More than this, he wanted to make sure after meeting her that she is not playing any political games with his sister, for he knew his sister was emotional fool to believe anyone easily and Meeramani seemed to have quite a sharp mind. Therefore, he wanted to meet her and form an opinion about her.

When King Neelkant reached the guest room, he realized that his friend hadn't touched any snacks as he had expected. His sister, Ambika, and wife, Padmavati, were also present there. The moment Rameshwar saw Neelkant, he hugged him and both the friends got emotional and continued to stay in each other's embrace for long.

Padmavati said, "Please have your snacks. Brother

Rameshwar hasn't touched anything to eat as yet and you've come so late. First have some food and then you may talk for as long as you want."

Listening to her, both the friends had their snacks. Padmavati knew that now that Rameshwar was here, both the friends would spend all their time with each other. They both used to share their happiness and sorrows like brothers and that's why, she arranged for the stay of Neelkant, too, in the guest room, without anyone telling her to do so.

When both the friends got some lone time, Rameshwar asked Neelkant, "Friend, won't you ask why I am here without any prior information?"

Neelkant answered, "I had thought about it that you must have some important work, but then I thought do you really need a reason to come to my house? Thus, I didn't ask."

Rameshwar got serious. He answered, "There was an important matter; that's why I had to come. This is a matter of our sister, Ambika's life."

Even Neelkant got serious. He asked, "What't the matter, Rameshwar? Tell me fast."

Rameshwar answered, "You know that my father, Gangeshwar Nath Shastri is very naive. He doesn't interrogate anyone much and that's why he doesn't know much about anything. He has committed a sin unknowingly or I must say he has been a victim of a conspiracy."

Neelkant was paying his full attention.

Rameshwar continued, "It's been more than 10 years. A businessman had come to my father and told him that his daughter was quite young and her in-laws were asking him to bid her adieu to their place. Since their daughter was quite young, they wanted a solution that could prevent her from becoming a mother till the time she didn't want to. So, father made a medicine like that. After that, these medicines have been going continuously till now. Surprisingly, they have been paying us four times the cost of the medicine till now, even after a period of 10 years. We supply these medicines twice every year; my father prepares the medicine for 6 months in one go. Once, my father had to go somewhere on an important task for one month with my mother and he gave me this responsibility. He had asked me to handover the box of medicines for six months and collect four times the cost. Since I am taking a majority of his work, I took over this responsibility, too. Later, I thought that the father who had come to ask to prepare the medicine didn't want his daughter to become a mother for some years, but it had been 10 years now. Even now, he had been paying four times the cost; why doesn't he want his daughter to become a mother, for she must have been mature now. I didn't find it quite right and I started investigating."

Rameshwar stopped for a moment and continued, "I appointed a spy to spy on the man who collected the box of medicines. I wanted to know where these medicines were going and why the person had been paying four times the actual cost since ten years. I thought somebody must be misusing our medicines and exploiting my naïve father. If these medicines were going to a lady who wanted to become a mother, I wouldn't have doubted anything, but these medicines were going so that a woman doesn't become a mother, that too for more than 10 years and that's why I decided to spy. The spy told me that the person who takes the medicines is Heeranand and he hands over the box of medicines at the borders of Jairajgarh. There, the army chief, Akroor Singh, takes the medicines from him and hands him great amount of money."

Neelkant got more serious upon hearing the name of Jairajgarh and Akroor Singh.

Rameshwar added, "When I heard the names of Jairajgarh and Akroor Singh, I got further investigations done and I got to know that Heeranand lives in a nearby village, Santpuram, and he is the brother-in-law of Akroor Singh. I wondered that the sister of Akroor Singh already had five children and even Akroor had four children, then who possibly might be consuming these medicines in Jairajgarh. Who's that wealthy in Jairajgarh who's been paying four times the cost of a medicine and who would benefit by someone not getting pregnant and I could fish out just one name, our sister, Ambika. It's been more than 10 years to her marriage and she has still not become a mother and Maharana Ranjeet is capable enough to pay not just four, but hundred times the cost of the medicines.

What is more serious is that these medicines had been going to Jairajgarh even before Ambika's wedding."

"So, this means that even the first wife of Maharana Ranjeet, Vaishali, was being given these medicines, as even she couldn't become a mother and she committed suicide of the accuse of being an infertile woman," Neelkant added in surprise.

"What's the story of Queen Vaishali?" Rameshwar asked in astonishment.

Neelkant reiterated the entire incident Ambika had told him and also about the truth behind Vaishali's death.

After knowing everything, Rameshwar concluded, "It's been confirmed that these medicines go to the royal palace of Jairajgarh for Maharana Ranjeet, so that his wives don't become mothers and he could keep marrying women. But, why doesn't he want his wives to become mothers? He doesn't have any successor to his throne as yet."

Neelkant agreed while thinking.

"I will tell you one more thing, Neelkant, probably you don't know. When your mother was alive, she had taken a medicine from us so that Ambika could become a mother soon. I had been wondering why Ambika hasn't become a mother as yet, because that one medicine has helped even infertile women become mothers. Then, your mother had passed away and my father reached on the conclusion that maybe Ambika haven't had the medicines. But, now, I know that these medicines couldn't work because of the other medicines being given to her. I have also heard that Maharana Ranjeet has married a young girl. I felt very bad for Ambika, but what could we do. What's written by Lord Vishwanath in her destiny shall happen."

King Neelkant said in rage, "Had he not been my sister's husband, I would've killed him right away. I am so angry for the great injustice he did to my sister."

"Calm down, friend! Lord Vishwanath will set everything right. We shall think and find a way in which Queen Ambika becomes a mother, so that no one can stop her from claiming the throne of Maharani and her son becoming the prince. We should take possible steps in this direction and turn the game of politics of

Maharana Ranjeet opposite. But poor Ambika, she must be sad on arrival of her co-wife. We should think of a solution to that, too." Rameshwar said.

"She is not sad, but very happy. I am going to drop her to her co-wife's place after two days," Neelkant added.

"What do you mean?" Rameshwar couldn't fathom anything when Neelkant told him everything what Ambika had told him.

After listening to everything, Rameshwar said, "From what Ambika have told, Meeramani appears to be an avatar of some goddess. She is giving her rights to be her co-wife. I am not able to fathom this. She might be a monk or a magician; we will get to know only when we will meet her."

"I am going to Sambhalgarh along with Ambika to figure this out. Ambika is foolish, anybody could fool her. I am planning to stay there for one week; why don't you accompany us, Rameshwar? You could go to Kashi from there. At least, we could be together is figuring the matter out."

"OK. I had anyway informed at home about my absence for 10-15 days. I will go to Sambhalgarh with you. I want to request you for one more thing; my father was naïve and has been caught because of this naivety. If he would get to know that he has committed a crime with a member of royal palace, he won't be able to live and I won't be able to see him die every second. Therefore, please forgive him if you can. He is a very sensitive person as you know. He has done everything unknowingly."

"Stop it, Rameshwar. He's like my father and I can never be agree that he can do anything wrong to anyone. He is that naïve that he won't be even able to understand if he would be made a part of some conspiracy. What has happened is history; let us take charge of our future now. Let's see what we could do now. One more thing, don't let Ambika know about anything. She is anyway madly in love with Maharana Ranjeet and won't listen to anyone, but her husband. If she will get to know about this, she will immediately disclose about this to Ranjeet and, thus, would spoil our plan. She cannot make a difference between an enemy and a friend.

Yes, you are right, Rameshwar said.

It's quite late, Rameshwar. Let us sleep now. Tomorrow,

even you make all the necessary arrangements, as we'll leave for Sambhalgarh day after tomorrow. Good night," Neelkant said in a tired voice.

"Good night, friend," said Rameshwar and progressed towards his bed.

Chapter 17:
The Union of Sambhalgarh with Ballabhgarh

The king of Ballabhgarh, Neelkant, his sister, Queen Ambika, and his best friend, Shiromani Pandit Rameshwar Nath Shastri, had arrived in Sambhalgarh. They were all impressed by the warm welcome offered by the king of Sambhalgarh, Surat Singh. The beauty and simplicity of Meeramani had impressed Neelkant and Rameshwar. Meeramani had returned after offering her evening prayers and both of them were compelled to join their hands before her looking at her cleric look. Ambika met Meeramani as if two sisters had met after a long time.

The inhabitants of Ballabhgarh loved Queen Meeramani and her family. They only couldn't meet the stepmother of Meeramani, Sheetla Devi, and her son, Somesh, as both of them had gone on a pilgrimage.

It had been four days since Ambika was in Sambhalgarh along with his brothers. Meeramani was noticing that Neelkant was trying to closely study her and was listening carefully to every word she said and was also keeping an eye on all her acts. Meeramani understood it's the love of a brother for his sister that was keeping him alert. Meeramani thought that she would remove all his doubts by tying a rakhi around his and his friend, Rameshwar's wrist after one day on the festival of Raksha Bandhan, and by promising him that his sister would be safe with her.

A day before Raksha Bandhan, Neelkant was strolling on the terrace of the royal palace of Sambhalgarh with Rameshwar when Meeramani came there with Malini to call them for dinner. She heard her name while she was still on the staircase and stopped to listen to their conversation. She gestured Malini to stay quite.

King Neelkant said, "I feel pity for Meeramani. Why Lord Shiva did such great injustice to her by tying her with a sinful person like Maharana Ranjeet."

Rameshwar said, "We have not been able to tell our sister, Ambika, about the truth as yet and now, poor Meeramani! How would she feel once she will get to know the truth behind her husband? She is still a newlywed girl; she still hasn't experienced the love of a husband. God hasn't done right with her."

Neelkant said worryingly, "I am so enraged; I wonder how such a sinful person has gotten such good wives. Maybe he's reaping the benefits of the deeds he might have done in his previous births; all he has done in this birth are bad deeds. Think of some way, Rameshwar. I was earlier worried for Ambika; now, I am even worried for Meeramani. She is too young and innocent to handle Ranjeet and he has a very bad character. He led Queen Vaishali to death and now his bad thoughts for Ambika are coming to light. Only God know what he will do with Meeramani."

Rameshwar suggested, "Let us tell the whole truth to Meeramani."

No, Rameshwar, we can't tell her anything. We have not been able to explain to our sister Ambika yet. Then how would we explain to a girl, who we have just met? Then, she might even think that we are telling her lies because of our sister, Ambika, and are trying to separate her from her husband. She has saved our sister's life. We can't break her dreams."

"Poor women, they are so sensitive. I pray to Lord Vishwanath that poor Meeramani gets all the happiness," Rameshwar said in a low tone.

Neelkant said in a low tone, "Rameshwar, I pray to God that their ordeal ends soon. Tell me, have you found any solution to the medicines being sent to Jairajgarh? The time for us to part is nearing and if we won't come up with a solution, the medicines would continue to be sent and the life of Meeramani would also be spoilt along with that of Ambika."

Rameshwar thought something and said, "Neelkant, do you know how Maharana Ranjeet is giving her medicines daily?"

"I tried to investigate, but she doesn't know anything. But yes, there's one thing, there's a maid appointed by Maharana Ranjeet himself and she gives her saffron-almond milk every night and it's crucial for her to have it every day. He said that the milk would help her become a mother soon, as he gave this to Queen Vaishali also. I wonder if he is giving the medicine in this milk," Neelkant said in a low voice.

"I bet he's giving the medicine in this milk, as this medicine has to be taken in warm milk. We must ask Ambika to stop consuming that milk and she will explain this to Meeramani, too, to not consume this milk when she's offered to," Rameshwar said in a hurried tone.

"You are a great physician, but an amateur politician. Ranjeet would get a hint when they both would deny having the milk and he would change his entire game plan. He would start giving them the medicine in some other manner. I had told you how he had killed his stepbrother. When his father had asked him to promise that he won't even touch him, he had changed his game plan and had his brother killed through Akroor Singh. What would he do to Ambika if he would get to know that we know his game plan? It has already taken us 10 years to understand his game plan; now, if he would change it, then it would take us our entire lives. You don't know about Ranjeet Singh, he is a big player. I know him since childhood and, thus, I know him. However, people who have just met him won't understand what he's from inside and what he appears form the outside. Let's both think what should be done. The onus of protecting our sisters is on us, brothers. Let's go downstairs now; it's quite dark. You never know if everyone would be looking for us," Neelkant concluded.

Meeramani gestured Malini and they both swiftly got down from the stairs. Meeramani wasn't able to understand what they were talking about, but she had understood that the history of Maharana

Ranjeet wasn't great, but as brothers Neelkant and Rameshwar, both were very good.

On Raksha Bandhan, Queen Ambika tied rakhi on the wrists of her three brothers, Neelkant, Rameshwar and the brother of Meeramani, Virat. They all blessed her and pledged to protect her all their lives and also gave them a lot of precious jewelleries. Meeramani said, "I don't want all these jewelleries because it keeps lying in my boxes. I don't want these things."

Queen Ambika said to Meeramani, "It seems as if Saint Meerabai of Lord Krishna has taken a re-birth in your avatar. Only your clothes are royal but from inside, you don't look materialistic, but spiritual."

Meeramani replied in a serious tone, "Ambika *jiji*, this is the religion of humanity. A person should be warrior by his acts and a monk by his soul. This way, there is no malice on the soul. All our relations are formed at our birth and end with our death. The birth of human is such that the whole world is a warzone of ethics and the human life is tied to the deeds he does. Every person has a fate, which is to amalgamate in Lord Shiva and be spiritual. Every person is a God person; we are all Lord Shiva-persons, or people of Lord Shiva. Then, who is our own and who's not."

"Then, what do you want, Meeramani. You could tell us without any hesitation," Neelkant asked politely.

"You have already promised me that you would protect me throughout my life; what else would a sister want," Meermani answered lovingly.

"If we wouldn't give you anything then the ritual of Raksha Bandhan won't be completed. We have to give you some gift being your brothers," Rameshwar persisted.

"Alright, I will suggest something to relive you of this burden. Please meet us in the Lord Shiva temple in the evening. I will think about what I want. However, since you have considered me your sister, I would promise you that I would always consider Ambika *jiji* as my elder sister and not my co-wife. Whatever is mine belongs to her first and I shall always protect her," Meeramani answered.

"Meeramani," Queen Ambika got overwhelmed and started

crying, "I should be promising this to you being your elder sister, but you have overwhelmed me by giving everything to me. Will I ever be able to raise my head before you? Meera, you are truly a great soul."

"Ambika *jiji*, I am just doing my duty and not a favor on you. You shall always stay like my elder sister," Meeramani said.

"I am not even worth the dust at your feet. If I had even one quality like yours, Queen Vaishali would have been alive today. I want to tell you everything today and get this load off my chest. I want to atone for my mistakes. Neelkant brother, you wouldn't stop me today as you know I don't know any politics. I am good as a fool, but I will tell the truth to Meeramani today." Then, Ambika told the truth behind the death of Vaishali to Meeramani.

Meeramani got serious and asked, "Did you never enquire about this from Maharana *ji*?"

Queen Ambika answered, "No, I was scared that if I'd tell him that I was listening to their conversation being hidden behind a tree, he might show his beast side to me, too. I neither told him anything nor asked. I told you this as you are my younger sister and our husband and in-laws' is the same. I wouldn't get sinned if I'd share my happiness and sorrows with you. Then, after some time, Maharana *ji* would be bored of you and would bring a new queen and you would face the same situation as me, the same situation what was of Queen Vaishali. Besides, Maharana *ji* didn't even allow me to see the Lord Shiva temple. He had got this constructed himself. I wanted to assist him, but he refused. He said Meeramani would step here first and offer her prayers first. He is confident that you would claim the royal throne and give his first son to him." Queen Ambika started crying again, "Don't think, Meera, that I am jealous of you as a co-wife. I would be happy if you would have a child. I would love your son more. I regret what I had done with Queen Vaishali. I wouldn't do the same with you. If Maharana *ji* would ask you to break all relation with me, would you agree? Don't do this with me, Meera. I have been alone for a long time and I don't want to be alone again. Don't part from me."

Meeramani got emotional and hugged Queen Ambika and said, "No, *jiji*, I promise you that I won't part with you."

All the brothers got emotional listening to the conversation of both their sisters. By the evening, before going to the temple, both Rameshwar and Neelkant had decided that they would tell everything to Meeramani.

* * *

In the evening, before offering prayers, Neelkant said to Meeramani, "Ask for anything, sisters. We would even offer you our lives."

"Neelkant brother, I want to know the complete truth behind the personality of Maharana *ji*. I have heard that you have been his friend since childhood. Please don't hide anything from me," Meeramani requested impatiently.

"We had already decided that we would tell you everything and not hide anything," Rameshwar bowed before the Lord Shiva and said, "Rest Lord himself is sitting here, he would do justice to all. He has the records of everyone's deeds and he would punish everyone accordingly."

"First of all, I would like to thank you, Meeramani, for saving our sister's life. You have done a great favor on us," Neelkant added.

"What is this, brother; on one hand you call me your sister and on the other, you talk about doing favors," Meeramani objected.

Neelkant furthered, "Whatever he have heard about you from Ambika and whatever we saw here, you are way better than that and we are proud to have you as our sister. You are our sister and that is why we are able to talk to you about this serious matter."

"Please don't hesitate, brother, you are my elder brother and would certainly desire my good," Meeramani assured.

"Meeramani, the time is nearing when you'd go to Jairajgarh; so listen to us carefully. Ambika is elder to you, but not as mentally mature as you. Virat is younger to you and, thus, you might not be able to say anything to him, but remember an elder brother is akin to father. Remember this brother if you ever get caught into troubles," Neelkant cautioned.

Meeramani got alert and started listening even more

carefully.

Neelkant added, "I know Maharana Ranjeet and Akroor Singh since childhood. We had received our education from the same Gurukul (seminary) and, thus, we were really good friends. Ranjeet is obstinate and pig-headed since childhood. He does what he determines to do without caring about anyone and Akroor Singh considers it as his duty to support him in all his wrong deeds. I was the friend of Ranjeet, but I never supported him nor motivated him towards doing wrong deeds and that's why our friendship couldn't last. His ego is most important to Ranjeet and he wouldn't see anyone above it. Now, listen to the real history behind Jairajgarh," Neelkant told Meeramani about everything including the parents of Ranjeet, the death of his siblings and mother, the murder of his stepbrother, the suicide of his stepmother and first wife Vaishali. Meeramani was in a shock.

Neelkant continued, "There's a poison of politics in the air of Jairajgarh. Stay cautious about all your steps there. Keep your eyes and ears open. One more thing, remember there is no way to safely exit from Jairajgarh. If you see any trouble in your life, then you could find the way through the jungle. However, no one in Jairajgarh knows that way except for Ranjeet and Akroor. You are new there and, thus, try to know each and every corner of the forest smartly and keep your eyes open always. You never know which way would come handy. Ranjeet is very clever and he wouldn't ever speak his heart out. He is a master in politics. Nobody knows what he says and what he means. His biggest weapon is his army chief, Akroor Singh. Always stay cautious of him. Never disclose any of your weaknesses to him as he is good at exploiting them and relishes exploiting one's vulnerabilities. You must be thinking that I am telling you all the evils of Ranjeet right at the beginning of your married life, but I am ashamed to admit that all of this is true. You will see for yourself when you would be there. Ambika has seen everything, but she is not ready to accept anything. She think accepting the truth is a sin."

Meeramani's face got grim upon hearing everything.

Neelkant said, "Ranjeet has been giving such medicine, which is preventing both his wives from becoming mothers. I am surprised to hear this. Ranjeet doesn't have any successor to his throne yet, but why does he want both his wives to not give birth to his child. What's the need of such medicines? You will have to figure out the truth behind this there. Rest Rameshwar will tell you."

Rameshwar said, "Yes, sister Meeramani. I will tell you the truth behind this medicine." He told Meeramani everything that he had investigated about the medicine.

He said, "I suspect he has appointed a maid who specially serves this medicine in warm almond-saffron milk to the queens. You will have to find out the truth for yourself. It's true that he gives the medicines to his queens, but we don't know why he doesn't want a child."

Neelkant furtherd, "I would also alert you to stay cautious of foolishness of Ambika. She tells everything to Ranjeet. Don't let her know that we have told you the entire history behind Jairajgarh, for she doesn't know it herself. I don't know if Ambika is foolish or if Ranjeet is shrewd. If Ambika asks you what we were talking about, just tell her that we were thanking you for saving our sister's life and convey the same to Ranjeet, too, for he is going to ask you if he'd come to know that we had come here. Rest you are smart. Sister, Lord Shiva will always protect you. Whenever you need this brother, I'd come running to you. It's a promise," Neelkant placed his hand on Meeramani's head.

Even Pandit Rameshwar Nath Shastri blessed Meeramani and said, "Even I promise that whenever you would need your brother, just remember me and I would never disappoint you. But Neelkant, we haven't found a solution to this problem yet."

"O Lord!" the eyes of Meeramani welled up with tears, "What is this plan of yours? Why doesn't Maharana *ji* want Ambika *jiji* to become a mother? Doesn't he want a successor to his throne and continue his dynasty? Or… or… or…" Meeramani had started to understand everything, "or he doesn't want his successor through Ambika *jiji*. It is confirmed that he gives medicine to Ambika *jiji* in warm milk. He didn't let Vaishali *jiji* become mother. This implies that Vaishali *jiji* had known Maharana *ji*'s reality. That's why she had said she was not a fool like Ambika. And even Ambika *jiji* was telling that he would choose the queen to mother his child as well as claim the throne."

Meeramani had started to figure out everything. She was able to understand Ranjeet's politics, but not the reason behind it.

"Lord Shiva has found a solution to this problem, brothers," She said.

"What? What's the solution?" Neelkant and Rameshwar said in chorus.

"Have the medicines been sent now?" Meeramani questioned.

"No, the box of medicines is ready and has to be sent probably by next month," Rameshwar answered.

Meeramani said to him, "Then, change all the medicines once you go back. Place those medicines which make even an infertile woman a mother. Then, Rameshwar brother, do something to make your father permanently hand over to you this responsibility of sending medicines to Jairajgarh. Thereon, send some powerful medicines which could make Ambika *jiji* a mother fast. The plan is that the medicines, which come from Kashi, would be entirely changed. She would become a mother fast. Keep all these things secret from your father too."

"Only Ambika would become a mother and you?" Why not, sister? Don't you want to give a meaning to your life by becoming a mother?" Neelkant was surprised.

"Now, this life would be only worthwhile when everyone would get their rights and we would change Maharana *ji*'s game of politics. I swear by Lord Shiva that the successor of the throne would only be born from Ambika *jiji*'s womb and she would be the one to claim the Maharani throne. This is my promise to you," Meeramani said with determination.

Rameshwar was surprised looking at this side of her. You are an avatar of Goddess, sister. Even a real sister doesn't show this true love to her sister that you are showing to your co-wife. I feel like touching your feet."

"This is the dilemma of our lives, brother. We women become happy by cheating with other women," Meeramani said with grief, "Instead of sharing each other's pains, we become the reason behind it. We experience happiness by harming each other and that's why we remain puppets in the hands of men because we don't want to realize our value, importance and the power in our unity. Thus, men keep us like a slave and we accept this slavery at our will. Then, we complain that men cheat us while the truth is that we women cheat ourselves."

Neelkant and Rameshwar were gaping at Meeramani seeing a new side of power, a new side of feminism. They considered her as an avatar of Goddess Chandi.

"Sister, are you truly from this world or you have come from heaven." Rameshwar was surprised. "A woman's thoughts, that too revolutionary. I promise you that no one would be able to misuse the medicines coming from Kashi."

Meeramani asked Rameshwar, "Could you also send the medicines to Sambhalgarh, which could help a woman become a mother fast?

"I have brought these medicines along. I thought Ambika might need them," Rameshwar answered.

"Alright, don't tell anything to Ambika *jiji*. I fear she might tell Maharana *ji*. Give these medicines to me. I will replace these with the ones Maharana *ji* is giving to his queens. This way, he wouldn't get to know and we would be able to turn his game," Meeramani said.

Neelkant added after thinking, "You had told me that my mother had asked for medicines from your father to help Ambika become a mother. I think Ambika must have told Maharana Ranjeet about this and he must have gotten the medicines replaced with his medicines."

"Don't worry, brother. Ambika *jiji* would start having these medicines from this moment and would become a mother soon. We would hear the good news soon by the blessings of Lord Shiva," Meeramani added.

"If you have said, then we would definitely listen to the good news. I completely trust you," Neelkant got overwhelmed.

Then, King Neelkant, Pandit Rameshwar and Queen Meeramani bowed before God to thank him and started preparing for their departure.

Everything was clear before Meeramani. She understood the various faces of Maharana Ranjeet and his game of politics.

Meeramani said to herself, “You’ve consummated women as much you have wished to and played with them as much as you desired to. You might have seen only one face of women till now, I will show you the other. You have forgotten the eight arms of Goddess Mahishasurmardini, whom your entire empire worships. It seems that you are not familiar with her great powers. Get set for a war of politics, Maharana Ranjeet Dev Pratap Singh, because this time you would have to fight with Meeramani.”

The next morning, King Neelkant bade everyone adieu and moved to his empire and Pandit Rameshwar Nath Shastri also set out for Kashi. However, before leaving, King Neelkant solved one more problem of Meeramani. He fixed the marriage of Virat with Sulakshana, the daughter of the maternal uncle of King Neelkant and Ambika, who was the current king of Kashi. Neelkant had sent the proposal of the marriage of Prince Virat through letter and Shiromani Pandit Rameshwar Nath Shastri had himself taken the proposal and that’s why he was hopeful that the king of Kashi would accept the proposal. Princess Sulakshana was an extremely beautiful and good-natured.

Queen Meeramani started preparing for her return to Jairajgarh along with Queen Ambika as their days in Sambhalgarh were numbered. Maharana Ranjeet could send his message any time to pick up both his queens from Sambhalgarh.

Chapter 18: The Arrival of Queen Meeramani to the Great Empire Jairajgarh

Maharana Ranjeet Dev Pratap Singh reached Sambhalgarh on time. After spending a few days at his in-laws home and finishing all the due formalities, he proceeded to leave for Jairajgarh with both his queens. King Surat Singh also bid adieu to his daughter by giving her all possible auspicious paraphernalia and gifts in dowry. Queen Meeramani took her maid Malini along with her in dowry as she had developed a good friendship with Queen Ambika's chief maid, Kaushika. Kaushika had also come along with Queen Ambika to Sambhalgarh. Maid Kushika had great respect for Queen Meeramani because she had saved the life of her Queen Ambika. King Neelkant had explained to Kaushika, before she left Ballabhgarh, that she should take utmost care of Queen Ambika, but should first obey the orders of Queen Meeramani.

Maharana Ranjeet Dev Pratap Singh reached Jairajgarh along with both his queens. The entire way from the boundary of the grand empire Jairajgarh to the palace was decorated magnificently and all the inhabitants were cheering for the king and his queens. The chariot of Queen Ambika had already reached the palace, so that she could make appropriate arrangements for welcoming the new bride.

At the entrance of the palace, Queen Ambika sang prayers

for Queen Meeramani and Maharana Ranjeet. Although Meeramani was happy with the honour and respect she had received; however, her heart was in deep pain. She was in emotional pain because of Maharana Ranjeet Dev Pratap Singh. On the outside, she showed herself to be calm, but inside, she had contained a lot of resentment. It was confirmed that Maharana Ranjeet would have his honeymoon with Queen Meeramani after the Rudrabhishek (special prayers of Lord Shiva) in the Lord Shiva temple and Queen Meeramani preferred to spend her first night in Queen Ambika's room.

The first thing that Meeramani did after reaching the palace was change the medicine bowl of Ambika with the help of Kaushika and Malini, without letting anyone else know about this. Now, Queen Ambika was being given the medicines which could help her get pregnant. Meeramani had a nice sleep after having done this task.

The next morning, Maharana Ranjeet reached the temple with both his wives at an auspicious time. Meeramani was extremely happy after having had the first look of the temple from outside. She looked with gratitude towards Maharana Ranjeet Singh and he, in turn, smiled with proud and love.

Maharana Ranjeet Singh said to her, "I want you to open the doors of the temple and step inside it first."

She replied with a smile, "No, Maharana *ji*. You should open the doors with your hands and I shall enter along with the tray of prayer paraphernalia; one should only do the tasks which he is expected to. You have got this temple constructed and it is your right to open it first."

Meeramani grabbed the tray for prayers from Ambika and said to her, "Draw a 'swastika' (holy symbol of Hindus) on both the sides of the doors. Since you are elder to me, this is your right." Queen Ambika looked at Maharana as if seeking permission. Maharana Ranjeet replied, "Do whatever Meeramani is saying. She is an ardent follower of Lord Shiva and she knows more than all of us." Ambika got happy having heard this and happily drew 'swastika' of Lord Ganesha with vermillion-sandal.

Meeramani lit two lamps and kept them on each side of the entrance. She then said to Maharana Ranjeet Singh, "Maharana *ji*, open the doors of the temple." She also gestured the priest to blow the conch shells. The chief priest blew the conch shells along with other priests. The sound echoed in the atmosphere and the entire Jairajgarh was filled with the prayers of Lord Shiva.

Maharana Ranjeet opened the doors of the Shiva temple. Queen Meeramani offered her prayers by laying on the floor and then making Queen Ambika ahead of her, said, "*Jiji*, please put your right foot forward and enter the temple." Maharana Ranjeet Singh was shocked listening to this. Meeramani ignored him and said to Ambika, "This is your right, *jiji*, please go ahead." Maharana Ranjeet Singh had already asked Queen Ambika to do as Meeramani said and thus, she put her right foot inside the temple. Meeramani entered the temple after her and asked Maharana Ranjeet Singh to enter.

Maharana Ranjeet was now irked. He was getting enraged at the audacity of Meeramani. He thought to himself, "I guess the first lesson that she will have to be taught would be that the results of disobeying her husband or Maharana of the grand empire was not right. I put in so much of hard work to gift her and how dare she do as per her wish. I wanted her to step inside the temple first; does she even respect my wishes? I am giving her respect, but she is in turn insulting me. She didn't do right by disrespecting me and my wish in front of Queen Ambika. Before I lose control over Queen Ambika, Meeramani will have to be taught a lesson. Now she is in Jairajgarh and this is my empire; here, whoever wouldn't accept my wishes, would be punished." Maharana Ranjeet Singh's anger was now mounting.

Meeramani reiterated sweetly, "Maharana *ji*, please come. Let's begin Rudrabhishek." In this ceremony too, she made Ambika sit first with Maharana and then took her seat.

Even the royal priest couldn't refrain from appreciating about Meeramani to Maharana Ranjeet Singh, "Maharana *ji*, you must have done a lot of virtues to have gotten wife like her. Your new queen is wise and worthy. With her stepping into the grand empire Jairajgarh, the first Lord Shiva temple has been established here. Just watch and see, she will also give you your first successor."

Maharana Ranjeet Singh was very happy listening to the

priest and his anger vanished away. Meeramani was very happy seeing the temple. She even touched Maharana's feet and thanked him for the wedding gift after the ceremony of Rudrabhishek. Maharana Ranjeet Singh had cooled down by now and the wisdom of Meeramani had helped him pacify.

After Rudrabhishek, Meeramani did something which left everyone stunned. Meeramani took off all her ornaments and put them at the feet of Lord Shiva and said, "Lord Shiva! You will have to keep up my respect. You've never turned down any of my wishes. I plead before you on the occasion of Rudrabhishek that the grand empire Jairajgarh should get its successor in one year. I want a successor to Jairajgarh. I pray that this becomes possible soon. I pledge that until you make me hear this good news, I wouldn't enter the royal palace and would serve you as a monk, have food once a day and would keep reminding you by staying here in this temple."

"What... what... how unusual pledge is this!" Every person was now wondering that if Queen Meeramani would stay in the temple then how would she give a successor to the throne."

Maharana Ranjeet Singh, too, said surprisingly, "What pledge is this and what madness! If you would stay here as a monk, then how would Jairajgarh get its successor? How would you give me a son?"

The royal priest said, "Daughter Meeramani, I had heard that you are an ardent Lord Shiva follower and wise. You have brought up your younger brother like a mother at a tender age. However, you have stunned me by your pledge. What wisdom have you proved by this pledge, can you explain?"

"I apologize to everyone," Queen Meeramani said politely, "I have stunned all of you by my pledge, but I have made the resolution. I have restricted myself to enter the palace, but not sister Ambika. It is not only the right of the younger queen to give successor to the throne, but the elder Queen Ambika too has that right. That's why we both sisters would try not to disappoint the grand empire Jairajgarh."

Everybody was overwhelmed listening to her reply. The priest blessed her and said, "You are indeed an avatar of Goddess. Whatever I had heard about you was less. The wisdom and sacrifice you have shown at such a tender age is very difficult to be found, my blessings are always with you." He then looked at Maharana Ranjeet Singh and said, "Maharana *ji*, it is the fortune of Jairajgarh that Goddess Mahishasurmardini has entered the empire in the form of Meeramani. Nobody can stop the growth of the empire now."

However, Maharana Ranjeet was again losing his cool. He was thinking about the tantrums being thrown by Meeramani. He was blabbering in anger, "I am blindly in love with her and she is taking advantage of my love. Even Meeramani appears to be foolish like Ambika. She would get insulted herself because I have been giving medicine to Ambika which would never let her become a mother. Then, what would her devotion do. Let me also watch this drama along with others. She is insulting me by doing as per her wish. When everybody would raise questions over her devotion, then she would get wisdom. For how many days will she stay in the temple and live like a monk, Ambika is never going to be a mother, no matter what Meeramani does. Maharana Ranjeet Singh smirked to himself, "When the entire Jairajgarh would laugh at her, then she would fall at my feet and seek apology. She is busy portraying herself as great, but at that time, I will tell her what I can do. I was planning to give her all the respect and rights of being a mother of my son and claim the throne of Maharani, but if she finds solace in this stupidity then let her be here."

Maharana Ranjeet controlled his anger and said softly, "Meeramani, your sacrifice is appreciable, but Ambika is infertile. When she couldn't conceive for ten years, then how can she now..."

"Now she will..." Meeramani interrupted in between and said with determination, "Now she has the blessings of Lord Shiva and support of her sister, Meeramani."

"May Queen Meeramani live long!" Everybody cheered and left the temple leaving Ambika, Meeramani and Maharana Ranjeet alone.

Tears welled up in the eyes of Ambika. She said, "Why you are taking so much pain for me, sister? What's the need of facing so much of pain? No sister does this for her real sister, then why are you doing this for me?"

Maharana Ranjeet answered for Meeramani, "She is crazy

to get famous as great. When she would get to know that you are infertile and cannot give birth to a child, then she would herself realize."

Queen Ambika started crying upon hear him.

Queen Meeramani said in a stern voice, "Maharana *ji*, you are talking big while standing in front of Lord Shiva. Don't challenge god by becoming blind in pride. This much of pride doesn't look good on you…"

"And being a woman, pride suits you?" Maharana shouted in between, "You keep disrespecting my love for you and all our rights in your pride.If you cannot do what you have been brought here in Jairajgarh to do, then I don't need you here. I strongly want you to deliver the successor to the throne of Jairajgarh within one year and claim the throne of Maharani. This is my wish and it is your religion to keep up the respect of my wishes. Just think, how powerful prince our son would be, who would claim such a huge empire and the throne of the king. Besides, he would have no competitor for the throne. I wanted to give you the pride to mother such a child. I thought you are smart, but you turned out to be even more foolish than Ambika that you want to give all your rights to your co-wife. Just think, if Ambika mothers the prince and claims the throne, then your worth would be akin to that of a maid." Maharana Ranjeet tried cajoling Meeramani.

"I am doing my deeds, Maharana *ji*. What Ambika *jiji* would do with me would be her deeds and she would reap its results. And whatever you do with us, you will bear the fruits of your deeds. She further said What would you do by winning the entire world with your powers? Wouldn't it be better if the whole world bows before you out of respect and not fear? For that, you would have to respect everyone's emotions. Love everyone. Cowards rule through their swords; if you don't have this sword, then everyone would stop respecting you."

"Queen Meeramani, stay in your limits. I have already listened to your lecture. If I am behaving nicely with you, then don't forget your place. You are only my wife. Whatever you are getting and whatever you will get, it will only be because you are the wife of Maharana Ranjeet Dev Pratap Singh. I am your husband. If I have given you the right to speak, then use that to only please me; don't irk me by misusing it. I won't tolerate any of your wishes from now. Learn the ways of living at your in-laws place. I can't stand a woman speaking uncontrollably in front of me. Bow down in front of me if you want to stay dear to me. I chop the heads which are raised in front of me. Don't force me to become harsh. Just focus on giving the successor to the throne. Mother a prince for the royal throne and raise him into a great and worthy Maharana. You have been made the queen of Jairajgarh for this purpose; so focus entirely on this and seize the throne of Maharani. Rest, I am still alive to take care of the rest of the governance and politics." Maharana concluded and exited from the temple.

This side of Maharana was new for Meeramani and she began to cry. Maharana changed his colors faster than a chameleon. He considers women weak and they are only objects of pleasure for him. Meeramani thought, "This person is not even worth giving love. He is far away from the definition of love and only knows the definition of lust. Love only knows giving and not snatching. If he had known the language of love, then giving him love was my duty; however, if he only knows the language of politics, then I will talk to him in that language." Meeramani wiped tears from her cheeks.

Queen Ambika was hearing their conversation; she hugged Meeramani and said, "Sister, if you want, even I could stay with you in the temple as a monk. Both of us, sisters, would spend our lives here."

"Then, what would happen to our pledge?" Meeramani asked while smiling, "Would you let me down before Maharana *ji*?"

"No, Meeramani, don't say that. I would rather die than letting you down, but I was thinking something else. Maharana *ji* is obstinate and arrogant. You have pledged, but he would do anything to win. Warzone or relations, both are same for him. Considering how arrogant he is, he wouldn't understand through any way, be it talks, money, punishment or politics and he won't accept his defeat. He just wants to win and rule over everyone at any cost and he wouldn't ever accept his defeat in front of a woman."

"God can make every impossible task as possible. If he has pride, then I have devotion. I pledge banking on that devotion, but he pledges to satiate his pride and egoism. Both the things are different. Now, this war is not with us, be it man or woman, but with Lord Shiva. Now we would only see that if someone is in war with God, then who would win," Meeramani said seriously.

"Everything is alright, Meeramani, but if he could do anything to win then he would make it a point to never come close to me and if that doesn't happen, then how would your vow be complete?" Ambika said while thinking.

"Completing our vow is in the hands of Lord Shiva, but," Meeramani smiled mischievously, "Would I have to teach you how to please your husband? When would your beauty and looks come of use if you are not even able to please your husband?"

Ambika and Meeramani started giggling together.

Queen Meeramani was trying hard penance and prayers in order to please Lord Shiva and Queen Ambika was trying her best to please her husband, Maharana Ranjeet Singh. Maharana had come to the temple several times in order to persuade Meeramani to leave her stubbornness as the consequences wouldn't be good, but she was not ready to accept as this issue had become a challenge for her, too. She knew that if she accepted her defeat, then it would be defeat of her trust in Lord and this time, it was more about the existence of Lord than her trust in him and she couldn't accept her defeat before Maharana.

On the other side, Maharana was losing his control before the beauty and youth of Queen Ambika. Then he thought that Ambika was anyway taking the medicine and cannot get pregnant; so, it didn't matter if he stayed in her room.

However, he didn't know that God had already shown his magic in the avatar of Meeramani and the game of Maharana had turned tables as the medicines coming from Kashi were being changed. Now, the medicines, which could make even an infertile woman as pregnant, were being sent by Shiromani Pandit Rameshwar Nath Shastri. Anyway, Ambika wasn't infertile, but a mere victim of politics of Maharana Ranjeet Singh. No matter how many moves a person makes, the last one is always by God and he would overpower the person who is always busy in making moves.

Chapter 19:
The Birth of the Prince of the Grand Empire Jairajgarh

It had been four months since the arrival of Queen Meeramani in Jairajgarh and she hadn't heard the good news as yet. Meeramani was wondering if brother Rameshwar Nath was sending the right medicines or if Maharana *ji* had come to know about our plan and if he had once again changed the game, then what will we do? She was lost in her deep thoughts when Queen Ambika entered the temple and bowed before the God. She then hugged Meeramani and whispered something in her ears which made her very happy. She fell at the feet of Lord Shiva and said, "O Lord! You have kept my respect. I knew you would never break my trust, my dear Lord Shiva! This servant of yours thanks you a lot."

Meeramani called out for her chief maid, Malini and said, "Hey Malini, do you hear?" The moment she entered, Meeramani told her the good news and said, "Go and get my makeup box. I will go to the palace with all the preparations and I would myself inform Maharana *ji* about this." She looked at Ambika and asked her, "Have you told Maharana *ji* yet?"

Queen Ambika said, "The penance is all yours. I wouldn't have told anyone before you and I have made all the preparations for you. I would myself get you ready and take you along with me to the palace."

Queen Ambika did prayers for Meeramani at the gates of the palace and took her inside the palace. Maharana Ranjeet was sitting in his room.

Meeramani said, "I would meet Maharana *ji* myself."

Queen Meeramani entered the room of Maharana Ranjeet Singh and she was carrying a tray of prayer paraphernalia in her hands and she was dressed up like a queen. Maharana Ranjeet Singh saw her and thought that maybe she had gained wisdom and she had come to him to seek an apology. "No issue, I would forgive her; after all, she is only half my age and would act like kids."

Queen Meeramani touched his feet and he gave her a puzzled look. Meeramani was glowing with happiness. She put a piece of sweet in his mouth and said, "Maharana *ji*, congratulations! With the blessings of Lord Shiva, you are going to become a father. The grand empire Jairajgarh is going to get its prince soon. Ambika *jiji* is going to be the mother of your first child."

Maharana Ranjeet was stunned for a second and shouted the next, "This cannot happen! This can never happen!"

"Why cannot it happen, Maharana *ji*? Aren't you happy to hear this good news? I thought you would dance like kids when you'd hear this," Meeramani pretended to be naïve.

"Because... because..." Maharana Ranjeet Singh was stammering; he controlled himself and said, "Because Ambika is infertile and she is not religious enough for God to bless her with a child and I thought you have come because..." Maharana Ranjeet Singh left his words unsaid.

"Man doesn't even exist before the will of God. What he would give and to whom and when is unknown to everyone," said Meeramani. "Devotion is not related to ringing bells in the temple or praying, it's related to the soul. If the soul is honest and guileless, then God listens to even the smallest of the prayers. Otherwise, even ages of devotion are waste. Ambika *jiji* is an honest woman; whatever she feels, she says. She doesn't know politics and that's why she loves you and doesn't ask for anything from you except love. She can sacrifice anything for your happiness and her love for you is honest. She doesn't worship God, but considers you as her God. She has always served you with all her body and soul; even

God is always close to such guileless woman. These are her deeds, Maharana *ji*, and whatever you do are your deeds. Every human has to face the consequences for his or her deeds, be it good or bad. Deeds are not tied to any relation, neither they are personal. Come with me, Maharana *ji*, Ambika *jiji* is waiting for you. I have made arrangements to ward evil eyes off her." Meeramani exited the room and Maharana Ranjeet Dev Pratap kept staring like a mannequin.

Each word of Meeramani was pinching Maharana Ranjeet Singh. The fort of his pride was being shaken by her clear and straight talks. Once again, God had shown the existence of his powers that no matter what a man does, he can never hurt his devotees. When a man deceits someone, who is a devotee of God, he forgets that God is standing behind his devotee, with all his forces. The war between human and God is a war of ethics and God always proves that human stands nowhere before Him.

* * *

Maharana Ranjeet called his chief commander and close friend Akroor Singh in his room and gave him the news of the pregnancy of Queen Ambika. Even Akroor Singh was stunned upon hearing this news. He said he would go to Shiromani himself to investigate how did this happen, but Maharana Ranjeet asked him not to go as whatever has happened, has happened now.

Then, Akroor Singh said, "Maharana *ji*, if you allow me, can I ask you something as a friend?"

Maharana Ranjeet Singh looked at him puzzled.

Akroor Singh said, "Maharana *ji*, your younger queen is, indeed, an avatar of a Goddess. Even the royal priest had said the same thing that day; in fact, the entire Jairajgarh is saying this. Everyone is bowing before her sacrifice and dedication for her duties. See how Lord Shiva has blessed Queen Ambika with a child. Maharana *ji*, I request you to accept the destiny written by God and end all this. This is the time to celebrate as you are going to be a father soon. It doesn't matter who is mothering the child as the child is yours. Many congratulations to you, Maharana *ji*. I believe that the grand empire Jairajgarh would only get a prince.

"Commander Akroor Singh," Maharana Ranjeet said in a stern voice, "If you feel like bowing before a female then you must take renounce. What would you do being our commander. Should I place you in service of Queen Meeramani? Carry her prayer trays and sit behind her in the temple. Have you gone crazy looking at her mania that you are seeing an avatar of goddess in her? She is full of immaturity and in that immaturity she has started to consider herself as goddess when someone called her so. She has forgotten that she's an ordinary woman. Or I should rather say that people have brainwashed her mind by calling her a goddess. Just naming one 'Meera' doesn't make her saint Meerabai. Females have just one task to do which is to keep their husbands happy and give birth to their children, that's it. No woman is born to become a monk. We, males, are there for that. We see politics, we see governments and we see wars. Can she ever be this powerful? I think Ambika had stopped taking the medicines, as she was in Sambhalgarh and Ballabhgarh for such a long time; that's how she could get pregnant and I don't know what magic you are talking about. Had Meeramani been a magician, she would have gotten pregnant herself; why would she help her co-wife get pregnant? Everyone has gone crazy by looking at her beautiful and innocent looks. Everyone is made to consider as goddess. Now, leave, Akroor, and let me think."

Akroor Singh bowed before him and left wondering what had happened to Maharana. He was wondering if he was explaining to him or to himself and if he had indeed turned blind to not notice the sacrifice and dedication of his younger wife.

Maharana Ranjeet Singh was experiencing happiness and sorrow all at the same time. He was happy for he was going to be a father after a long time and was sad at the same time because it wasn't Meermanai's child. He thought that his children with Ambika would be jealous of those with Meeramani. He thought that anyway Meeramani was adept in politics, nobody knew what would she conspire and that's why he didn't want any to her children with his other wives. No matter how many women he would consummate with, he would have children with only one wife so that peace sustains in his empire. But, God spoiled his plans. He thought he would have to face the consequences of his mistakes like his father,

Surya Dev Pratap Singh, did.

Lost in thoughts, Maharana reached Ambika's room. The maids left the room while congratulating him. Ambika was turning red while blushing. She stood up and touched his feet and said, "Congratulations, Maharana *ji*! God has blessed us for the penance of Meeramani."

He hugged Ambika and said, "Which month is it?"

Queen Ambika answered, "Third month. This is all a result of devotion and penance of Meeramani. She only had assured that I would give Jairajgarh its prince. She is an ardent followed of Shiva and even he couldn't turn down his wishes and blessed me with the fruit of her devotion." She hugged Meeramani and said, "You are more than a real sister. I am indebted to you for life."

Meeramani answered, "Don't think rubbish, *jiji*. Now, only think about ethics and talk about ethics. The thoughts of a pregnant woman affect her child. The better the thoughts, the better the child."

Maharana Ranjeet Singh thought to himself, "Meeramani is so clever and shrewd. She wouldn't let her jealousy come out. She is unmatchable in politics. I will have to save Ambika from her till her child is born. What if she does anything dangerous! I don't care about Ambika, but the child in her womb is mine; I will have to protect him. He ordered the maid Kaushika, "Ask the messenger to call the chief royal doctor now and ask him to meet me in my personal room."

The maid, Kaushika, bowed and left the room.

He said to Ambika, "Take complete rest now. I will go meet the royal doctor and would make all the necessary arrangements for your comforts." Maharana Ranjeet exited the room and progressed towards his own. Ambika was going crazy looking at Maharana's love for her and Meeramani was happy to see her sister happy.

Maharana Ranjeet was sitting in his room wondering how to keep Meeramani away from Ambika. It wouldn't be possible in Jairajgarh. Then he remembered that the first child of a woman is born at her maternal place. "It would be fine if she goes to her home and Meeramani stays here with me." Maharana Ranjeet took deep breath thinking about this.

Then, the chief physician, Jagdish Raj, entered his room and greeted him.

Maharana Ranjeet said, "Please come, Jagdish Raj; I have called you for a purpose. It's the first trimester of Queen Ambika. I think Jairajgarh is going to get its Prince soon. I want you to check her up and tell me about her condition so that I could send her to her maternal home as according to the customs, the first child takes birth at his mother's place."

"Congratulations, Maharana *ji*, after the construction of the temple, I am confident that Lord Shiva will bless you with a son soon. Your youngest Queen Meeramani is an avatar of Goddess. Everything has been possible from her penance. Kindly send this message to Queen Ambika so that I could check her up," Jagdish Raj said cheerfully.

"Come, let's go together," Maharana Ranjeet Singh said.

The chief physician checked Ambika and told that she is healthy and is fit for long journeys. Maharana, then, said, "Alright, then I will quickly inform King Neelkant in Ballabhgarh that Ambika would be coming there for the delivery of her first child. Our commander, Akroor, would go along with a unit of soldiers and doctors so that Ambika doesn't face any problem in the way." He then said to Jagdish, "You may leave now; we would inform you about going to Ballabhgarh."

After the doctor exited, Ambika said to Meeramani, "Make all the preparations, even you have to come along with me."

Before Meeramani could say anything, Maharana said, "No Ambika, somebody has to be here to take care of me. There would be many people around you, but I would be alone without my wives."

Queen Ambika got upset hearing this. She persisted, "But Maharana *ji*, she is my sister and I need her right now. You would have to promise me that she would be close to me before my child is born. I want her to see the face of the child first, even before me. I had pledged before God that I won't see the face of the child before her. Even if I am pregnant, it is all because of her dedication. I won't leave before you promise me."

"Alright, don't worry, Ambika. Meeramani would reach you before the childbirth. I promise you that she would reach you in your last month. You both have forgotten me and have done an alliance amongst yourselves," Maharana assured.

After some days, Queen Ambika left for her home to Ballabhgarh along with a unit of servants and soldiers under the leadership of Akroor Singh. Meeramani got lonely upon Ambika's departure. She started spending most of her time in the temple. Maharana Ranjeet wanted to spend time with her, but she used to stay silent and upset. She had even started to consume the medicines which were earlier being given to Ambika because she didn't want to get pregnant before Ambika.

One day, she received an invitation to the marriage of her brother, Virat Singh, with Sulakshana, the princess of Kashi. She got happy hearing this and started persisting Maharana Ranjeet Singh to allow her to go to her home. Maharana Ranjeet left for Sambhalgarh along with her.

The marriage of Prince Virat had happened successfully with Sulakshana. They both had persuaded Maharana Ranjeet Singh to let Meeramani stay there for some time and Maharana couldn't refuse as he had seen Meeramani happy after a lot of days.

King Neelkant from Ballabhgarh had also come to attend Virat's wedding from the bride's side as Sulakshana was his cousin. He informed Maharana Ranjeet Singh that eighth month of Ambika had begun and she was calling Meeramani; therefore, Maharana Ranjeet Singh asked Meeramani to go to the maternal place of Ambika from there. He also told her that he would come there with a procession after the birth of the child. He returned Jairajgarh alone.

* * *

The ninth month of Ambika's pregnancy was coming to an end and, thus, Meeramani reached to her with his brother having done all the preparations. Upon their arrival in Ballabhgarh, they were welcomed by King Neelkant. Queen Ambika was very happy and content to see Meeramani. He thought that Meeramani would take care of everything. Meeramani had brought a famous midwife of Sambhalgarh, Sankula Devi, along with her. Sankula was an experienced midwife and she had an experience of successful deliveries in bad pregnancy situations, too. She didn't want to take any chance for Ambika, and she trusted this experienced midwife. Neelkant had also called Shiromani Pandit Rameshwar as it was Ambika's first delivery and he didn't want to take any chance too. He wanted everything to happen peacefully so that Maharana Ranjeet Singh didn't get any reason to complain.

Padmavati Devi, wife of King Neelkant, had gone to her maternal place along with her three kids for the coronation of her brother. King Neelkant didn't go there looking at his sister's condition, but he was going to pick them up after a few days.

All the well-wishers of Queen Ambika reached to her with the beginning of her ninth month. Queen Meeramani from Jairajgarh, Prince Virat Singh from Sambhalgarh, Shiromani Pandit Rameshwar from Kashi and her brother, Neelkant, were already there.

After dinner, Queen Ambika went to her room to sleep, while others went to the terrace to stroll. They all were discussing various topics.

Then, King Neelkant held Meeramani's hand and said, "Sister, I shall never be able to pay off the favour you have done for Ambika; I am indebted to you for life. You are my younger sister, but I bow before you for your greatness and sacrifice. You had made one promise to Ambika that she would be the mother of the prince and would claim the throne of Maharani and Ambika has made one promise to herself that she would ask for the throne of Maharani from Maharana for you and she considers it right that she doesn't deserve the throne. The only woman who deserves the throne of Maharani is you; therefore, don't turn down her wish and respect the throne by claiming it. Everybody, including Ambika and your brothers, Virat, Rameshwar and me would feel proud to see you sitting on the throne.

Meeramani's eyes got wet, seeing so much love for her. She said, "Till the time I have brothers like you, I don't have to worry about anything. I am grateful to get a sister like Ambika *jiji* and brothers like you. My life has become meaningful."

"We have been obliged to get a sister like you, Meeramani," Rameshwar said.

Virat Singh wasn't able to understand anything. He asked his sister about what was happening. He asked her to explain the situation to him.

"Meeramani, you haven't told anything to Virat as yet?" asked Rameshwar.

"No, brother, I didn't get a chance, but I feel today is the day. Both of you brothers tell the entire story to him while I would sit with Ambika *jiji*. But Virat, keep this confidential and make sure that this remains between four of us, not even to Sulakshana and definitely not to our father Maharaja," said Meeramani.

"I know, *jiji* Ma, your every word is a command for me," said Virat.

Meeramani smiled and left the terrace. King Neelkant and Pandit Rameshwar told the entire story to Virat, who was very angry by the end of it. He shouted, "I swear by Lord Shiva, had he not been my brother-in-law, I would have chopped his head off."

"Calm down, brother. We have been seeing this since childhood. We have been keeping calm since it is our sister's house. When someone treats our sisters badly, as they have been brought up so lovingly, or their husband mistreats them, our blood comes to a boil," said Neelkant.

Rameshwar added, "But when the sister is like Meeramani, who is a warriors by acts and an ardent follower of Lord Shiva by soul, then these worries start to lessen because we know that she is an avatar of Mahishasurmardini and would set everyone right. Ambika has made a great decision by letting Meeramani claim the throne of Maharani as Jairajgarh needs a Maharani like her."

"Yes, Rameshwar brother, you are right. Now, I am confident that Meermanai would turn tables for Jairajgarh. We are with her anyway. Maharana won't be able to do the same with her as he had done with his first two wives. We won't ever let this happen to Meeramani," King Neelkant said.

King Neelkant, then, stretched his arms and let out his hand. Pandit Rameshwar put his hand over the hand of King Neelkant and Prince Virat placed his hand over them.

They were still talking when Meeramani came running to them and said, "Ambika *jiji* is experiencing labour pain; I think it is the time to hear the good news. I am going to her room with the midwife; all of you should also come downstairs."

All of them ran downstairs.

* * *

They all heard the cries of a baby and they all hugged each other in excitement. They then waited to hear the good news. Meeramani was still inside along with the midwife, Sankula, Kaushika, and Malini.

It had been quite some time and Meeramani hadn't come out yet. All three were tensed now. After quite some time, Sankula Devi came out and said, "Meeramani is calling you all inside the room."

The room of Queen Meeramani was beside that of Ambika and its one of the doors opened to the room of Ambika and the other to the outside. All the brothers turned towards the outside door. The moment they entered, they saw Meeramani sitting on the bed with her hands on her head.

They got worried and asked, "What happened, Meeramani? What's keeping you sad at this time of happiness? Is Ambika alright? Are both the child and the mother alright?" The voice of Neelkant was now getting heavy.

Meeramani started crying and said, "I don't know what and why Lord Shiva is punishing us for. We haven't got the prince of Jairajgarh. Meeramani ordered the midwife, Sankula Devi, please get the child here."

Neelkant said to Meeramani, "It is not an issue even if it is a princess, Meeramani. It is still a grace of God that Ambika got a chance to become a mother. Maybe Lord Shiva has written this in your fate to become the mother of the prince of Jairajgarh. We value both our sisters."

Even Rameshwar added, "Neelkant brother is right. No matter who gives birth to the prince of Jairajgarh, he or she will have two mothers and three uncles. So, it really doesn't matter who mothers a son and who mothers a daughter."

Then, Sankula Devi got the child. The child was very beautiful and healthy and had brightness on his face. All the uncles were happy upon seeing the child. Meeramani gestured the midwife to give the child to her. Meeramani took the child to the room of Ambika, where Ambika was still in a semi-conscious state.

Queen Meeramani removed the cloth from the baby and said, "The child is neither a boy nor a girl, but a EUNUCH."

"What!! What??" Everybody was stunned.

"What would happen now?" Neelkant sat on the floor holding his head.

Even Rameshwar was standing stunned.

Virat was silent.

Silence prevailed in the room!

Pin-drop silence.

Chapter 20:
Queen Meeramani's Plan

Everyone was sitting silent.

Neelkant broke the silence and said, "Does Ambika know this?" He left his sentence incomplete.

"No, brother, she is not conscious yet because of the intensity of the pain," said Meeramani.

"She shouldn't even get to know this, Meeramani, she is extremely sensitive. She won't be able to stand this," Rameshwar suggested.

"She wasn't able to stand the news of Maharana Ranjeet Singh getting remarried and had almost planned to commit suicide. Now, this is a matter of her child. This trauma would kill her," Neelkant expressed in grief. "God has played a joke with us. Lord Shiva could have given her a daughter instead," Neelkant started crying.

"What would happen to all of us, brother, if you would become weak?" Meeramani stood up to wipe the tears of Neelkant.

"Don't let Ambika *jiji* know that her child is a eunuch. Sankula is from our empire; I would handle her and would also pay her for keeping quiet about the whole thing," Virat spoke for the first time.

Neelkant expressed his grief, "No, Virat. This won't be

possible. You cannot hide a child from his mother and in sometime, eunuchs would come to congratulate; how would you hide from them? The biggest problem is Maharana Ranjeet Singh; how would we tell him? He wouldn't take Ambika back with him. And Ambika wouldn't be able to live in this anticipation; I know Ranjeet since childhood. He destroys everything that no longer serves his purpose. He only values people who are of some use to him; Ambika is no longer of any use, neither as a wife nor as a mother of his children. If it had been a daughter, he would still have understood, but now he wouldn't. He wouldn't understand Ambika and would instead punish her for mothering a eunuch. He wouldn't even take her along with him and you all know the position of a woman in society who is dumped by her husband. So, nobody can save Ambika now, not even God. The days of her life are now over."

"Neelkant, brother, control yourself," Rameshwar said, "There is no problem which doesn't have a solution. We are still alive and would definitely find a solution. Nothing would happen to Ambika; she is our sister, too. Meeramani, go and explain to Sankula now to not let anyone know about this and when Ambika gains consciousness just tell her that the baby is not well that's why the baby cannot be shown to her. Everybody think about this problem and pray to God. Let us all meet at the terrace at night. If anyone comes up with any solution, we will together take the decision. Till then I will make the child's Janam-Kundli (horoscope), let us see what is written in his destiny," he added.

The fact that Ambika had given birth to a eunuch was familiar to only a few people - King Neelkant, Prince Virat, Shiromani Rameshwar, and Meeramani, along with the chief maids, Kaushika and Malini and midwife Sankula Devi. Rest everyone was trustworthy, who needn't required to be told anything. However, there was just one person whose mouth had to be shut, and she was midwife Sankula Devi.

Queen Meeramani explained everything to Sankula well, gave her a lot of wealth and also promised to give a lot of land to her sons. For keeping the whole thing as a secret, whatever was being given to Sankula was beyond her expectation. She wouldn't have got all this had it been a prince and that's why she agreed to keep shut.

Virat even threatened her that he would put her family in prison if she ever disclosed this. Sankula Devi found it worthier to stay mum and she swore that she would declare outside that it was a son and would take care of the child till a solution is found.

Pandit Rameshwar Nath prepared a medicine to help Ambika get well soon and would also sleep more as an effect of the medicine. The moment Ambika gained consciousness, Sankula told her that it was a prince and gave her the medicine. She got very happy and slept again under the effect of the medicine. King Neelkant had guarded the rooms of Meeramani and Ambika heavily. He had declared that nobody is allowed inside as Ambika and the child were not well. Apart from the royal family, only Malini and Kaushika, could enter and Sankula, who was taking care of the mother and the child, was already inside.

They all met at the terrace at night.

Neelkant said, "I couldn't find any solution to this problem neither my brain is working. You should decide amongst yourself. I would agree with your decision."

Pandit Rameshwar added, "I want to share a good news before you arrive on any decision." Everybody looked at him with questionable expression.

Rameshwar Nath added, "I have prepared a birth horoscope of the child and it is written that he would be a king. He would have a comfortable life and would prove to be a good king. He would be a warrior by acts and a saint by heart. There are two problematic times in his life – one i.e. from his birth till he attains 5 years of age, and the other from 17 years of age till 22 years of age and unfortunately this bad time seems to be cropping because of his father. That's why we would have to keep him away from his father during all such times. He would always stay ahead and would be known as a great Maharana. I suggest we should plan in a way that he is safe and gets the best education being a royal child. Good up bringing and good education can make a child into something no one could even imagine. Now, who would take the responsibility, we have to think about this."

"It is waste to expect this from Ambika; she cannot decide anything in life. She is anyway a puppet in the hands of Maharana. He makes her act the way he wishes to and she agrees to him. She doesn't use her brain much; she is very sensitive too," Neelkant added.

"Don't forget Neelkant brother," said Meeramani, while adding, "Your younger sister is not weak –neither from mind nor from heart. I am sorry, but you have made her weak by telling her so. She is a woman and even God bows down before the powers of a woman. The fact that she believes anyone easily and that she is guileless, reflects her honesty and not weakness. She has been bowing down before her husband because of our rituals and customs or may be because she loves her husband too much and loving someone is not a crime. When the life of her child is at stake, a mother would fight till her last breath."

Meeramani added, "Rameshwar brother, you have changed the direction of my thinking that if a child gets good upbringing and education then he could do anything and become anything, even if he is a eunuch. Deformity in a body could be anywhere so how is the child responsible for it, if he is a son, a daughter or a eunuch, but isn't he still the child to his parents? A body of a eunuch is also made of five things, which compose every human body. He can be anything for society, but for his parents he is still their child and separating a child from his mother or father is a shame on humanity as well as society. I pledge today that I would train the child in such a way that he would prove his credibilities in order to claim the throne and he would prove that a child could do anything if he gets good education. He cannot take the generation ahead, but the same could be true for an infertile man or a woman also. Does the society take away their rights, then? Every drop of blood in his body and every part of his body says that he is a human."

"This is the dilemma of our society, said Meeramani sadly while taking a deep breath. We pray to the Brahmacharis (Celibate) because he is a saint and is on the way to God, but the ones whom the God has himself made saints, we ridicule them and don't even give them respect similar to animals and never give them love even after seeing them as humans. We laugh at them and take pleasure out of their pain. We get pained looking at other's pains, but why don't we get affected by their pain? I would change the definition of this word, 'EUNUCH'," Meeramani expressed.

Everybody was surprised looking at this side of Meeramani. It always seemed as if an avatar of goddess is speaking. She becomes like Mahishasurmardini. No beast can now stand in front of her. She opens the arms of her brain like a warrior and no enemy can even stand in front of her. The plan was set. Meeramani said, "Now, we would fight the battle of ethics in the warzone of the world and we would execute this plan." Meeramani disclosed her plan:

"The first step of this plan is: Rameshwar brother, you would go to meet Ambika *jiji* first and would explain to her that according to the birth chart, she seeing the face of her child could prove to be harmful. Therefore, she shouldn't see the face of her child till the planets are made calm. Tell her about the child becoming a king and everything written in the birth chart truly. Just don't tell her that the child is a eunuch. Tell her that she can feed the child by blindfolding herself. Sankula would make sure that she is not able to see the child.

Meeramani further said, "Rameshwar brother, you will have to do one more work. You have to make another birth chart which would say that till the child attains the age of 5 years and if the father sees the face of his child it could be perilous for the child and could even kill him. Make an accurate birth track as Maharana does not believe anyone and he would show the horoscope of the child to the royal priests and that he could not find out any shortcomings in it, you will have to take care of this."

"Don't worry about that, Meeramani, no one can question a birth track stamped by the Shirmomani family. Great priests come to seek education from us," said Rameshwar.

"This is nice." Meeramani was now content.

"The second step of the plan is Neelkant brother, in a day or two, call the eunuch chief of your empire and arrange for a great wealth for him. Rest, leave everything to me. They wouldn't open their mouth ever. One more thing, is it possible that your wife doesn't come back here for another one or two months?" Meeramani asked.

"Of course, it can be possible. Which woman wouldn't be happy by this; this should be a great news for her anyway that she can stay even more at her maternal place," Neelkant said.

"This is fine. I would devise a plan in a few days that where would Ambika *jiji* stay with the child for five years. We can either leave her here, and if Neelkant brother faces any problem, we can then send her to Sambhalgarh along with Virat, they will be safe there." Meeramani said.

"What are you saying, Meeramani? Could any sister be a trouble for her brother?" Neelkant said lovingly.

"No, brother, I was mentioning as your wife would be back after some time and it would be tough for us to keep the secret and we have to keep her away from Jairajgarh for the next five years also,"Meeramani explained.

"Don't worry about that. She is anyway very finicky. I would put a doubt and she wouldn't even come close to Ambika or her child. I have a plan. I would make the arrangements of her stay in a guest house built close to the palace. As soon as Ambika recovers from her illness, I would make all the necessary arrangements for her to stay there. Nobody would go there and she would also get some lone time to take care of her child. I would go there to meet her daily so that she could share her problems with me," Neelkant added.

"Then, it is fine, Meeramani said happily. I would explain to Ambika *jiji* myself. Till then, her love for her child would be completely born within her and she wouldn't ever be able to live away from him, even if it is a eunuch. Later, we would also make Ambika *jiji* a part of our plan. Then, it won't be possible that she doesn't stand for the security of her child against her husband. Make arrangements for sending the message to Maharana *ji*; you never know if he comes here with a procession upon listening to the news of the birth of his child. Once Ambika *jiji* is fine, I would make everything fine upon my return to Jairajgarh. I would explain to Maharana *ji* to not even try to see the face of the child for the next five years."

"What are your orders for me, *jiji* ma?" Virat asked.

"An important instruction for you, my brother, is that you

would have to go to Jairajgarh before Sambhalgarh as Maharana *ji* doesn't trust Neelkant brother completely and thus you would go there and confirm that it is a beautiful child and reassure all the things I would tell to the messenger. He would be assured that whatever he is being told is true. You were anyway asking to leave. So, get ready and also assure Sankula that we would give her the promised wealth upon reaching Sambhalgarh," Meeramani said.

Everybody was now content listening to the plan.

"Now, Neelkant brother and Virat, both of you should take rest; everything has been solved. I want to talk more with Rameshwar brother on this issue," Meeramani added.

After their exit, Meeramani asked Rameshwar, "Is it a she-enuch or a he-eunuch?"

"It is a he-eunuch," Rameshwar answered.

"What health problems could he face in the future? Please tell me in detail about this Rameshwar brother," Meeramani questioned.

"There cannot be any major health issues," said Rameshwar, "but at times after growing up a bit, a few female qualities start arising in he-eunuchs, be it in their voice or behavior."

"Can we not stop those female qualities from arising, either through medicines or herbs?" asked Meeramani.

"Yes, it is possible; there are some herbs which increases masculine properties. We use these medicines to cure infertility in a man. We could give those medicines to him so that male qualities overpower that of a female. However, he would still not able to produce a child, and not even consummate with any woman."

"That is not required," said Meeramani, "I was asking just to have an idea that while bringing him up which qualities would overpower more so that accordingly we would take care of him. When can we start giving these herbs to him?"

"We can start giving these herbs anytime from the age of five years to seven years," said Rameshwar Nath.

"Everything will be alright by the grace of Lord Shiva," Meeramani said while looking up at the sky with folded hands. "God has sent us this child with a special motive. His birth would be a boon for society, not a curse. He will be an example, a living message for the society. Maybe other eunuchs would get inspire from him to fight for their rights. Maybe their parents wouldn't separate themselves from their child as it is not a shame to give birth to a eunuch. We could make a child into anything with our proper upbringing."

"What would we name him, Meeramani?" asked Rameshwar Nath.

"His life is like a war with ethics and thus we would name him 'Samar', Samar means war. "Samar Dev Pratap Singh". Meeramani declared.

After a few days, Ambika was alright and she had developed great love for her child after feeding him. She used to embrace her child all the time and that's why explaining things to her didn't turn out to be difficult. Although she was upset as expected in the beginning, but after everyone explained her she kept silent as she understood that going with the lie was beneficial for her and her child. She trusted Meeramani the most as Meeramani told her that she would make everything fine so she trusted her as whatever Meeramani said, she definitely fulfilled it.

King Neelkant made his guesthouse, Ambika's home for the next five years.

Virat set out for Jairajgarh with a letter written by Ambika with the help of King Neelkant:

"Greetings to Maharana *ji*,

Congratulations on the birth of the prince of the grand empire Jairajgarh.

According to the placement of some planets and constellations, the father cannot meet the child for the next five years. While coming to Ballabhgarh from Jairajgarh, you had promised me to give anything I would ask for upon the birth of a son, so fulfill your promise by making my younger sister, Meeramani, sit on the throne. I am happy being your wife and a mother to your child. A worthy ruler increases the worth of the throne; I was never good in politics, but Meeramani has all the qualities required for the Maharani throne. One more reason is that while the birth of the child, his life was in danger and if Meeramani hadn't been there I wouldn't have saved his life. Thus, she has the first right on the child. He is more a son of Meeramani than me. I have just given birth to him, but have given all the rights of a mother to her. She is the mother, so anyway she has the right to the throne. Meeramani doesn't know anything about this, so you must explain to her. She wouldn't agree ever as she doesn't believe in snatching other's rights. Show this letter to her so that she is convinced that I have willingly given my rights up and she should keep the respect of my wish. Meeramani has named your son "Samar Dev Pratap Singh". Please let this name remain. We shall meet each other after five years, but please allow Meeramani to meet me in Ballabhgarh.

Your Queen, Ambika.

Everything was going perfectly as per the plan.

Chapter 21:
The Maharani Throne of Meeramani

Prince Virat had reached Jairajgarh and had given Queen Ambika's letter to Maharana Ranjeet Singh. Maharana Ranjeet Singh was very happy. Having a prince for Jairajgarh and after reading the letter all his worries had come to an end. Everything was happening the way he wanted it to happen. He wanted Meeramani to claim the throne of Maharani and by giving her the responsibilities, Ambika had also given the responsibility of bringing up the child to Meeramani; his happiness knew no bounds. He consulted with his chief minister Shambhu Dev Singh and other courtiers and ministers if anyone had any issue if Meeramani claimed the throne, but nobody had an issue as Queen Ambika had herself given her rights to Meeramani happily and everyone knew that Meeramani was worthy of becoming a Maharani.

Maharana Ranjeet Dev Pratap Singh had shown the horoscope of his son to the royal priests. All the royal priests had done the same predictions what Rameshwar Nath Shashtri did.

Maharana Ranjeet had sent Chief Commander Akroor Singh and Chief Minister Shambhoo Dev Singh to Ballabhgarh to bring Meeramani back safely and he also sent a lot of gifts for Queen Ambika and his child.

Upon reaching Ballabhgarh, Commander Akroor Singh

and Chief Minister Shambhoo Singh expressed their desire to see the prince, but Meeramani diplomatically declined their request. She said that the father has the first right to see his son and he would only be able to see him after five years. Therefore, even the inhabitants of Jairajgarh won't be able to see him before that. King Neelkant was impressed by the politics of Meeramani. Meeramani started from Ballabhgarh at the right time, but left her maid, Malini, and midwife, Sankula Devi for Queen Ambika so that she doesn't face any problems in bringing up the child. She didn't trust anyone except them. She had instructed both her maids, Malini and Kaushika, and midwife Sankula. She had also promised Ambika that she would reach there before every birthday of the prince.

Queen Meeramani was welcomed dearly in the grand empire Jairajgarh; however, she was not able to understand that why was she welcomed that dearly. Maharana Ranjeet Singh had instructed her to reach the court directly. She found this surprising. The moment she entered the court flowered were showered upon her and everyone cheered and greeted her by calling her ‘Maharani Meeramani‘.

Meeramani stood nonplussed. She bowed before Maharana and asked, “Why am I being asked to come inside the royal court?”

Maharana Ranjeet Singh answered, “Because, now you would sit here on the throne of Maharani and today is your coronation.” Maharana Ranjeet Singh showed her the letter sent by Queen Ambika and said that all the courtiers too agree on this.

After reading Queen Ambika's letter, Queen Meeramani didn't protest to this and her coronation thus began. Maharana Ranjeet Singh happily crowned Meeramani himself and also gave the sword of Maharani while inviting her to claim the throne.

The conch shells were being blown in the court as the throne, which was vacant since years, was finally claimed. Long live, Maharani Meeramani! Long live, Maharani Meeramani! All the four directions were filled with this chorus and Maharana Ranjeet was feeling more proud than Meeramani as God had fulfill all the wishes of Ranjeet Singh. He had got the successor to his throne and had also made Meeramani claim the throne, which he always wanted.

Meeramani did a lot of welfare after claiming the throne, contributed in a lot of religious tasks and also stopped violence against women completely. Maharana Ranjeet was so happy with her that he didn't want to interfere in Maharani Meeramani's tasks as he trusted the wisdom of Meeramani and had understood that she doesn't hate her stepchild, but loves him like her own son. She is a responsible woman and her love for Queen Ambika was also not fake, both really had sisterly love amongst themselves. This doubled his happiness. Gradually, Maharana was letting all his responsibilities rest on Meeramani and was getting content because he trusted her completely. Even Meeramani was doing everything with great interest and she hadn't given Maharana Ranjeet Singh any reason to complain.

Maharana had informed the courtiers to discuss all the matters with Meeramani and keep her informed, too. She was given the responsibility of internal security, finances and treasury. Even chief minister Shambhoo Singh informed her directly. Meeramani had made the empire prosperous as well as happy in a span of mere 1-2 years. She was the first person to run the empire ethically and systematically without being dependent on Maharana.

Only the entire security of the state rested with army chief Commander Akroor Singh, who had been with Maharana since the beginning and on whom Ranjeet used to trust a lot as he was also his childhood friend. Only he had the right to inform Maharana and not to Maharani.

Although Meeramani was very busy, but she never forgot taking out time to attend the birthday of Samar Dev. Prince Samar used to call her Ma and Ambika as Badi (elder) Ma. Meeramani used to tell about Samar's playful activities to Ranjeet. Maharana always used to regret not being able to meet his son being his father. He was dying to hug him. He had been waiting since long only to have a glance of his son. Maharani Meeramani started taking Maharana Ranjeet Singh to Shiva temple with her every morning and Maharana Ranjeet Singh also took Maharani Meeramani for hunting to the forests along with him.

Time was passing fast and the wait came to an end.

On his fifth birthday, Prince Samar Dev was going to return

to Jairajgarh along with his mother, Queen Ambika. King Neelkant was himself going to come along with his family to Jairajgarh to drop his sister Ambika and nephew Samar Dev pratap Singh. Meeramani had even sent a message to her brother, Virat Singh, and his wife, Sulakshana, who had a son by now.

Maharanai Meeramani had arranged for a grand ceremony for Prince Samar. She had even invited kings from the friendly empires and this ceremony was supposed to go on for three days.

Finally, the auspicious day had arrived. Since morning Maharana Ranjeet Singh was nervous as he would see his son for the first time today. While Maharana was eagerly waiting to see his son, he was also getting apprehensive by imagining his looks. Today, he wasn't the Maharana, but a father who was dying to see his son. He hadn't even slept the entire last night out of anticipation. Meeramani had reached the temple early morning as she wanted Rudrabhishek (Lord Shiva special prayers) to be done by the hands of Prince Samar. She didn't want to leave any stone unturned for the preparations.

Maharani Meeramani had told Maharana Ranjeet Singh that he must declare Samar as the prince of the grand empire Jairajgarh as his birthday gift. Although this ceremony is done when a prince is young enough to sit in the court, as he then has to participate in the entire decision making. He was too young for this, but Meeramani wasn't ready to agree; she wanted Maharana to make Samar wear the crown and bless him. She gave her own example how she had started to learn war tactics as well as politics since the age of five and she was an expert by the time she attained 16 years of age. She wanted the same for Samar so that he could become worthy warrior to claim the throne.

It has always been tough for Maharana to find a counter to Meeramani's politics and that's why he had never been able to refuse to what she said. Moreover, she was not saying anything that could invoke Maharana to object.

Finally, the wait of the grand empire Jairajgarh came to an end and Samar Dev entered the boundary of Jairajgarh along with his uncle, King Neelkant, and mother, Queen Ambika. The inhabitants of Jairajgarh were dying to catch a glimpse of their prince and were cheering for him and Queen Ambika. Queen Ambika was overwhelmed by the welcome and was bowed before Maharani Meeramani, who had shown her this day.

Prince Samar Dev's chariot reached the big house adjacent the Lord Shiva temple as he could enter the royal palace only after the Rudrabhishek. Prince Samar was a true copy of how Maharana Ranjeet Singh looked when he was a child, the elderly people was talking about this among themselves. His fair complexion and deep eyes reminded them of a young Ranjeet. His smile was as attractive as his mother. His face was innocent and pretty that it could lure anyone. Meeramani was standing at the entrance of the big house holding a tray for prayers. Prince Samar only knew Meeramani and came running to hug her. Meeramani handed her tray to a maid and hugged her while crying happily. Everyone's heart melted seeing this. Such love of a mother and her son; that too from a stepmother, every onlooker was surprised. Even Queen Ambika and Neelkant could not help, but cried happily seeing the love of Meeramani and Samar.

Maharani Meeramani did *tilak* of Samar and sang prayers for him. She even warded off evil eyes off him. She even prayed for Queen Ambika and touched her feet and welcomed her to Jairajgarh.

Ambika couldn't say anything; she started crying and hugged Meeramani in return. Her tears said everything she wasn't able to put in words. She then asked while wiping her tears, Meeramani, "Where is Maharana *ji*?"

"He will meet you and his son only after the Rudrabhishek," Meeramani giggled. "Welcome, Rameshwar brother and Neelkant brother!" Meeramani took both of them inside.

Prince Virat Singh had already arrived along with his wife, Sulakshana, and his child. Everyone was happy upon seeing each other. Meeramani told Neelkant, "Please take care of my prince, he is still a child now, and make sure that nobody can reach to him without the permission."

"Don't worry; we are keeping an eye on him," Neelkant said.

After some time, a chariot pulled by 8 horses stopped outside the Lord Shiva temple. Queen Ambika was getting restless to see him, while Maharana Ranjeet Singh was getting restless to see his son. Lord Shiva'Rudrabhishek' had begun in the temple and all the family members were seated. There was a curtain through which Maharana could see Ambika sitting with her son, Samar. The royal priests had ordered Maharana to see his son after the prayers. During Rudrabhishek, Maharana could see a small, fair hand rising to put prayer paraphernalia into the fire. The restlessness of Maharana was clearly visible. Meeramani was happy seeing his condition as she thought that the more Maharana would long to see his child, the more he would love him and the more he would be compelled to love him even after knowing the truth. She wanted him to look at Samar as his child from the eyes of a father, who only knows love. He shouldn't consider him as a son or a daughter.

The Rudrabhishek had ended and the moment of the meeting of the father and the son had arrived. The curtains were removed and Maharana could see a beautiful little boy standing holding the hand of his mother and looking at him with surprise. Maharana Ranjeet Singh remembered his childhood and his eyes were filled with tears. He called his son to hug him, by opening his arms in embrace, but Samar didn't progress as he didn't know his father.

Queen Ambika moved towards Maharana and touched his feet while crying happily. She asked, "Maharana *ji*, are you alright?"

Maharana hugged Ambika and said in a heavy voice, "Ambika, I am indebted to you and to Meeramani. I and Jairajgarh would be indebted to you for gifting a son to me. The grand empire Jairajgarh would always be indebted of the efforts you both have made."

By then, Prince Samar had embraced Meeramani, all confused. He was unable to understand anything. Meeramani asked him to touch his father's feet while introducing him to his father.

Upon receiving his mother's command, Samar Dev progressed towards Maharana Ranjeet Singh and touched his feet with his little hands. Maharana picked him up and fondled him that everyone around started crying with too much of happiness .

Neelkant, with tears filled in his eyes, moved towards Meeramani and said, "You are a figure of sacrifice, Meeramani, you have done what nobody of us could have imagined to do."

Everybody had tears of happiness in their eyes. During that one second, there was one stone-hearted person who was crying too and this person was army chief Akroor Singh. Nobody could see, but he had bowed before Meeramani from inside, out of deep respect.

Then, everybody progressed towards the court according to the plan of Meeramani of coronation of Samar Dev as a prince. Maharana Ranjeet Singh has also crowned Prince Samar Dev Pratap Singh. All the inhabitants of Jairajgarh were cheering for their new Prince Samar Dev.

All the three days, there was an atmosphere of a festival in Jairajgarh; everybody was singing and dancing and everybody returned to their houses only after three days.

Only close relatives were left now. Even Rameshwar had bid adieu after three days as he didn't want to come under the eyes of Maharana Ranjeet Singh as he was sending medicines for Meeramani. While blessing Meeramani, he told her slowly that he had got medicines for Samar and had given them to Neelkant and she should take those medicines from him secretly. He also told her to give two doses of the medicines per day and whatever she wanted would happen. After saying this, Rameshwar Nath bid adieu and left for Kashi.

Meeramani's brother Virat had also left with his wife and son for his kingdom. Only the family of Neelkant had stayed upon persistence of Meeramani. Neelkant had accepted to stay in a building as Rajputs never stayed in their sister's house. He had brought his food and chefs along with him.

Meeramani entered the building along with Samar and Queen Ambika who she hadn't left along with Maharana despite his persistence. Queen Ambika was talking to Padmavati, wife of Neelkant. Both their kids were playing and Meeramani was talking to Neelkant.

Neelkant said, "This building is very beautiful, Meeramani. The cool breeze and the greenery here along the lake is making me feel happy. Have you looked at the forests after becoming Maharani?

"Yes, brother. While going for hunting with Maharana *ji*, I have studied the forest area carefully," Meeramani answered.

"Listen carefully Meeramani, said King Neelkant, "There is a way in this building which leads to the forest."

"But I looked at Maharana *ji* on the day of Rudrabhishek; he looked like a meek father who cannot do anything wrong," Meeramani said emotionally.

"I pray that you are right; however, you should be cautious. Don't forget that he is a strong politician and he still doesn't know the truth of Samar, so you can never predict the future." Neelkant expressed his concern. "Politics say that a king should be cautious of his boundaries. He shouldn't wait for the enemy to attack first and then he secured his boundaries. He should make sure that even if an enemy comes, he should return empty-handed. That's the quality of a good king."

Neelkant added, "You are anyway a Maharani and should be ready for all the games of politics and all wars. Emergency doesn't come after informing anyone; therefore, prevention is always better than cure."

"You are right, brother, then, what should be my next step," Meeramani asked.

"This palace is close to the jungle as well as the lake and according to my understanding if we dig the land here, we can make a tunnel underneath. There are two-three good workers in Ballabhgarh, who are proficient in the art of digging tunnel. I will send them dressed up in women's attire. You hide them in the palace and keep them engaged in some work. They would dig a tunnel from here towards the jungle. In case of any emergency, it would be easy for you to go from the palace to the jungle and from the jungle to the palace," said King Neelkant seriously. Don't tell about all this to anyone, especially to Ambika. No doubt that Ambika has changed a lot, and have attained wisdom, but she still doesn't know the politics of your level. Always remember, you are the Maharani of Jairajgarh, not her.

"Alright brother, I will always remember this,"said Meeramani while adding that, I know you have not left me alone. Please don't take too much tension. Come lets have food.

King Neelkant stood up to have food.

After two days, King Neelkant left for his kingdom along

with his family. Queen Ambika was back to her daily chores and Maharani Meeramani got busy with Samar's education. Maharana Ranjeet Singh was very happy to see the love between both his queen and seeing the bond between Meeramani and Samar made him happier. He was even more happy to see the way Meeramani was taking care of Samar. He then stopped interfering with whatever Meeramani was doing for Samar and how she was bringing up him.

One day, while sitting at the court, Maharani Meeramani got unwell. When the doctor was called in to examine Meeramani, he gave a good news to Maharana Ranjet Singh that Meeramani was expecting. Upon hearing this, Maharana Ranjeet Singh got very happy and Queen Ambika was also very happy, but Meeramani was a bit tensed. She got worried for Samar as she knew that according to ritual, she would have to go to her maternal home for her delivery and then who would take care of Samar.

One day Meeramani was meditating at Lord Shiva temple to find out the solution to her problem. Queen Ambika came there and sat besides Meeramani. Ambika asked Meeramani that wasn't she happy with the good news?

"I am very happy *jiji*, but I am also worried about Samar,"she said.

"I will take care of Samar, Meeramani, I am his mother too. You don't worry,"said Queen Ambika.

Meeramani said, "Being a mother you would take care of Samar, but you won't be able to deal with Maharana's politics."

"I have an idea *jiji*,"said Meeramani to Ambika. "When the time comes for me to go, you stay adamant with Maharana that you would also go along with me as you cannot leave me alone and you would take care of me. You stay stubborn infront of him. If he says that Samar would not go, you accept it, rest I will take care of everything," she added.

"OK, OK,"said Queen Ambika happily, "Everything will happen as per your wish, but now stay happy."

Maharani Meeramani also started laughing with Queen Ambika.

Then whatever Meeramani wanted to happen, it happened the similar way. Queen Ambika got her wish fulfilled by Maharana.

He wanted Samar to stay with him, but Meeramani told him that how would Samar stay without his mothers. She told Maharana, "If Ambika *jiji* was being adamat, atleast you are behaving like a mature man and should understand that how would a little child stay away from his mothers. Moreover, you would be busy with your court work and would go out, but we don't want to take any risk for Samar. So if Ambika *jiji* wants to come with me then Samar will also come along. This is my final decision."

Whenever Maharani Meeramani decided upon something, Maharana Ranjeet Singh was never left with any option, except accepting her demands. Maharani Meeramani left for her maternal home in Sambhalgarh along with Queen Ambika and Prince Samar.

Chapter 22:
The Birth of the Children of Meeramani and the Problem of Prince Samar Dev Pratap Singh

Maharani Meeramani was blessed with twins – a son, Rudra Dev Pratap Singh, and a daughter, Amritamani. Queen Ambika had made Amritamani as her own daughter. She had told Meeramani, "Both the sons are yours; you could teach them war tactics or politics, but the daughter is mine and would stay with me." Ambika was very happy to get a daughter. Both the kids were seven years younger than Samar Dev.

It had been six months for Meeramani to have come to Sambhalgarh and her children were now three months old. Her brothers, Rameshwar Nath, and Neelkant, had come to Sambhalgarh to see her children and gift her a lot of presents.

They all started their conversation in private.

"How is the training of Shiva-Jan army going?" Meeramani asked King Neelkant.

King Neelkant answered, "Shiva-Jan army is getting super-trained, sister, and you will be happy to hear that even Rameshwar Nath has made a huge contribution in this, not just in the form of money. He has admitted a lot of people into the army from Kashi and nearby states and he is even imparting them knowledge regarding medicine as a result of which, a lot of Shiva soldiers have now become physicians. Your Shiva-Jan army is expanding and is getting trained, too. We have heard that you have gotten a few warriors from the Shiva-Jan army admitted into the army led by Akroor Singh and these people keep giving you inside information from there."

"You have heard it right, brother. We have spread a lot of informers in the entire state and they keep giving me information," Meeramani informed Neelkant and then thanked Rameshwar Nath, "Thank you, Rameshwar brother, you have selflessly done a lot for this empire and all of us. We are indebted to you for that."

"Don't be so formal sister Meera. We all are a family and one doesn't oblige family members. People thank only strangers. Whatever you are doing, we cannot even match to that. By creating this Shiv-Jan sena you have performed a great task for which God will always bless you."

"Meera now listen carefully," king Neelkant said in a serious tone. "I have brought with me four very well trained soldiers who are extremely good at digging a tunnel. They are also good at disguising themselves so you take all four of them to Jairajgarh . How and when will you start the digging process that you decide on your own. From your big house to the jungle a tunnel can be made, so you start that work soon. Whatever time it takes. You are now well enough to travel also, so you get ready to leave for Jairajgarh. Go before your empire might come in danger with your absence."

"You are right brother," said Meeramani, "I will talk to sister Ambika and will make preparations to leave."

Queen Ambika entered the room and said to everyone, "If you all are done with your important political discussion, can I also talk to you about something?"

"Sister Ambika without you, nothing can happen; come inside," Meeramani said with a smile.

Queen Ambika said, "I have to talk something important to you all, but before I begin I join my hands and request you all that don't feel bad or get angry on whatever I say. I am afraid to even talk to you all. Brother Neelkant I am saying this for you specifically, don't say that I am a fool and that my talks are baseless and stupid."

"What happened Ambika? Why are you talking so differently? Hurry up and say whatever you want to," said Neelkant with a smile.

"You all have made Ambika *Jiji* so scared of you." Meeramani smiled and said, "Come sister, sit here and say whatever you want to say without any hesitation."

"Meera, actually I only want to speak to you, but if you feel bad then please forgive me. Also, don't be angry from me. I want to say that with the blessings of Lord Shiva now we are blessed with a boy and a girl. So can we declare Rudra Dev as our successor for the throne and let Samar Dev grow as a child. We can tell the truth about Samar Dev to Maharana, maybe in lieu of Rudra Dev he might not be so angry and forgive us also. In this way we all can end our worries. Else I am always worried about Samar Dev, but doing this might take that fear away from us."

King Neelkant got up and patted his hand on Queen Ambika's head and said, "Ambika you have become very intelligent, this is a great idea; what do you say Meera?"

Meera looked at Rameshwar Nath and asked, "What is your take on it brother?"

"I too think that the idea is appropriate," Rameshwar Nath said.

Meera said in a serious tone, "Tell me one thing sister Ambika, Rudra Dev and Amritamani are born from my womb so do you consider them as separate from your kid or as stepkids?"

"What are you talking Meera," queen Ambika said in anger; "Do you feel that the twins are stepkids for me? I love them so much, cannot live without them; they are the my life," Ambika said wiping off her tears. "What I told you and what are you replying, hurts me so badly."

"But Ambika did not say anything wrong Meera," King Neelkaanth said in a serious tone, "You should not be emotional, rather think practically." It was for the first time that Neelkant had supported Ambika and she was happy about it.

"I am not thinking out of my emotions brother," said Meeramani, "I am thinking with all my brains and politically. All the three children are ours, Ambika *jiji* and my. So our eldest child is Samar Dev. Rudra Dev is the younger brother and once he grows up, he would prove his capabilities, but whatever teachings we are giving to Samar Dev, can anyone of you tell me that why is he not capable of being a king. If he doesn't qualify to be the king, I will do as you all say. Because I want him to sit on the throne because of his capabilities, not out of emotions. God forbids but what if in the future if Rudra Dev gets deformities in his hands and legs and any of his body parts, wont he be my son. Similarly, the deformity in Samar Dev should not be a cause of hindrance of him becoming the king or Maharana. His problem is a very personal matter."

Meeramani further said, "Let's go back in history and see that there have been some kings, who were unable to give birth to a child, so did their queens not gave birth by taking an alternate route and gave the kingdom a prince? Let's take the case of Mahabharata. Maharaja Pandu due to his physical limitations was not able to have a child of his own. That time, when Maharani Kunti gave birth to 5 children, were they not Maharaj Pandu's children or if he was unable to birth his own child was he declared unfit for the crown? Just in the same way, our son Samar Dev is also incapable of giving birth to a child, but that does not mean he is incapable to take over the kingdom as their next king. First, let him complete his education and training, if he does not come up to our expectations then I will do as you will say. But, it's very important to give him a chance as he is our eldest child too. Till then Rudra Dev will also grow up. Once both are grown we will decide who will acquire the crown. Whosoever deserves will get the crown. Till then we won't let any injustice happen to any of our three kids."

"I am fully convinced with sister Meera," said King Neelkant.

"After a few minutes of thinking, I too support this," said Pandit Rameshwar Nath.

Queen Ambika got emotional and wiped her tears.

Next morning King Neelkant left for Ballabhgarh and Pandit Rameshwar Nath also left for Kashi. Maharani Meeramani too was eager to reach Jairajgarh because she did not want the administration of the kingdom to deteriorate. She had worked really hard for the happiness and prosperity of it. Even though Maharani Meeramani was living in Sambhalgarh, she could still fetch out all information of Jairajgarh with the help of her spies. The only worry she had was that she did not want Maharana to take full control of the kingdom in his own hands in her absence. She did not want that her administration and her relations with the employees of the palace get spoil. Specially, her equation with chief minister Shambhu Dev Singh, who treated Maharani Meeramani as his own daughter and believed in her political skills. He never did anything without asking her. She did not want that Shambhu Singh should go to Maharana for any advice or help in case any problem arises. Though Maharana Ran*jit* Singh was a very good politician, but he was very arrogant and egoistic. He never liked to hear anyone's problem; he only liked to give orders. This was the thing that Meeramani hated about him. Due to this attitude, the kingdom could go against him anytime. Listening to others first and then passing on judgment was the best way to deal with a situation, Maharani Meeramani could not make Maharana understand this.

Maharani Meeramani sent a message to Maharana Ranjeet Singh in the name of queen Ambika. The letter had the message that everything is fine here, now you please come and take children and us back to Jairajgarh. It seemed that Maharana was waiting for this message. He reached Sambhalgarh as soon as he got the message, stayed for four days and then brought his both the queens and three children back to Jairajgarh

Maharana Ranjeet Dev Pratap Singh along with his queens and the children were on their way back to Jairajgarh, and with them were the disguised soldiers, who had to dig the tunnel.

Meeramani started taking care of her throne upon reaching Jairajgarh and started staying busy. The work of digging the tunnel was in its full speed. No one used to come to the building. Maharani Meeramani had kept all the necessary items to be used for temple in the building, so there wasn't any chance of Maharana Ranjeet Singh going to the building. Four anchoresses were made to stay in the building, who were celibates. They took care of the temple, that's why Maharana Ranjeet Singh had nothing to do with them. The four women anchoresses were actually the Shiva-Jan soldiers who were digging the tunnel, they changed their appearances so that no man entered in the building. Maharani Meeramani Devi had ordered that till the time the four celibates stayed in the building, no man should enter the building that's why the building used to remain closed and no one used to go there.

After the hard work of three long years the tunnel was complete. That would open to one of the caves in jungle. Time taken to travel from the royal tents of Jairajgarh that were located in the jungle to the building would usually take 3-4 hours. But now it would take only 30 minutes due to the tunnel. Once the tunnel work was complete, all the four disguised men left the palace by chanting Lord Shiva's name under their veil in their disguised form. No one doubted them. Only three people knew about the tunnel: King Neelkant, Maharani Meeramani Devi and Pandit Rameshwar Nath Shastri. No other person knew about the tunnel.

Time was passing by quickly and things were changing. All the children were grown up and their education and training was also going at a fast pace. Prince Samar Dev was becoming perfect in the art of war. On the orders of Meeramani, Akroor Singh was also teaching him how to use tricks of the sword. Samar Dev's training and education was always under her guidance only.

Maharana Ranjeet Singh was very satisfied with the growth of his children. He was very proud of the way Samar Dev was growing as Meeramani was teaching him everything under her guidance. He had initially thought that once Meeramani will have her own kids she will not take care of Samar Dev, but the way she was training him it was sure that the prince was going to take charge of the throne very soon. Maharani Meeramani's full attention was on Samar Dev only. Queen Ambika and King Ranjeet Singh were busy with Rudra Dev and Amritamani.

Time passed on and Samar Dev was growing physically. He had stepped into youth from being a child. Shiromani Pandit Ramdas' medication was working wonders. Samar Dev was 6 feet tall and had a fair complexion. He had started growing his moustache and beard. His masculinity was clearly overtaking his feminine side.

Right in front of the eyes prince Samar Dev was a 17-year-old young man. He was very handsome. He was very well versed in politics and war. He had learnt the skills of sword from Maharana Ranjeet Singh and commander-in-chief Akroor Singh. No one in the entire kingdom or nearby kingdoms could ever stand in front of Maharana Ranjeet Singh and Akroor Singh's sword and same was the case when Samar Dev would fight. Just like his mother Maharani Meeramani, he had the knowledge of the Vedas and was a devotee of Lord Shiva. His face and complexion was just like when Maharana Ranjeet Singh was young. But Maharani Meeramani had modified a few things in him. She had taught him to forgive, to pity, to respect and had given him the knowledge of Vedas.

She also taught him that, "Never misuse your power. Always use your sword to take care of the good and to ward off the evil. If a person has not done anything bad to you then do not show your power to him/her. People who do this are the ones who have ego and arrogance and you never let these virtues go to your brain. Always be disciplined. It is very important for the kingdom not to go on a war at first. But if someone challenges you to have war with him/her then you should act upon that. That is not peace; it's weakness. Once you have entered the battlefield, your enemy's head should be in your feet. Do follow what your mother has taught you."

On the other hand Maharana Ranjeet Singh was trying to study prince Samar Dev. He observed that though Samar Dev was a very handsome prince and girls were attracted to him, but he never showed any interest in them. It was difficult for Maharana to understand that though Maharani Meeramani is giving him the best training and education why is she turning him into a monk? He tried to discuss this with Meeramani. She laughed at this thing and said he is just a kid and will be fine on his own. Maharana Ranjeet Singh also tried talking to Queen Ambika about this situation, but she avoided it by saying that Maharani Meeramani is taking very good care of him and she is the only one who is responsible for Samar Dev and that Ambika has no say in this. Samar Dev had no friends, Maharana Ranjeet Singh thought. He only talks to his mother. Maybe the mother-son relationship is coming in between and increasing the problems. It might be the case as Meeramani would not talk to Samar Dev about this openly and he is so shy with me.

The nearby kingdoms would send marriage proposals for Samar Dev. Maharana thought that by getting him married he would start enjoying the marital bliss and his problem of shyness might go away. But Meeramani had a clear understanding of Samar Dev's physical structure; she would be always worried that something bad might happen one day. Samar Dev was no more a child. Maharani Meeramani decided that this was the correct time to tell the truth to Samar Dev about his body. She sent a message to king Neelkant that she was coming with Samar Dev for some important work.

As Meeramani left with Samar Dev for Ballabhgarh to see King Neelkant, and Maharana Ranjeet Singh finalized the marriage of his son Samar Dev with princess Sukanya, who was the daughter of Satyaraj Singh—King of Garudgarh. He was Maharana's friend. Queen Ambika tried her best to stop him but he did not listen to her.

Chapter 23
Yuvraj Samar Dev Pratap Singh's introduction with the truth and the secret of Shiva-Jan Army

On one hand in Jairajgarh, celebrations were going on the occasion of finalizing the marriage of Samar Dev Pratap Singh, and on the other in Ballabhgarh, King Neelkant was explaining Samar Dev the truth about what has happened since his birth. There was only one thing that was hidden from him because Meeramani did not want Samar Dev to think negatively about his father Maharana Ranjeet Singh. Hence, Neelkant did not tell Samar Dev that his life was in danger from his own father. Samar Dev was explained that this truth was not told to Maharana *Ji* because he might have thrown out Queen Ambika from the kingdom and also the mothers were afraid that if the king ordered, the eunuch might take the prince away and in that case the queens would not be able to do anything. Keeping in mind about this, the king was not told the truth.

After listening to the entire truth Samar Dev was taken over by inferiority complex. He thought that this was something really big of a weakness and he went upstairs on the terrace. King Neelkant went upstairs to console him and make him understand not to feel so bad. Meeramani could not see her son in this situation; hence she also went to the terrace. She patted his head and Samar Dev started crying hysterically. He said, "Why did this happen to me, why me? Why did God not make me a normal person?"

Mother Meeramani's heart moved while seeing Samar Dev's situation. But she did not want him to feel weak; he was not made to be weak. His tears were ruining all his hardwork. It was difficult for Meeramani to see this. She made up her mind that now she had to be strict and deliver a strong lecture to Samar Dev so that he comes out of this shock.

"Stop crying like a weak person Samar," Meeramani said in an authoritative tone. "You are a Kshatriya (warrior caste). Do you know the meaning of this? It means that you are a warrior and one who cries in the battlefield are not known to be warriors. You have royal warrior blood running in your veins. You come from the family of Maharanas, who were so powerful that people would be willing to lose their lives than to fight with them. Their son cannot be so weak. If you cannot control your emotions, how will you control the kingdom.... Do the royal queens wait for this day and feed their children with their milk and blood so that once the child grows up he can disrespect them. Samar Dev this is weakness; you are being vulnerable. You are asking me that why did God not made you a normal person, by asking a question like this you have already shown your weakness. You were an extraordinary child Samar, you were incomparable, but after saying words like why did God not made you normal, you ruined everything for yourself. But I am not an ordinary woman, Maharani Meeramani is not an ordinary woman and I could not have made my child a normal and a common child. Though you were given birth by queen Ambika, but I have raised you, you are the result of my austerity. You are Maharani Meeramani's child. I have full faith on my austerity and Lord Shiva and know that he would never do anything wrong with me."

"Tell me what is troubling you," Meeramani further said. "It is the thing that you are a eunuch, you cannot marry and give birth to children. It's just this thing, right? What else do you think is your weakness? You developed a feeling of inferiority complex just because of this small thing?" Meeramani said in anger. Consummating females or giving birth to children is a very small thing; anyone can do it; birds and animals do the same. You cannot enjoy the pleasures of a married life, only this is the reason for your worry?" "Do you know who is the greatest figure of a kingdom? That person is the King. Everyone bows down his or her head in front of him. But a King only bows his head in front of a saint or a monk or a celibate except God. Do you know who a celibate is? They are those, who denounce marital bliss just to walk on the path of God. To become such a soul, a man has to overcome his sexual desires and a woman too has to denounce all her sexual needs. They have to give up on family, sexual relations, ego, and arrogance; without doing so they cannot attain God. Now answer me, who is greater than God? Answer me Samar Dev," said Meeramani.

"No one and nobody is greater than God," said Samar Dev in a deep tone.

"Just to attain God, people become celibates and denounce all wordily pleasures. They leave their houses, their children, ego, and arrogance. They leave all those things that can act as an obstacle in the way of God. The thing that one has to leave to attain God, do you think that thing is so important in human life?" she further said.

"God has made you people specially to show this to the world that you are his people, his devotees. You are walking on the path of God and so he has made you a celibate. This is a message from God, Samar. So get up and recognize who you truly are Samar Dev Pratap Singh. You are a warrior; this world is a battlefield of religions. If someone will try to take over your right to religion, will you start crying in the battlefield? One has to fight for his or her rights. A person who can fight for his or her rights can also fight for the rights of others," said Meeramani.

"When we all believe that God is omnipresent then do you really believe that he would not be inside in eunuch? They are also a part of the universe. Lord Shiva has a snake around his neck just to show that all creatures need to be respected. If God has accepted a creature, who can dare to go against him? We all are his children. Many people have forgotten this thing in today's world. People do not realize that every human has his or her special purpose in life; we have to fight to make them realize this, this battle is the battle of dharma. This battle cannot be fought with weapons only. One has to strictly adhere to his or her good deeds. I was adamant being a woman also I was immovable because I always thought that I am powerful. I never believed that I am weak, but today my child, whom I have given all my virtues, feels so weak. Maharani Meeramani's child cannot be so weak."

"I have taught you everything, virtues of war, politics, niti *gyaan* (ethics knowledge), but I had left one of the *gyaan* (knowledge) for the end. But I feel I have made a mistake. That *gyaan* (knowledge) should have been given to you in the first order... *gyaan* (knowledge) to read Mahabharata and Bhagwat Gita so that you could have realized your truth and the truth of the entire world. Once you get this *gyaan* (knowledge) all the darkness within you will disappear."

I had thought that I will make you the representative of eunuchs , will make you a role model for society to see that if any part of our body does not function that does not deter us to disapprove that human being. But your weakness today has weakened me from inside. Your words force me to think that if we cannot make sexual relations with a man or a woman or if we cannot give birth, then we are not worthy of living in this society. Are these things so big that nothing can overcome them; does life ends with this? This relationship between a man and a woman is only for a few minutes. After that they do their respective jobs. Life does not depend on consummating. Life is more than that and we all have to fulfill our duties. Every human being has to fulfill his or her duties alone. Relations, sex, fun, and alcohol everything is given to us by society and they will end in this society only. Human being only takes his deeds with him to an eternal path. There is a lot to do in this world; everything doesn't end in a single relationship. Everyone lives selfishly, but one who lives for the well being of others, who help others without any personal benefit, lives the crux of life.

"If you can understand what I am trying to say then get up like a warrior and like a soldier, put that to use and if still you don't understand then keep on crying here like a loser. I am strong enough to fight with this society. It's a shame to those parents who sacrifice their kid just because he is a eunuch... shame to those eunuchs who take away a child from the parents forcibly because the child needs to live a life in hell. Shame to those people and to this society and their disgraced thinking who reject a child just because he is incapable of making sexual relations and giving birth."

King Neelkant was quietly listening to thc conversation between Maharani Meeramani and Samar Dev. He then said, "If parents give their children the right upbringing and a good thought process then be it a boy or a girl or a eunuch, that child can become anything. That's why it is very important to make society realize that it's important to give good upbringing to the children, so that they can be a part of the betterment of society. Traditions and cultures of a society should be positive and not negative."

"Today I will show you what all can eunuch do, come with me," King Neelkant said. "Meeramani you go and rest now as you have to leave for Jairajgarh early in the morning. It is time for me to tell everything to Samar Dev, hence I am taking him to the secret organization of Shiva-Jan."

"Go Samar, go with your uncle and see yourself what all eunuchs are capable of and live a normal life,"said Maharani Meeramani. As he got the orders from Meeramani, Samar Dev greeted her and left with his uncle Neelkant. Maharani Meeramani also went to sleep in her room.

Shiva-Jan army's introduction:-

When Samar Dcv was born and eunuch had come to Ballabhgarh to congratulate, their chief-head was Mungeri. When King Neelkant and Maharani Meeramani had shared their problem with him, he was astonished to see that Meeramani was being so helpful to Queen Ambika, who was her husband's first wife. He was surprised to see that though she was a stepmother still she was doing all of this so selflessly. He fell on her feet with respect. He promised her that this would forever remain a secret and that he would protect the prince all through his life. Maharani Meeramani had also promised that she would work towards giving eunuchs a better life. She would also work to get them respect from society. Maharani did fulfill all her promises. Mungeri had faith that God had sent prince to become their representative, and due to him they would be respected in society.

King Neelkant and Queen Meeramani made a plan that all educational and practical knowledge will be provided to eunuchs. They will be trained to become spies. Both the king and the queen gave them so many patriotic speeches that they started seeing a purpose in their lives. Their chief—Mungeri also collected a few eunuchs and gave lectures on self-love and patriotism. King Neelkant also opened a secret organization where they would train the eunuchs about weaponry. The main reason for this building was that King Neelkant wanted to celebrate his nephew's birth, also because he wanted them to keep the secret. In the eyes of his empire, it was just a building that was given to eunuchs on the occasion of the birth of king's nephew.

In the process of setting up this entire secret organization, Maharani Meeramani's brother Virat Singh played a very essential role. He supplied armory and loads of money that would help the organization to run successfully and effectively. Later on, they made Mungeri as the head of the organization. Rest all the eunuchs who would enter the premises of the organization would take an oath of secrecy. Mungeri would personally take care of this. Mungeri had two personal helpers, Kokila and Chanchala. Apart from these three people, no one knew about King Neelkant, Maharani Meeramani and Virat Singh. Every three months, the Kingdoms of Ballabhgarh, Sambhalgarh and Jairajgarh would donate a large sum of money for the well being of the organization as was promised by Maharani Meeramani to Mungeri.

The chief Mungeri and his helpers Kokila and Chanchala had fixed a monthly wage for the training, just like any soldier would get. It was done so that they could also earn their food with respect. When they would be employed by any of the three kingdoms, their monthly wage would come from that particular place and the organization would no longer pay them. These people had no families of their own they only needed bare minimum clothes to cover themselves, food only to fill their stomach and a roof above their heads. Otherwise also a human being only needs money to fulfill the wishes of the family; else a single person only needs food, clothes and a house. More than this is not required. If he wishes anything more than this then he is being selfish. Gradually, they had also brought eunuchs from the neighboring kingdoms. They would train among themselves. And with time they were increasing in numbers. They were named as "Shiva-Jan Sena". Maharani Meeramani gave the name. Shiva-Jan Sena means army of Lord Shiva.

When Samar Pratap Singh was five years old, he returned to Jairajgarh. King Neelkant also joined along with a small team of Shiva-Jan army. They were disguised as soldiers, hence no one could make out that these were eunuchs and the members of Shiva-Jan. Maharani Meeramani spread them like spies in the nearby kingdoms. No one knew about their true nature. Sometimes they would dress up as eunuchs and would celebrate in good times and other times they would become soldiers. They had mastered in the art of war. They were also good in disguising themselves and could make different types of sounds; hence were not caught by anyone.

There were two main tasks of the Shiva-Jan army. First and the most important was to secretly take care of the safety of prince Samar Dev and Maharani Meeramani's kids prince Rudra Dev and princess Amritamani. These Shiva-Jan soldiers were spread in the entire palace, some as cooks while others as soldiers. They had different faces every time. They would keep an eye on everyone without anyone knowing about it.

The second task was to collect news from Jairajgarh and its nearby kingdoms and pass it on to Maharani Meeramani. They would have their meetings in a building behind Lord Shiva temple that was always empty.

Out of the entire Shiva-Jan army, only five important people were allowed to talk directly with Maharani. Their names were Phoolan, Chammo, Gola, Gannu and Kaalu. These five would order the army also. The rest of the army had no clue about Maharani Meeramani. The Shiva-Jan army in Jairajgarh would consider these five people as their chiefs.

In Ballabhgarh also King Neelkant would only give orders to Mungeri, Kokila and Chanchala. And in the kingdom of Sambhalgarh, Virat Singh would give orders to army chief—Kajri, Chameli and Shabbo. Virat Singh has taken over the throne of Sambhalgarh because King Surat Singh had taken up retirement. King Surat Singh also had no clue about this Shiva-Jan army.

In honor of Samar Dev's return after five years, there was a huge celebration in Jairajgarh. Among the guests was present Shiromani Pandit Rameshwar Nath Shastri from Kashi. During his visit King Neelkant, prince Virat Singh and Maharani Meeramani informed him about the Shiva-Jan army . Pandit Rameshwar Nath was astonished to learn about their activities. He decided then and there that he would fully support in this endeavor. When he returned to Kashi, he met the eunuch chief, Gokul. He sent Gokul to Ballabgarh on his own expense so that he meets Mungeri there and learn about their work and instill the feeling of patriotism in himself. He can also fulfill his life as a eunuch. Gokul met Mungeri, Kokila, Chanchala and when he saw the Shiva-Jan organization he was impressed and promised to surrender himself completely in this work. He took an oath of maintaining privacy and becoming a true patriot. He also promised to bring more eunuchs in this organization. Shiromani Rameshwar Nath started teaching medicine to all those who were interested in learning about it. Shiromani Rameshwar Nath Shastri made such medicines that made eunuchs more powerful.

There were many departments in the Shiva-Jan army, the primary ones were: weaponry and spies. Second department had people to make great food and were good in chores of the home and now the third department of healthcare was the one opened by Shiromani Rameshwar Nath Shastri. In the Shiva-Jan army, a few had become skilled warriors, some were great spies, a few were medical practitioners, some had become chefs and a few were employed by the state.

"Jai Shiva Shankar, Jai Shiva-Jan" was their slogan that they would use to recognize one another in their disguised look.

Everything was done in secrecy because the state was corrupt and the minds of the people were tarnished. They would have never allowed the eunuchs to stand beside them as soldiers of an army. But a few people, who were helping them to grow, made eunuchs able to establish themselves successfully.

Maharani Meeramani got up early in the morning and was ready to leave for Jairajgarh when she saw that Samar Dev was also ready and was walking towards her. He touched her feet and asked for forgiveness. He said, "Forgive me mother for I disrespected and disregarded your traditions. Yesterday uncle Neelkant took me to the Shiva-Jan organization and I was astonished to see them. This is all your hardwork and dedication. Today, I take an oath and promise you that I will become Samar Dev Pratap Singh—a role model for society. I will teach them that no one is unworthy in this society. We eunuchs are also the children of God; and hence are a part of society. Our life has a motive too, we are not born to sing and dance on special occasions rather we can do all the work that any person does. Our heart, mind and body works exactly like any other human being. We will prove ourselves and this society will have to accept us with equal rights and respect. We are celibates .... we are monks.... we are saints... we are Shiva-Jan.... now I am completely ready for this righteous war."

Maharani Meeramani hugged Samar Dev and said, "I know that you are incomparable and extraordinary. I haven't kept your name Samar just like that. Samar means "war" and you are an unbeatable warrior and combatant. You cannot give up until the success falls on your feet."

It was time to go back to Jairajgarh. Samar Dev Pratap Singh was on a carriage with six horses. Behind him was a royal carriage for the queen with eight horses. The carriage was closed from all sides and had a door on the left side and a window with a satin curtain on the right side.

"What you are saying is absolutely right brother, it is time to tell the truth to Maharana *Ji*. I will see the right time and then will talk to him," said Meeramani, while adding further, "Though his heart is that of a father filled with love for his child, but the danger has not yet completely disappeared. Do you remember what Shiromani Rameshwar Nath brother had said when he made Samar's horoscope. He had said there would be two lethal time frames in his life. First one will be from his birth up to five years and the second one will be when Samar turns 17 till the age of 22. The danger comes from his father. So he has to be separated from his father during that time. I took care of the first time frame from birth till 5 years, but now Samar has turned 17 and one year has already passed. But the fatal time has started and we all should pray that till he completes 22 years of his age, everything should remain peaceful. I am trying to think of a plan. You also think about this and devise a plan of how to keep Samar Dev away from his father Maharana Ranjeet Singh for 5 years.

"Hmmmmn..." , King Neelkaanth took a deep breath and said, "Well I will have to think about this Meeramani because Shiromani Pandit Rameshwar Nath's predictions never go wrong. It's ok Meeramani you don't worry, I will think something. You also think and solution will come to your mind. Now you start for Jairajgarh. The route is long; you should not be late."

"Ok brother," Maharani Meeramani bowed and greeted her brother and went inside her royal carriage.

Prince Samar Dev Pratap Singh ordered the army to start the journey for their kingdom of Jairajgarh.

Chapter 24
The Anger of Queen Ambika

Maharani Meeramani and prince Samar Dev Pratap Singh had reached Jairajgarh.

After taking permission from his mother, Meeramani, prince Samar Dev left for his room to relax, but before Maharani Meeramani could reach her private room her chief maid Malini in the midway stopped her and informed that Akroor Singh had sent a messenger a few times.

"Why, what disaster has happened," Maharani Meeramani said while walking towards her room.

"He has sent the message through his messenger that something very important needs to be discussed; hence he wants to meet Maharani. If this wasn't the case he would have never dared to disturb her when she is tired," chief maid Malini said.

"Hmmmn..." Meeramani thought in her mind that if it wasn't something urgent and important, Akroor Singh would not have sent the messenger so many times. He is not the person who will worry for no reason or will trouble someone without a cause. But if something is so urgent and important why didn't he discuss it with Maharana *Ji*? Meeramani thought for a while and said, "Send the message that I am back, but I am very exhausted and so will only meet Akroor Singh in our private meeting room."

"As you order Maharani *ji*," Malini said and left the room.

The 'private meeting room' was a humongous room. It was designed in such a way that one room will open to their bedroom and the second one to the exit. Whenever in the night or during an emergency situation when he does not wish to go out in his royal meeting room this private room was used and people were called in this room. He would go outside his bedroom into the meeting room and once the meeting was over he would go back into his bedroom. This facility was accessible to Maharana and Maharani only.

Meeramani had not even reached her room yet when Maharani Ambika rushed inside the room and worriedly said, "Something terrible has happened, I could not do a single thing."

Meeramani got worried too and asked her sister Ambika, what had happened and why was she worried so much.

"Maharana *ji* did not listen to me for once also and he fixed the alliance of prince Samar Dev with princess Sukanya," Maharani Ambika said.

"Whaaatttttt…," Meeramani shouted in surprise. "What did Maharana *ji* do….. He could have waited for me…. What was the hurry to do this? What was the requirement for this….," Meeramani said in an angry tone.

"I tried to make him understand Meeramani," queen Ambika said with tears in her eyes, "But he did not listen to me for once also. I told him that you will be here in two days so we can wait for you, we can then discuss this with you as this is such an important matter. But he did not respond to me. He said when the time would come for Rudra Dev or Amritamani then he will discuss with you as you are their mother. Maharana *Ji* further said that I have told you because you are Samar Dev's mother and that's all. You know Meeramani, till date he doesn't listen to me at all, he never agrees to what I say, he just wants me to be his submissive. I am always quiet," Queen Ambika said in a sad tone.

"Don't worry sister, it seems that the time has come to discuss things with Maharana *ji* in a one-on-one," Meeramani said in an angry tone. "Go and sit calmly in your room, I will go and talk to Maharana *ji* right away," Meeramani said angrily and went outside her room.

As Maharani Meeramani reached outside Maharana Ranjeet Singh's room, she calmed herself down and took a deep breath. She went inside and said, "Greetings Maharana *ji* from Meeramani."

"Come Meeramani come," Maharana Ranjeet Singh said in a happy voice. "I, myself was going to come to your room to tell you a good news that we have fixed Samar Dev Pratap Singh's marriage. Here, take this sweet," Maharana picked up a sweet and put it in Meeramani's mouth.

"What was the reason for this hurry? You could not even wait for me," Maharani Meeramani said complaining.

"What is the matter Meermani, I had thought that you would be ecstatic to hear this news, but what I am seeing is the other side. Are you overpowered by the feeling of a stepmother," said Maharana Ranjeet Singh.

"Maharana *ji*," Meeramani said loudly in an angry tone.

"Meermani lower your voice. You know that I don't like anyone speaking to me in a tone like this." Maharana said angrily. "What are you angry about; he was supposed to get married one day. I fixed his marriage today itself. I am his father, getting him married is my responsibility. You have fulfilled your responsibility by training him to take care of the royal throne in the best possible way. More than that, you have no more responsibility when it comes to Samar Dev. You take responsibility of Rudra Pratap."

"My responsibility towards Samar Dev is over and I should now concentrate on Rudra Pratap. Maharana *Ji*, today you have crossed all limits of calling me so selfish. You put a name on my motherhood and my sacrifice and called it a responsibility. I was not taking responsibility of your son. Samar Dev is my child too; he is my honor. If today I ask him to say no to this marriage, he will do so."

"Meeramani, stay in your limits. Do you want to teach my son how to go against me? Before that will happen, I will slit your head from your body," Maharana's temper had reached its limit.

Meeramani argued in a high tone in anger. She said, "If you want to slit my throat, then do so. What else have you done in your life? You have never loved someone so much that they would bow their heads in front of you in love or respect. You have used the medium of politics not only to save your throne, but also in relationships. That's why you could never get someone's love. This is the reason why everyone is afraid of you; it is because of your mighty sword, no one loves you. Once you don't have the power in your hands you will see the real face of everyone in regard that how much they love you."

"Okay, so you hate me so much inside your heart. You have become a poisonous snake. And before you start to spread this poison into my family and me I will kill you." Saying this Maharana grabbed Maharani Meeramani's throat.

"Wait Maharana *ji*," queen Ambika entered and her loud voice echoed in the room. She entered Maharana's room while holding prince Samar Dev's hand.

"Stop playing this dirty game of yours," queen Ambika said angrily. "Here is your son Samar Dev Pratap Singh, take him and do whatever you want to do with him. If you wish to kill him, then do so. Do whatever you want to, but you dare touch Meeramani. Do not forget that I have witnessed the entire truth about queen Vaishali and if that comes out, your entire truth about relationships will come out too."

"Shut your mouth Ambika," Maharana yelled in anger. "It seems you are going to die today too."

"Even if I have to die today I will not stay quiet. You cannot make me quiet," Ambika yelled in anger. "Have heard you saying such things to me for long and I have always loved you, hence remained quiet and obeyed to your orders. You thought my love was my weakness. Yes, you do play politics in your relationships. You played politics with me, you did the same with Queen Vaishali and Queen Meeramani. You have never loved anyone, so now you will also not get love from anyone in return."

"What rubbish are you saying Ambika?" Maharana shouted once more in anger.

Queen Ambika yelled in anger and said that queen Vaishali had cursed you. "I cannot forget that ill-fated day, but selfish men like you will not remember anything. It's ok if you don't remember; I will make you remember all that she said. Let's go back to the day near the lake Sapta-Sangma where queen Vaishali committed suicide by submerging herself into the lake. I was hiding behind a tree close to that and saw and heard everything. I saw what you did not see. When you walked away, then queen Vaishali had dived into the water and she cursed you, listen everybody, today everyone in this room will listen to the truth, listen to the truth about Maharana Ranjeet Singh's character..." and then Maharani Ambika told everyone the truth behind Queen Vaishali's death....... "I was terrified after seeing that side of you; I held my breath and stood still behind the tree. I was afraid that if you will see me you would show me your worst side. Queen Vaishali was sitting on the ground and crying for her honor, and then she stood up. It felt as if she was not in her senses. Tears were falling from her eyes ceaselessly; she looked as if she was in a great pain. Her dupatta was in the ground, her long hair were open; she walked slowly towards the Sapta-Sangma lake and joined both her hands in the air and pleaded, "Hey Maa Chandika, hey Maa Mahishasurmardini, your presence and powder was disrespected so badly that I cannot even breathe here, to stop this dirty game now you will have to send one of your powers, if I have ever done any good deed then you make sure that this arrogant man is never loved by any woman and make sure that this man cannot touch my dead body; praying this I sacrifice my life in your feet, "Jai Maa Mahishasurmardini", she said this and jumped into the lake. She died, but it did not even affect this selfish and arrogant man. When queen Vaishali died then Maharana started playing his dirty games with me and when he was bored with me he tried doing the same with Maharani Meeramani. But because he is not succeeding in his selfish motives with Meeramani, he wants to give her a bad name and hence is accusing her."

"Stop it *Jiji*, now please calm down," Maharani Meeramani said this to queen Ambika and hugged her and said, "Why have you come here? I had told you to stay and be calm in your room and that I will come here and talk, then why you came here?"

"Leave it Meermani," Maharana disregarded and said, "I clearly understand what kind of character women like you have. Why you don't want Samar Dev to get married, do you think I do not understand your politics? It's because you don't want that Samar Dev should get married and he could give birth to the heir of this throne. You want him to become a monk and you keep him away from the girls.... because you are overwhelmed with the feeling of stepmother. You want Rudra Dev to acquire the throne. That's the reason you are behaving like a saint and making a fool out of Ambika, she is a fool anyway, but I am not a fool, Meeramani. My son Samar Dev will now do whatever I will say."

"Once you consummate with any women, she becomes fool for you," queen Ambika said. "You were the one who went to ask for Meeramani's hand in marriage. And the same was for me too. We both had not begged you to marry us, nor our fathers or brothers came to you to marry foolish ladies like us. Now that you have consummated the marriage with us, we seem foolish and selfish to you."

"Queen Ambika, stay in your limits," Maharana growled with anger. "You have lost all your limitations to the ground. Your son is a youth and is standing here and how and what are you saying to me."

"Youth son Maharana *Ji*," queen Ambika laughed. "It was Maharani Meeramani who made him a youth, the lady who is standing in front of you; the one whom you are calling stepmother again and again. You are abusing her motherhood. Have you been a part of his growing ages?"

"Meeramani we have heard enough of what this man, who appears to be our husband, has said, now it's time to listen to our son. This will clear all our misunderstandings in one go. So prince Samar Dev Pratap Singh," queen Ambika said with a taunt, "your mother queen Ambika and your stepmother queen Meeramani does not want you to get married; however your father Maharana Ranjeet Pratap Singh wants you to get married. Now you have to decide and answer right now. Let me clear one more thing, be careful if you go against our wishes, your life will not be in any danger, but if you go against your father's wishes your life will immediately be endangered. Your father will not be able to digest the fact that you can go against his wishes and can sentence you to death also. Now think and then reply."

Price Samar Dev looked at his father, and then he looked at his mothers' and said, "If disagreeing to my father's wishes will bring death upon me then I accept that. I cannot bear my mothers' getting insulted. I am what I am today because of their hard work and love. Hence I promise today that till the time I am alive I will not marry. I will take care of my mothers and will conduct as per their orders; this is the only aim of my life." Samar Dev looked at his father whose face was filled with the clouds of insult.

Maharani Meeramani raised her hand and kept it on Samar Dev's head and ignoring Maharana Ranjeet Singh, she left the room.

Once Maharani Meermani had left, queen Ambika looked at Maharana Ranjeet Singh with a faint smile and proudly walked out of the room.

Samar Dev looked at his father and asked with respect, "What order do you have for me?"

"Now you don't need my orders Samar Dev. By supporting and agreeing to your mothers you have shown disrespect towards me," Maharana said sadly. "Go away from my sight and leave me alone."

Prince Samar Dev bowed with respect to his father and left the room.

Meeramani was walking towards her room, when queen Ambika called out her name and said, "Wait for me sister, I am also coming with you." They held each other's hands and both of them went to Meeramani's room.

Once they were inside the room, queen Ambika smiled and said Meeramani, "I am feeling very light today. Till today I never dared to speak a word in front of Maharana *Ji*, but today what all I said made me feel so light hearted. I am very content now. Say something Meeramani, but don't say that I made a mistake by arguing with Maharana *ji*."

"No *jiji*, I was astonished to see you today. I could not believe from where you got into the soul of Goddess Chandika. You were full of courage and strength. I am so happy that finally you have learnt to speak up for yourself and your rights." She hugged queen Ambika. "But I am a little worried for Samar Dev. Didn't you notice Maharana's face? It was filled with emotions of insult and disrespect. You know how egoistic he is. And we have hit his ego hard today. He will not accept this behavior of ours. He doesn't seem to think about anyone more than his ego. Now we will have to plan our next move."

"It's a shame to be such a man who cannot regard his relationships with his children and wives more than his ego. What's the use of this ego and arrogance? Now let him be alone. I will not go and try to persuade him anymore. You also don't go Meeramani and now leave all of this and tell me, did you tell Samar Dev that he is a eunuch and that he cannot marry."

"Yes *Jiji*, I explained and made him understand everything," replied Meeramani.

"God bless my child," queen Ambika said emotionally. "Was he really upset once he got to know the truth?"

"Yes *Jiji*, he was really upset once he got to know the truth, but I explained him everything and made him understand. He is fine now."

"One thing that you always say that "solutions are hidden in the problem", one similar thing happened today also. Samar Dev promised not to marry in his entire life. This saved us from telling Maharana *Ji* that Samar Dev is a eunuch. Also, because of Samar Dev's promise no one will ask him to marry again."

"Ohh yes. This is so true. I did not think about this. Truly this was a solution to our problem. Nice work, now you are getting good at understanding all this. Now you please take the Maharani throne from me and start acting as a Maharani. Take your responsibility and free me."

"Till the time I am alive how can you be free," queen Ambika said. "Also it's good that we got over with this problem. Now this secret will remain between the two of us and no third person will ever come to know about this."

Both queen laughed out loud. Maharani Meeramani and queen Ambika had no clue that the news was leaked to a third person. Someone was hiding and listening to all their talks. That person was in the private meeting room that was only separated by a door to Maharani Meeramani's bedroom. That person was none other than the commander-in-chief Akroor Singh, who had come to see Maharani Meeramani and about whom Maharani had completely forgotten.

Akroor Singh left the room quietly and went to Maharana's room.

Once he reached there, a messenger went inside Maharana's room and told him that Akroor Singh wants to see him immediately. Maharana Ranjeet singh refused to see him and told the messenger to ask Akroor Singh to meet in the royal courtroom in the morning.

The messenger came back to Maharana and said that Akroor Singh has said that it's very important and urgent.

Maharana *ji* thought to himself that now even Akroor Singh is not taking my orders. At last, he ordered the messenger to send Akroor Singh inside the room.

Akroor Singh greeted the Maharana and even before the king would say something, Akroor Singh told Maharana whatever he heard. After hearing all, Maharana Ranjeet Singh's face had turned pale. It was clear from his face that he was in shock. He lost control over himself and was about to fall before Akroor Singh instantly offered him support.

Akroor Singh picked up a glass of water from a nearby table and offered it to Maharana. He drank a little bit of water and then handed over the glass to Akroor Singh and said in low tone, "God is making fun of me. My senses are not working Akroor Singh. What am I suppose to do now. I cannot believe that my queens will lie to me about this. I am so angry that I can go right now and kill them. Tell me Akroor Singh, what am I suppose to do now."

"Right now be patient Maharana *Ji*. Haste is the work of devil, let's remember this. We will have to think through this and act very carefully as this is a family matter. This is not a situation of an enemy. It's about the family and we will have to deal patiently with this. I will take your leave now, you rest for sometime and we will discuss this tomorrow. This is a suggestion from a friend as well as from the commander-in-chief,"Akroor Singh said this and left the room.

Maharani Meeramani remembered something and got up while queen Ambika was talking to her. She said, I forgot that I had to complete some very important official work.

Meeramani left her room and called her maid Malini. She asked her that the messenger has not yet gone and called Akroor

Singh to the room.

"He is waiting for you in your private meeting room from long," Malini said.

"Sitting in my private meeting room, since when?" Maharani Meeramani asked.

"Since you left for Maharana *Ji's* room," replied Malini.

Listening to her answer Maharani Meeramani got worried, "But he is not there. I just checked myself. I am coming from the room. If he is not there then where did he go without taking my permission? Did he inform someone?"

"No, he did not say anything," said Malini. "I myself escorted him to the room and had told him that you have gone to see Maharana *Ji* and will be back in sometime and that he can sit in the room and wait for you. I told him all this and then came outside the room. I asked him if he would like to drink anything, but he had said no. Now you are saying he is not in the room. But how can he leave without taking your permission. How can he go without informing you…."Malini was shocked at this behavior of Akroor Singh, but Maharani Meeramani had understood that the arrow has already left the bow.

Maharani Meeramani said to Malini in a serious tone. "Go… run fast and as you find any soldier from the Shiva-Jan army, be it Chammo, Phoolan, Gola, Gannu or Kaalu whomsoever you find inform them that this is an emergency situation and that I will go to the temple in the night." Going to the temple meant that Maharani Meeramani would be meeting them in the temple.

"As you say," Malini said and ran to find the soldier.

The soldiers—Chammo, Phoolan,Gola,Gannu or Kaalu—all were the soldiers of Shiva-Jan army. They were her personal eunuch spies.

Maharani Meeramani then along with queen Ambika went to prince Samar Dev's room. He was in a deep thought. Seeing them he said, "Why did you took the trouble and come here, you should have called me to your room."

Maharani Meeramani said, "Samar, my child, are you fine, please don't take your father's words seriously. Don't take them to your heart."

"Please don't worry mother, I am absolutely fine," Samar Dev said with respect.

"Ambika *Jiji* I will have to take your leave now, but you stay here with Samar Dev. Spend some more time with him and make him understand." Maharani Meeramani left the room then.

Queen Ambika said to Samar Dev, "Why are you sitting here alone? Let's go to park, both the kids are asking about you. Amritamani is repeatedly asking when will brother Samar come? Come, let us go and meet the kids. Spend some time with them, you will also feel better."

Samar Dev got up and went to the park in the palace, along with mother queen, Ambika.

Chapter 25:
The Conspiracy of the Murder of Prince Samar Dev Pratap Singh

During the night Maharani Meeramani picked up the worship plate and went to the temple along with her maid Malini. On her way she asked her, "Whom did you deliver the news?"

"Phoolan and Kaalu," said Malini in a low tone voice and to the point.

"Hmmn.." Maharani Meeramani took a deep breath.

Once they reached the temple Maharani asked the maid to go outside and guard the temple and close the gate. Malini quickly followed the orders. Maharani Meeramani started worshiping Lord Shiva, she prayed for a few minutes and then picked up the shankh (shell) and blew it loudly. The entire environment was filled with the holy sound... This was also a clue that Maharani Meeramani was in the temple and was being guarded by Shiva-Jan soldiers. No one will be allowed to even go near the temple now.

The second signal was for those Shiva-Jan soldiers who wanted to meet Maharani. They were hiding in the nearby building. They could now go and see her. After a few minutes, two dark shadows went out from the building and started walking towards the temple. The back door of the temple was the same as the back door of the building. They opened the door and closed it once they were inside. They greeted the Maharani. They were Phoolan and Kaalu.

The whole of Jairajgarh knew that Maharani was a great devotee of Lord Shiva. Hence, she would go the temple whenever she wanted. No one would ever be surprised about her visits to the temple. Everyone knew that there was no specific time for her prayers. She would go whenever she wanted to. If she was happy or sad, she would go to the temple. Be it in the morning or in the evening, afternoon or night, she would visit the temple at anytime. Because of this no one was allowed to visit that temple. It was her private place of worship. She would close all the doors from inside so that she is not disturbed by anyone. No one should come between the God and his devotee; hence no one ever questioned her visits to the temple. It has been many years since this tradition was being followed. It was due to this reason that no one ever got to know about the Shiva-Jan soldiers. Because whenever Maharani wanted to talk or discuss anything with them she would do it behind the closed doors of the temple.

Phoolan and Kaalu greeted the Maharani and asked her what were the orders.

"I want all the information about commander-in-chief Akroor Singh everyday 4 times," Maharani Meeramani said in a low tone.

Both the soldiers nodded their heads in agreement.

Whenever Maharani Meeramani met the Shiva-Jan soldiers in the temple, there talks would contain less words, and they maintained a low tone. In this case Maharani Meeramani meant that she needed all the information on Akroor Singh at all the four times of the day. She needed information on all his moves throughout the day. If she ever needed to discuss things in detail, she would do so in the building and not in the temple. For that she would first send a message to the soldiers. She would then appoint a time and would go inside the building where the soldiers would be present.

Maharani Meeramani picked up the worship plate and turned back to the soldiers and said, "Increase security for prince Samar Dev. Then she instructed the soldiers to go into the building", they nodded and opened the door and entered the building. Maharani opened the temple door and went outside.

The next day in the royal court Maharani Meeramani asked Akroor Singh in an angry tone, “Yesterday you came to meet me in my private meeting room and left without taking my permission, expain me the reason.” Maharani Meeramani said this in an agitated tone.

“I am very sorry and would like to apologize for yesterday, but Maharana *Ji* had called me for some very urgent and important work. I could not meet you because of this reason. Later, I was sent away for some important work by Maharana *ji*.”

“You could have informed me about this to my maid Malini, who was just outside the room,” Maharani Meeramani said in anger. “Being a friend to Maharana *ji* does not give you the liberty to cross your limits and disregard me. You should not forget that I am a Maharani of the empire. What was the important thing that you wanted to meet me for?”

“I once again apologize,” Akroor Singh said with a modest tone. “The important thing was that from the past few days there has been some activity in the jungle and near Sapta-Sangama lake, because you head the internal security and if you allow us can we look into the matter to see what's going on?”

“I am surprised to know why are you so interested in the internal security, though you are the head of the external security. Because you are the commander-in-chief of our army and also you are Maharna's close friend, in this regard you are like my brother. So I will explain you. But it's surprising, how come you have information on the activities that are taking place in the jungle. For your kind information, it came to my attention that a few dangerous animals were hunting in the jungle and would enter the kingdom in the night. This would put the lives of innocent men at danger. So I wanted to put some kind of security walls that would prevent these animals to enter the kingdom. Are you convinced with the answer or you would want to look into the matter yourself and get the orders from Maharana *ji*?” Maharani said in a harsh manner.

“I am completely convinced Maharani *ji* and from next

time onwards I will be very careful to stay within my limits. I once again ask you for forgiveness," Akroor Singh said in a polite manner and walked out.

Before Maharani would walk inside the royal court she saw that one of her Shiva-Jan soldier Kaalu was disguised as Maharana's soldier and was standing behind. He looked at Maharani and made a gesture with his eye. Maharani in no time understood that something very urgent has come up.

Maharani Meeramani turned to a soldier and said in a loud tone to go to her maid Malini and tell her to prepare her worship plate and that before lunch she would want to go to the temple. She also said to tell Malini to wait for her outside the temple. She quickly walked towards the royal court.

Shiva-Jan soldier---Kaalu had the information now that Maharani would meet him inside the temple before lunch. He escaped quickly.

Maharani Meeramani like always closed the temple gate and Malini stood outside the temple like a guard.

As Maharani Meeramani blew the conchshell, Kaalu came inside the temple and said that very early in the morning, even before the dawn Maharana had called Akroor Singh into his private room. Maharana *ji* said that he would like to come for a dinner today at Akroor Singh's house. Then Akroor Singh instructed his cook at home to prepare delicious and lavish food for the king. After saying this the soldier stood still and his head was bowed down.

"Is there any arrangement of our soldiers at commander-in-chief's house?" Maharani Meeramani asked.

"Yes, we have made arrangements," Kaalu said.

"Expalin in detail," Maharani said.

Akroor Singh's head cook was made to stumble down which led to a fracture in his right hand in the morning. Chammo did this. The cook was given a lot of money then and was asked for forgiveness. Chammo also told him that he would call his cousin, who is also a chef to help in preparing the food. The cook agreed to this, partly because of the pain and partly because of the money he was given.

This brought a smile on Maharani's face. Maintaining a

serious face she asked, "Who is the cook then?"

"Phoolan," Kaalu said.

"Tell Phoolan to disguise himself carefully because Akroor Singh has seen him numerous times. Also will Phoolan manage to travel from the kitchen to Akroor Singh's private room alone?" asked Maharani.

"Yes Maharani. Gannu will also be present near the private room, disguised as a soldier," Kaalu said.

"I would immediately need all the information about Maharana *ji*'s and Akroor Singh's meeting. Whatever time it would be, inform me at all costs. Even if you have to come inside the palace, do so. But I would need all the information without any delay. I will be waiting to hear the details. She instructed the soldier to go back."

"As you command," Kaalu said and disappeared in the building.

As Maharani Meeramani reached back to her palace she got the news that Maharana is resting in his bedroom. His health is not good today; hence he returned to the palace early and was asking about Maharani. Listening to this, Maharani Meeramani went to see Maharana *Ji* instead of going to her room.

When Maharani Meeramani reached Maharana *ji*'s bedroom he was laying on the bed and both of his eyes were closed. Tears were falling from the corners of his eyes. Maharani Meeramani was worried. She went up to him and wiped his tears and asked what happened, why are you so sad today? What is the problem please tell me.

"Come Meeramani," Maharana got up and said. "No, there is no reason to worry. Come and sit here."

"You had called me. Is there something important you wanted to talk," Meeramani asked.

"I do have something important to say. Do not send prince Samar Dev outside the kingdom for a few days without informing me. And also today Akroor Singh has invited me to his place for dinner, so I will not be available in the palace at dinner time."

"What's so important today that the commander-in-chief Akroor Singh has asked you to have dinner with him at his place," questioned Maharani Meeramani.

"He has not asked me as a commander-in-chief. He has asked me as a dear friend to join him over dinner at his place. Do you have a problem with that?" Maharana asked with a stare.

"What are you saying Maharana *ji*, why would I have a problem with your friend inviting you over dinner. But why are you asking me not to send Samar Dev outside the kingdom?"

"Nothing serious, it's just that he would be upset with all the tensions in the family. Hence, I wanted him to stay in the palace till everything is sorted out."

"Ok. Everything will happen as you say. I will take your leave now," Meeramani greeted him and walked outside his room.

Maharani Meeramani left Maharana Ranjeet Singh's room and started walking towards her room. She was thinking that Maharana *ji* doesn't look fine. It's difficult to guess what's going on in his mind? Haven't seen him like this before.

Seems like he is broken from inside, also it's not possible that he called Akroor Singh early in the morning just to ask him to have dinner together at his place. He could have asked him that during his visit to the royal courtroom. Maharana *ji* said that Akroor Singh invited him to his house, but Kaalu informed that Maharana *ji* himself called Akroor Singh and said that he will come to his place for dinner. Both these sentences are way too different. His emotional side for Samar Dev is also not usual. This means that something big is going to happen. We will have to be extremely careful rather now we will have to take care even more than ever.

Maharani called her chief maid Malini to her room and told her that something very big is going to happen. She could smell politics and negativity in the air. Please be very careful and if you anytime and anywhere feel something unusual is happening, do not hesitate to inform me immediately. Do not think that I would be resting in my room. Whatever time it may be, just inform me. Go and tell Kaushika about this, this is very important. You understood."

"Yes Maharani *ji*, I understood everything," Malini greeted Maharani and went out of the room to explain everything to the other head maid Kaushika.

Maharana Ranjeet Pratap Singh was getting ready to go to his dear friend--Akroor Singh's house. The day Akroor Singh had told him about Samar Dev, since that day Maharana could not rest. He was very upset and sad that how could his queens hide such a big thing from him. If they had told him in the beginning, things would have been easy that time, as he had no attachment to the new born. But now after so many years he loved the prince. He could not imagine the prince getting hurt even with a prong, how would he give order for his throat to be slit.

Maharana Ranjeet Singh was feeling like all his enemies, rulers around his kingdom and all those people who used to bow their heads in front of Maharana were today laughing at him. They were taunting him and saying that your reputation today was that you gave birth to a eunuch. Maharana Ranjeet Dev Pratap Singh had decided that he would not be able to tolerate if anyone raised a finger in front of him. He could not even think about that. If the news went out in public, everyone would raise a finger against him, his entire family, his throne. Even if he punished both his queens for hiding such a big thing from him then also his reputation would not remain the same like it was before. This will also bring out the entire truth. If the queens have got courage to hide the truth about their son and to argue with the king, he could not imagine what would be their next rebellious move.

Maharana Ranjeet Singh thought, starting with his queens first, then his empire, kingdom and enemies everyone would start rebelling against the wishes of the king. And he would not tolerate this. He would kill everyone, even before anyone tried to raise a finger against him also. He could not bear anyone raising their voice in front of him. He had also promised King Satyaraj Singh that his daughter princess Sukanya would marry Samar Dev. Now if they got to know the truth about Samar Dev how would Maharana make an eye contact with him?

"And my child...Samar Dev" once again Maharana's eyes got filled with tears. "He is so handsome. He looks like me. Whatever a father expects his son to be, Samar Dev is the same. He is a great warrior, a great prince, good in politics. He can become a great ruler; there is no doubt in that. He is such a kind-hearted ruler and the entire kingdom loves him. I too love him a lot; maybe I won't be able to live without him; but in order to save my family's honor and respect I will have to take this step."

"The grand empire Jairajgarh is testing me; it's asking me to pay the price of the throne. I will have to repay it. I cannot step back now, cannot embarrass myself. I cannot disrespect my throne, my ancestors and myself. If this throne wants the blood of the prince and wants to satisfy its thirst with the prince's blood and if this is the only means for its prosperity then as the ruler I will have to do so. I will have to sacrifice my son. Between a king and a father, a father will have to lose the battle. He has to make his heart strong and will have to sacrifice Samar Dev...sacrifice...sacrifice."

In the end between the battle of a father and a king, the ego of the king won and the love of a father lost. Maharana got determined, picked up his sword and headed over to Akroor Singh's home to announce his final decision on the life of prince Samar Dev Pratap Singh.

Chapter 26:
The Important Conversation between Maharani Meeramani and Commander Akroor Singh

Maharani Meeramani was standing at the window of her bedroom while staring outside in the night. She was worried. It has been a few days since Maharana Ranjeet Singh returned, but still there was no news from Kaalu, Gannu and Phoolan. What would have happened there? What conspiracy would have happened? No one informed about what all happened. How did this happen? Either they did not get the news or they were not able to know about it. But our Shiva-Jan army is not like that. They will let their throats get cut, but will not step back for Maharani's work.

Maharani Meeramani was deeply drowned in her thoughts, when the chief maid Malini came and reported, Maharani *ji*, this maid has a severe stomach ache, she wants a few days' vacation and wants some money from you for her treatment.

"Give her whatever she needs, Malini. I am worried right now," said Meeramani without even looking at her servant.

"This servant is not ready to listen, please listen to her. She is saying that she only needs help from you. It's somc women related big problem. Without telling you about it she won't leave. She wants to speak to you in privately,"said Malini.

"This is so troubling," Maharani Meeramani said in anger. The moment she saw the face of the servant in lamp's light she was astonished. It was Phoolan from Shiva-Jan sena. "Malini close the door on your way out, let me listen to this maid's problem," said Maharani Meeramani.

Malini closed the door and sat outside the room to watch over. As she left, Maharani Meeramani turned to Phoolan and asked her "What's the news, tell me fast."

"The news is really bad Maharani," said Phoolan.

"This isn't the time to puzzle me with your talks, tell me everything hastly," Maharani said.

"Maharana *ji* has made a full proof plan to kill prince Samar Dev," said Phoolan. The plot goes like this:

"Maharana *ji* has ordered his commander-in-chief Akroor Singh that day after tomorrow he will send prince Samar Dev to the jungle. He will tell him that there is sure-shot news that some people have encroached on our land and are hiding in the jungle. You find them and then kill them. Maharana will further tell him that because Akroor Singh is looking after the safety of other borders, prince Samar Dev will have to go immediately. But the main thing is that Maharana *ji* has already got to know the truth. He has also said that he does not want Samar Dev to see or meet any of his mothers, hence he will call Samar Dev late in the night tomorrow and tell him that an emergency situation has arrived and that he should leave immediately early in the morning. In this way he won't be able to meet you or tell you anything. His conspiracy plan is complete. According to the Maharana *ji*'s plan, someone who fixed by Akroor Singh will meet the prince in the jungle and will offer him a drink, which will have poison in it. The drink might kill the prince or it will leave him completely unconscious. In any case when it's late in the night, he will then slit his throat and throw the body in that part of the jungle where lions rule. In this way his plan will also succeed and no one will doubt him. Maharana *ji* does not want that his dead body should be discovered by anyone, because in that case everyone will get to know that he was a eunuch. He will tell his kingdom that prince Samar Dev was following the encroachers and he went deep inside the jungle in the area where lions live. The prince and his two soldiers were attacked by a pride of lions and they were killed. Their bodies were not found also. This way Maharana *ji* will save himself from the humility. Once the news of prince Samar Dev's death will settle, Maharana will then declare prince Rudra Dev Pratap Singh as his successor."Maharani Meeramani held her head with both her hands and she sat on the couch. Phoolan hurriedly gave her a glass of water.

After a few minutes Maharani drank the water and asked, "Who is going to kill the prince?"

For this task Maharana *ji* and army chief Akroor Singh have selected prince Samar Dev's chief soldier Sushant Singh, Phoolan replied.

"Will Akroor Singh not do this task for Maharana *ji* this time," Maharani asked in a state of shock.

"They have planned it like this because Maharana *ji* does not want to stay when the news of prince's death will come out. He said that he won't be able to face his two queens. To this concern, Akroor Singh suggested that they would go to a war and once they are back, the news of the death would have settled and also the queens would have accepted the fate. In this way no one will doubt Maharana *ji*, and also Maharana *ji* will not have to face both the queens," Phoolan told the entire truth to Maharani.

"Hmmmmn...." Maharani started thinking seriously. Suddenly Malini came inside. She was terrified. She told Maharani Meeramani that Akroor Singh's messenger has come and says that there is an emergency situation and Akroor Singh would want to talk to you privately. He is sitting in his chariot downstairs, and if you permit he would like to see you secretly in the private meeting room. This is very important.

"What is this happening Malini, my mind is getting dizzy. I am already in the middle of some very urgent and important talks and now what would Akroor Singh want to tell me."

"What would you like me to do," asked Malini.

"Tell the messenger that I have permitted Akroor Singh to come and see me in my private meeting room," said Maharani Meeramani.

Malini went out after getting the orders from Maharani

Meeramani. Maharani then turned to Phoolan and asked him to hide in the room, as they need to make a plan right away.

Maharani Meeramani calmed herself and went to the meeting room where Akroor Singh was already present. He was walking around the room in haste. He looked very worried and terrified.

As he saw Maharani Meeramani, he greeted her and said, "I apologise to disturb you at this hour. Would not have done so, if it wasn't an emergency situation."

"Akroor Singh *ji*, I am not feeling well right now. My head is in a state of turmoil. Whatever you have to say be quick and to the point," Meeramani said.

Maharana visited my house today for dinner, and then Akroor Singh told her the entire plot that they discussed to kill prince Samar Dev. He told her the exact plan that Phoolan had already told her.

Maharani was speechless. She was not able to understand what side of Akroor Singh was this. She was not able to understand why would he do such a thing and get punished by Maharana. She said, "Are you out of your mind? Do you even know what you are saying? Why would Maharana *ji* kill his own son? Why are you telling me all of this and opening yourself to Maharana's anger and punishment. You are his dear friend and the commander-in-chief of his army. Why will you become a traitor in his eyes? What is going on in your mind Akroor Singh, explain clearly."

Akroor Singh told that he had heard Maharani Ambika and Maharani Meeramani's discussion in the meeting room. He went to Maharana *ji* and told him whatever he had heard. Maharana *ji* was very upset. He called me to his room in the morning and said that he would like to have dinner at my house. During dinner, Maharana *ji* told Akroor Singh the entire plan. While talking, Akroor Singh got teary eyed. He wiped his tears in hurry. Maharani was shocked to see this side of Akroor Singh. He said he loved Samar Dev as his own son and had no clue that once he will tell Maharana the truth about Samar Dev, he would want to kill the prince.

Maharani Meeramani said, "You took such a big risk to come here and tell me all of this. Do you know if Maharana *ji* gets to know about this he can give you a death penalty."

Akroor Singh said, "I am his best friend and will not shy away in giving up my life for his sake. But I cannot let him live with the guilt of killing his own son. I want to save Samar Dev. Maharani *ji*, I want to save his life because I know Maharana *ji*. He will not be able to live with this. He might be strong from outside, but he loves his family to death. He has got blind in front of his arrogance and ego. Once he will realize what he has done he won't be able to survive. He will be very guilty later on. I am just trying to save him from this guilt. I know that he is already very sad and guilty of his step brother's death. He won't be able to survive the death of Samar Dev Singh. I want to save him from this bad deed. I respect you a lot Maharani *ji*. The way you have respected and loved both your husband's second wife Queen Ambika and her son Samar Dev, it's remarkable. I bow down to you in respect. We have to save Samar Dev, even if during this I lose my life."

"But you have promised Maharana *ji* that if you won't be able to complete any of his work, you would kill yourself. Then now that you will fail to complete this work, won't you will have to kill yourself," asked Meeramani.

"If I have to sacrifice my life for Maharana *ji* or his family, I would happily to do so. But in this case, I have made no promise to him. This work will be done by my son Sushant Singh. Maharana *ji* when explained me the entire plan, I told him that I will not be able to do this. I said to him that we should let Samar Dev's chief soldier Sushant Singh complete this task. Hence, neither has Maharana *ji* directly given any orders to Sushant Singh, nor has Sushant Singh promised to do anything for Maharana."

"What's your plan, how will we save the prince," Maharani Meeramani asked with courage.

"So the plan goes like this: Sushant Singh will arrange for a corpse and he will hide that below Samar Dev's camp in the jungle. He will disguise the prince and help him to flee. Samar Dev will have to give his clothes and ornaments to the corpse, which we will return to the Maharana *ji*. In this way, he will be confident that his plan is successful. However, I have not yet thought about where will the prince go and how will he go. You will have to plan all of that. I have come to you for this help only. I need your help for this. Also, I have no clue as to how to disclose all of this to Prince. You are the only one who can understand him. So you please let him know, where he will go and why. I and also my son Sushant, promise you that we will not let him die. Sushant Singh will lie to the Maharana *ji* about his death, as like your big brother, I can only help you this much," Akroor Singh got emotional while saying this.

"Please forgive me. I always had such wrong idea about your image in my head. But, you are so truthful and loyal. I really don't know how to thank you," said Meeramani.

"Thank you Maharani *ji*," Akroor Singh said with emotions. "The way you have taken care of this family and the entire empire, it's truly remarkable. It shows your selfless nature. We have to bring back Maharana *ji* on the right path, so I request you, because only you can do this. Please allow me to take your leave now. Now you have to take care of everything."

"Bhai *ji*(brother) please be very careful while going out. These days Maharana *ji* doesn't sleep," she said.

"Please don't worry Maharani *ji*. When Maharana *ji* had come home for dinner, I offered him some almond milk. I had added sleeping pills to that. I have an idea that he has not slept for many nights. So I had to do it. Do not worry, he will sleep the entire night and will only wake up in the morning," Akroor Singh said with a smile.

Maharani Meeramani also could not stop herself and smiled.

Now Meeramani had already thought about a plan to save Samar Dev's life. With the help of Akroor Singh it had become easy. She went to Phoolan and asked him to tell Gannu and Kaalu to go day after tomorrow and hide in our secret cave that opens in the jungle. We will take out the prince safely from there and take him to the safe room. Send one of our spies with this letter to King NeelKant in Ballabhgarh. Hurry so that he gets the letter in time. Meeramani after saying this started writing the letter.

Handing over the letter to Phoolan, Meeramani said, "Guard this letter with your life. It is important than all our lives. Hence, send only efficient Shiva-Jan soldier with this letter so that he can take care of it more than his life. That's it. Now you go. Rest we will all gather up for the meeting tomorrow night at the same place where we always meet."

As soon as Phoolan left, Maharani Meeramani called Malini and started explaining her the plan. "Go to prince Samar Dev's room and tell him that Maharani Meeramani has ordered him to dress like a maid and you will help him for that. You get her a lehnga (long skirt), dupatta (big scarf) and most importantly ask him to do a veil. Once he has disguised himself as a female, ask him to go to Maharani Meeramani's room and don't utter a word until she says him to. After you explain him all of this, hand him a pooja plate and tell him that until he will return you will be hiding in his room. Also explain him that even if Maharani Meeramani says anything to him he should not utter a word and just nod his head. Do as explained."

Malini registered every word in her brain that Maharani Meeramani told her. Prince Samar Dev too obeyed all the instructions that were given by his mother Meeramani.

Prince Samar Dev reached inside Maharani Meeramani's room. She instructed him and said Malini, lets go to Shiva-temple. He quietly started walking with her. She took Samar Dev in night to her kingdom's Shiva-temple. Once they reached the temple she instructed him to close the temple gate. Samar Dev did what she said just like a servant. He did not utter a word. Maharani Meeramani did not say a word for a few minutes and kept inspecting the temple, looking behind the walls and idols just to double check that no one was listening to their talks. Once she was convinced fully that there was no one present apart from her and Samar Dev, she instructed him to pull up his veil just a bit. Samar dev was perplexed. He was unable to understand anything; all he knew was that his mother Meeramani never utter a word without making sense. Whatever she says has a reason. She would not joke about all of this. Samar Dev blindly trusted his mother and without uttering a word lifted his veil just a bit. As soon as Maharani Meeramani saw his face, she said, listen my child now is the time when you will have to live an unknown life. I don't know when will I be able to call you back to Jairajgarh. But listen carefully because I have no time to repeat things to you."

Samar Dev bowed his head in acceptance.

Maharani Meeramani said, "Tomorrow morning Maharana *ji* will call you in his room and ask you to go to the jungle. You listen to him carefully and do not try to argue with him. Whatever he asks you to do or wherever he asks you to go, you silently agree to his order and do not try to go against him. Once you reach your camp in the jungle, order all your soldiers to go out of your camp. Tell them that you are really tired and want to rest. Once everyone goes out you look below your bed. You will find a corpse dressed up in royal clothes. You pick it up and carefully lay it on your bed and take out your ornaments and put those on the corpse. You will also find some other clothes that will help you to disguise yourself. Wear them and then leave the tent from the backside and drop a red handkerchief once you exit. You will find the handkerchief on your bed."

Maharani Meeramani further said, "Once you are out of the camp run quickly towards north. Running in that direction will take you miles away from the soldiers. When you will be running in the direction you listen carefully, you will hear the sound of falling water. This will tell you that there is a waterfall nearby. You will find few caves and tunnels there. One of the caves will have a few logs of wood and some dried flowers over them in the front. Remove logs from there and you will find matchsticks and some torches. Carefully pick up 3 or 4 torches from there and as you will leave the cave you will find a pot on your right hand side filled with oil for the torch. You dip your torches in that oil and then enter the cave from right side."

"You will find two spies hiding inside the cave- Gannu and Kaalu. One of the rocks will easily slide and from there you will find your way ahead. There will be an underpass just before you get into the cave. Handover the torches to the spies and they will lit those themselves. One spy will walk in front of you and the other will walk behind you. You will stay in between them. This cave will end at a secret room inside a building that is behind the Shiva-temple. The room is fully furnished and a secret room. No one knows about that apart from me. The spies will leave from there. Until my next instruction comes, you rest in there. Don't even try to go out of that place. One of the spies will arrange food for you. As I will get time, I will come and see you. Till then you will live like an unknown person and do not try to contact anyone, especially me."

"Should I repeat anything to you or have understood everything?" asked Maharani Meeramani.

The prince replied, "I have understood everything mother."

Maharani Meeramani said, "Now we will return the same way we came here. Rest Malini will explain you everything. You go to your bedroom and pretend to sleep, but don't sleep tonight Samar, You have to be very alert and cautious. Be ready to fight against any emergency danger also. For your safety I have appointed Shiva-Jan soldiers. They will be alert and are powerful, but then also you be very careful."

Samar Dev nodded in agreement.

Maharani Meeramani hugged Samar Dev and with teary eyes said, "Samar my child you are very precious to all of us. Please be very careful and alert and take very good care of yourself. I don't know when will we see each other next."

Prince Samar Dev touched his mother's feet and said mother you also take very good care of yourself.

Maharani Meeramani hugged him tightly and said, "Let's go now. We don't have much time with us."

Both mother and son went back to the palace in the same manner in which they had come.

Chapter 27:
The Plan to Save Samar Dev Pratap Singh

Meanwhile in Ballabhgarh, King Neelkant was asleep as it was still very early morning. One of his chief servants came into his room and said that a messenger had come who didn't disclose his reason for coming here, he only said that he had a very important message for you from your sister and would like to see you without any further delay.

King Neelkant immediately understood that the message cannot come from sister Ambika, so it must be from sister Meeramani. He ordered to send the messenger to his personal meeting room immediately and that he would join him soon.

As the King reached the meeting room, a Shiv-Jan soldier eunuch Gola was waiting for him. As the king saw him, he asked, "Gola, is everything fine?" In his reply, the messenger handed over a letter to him. The letter was from Maharani Meeramani.

The king opened the letter and started reading. While reading the letter, his face showed strong emotions. The letter was-

Greetings to King Neelkant from his younger sister Meeramani.

Dear brother, I don't have much time to write a lot. An emergency situation has emerged. Maharana*ji* has come to know the truth in a very brutal manner. He has not yet uttered a word to anyone. Though, he is completely quiet, but he is going through a tough battle inside. Resultant to which, feelings of a father have lost to that of an emperor. His ego has won. He has already planned a plot to kill Prince Samar Dev. The day you will receive this letter be prepared to leave one day after that. In the eyes of Maharana, by that time, he would have killed Samar Dev. Get here with only one small army of Shiv-Jan soldiers and an empty carriage of your queen. No one should be aware of the empty carriage except you and me.

Rest we will talk once you are here.

Your younger sister,

Meeramani

After reading the letter King Neelkant asked eunuch Gola to go to Shiv-Jan organization. "Ask the organization's chief Mungeri to get ready for day-after tomorrow, we have to leave for the kingdom of Jairajgarh and we only need a small, but fully equipped army. Apart from this, what else has Maharani Meeramani has asked you to do?"

He said."I have to reach Jairajgarh by evening because Maharani Meeramani would conduct an emergency meeting with 5 chiefs of Shiv-Jan at night," said Gola.

"Okay, once you deliver our message to the Shiv-Jan organization you leave for Jairajgarh and tell Maharani Meeramani everything will happen according her instructions," said King Neelkant and left the meeting room.

It was already night in Jairajgarh. As Maharana called Samar Dev into his room, Maharani Meeramani also came out of Lord Shiva-temple and left for the emergency meeting. As she reached inside the building all the five chiefs of Shiv-Jan, eunuch-Phoolan, Gola, Gannu, Kaalu and Chammo, were already present.

Firstly, Maharani Meeramani asked Gola if he had safely delivered the letter to her brother Neelkant and what was his message.

Gola greeted the queen and said that King Neelkant had said that everything would happen as she wished.

Maharani then turned to everyone and said that an emergency situation had arrived and everyone should listen very carefully what they have to do. She had no time to repeat.

Maharani Meeramani started telling them about her plan:

"Gannu and Kaalu- both of you start your way from the building into the secret cave and leave where it ends in the forest. Stay inside the cave and wait patiently for Samar Dev to light the torch. This will be a signal for you to bring him between yourselves. The prince will walk in between you two and from that cave bring him to the safe building in the secret furnished room."

"Phoolan and Chammo, both of you start from the building in the morning and reach the forest. Once you reach the safe place, keep a red handkerchief on his bed. Maharani handed them a red handkerchief. Then wait there till the prince reaches. After that you also merge with the army of soldiers and stand strong outside the prince's building. Once you are there, secretly tell the chief of army, Sushant Singh, that he should only start working once he sees a red handkerchief fallen behind the building, before that he cannot start, also tell him that both of you will stand outside the building as per my order."

"Once the prince reaches the building and says that he wants to rest for sometime keep in mind that only chief-Sushant Singh should enter his room. Be very careful about this thing."

"And Kaalu you deploy all the Shiv-Jan soldiers for the security of this building. They will protect the place from inside. No one from outside should get an idea about all of this.

And all of you listen to one thing, saam-daam-dand-bhed (Content, price, penalty, distinction) whatever it takes, our first aim is to protect the prince's life. If anything changes suddenly, you all can take decisions independently. Hence, your weapons will always remain with you. We want the prince to be alive at any cost. For this even if you have to slit someone's throat or kill them—do it. Think that Maharani has ordered you to do so. Now you all leave and start doing your work. Maharani shouted the slogan- Jai Shiv-Shankar... Jai Shiv-Jan!"

Everyone repeated the slogan and went ahead to do their respective duty.

Next day even before sunrise and as per his plan to kill the prince, Maharana Ranjeet Singh asked Samar Dev Pratap Singh to start walking towards the jungle with small army and its chief Sushant Singh. As per the order, the prince did not utter a word nor did he met any of his mothers.

According to Maharana's plan, he did not want to stay in his kingdom when he gets the news of prince Samar Dev's death. So he was marching towards a battle. But according to Maharani Meeramani's plan, she wanted the king to stay in his kingdom when they get the news of prince's death. She wanted the king to feel confident that his plan was successful. Maharani also wanted to see how the king would react on hearing about his son's death. She wanted to see the pain on his face. It was important for her to know if the king really cared for his son and was sad about his death or not. This was crucial for her next plan.

The entire kingdom was mourning the death of their prince Samar Dev.

Maharana Ranjeet Singh was satisfied that his plan was successful and so was Maharani Meeramani. She had already counter attacked the king's plan and knew that the prince was alive. The prince had already reached the safe building and was in the secret furnished room.

When prince Samar Dev reached inside the room, Maharani Meeramani was already there. She hugged him tightly and started crying. She then asked him that I am doing all of this just to save your life. Please have trust in me and don't ask any questions. I won't be able to answer them right now. Also, I won't be able to come here often. I am trying to send you to Kaashi. You will remain safe there. From now on you will have to live an unknown stranger's life. I have to make preparations for you to leave Jairajgarh safely also.

Maharani handed a red bag to the prince and said, "There are two books inside this, Mahabharata and Chanakya Niti. You will have ample of time to read these. These books will answer all your questions. Your time will also pass. Once you reach Kaashi keep reading these books very carefully. Till the time you are here you will get food and fruits and also there is a small Shiv-Jan army soldiers here, who will take care of your security. Do not try to leave this place once also."

After this Maharani Meeramani went back to Lord Shiva

temple and from there went back to her palace, to plan her next move.

When the entire kingdom of Jairajgarh was mourning the death of their beloved prince, Maharani Meeramani was waiting for King Neelkant to reach the kingdom and take away prince Samar Dev safely with him.

Next day King Neelkant had reached Jairajgarh with a small army of Shiv-Jan and an empty royal carriage, as was planned. As the king reached the boundary of Jairajgarh, he received a letter from Maharani Meeramani. Shiv-Jan soldiers delivered the letter. The letter said—

Greetings from sister Meeramani to brother Neelkant.

As you know the entire kingdom is mourning the death of prince Samar Dev, I would request you to please visit the Lord Shiva temple first. I would want to see you there first.

Your younger sister,
Meeramani

* * *

King Neelkant gave order to his army to start walking towards Shiva temple.

As the king Neelkant reached the temple, Maharani Meeramani came out of somewhere and closed the doors of the temple.

Queen Meeramani greeted the King Neelkant and told him the entire plan, from start to the end. She also told him that the commander-in-chief Akroor Singh and his son Sushant Singh are on their side and helping them to save prince's life. Further, she told him, "The prince is safely resting in a secret room inside a safe building. The royal carriage was brought, so that the prince could disguise himself as your queen and sit in that carriage and leave the kingdom of Jairajgarh. Once you are out of the boundary of this kingdom, send the prince to Kaashi. He will be safe there. I have got information from Akroor Singh that Maharana Ranjeet Dev Pratap Singh has his spies all over Ballabhgarh and Sambhalgarh. I will take you to Samar Dev in a few minutes. Secondly, Queen Ambika is in a state of shock. She has fainted. I am afraid of her health so you take her also along with you. Once you take her out of the boundaries of Jairajgarh, then only tell her that the prince is alive. I am pretty sure she will not be able to hide her emotions. Her face might tell the entire story to Maharana *ji*. He might know the truth then. I am really worried for her health, so we will have to disclose her that prince is alive, but tell her that she cannot meet the prince. Also do not tell her that the prince is in Kaashi. If queen Ambika gets to now that prince is in Kaashi, she would go and see him there and at this point I have no clue how many spies are there. Akroor Singh has promised that he will be calling all spies from Kashi back to Jairajgarh. But till the time, I am not confident and sure, please don't send Queen Ambika back to Jairajgarh."

"Ok Meera, I have understood the entire plan carefully,"said King Neelkant.

"Come this way brother and meet Prince Samar Dev Pratap Singh. Let us explain him the entire plan also. Do not suggest him to go to brother Rameshwar. But do tell him that whenever he sees a red flag on the terrace of Shiromani palace he should knock on the door and ask if his maternal uncle has come to see him,"she said.

Meeramani further said, "Brother Neelkant, you please take care of sister Ambika in Ballabhgarh and rest I will take care of Jairajgarh. Now when Akroor Singh has joined hands with us, it seems the entire kingdom is with us."

Listening to sister Meeramani's talks, king Neelkant got emotional and hugged his sister.

King Neelkant along with sister Maharani Meeramani went to see Samar dev. King Neelkant ordered Samar Dev to wear the clothes of a queen and asked him to disguise himself as a queen. He was also asked to hide his face with a veil. Once he disguised himself under the clothes, there will be an empty royal carriage outside the building and the prince will quietly sit inside it. Once they cross the border of Jairajgarh, King Neelkant would explain him everything. For now the prince should only obey his orders. Samar Dev greeted his mother and did as per his uncle had told him to do so. He disguised himself as a queen and crossed the border of Jairajgarh.

The border of Jairajgarh was long gone. King Neelkant and his convoy had reached a safer place. He asked his entire convoy to stop and leave Queen Ambika, her main servant Kaushika with the king. He ordered everyone else to move away from them. King Neelkant then went to Queen Ambika and tried to bring her back to conscious.

He said, "Get up sister Ambika, see, your son Samar Dev is alive. Open your eyes."

Queen Ambika was lying in her carriage unconsciously. Kaushika supported her to sit and said, "Get up queen and see prince Samar Dev is alive. Please open your eyes."

Queen Ambika opened her eyes and saw prince Samar Dev. She hugged him and started crying.

When she had gained full consciousness she asked King Neelkant if all of this is a drama. She was not able to understand anything.

King Neelkant told Queen Ambika and prince Samar Dev about the evil plans of Maharana Ranjeet Singh. Ambika was filled with anger. She was furious. On the other hand, the prince had tears in his eyes. Ambika wanted to go and confront Maharana Ranjeet Singh for his evil thoughts, but King Neelkant explained her how Queen Meeramani has saved Samar Dev's life and we should not let her sacrifice go in waste. We should wait till Queen Meeramani takes care of the situation in Jairajgarh."

King Neelkant told Samar Dev to never leave Kaashi. "We will recognize you even if you disguise yourself 100 times. Also go to a very famous Shiromani palace every now and then and check if you see a red flag on its terrace. If you see one, then knock on the door and ask anyone if your maternal uncle from Ballabhgarh has come. And then come inside. We will meet you there. Apart from that, just understand that you are all alone in Kaashi and that you are the son of Baba Vishwanath. Also remember, you will live an unknown life of a monk. Don't even go near the palace in Kaashi."

Samar Dev's face turned sad after hearing all of this. Living away from his parents and home, one could clearly see how sad he was. Then Samar Dev was explained about the rest of his travel. Two Shiv-Jan soldiers were ordered to safely leave Samar Dev to

Kaashi. Neelkant also handed him a bag that had some money and a few clothes. He told Samar Dev to change his appearance such that everyone thinks of him as a local Kaashi guy.

Everything had happened as per the plan. Queen Ambika was healthy now as she knew that her son was alive. Also, to protect his life she had understood it's better to stay away from him.

Maharani Meeramani was trying to bring back the kingdom systematically once again. She left no stone unturned in the education of her two kids. Apart from discussing about the goodwill of the kingdom, she did not like talking to Maharana. She also paid visits to Queen Ambika and her brother King Neelkant. She would console her that she would make everything fine and the kingdom would be a much happier place than it was before. Queen Ambika and King Neelkant had full faith in their sister, Meeramani. They were proud of her.

Queen Ambika was living in Sambhalgarh and was trying to cope up with the reality. She did not want to even hear Maharana Ranjeet Singh's name. She could not believe how a father could plot to kill his own son, whom he loved so much for so many years. She hated him. She would only curse him. It seemed that her curses had started to work on Maharana Ranjeet Singh.

Maharana Ranjeet Singh had started to fall in his own bad deeds. His health was deteriorating day-by-day. He used to be sad all the time. He had closed himself in a dark room and would often cry thinking about his son, Samar Dev. He had announced his younger son Rudra Dev Pratap Singh as the Prince of the kingdom. Maharani Meeramani had not objected to this as she wanted to see what was Maharana Ranjeet Singh's next plan. She could see that Maharana had already started paying for his bad deeds. But she wanted that his ego should get washed away with his tears and that his guilt would break all his arrogance.

Maharana Ranjeet Singh would cry while remembering his wife Ambika. Maharani Meeramani was so busy dealing with the work of the kingdom that she never had time to look after the king. Both her children were also very close to their mother. Only daughter Amritamani would go to his room everyday once to see if her father was doing fine. She would often ask about her mother Queen Ambika Devi. She wanted to know when would her mother return. Maharana Ranjeet Singh had no answers to her questions. He would just pat her head with teary eyes. He would often ask Maharani Meeramani about Queen Ambika Devi's return, but she would always say that she does not want to come back. You should go and try to convince her to come back to the kingdom. But Maharana Ranjeet Singh was full of guilt. He was not ready to face Queen Ambika. He thought to himself that the queen loved me with all her heart and I took her for granted and did not pay any respect to her feelings. I never reciprocated her love also. Queen Ambika always loved him selflessly, she always wanted to live by his side. But Maharana Ranjeet Singh snatched and killed her son also. It would have been better if he would have gone away with Queen Ambika and Samar Dev to some other place and left the kingdom to Rudra Dev and declare him the next king. By doing this, he would have atleast saved himself from insult and would have saved his family too.

Today, Maharana Ranjeet Singh was all alone. He was under a heavy burden of his own bad deeds. There was no one besides him to take care of him. He had no one with whom he could discuss his feelings and that would have given him some satisfaction. It's true that time changes everything. All through his life Ranjeet Singh thought he did not need anyone in his life. But his ego had waged a war against God and now he had to live under this burden.

Maharana Ranjeet Singh was now remembering his father Surya Dev Singh's words. In his whole life he never agreed to anything apart from his selfish nature, anger, ego, arrogance. He wanted that the whole world should be under his feet. First he would not love anyone,, now no one loved him. He never wanted to hear anyone, now no one was there to hear him. He would make people dread in his fear, today he was dreaded by his own loneliness. He never wanted anyone to raise their heads to him, never wanted anyone to speak in front of him. Today he wanted someone to sit with him and listen to him and talk to him, but he had no one by his side. Today he was longing for anyone to come and sit with him in this dark and lonely room that he made for himself. Due to his bad deeds and arrogance, he was now living in this dark room all alone. This darkness was killing him day-by-day. But he had brought this entire thing onto himself. He had made his life this way and now there was not any ray of light that could come inside his dark gloomy life.

Chapter 28:
Samar Dev Pratap Singh in Kashi

It was raining heavily and the storm was at its full pace in Kashi. The sun was setting down and slowly the night was getting darker and the storm at this time was terrifying. Tension prevailed in the Shiromani palace as the son of the palace, Shiromani Pandit Gopaleshwar Nath Shastri, had gone to pay a visit to Kashi's royal family of King Gangdev's wife because she was not feeling well. When king Gangdev had sent the message that the rain was light and was drizzling, he had also sent the carriage for his travel. It was not possible to avoid the order of the king, but Shiromani Palace's leader- Shiromani Pandit Rameshwar Nath Shastri was not feeling well and hence his son, Shiromani Pandit Gopaleshwar Nath Shastri, had to hurry to the palace's order..

It was long since Gopaleshwar Nath Shastri had left for the palace and the rain was pouring heavily now and also there were occasional thunderstorms. It was very difficult to track the time in this stormy weather. During all of this, Gopaleshwar Nath's son- Shiveshwar Nath, aged 8 years, was being adamant making it difficult for the entire house. The child's grandfather Rameshwar Nath was roaming in his front yard in this troubled time.

The child, Shiveshwar Nath, had a lot of reverence in Lord Shiva. His faith in the temple of Baba Vishwanath was immense.

His faith at this young age had astonished everyone. At the age of 6, he had promised that till the time he was in Varanasi, neither he would eat anything till he visited Baba Vishwanath's temple nor he would visit the temple until he had taken a bath in the holy Ganges river. Initially, no one took his promise seriously, but the child did not give up on his covenant and continued to pay regular visits to the temple twice everyday even in adverse weather conditions. But today was a different case as firstly it was stormy outside, secondly his father was not at home and lastly his grandfather was not feeling well.

The rain was pouring heavily. Shiveshwar Nath's mom, Kamala Devi, scolded him and said that whatever happens he would not step outside the house. Agreeing to his mother, he sat inside his room and did not eat a single grain of food. After failing to persuade him, the mother went to his grandfather and complained about the child.

Grandfather Rameshwar Nath Shastri went to Shiveshwar Nath and keeping the dinner plate in front of him said, "Enough of your tantrums. We all thought at first that you are being childlike and will understand as you grow old, but now the limit is crossed."

He further said, "Eat your food quietly. It's pouring heavily and the waves are rough in the holy Ganges river. He explained the child that if in this weather, he goes out and something bad happened to him, what answer would he give to his son.

Shiveshwar Nath greeted his grandfather and said his life belonged to the family and if someone ordered him then he could give up his life to them anytime. But he could not break the promise that he had made to Lord Vishwanath. He further said, till the time he was on the soil of Varanasi, he would not eat anything until he visited the holy temple. They could send him somewhere else or could kill him, but he would not give up on his promise.

After hearing to Shiveshwar's words, the grandfather was very upset and said, "Are you an avatar of 'Bhishma Pitamah' that you have taken such difficult promise."

The child smiled from within keeping a serious face. His mother, Kamala Devi, and grandmother, Leela Devi, after hearing the child, they said, whatever be the case he was a little kid and till the time he would not eat the food they too would not eat anything. They silently wept.

In the end, Rameshwar Nath had to bow down to the stubbornness of all three of them and he took his umbrella in his hand and stood up to go out. He said to kid, "Let's go fast. Get up. I don't know who will be waiting for you with doors open to Baba Vishwanath's temple."

He further said that Shiveshwar had become really stubborn and once his father was back from the palace, he would talk to him about it.

Shiveshwar got up quickly, changed his clothes and held his grandfather's finger and walked outside.

The temple was not too far from the Shiromani palace, but heavy rain and dark night had made it look dangerous. The rough water was making noises in the river. Grandfather had never seen such rough waves in the water and was afraid that the kid might not get trapped in this stormy river water. He thought to himself that Shiveshwar was the only grandchild he had and hence prayed to the Holy river and Baba Vishwanath to take care of his devotees.

Praying for their safety, both the child and his grandfather reached the wharf of the river. There was no one in the area. After all, who would risk his life in the stormy weather near the river. Shiveshwar was very happy as everyone had agreed to his demands. He thought that now he would take bath in the holy river and would then visit the temple and then would rush home to eat the delicious food that his mother had made for him. He was hungry; after all he was just a kid. He started walking down the stairs towards the river.

Seeing his hastiness on the stairs, his grandfather shouted at him to be very careful as the stairs would be slippery. He alerted him not to go far in the rough river water.

On the other hand, Shiveshwar was very excited and he started to go down the stairs very swiftly. Just as he was on the stairs, a voice startled him and someone shouted at him and said to stop at the very point where he was. Shiveshwar stopped and looked back and saw an Aghori sage walking towards him. The sage had long black hair, and was holding a kamandal in one hand and tongs in another. He had a long beard and a moustache. He kept the kamandal and tongs on the banks of the river and jumped towards Shiveshwar. He held the kid in his hands and started walking towards the temple. Shiveshwar tried to get out of his grip, but the sage was very powerful in comparison to the child. He would be at least 6 feet tall.

When the grandfather saw that the aghori sage had held the kid, he shouted that Shiveshawar was his grandchild. He yelled at him and said, "Where are you taking him? He is with me."

But it seemed as if the sage did not hear a single thing and he took the child to the temple and left him on the front yard.

The grandfather ran as fast as he could behind the sage saying that the child was his only heir and to leave him. He saw that the sage had left Shiveshwar at the front yard of the temple and he hurriedly jumped towards him.

The sage laughed at Rameshwar Nath. His face and eyes were red. Seeing this Rameshwar whispered that this sage might be under the influence of drugs.

Seeing the condition of Rameshwar, the sage turned to Shiveshwar and said to him that do you not pity to see your grandfather's condition. He said that I would help you in fulfilling your promise. As he said this he poured all the water from his kamandal onto Shiveshwar and said that now that you have taken bath in holy water go inside and visit Baba Vishwanath's temple.

Shiveshwar greeted the sage and ran inside the temple.

Rameshwar Nath was Confused and wondered who was this sage and how did he know so much about the kid. Once Shiveshwar went inside the temple, the sage turned to Rameshwar and said to get some heat from the nearby bonfire as he was all drenched in the rain. He asked him to do so else he would fall ill and would have to take his own medication.

Rameshwar looked at the face of the sage through the light of the fire. He saw a handsome young man, somewhere around 18-20 years old, and who did not look like aghori sages. He was fair and was charming and polite to talk to. Rameshwar thought to himself that this man looks as if he is from a good family and looks familiar too. He was confused as to how does this man knows so much about Shiveshwar and the family. He also thought that this sage could be

Baba Vishwanath's descent. Finally, he asked the sage, "How do you know so much about Shiveshwar and my conversation? Are you a psychic?"

Hearing this, the sage smiled and said, "Some answers come with time. Time is very powerful. It can make a king into a slave and vice-versa. One should leave a few answers to time."

Rameshwar was trying hard to read the face of the sage. He thought to himself that this man has lost his brains. Conflicting to his own thoughts, Rameshwar then realized that this sage's talks are very meaningful, his face had a glow and his body looked firm and powerful. His hands were firm and looked as if he had practiced weaponry in the past. But his face and his thoughts did not match. Is he a clueless caveman or a kidnapper? These days kidnappers are also increasing in Kashi, Rameshwar thought to himself.

As he was still juggling with these thoughts in his mind, Shiveshwar came outside the temple.

"Hey come here Shibu and take some heat from the fire," Rameshwar said to his grandson.

As Shiveshwar came closer to the fire, Rameshwar grabbed him and made him sit on his lap so that the sage could stay away from the child.

Agori sage had sensed the fear in Rameshwar's mind, he smiled.

Shiveshwar opened his fists and gave some prasad to his grandfather. He also took a piece of sweet and offered to the sage and said, "Take it, it's lord Shiva's Prasad."

Aghori sage took the Prasad with his both hands, then touched it to his forehead and started eating it.

Rameshwar was still trying to closely watch the sage's actions. He thought that the sadhu ate the prasad very nicely, hence he seemed to be from a nice family. It might be the case that someone kidnapped him and made him the aghori, Rameshwar thought.

After finishing eating his prasad, the Aghori wiped his face from his clothes properly and turned to Shiveshwar and asked him, "Tell me one thing that if you have made a promise to God, then what is the fault of your family, is it ok to trouble them?"

"I understand this completely, but I am a small kid and my

family would not allow me to go out alone," Shiveshwar replied with seriousness.

Listen Shiveshwar, Aghori said to him, "Just like if someone else eats the food, it will not benefit another, mentally or physically, similarly prayers have their own place too. If you bring trouble to other people because you have to pray, you will get no blessings from God. Troubling any human being makes god sad. Being stubborn will not lead you to get blessings from God. Sacrificing our likes, interests, ego and all such things that bring sadness to other people is what God wants from us. God speaks the language of love, hate is the language of evil."

"Do you see the snake that goes around Lord Shiva's neck, why do you think he has the snake?," Shiveshwar and grandfather, both nodded and said no.

Aghori smiled on this reaction and said, "That's because Lord Shiva wanted to send a message to the world that everyone had to be respected in this world. If you were respectful towards a snake, even he won't bite you. A snake would not bite you unless you trouble him. He would only bite you in self-defense or when he is hungry. If one has a full appetite no will trouble anyone, or else human will also bite other human, meaning that a human can also kill another human. Upper class, middle-class, all of these things are society's bad customs which can make anyone adverse. Lord Shiva, by keeping the snake around his neck, tells the world that anyone with worst behavior also can be calmed down with love. Even birds and animals can understand the language of love. The human unlike animals and birds has the power to speak so he/she should speak with love. If he does not then he/she is evil."

Aghori sage further continued, "God is present everywhere, the five elements that constitute the human body, he is in all those elements also. This means that God is within us. Prayers and worshipping God hold an important place in our lives. It is good to have faith in God, but ritualism does not bring us closer to God and stubbornness is totally wrong. Every soul has God in them, you can see Baba Vishwanath everywhere. Learn to be disciplined not stubborn."

"But Baba," asked Shiveshwar, "If I make a promise and

doesn't stick to it, won't the God get angry with me and punish me?"

Aghori sage took a deep breath and said, "If you make a mistake, do your parents punish you or are happy to punish you?"

Shiveshwar nodded saying "No".

"So, in the same way, God who has created this world and whose we are his children, he can never feel good or can be happy by punishing us, this can only be the case with evil," said Aghori.

"God only knows how to love. We get pain due to our own bad deeds. God has given us freedom to do our deeds; we are responsible to face repercussions of our good/bad deeds."

Along with Shiveshwar, grandfather Rameshwar Nath was also listening all of this very seriously. He thought to himself that maybe this is Lord Krishna disguised as Aghori sage and explaining the Holy book Gita. His voice was peaceful to the ears. It had almost stopped raining and was drizzling, but Rameshwar Nath had lost track of time. He was enjoying himself in the deep knowledge of Aghori sage.

"Now answer one more question," Aghori sage asked Shiveshwar, "The water that you get at home, where does it come from?"

"It comes from the holy Ganges river that flows locally, whole of Kashi get its water from the river, the pure and holy river provides water for everyone," Shiveshwar replied showing that he knew everything.

Aghori sage smiled and asked another question, "Tell me if someone takes out the water from the Ganges river in any vessel, will the water become pure or impure?"

Shiveshwar replied thoughtfully, "Water from the holy river Ganges is so pure that it eradicates all impurities, hence it cannot be impure. It purifies everyone so it will obviously purify anyone."

"That's a correct answer, you are an intelligent boy, but even after being so wise how come you don't understand that the water that comes in your house flows from the holy river Ganges, so can you not take bath and be pure at home only. Do you really think there was a need to trouble your family in this stormy night. You could have taken bath in your home in the holy water and become pure."

Shiveshwar nodded in agreement. His grandfather Rameshwar Nath was deeply into Aghori sage's wise talks.

"Ok, now answer another question," said Aghori sage, "You are such a deep devotee of Baba Vishwanath. If you have to go out of Kashi, will you forget him?"

Shiveshwar nodded in disagreement.

Hmmnnn.. Aghori sage took a deep breath. He said, "Dear Shiveshwar, like I have said before, if you have to live anywhere, do anything in life and have God inside your heart and his teachings inside your brain, you will see that the entire planet has Lord Shiva in it and every element/human being too has Lord Shiva in it, everybody is a Shiva-Jan (Lord Shiva people)"

"Shiva-Jan???, Baba?" Shiveshwar asked in surprise. Rameshwar Nath also looked at Aghori sage in surprise.

"Yes Shiva-Jan," Aghori sage said, "Shiva-Jan means people of Lord Shiva and everyone has a special place be that God-Goddess, birds-animals, humans, insects, none of the living objects have been left untouched. This is the true worship of Lord Shiva, Baba Vishwanath's true devotee will no longer have to go miles to search for God. You can find God in your own hearts. If you do service for anyone that will mean that you did that for God. If you want to observe a fast, then sacrifice your food and give it to someone who is hungry. This is called selfless service. Staying hungry will only hurt you physically it will not bring you closer to God."

Aghori sage took out two books from his bag. The first one was holy book "Bhagvat Gita". He gave that book to Shiveshwar and said- this book would be worshiped in every era.

"There is no age of reading this book. At times people at the age of 40s or 50s do not get wisdom after reading this book, and sometimes a child can gain all the knowledge after reading this book and become learned. This book will be worshipped in every era and till the time this universe exists. You will find answers to all your questions in this book. If you have any trouble in your life, you will find the solution to it in this book. The second book is Chanakya Niti. This book is a mixture of politics and power of worship. This book has knowledge of Niti *gyaan* (Policy knowledge)."

"No friend is greater than books. They not only give you

knowledge, but also offer it for free. No costs attached. They do not even ask for any fees. . Rest everything in this world has a price attached to it, even our breath,"the sage added.

The rain had stopped completely, the sky was getting clear and the stars were peaking through.

Aghori sage said, "You must go home now. Your mother must be waiting for you. Also, you must be hungry. My talks can only feed your brain, but not your stomach."

Grandfather Rameshwar stood up and all his fear had disappeared by now. He bowed down before the sage and asked him to accompany them to their home and have dinner.

He said, "Though you look younger than my son, your knowledge is greater than my grandfather. No one gets respect if he or she is older, only a knowledgeable is respected and this you have made so clear today. Please oblige us and come to our home with us."

The little boy Shiveshwar touched both the books to his forehead and then touched the feet of Aghori sage.

Aghori sage touched his forehead and said, "I bless you that you achieve your greatest aim, be sure that everyone gets what they deserve and always keep trying to fulfill your aim, don't lose heart until you find your goal."

Shiveshwar requested the sadhu to accompany him to his house and have dinner.

"This is not the right time. I will surely visit you one day, but not today," said Aghori sage.

"It's getting late in night, you both go home," said Aghori sage and started saying, "bum-bum bhole" and went into another direction.

Rameshwar Nath shouted and said, "Baba atleast tell us your name, how will we search for you in future?"

Aghori turned towards them and smiled and said, what difference does a name makes? God recognizes us through our deeds, not by our names. You call me whatever name you like. He said this and started walking again.

Rameshwar Nath mumbled that who is this secret Aghori sage. He seemed familiar to the Kshatriya caste. Isn't he the one?

Due to his long hair and beard and moustache I couldn't see his face clearly, but his talks are familiar and his thoughts are fiery. Whatever be the case he is the child of Maharani Meeramani... But he had died......

Samar Dev Pratap Singh, Rameshwar Nath shouted in the dark making a guess, and asked him, "Is your mother's name Meeramani Devi?"

Aghori sadhu froze where he was standing. He turned back and walked fast towards Rameshwar and said, "Don't take the name uncle, I am living as unknown habitants."

"Is he truly that person," Rameshwar thought to himself in surprise. "But what is he doing here? They say that he died while fighting with his enemies in the jungle. Is he alive, and if so then why is he not living in his kingdom? How is this possible? He is living here and his entire kingdom is mourning his death. Does Ranjeet Singh know the truth..."

"Now you cannot say no," Rameshwar smiled. "Now you will have to agree to have dinner with us. You have to come to our house and tell me the entire story, then I will know what the truth is and empty stomach we won't be able to talk so long."

"So come Prince Samar Dev Pratap Singh, you are welcome to your uncle's house," Rameshwar smiled and said.

Aghori Samar Dev Pratap Singh did not show any resistance, but he did requested that he was living as an unknown habitant and he should not be called out by his real name or his family's name. He further said he had come here hiding from everyone and hence he had to change his entire look.

"Until our conversation is over, I request you to please not tell your family about my real identity. If my mother and uncle had felt that I would have been safe at your house, they would have sent me to you. If they haven't done so and have told me to live an unknown life, then they would have known that I was safe like this," said Samar Dev.

Hmmmnnn... Rameshwar sighed deeply. "This means that your father Maharana Ranjeet Singh has played his game,"said Rameshwar Nath in a serious tone.

He now understood the seriousness of the situation.

He took Aghori sage along with him to his house.

On his way, he thought that sister Meeramani and Neelkant knew this that for Samar Dev only three places were safe- Virat Singh's palace in Sambhalgarh, NeelKaant's palace in Ballabhgarh and our Shiromani palace in Kashi. But, if they have thought thoroughly on all three places and decided none of these were safe for him that means he was in grave danger.

Thinking about this Rameshwar said to Samar Dev that there was a door in the back lane that opened inside a clinic. You wait for me there. I would hide you there and get you the food and then would talk in detail.

"Ok uncle,"said Samar Dev and turned to the back lane.

Both of them finished their food. Rameshwar had already instructed his family that someone special was coming to get the medicine and hence he should not be disturbed at all. This was not the first time that Rameshwar had done this. Every time someone special would come to get the medicine, Rameshwar would stay in the hospital and hence his family would treat this as a normal incident.

Rameshwar asked Samar Dev, For how long have you been staying in Kashi?"

"It's been almost more than a year now. Neelkant uncle had said no matter what, do not leave Kashi. Even if you change your appearance hundred times we will be able to recognize you. He had also said that whatever news I hear about them, I should not contact them, whenever it would be possible they would contact me. Apart from that I always had to believe that I am Baba Vishwanath's child and I am here to learn how to live a saint's life,"he said. While saying all this, his face turned gloomy and it clearly showed how much he missed being away from home and from his parents. He said, "Whatever was told to me, I just kept on following those instructions."

"Did your Neelkant uncle told you how will they contact you?" Rameshwar asked.

"Yes," replied Samar Dev. "He had asked me to go to a very famous Shiromani palace every now and then and check if you see a red flag on its terrace. If you see one, then knock on the door and ask anyone if your uncle from Ballabhgadh has come. And then come inside. We will meet you there."

Rameshwar said in a serious tone, "First of all if Meeramani has sent you here and has asked you to live an unknown life then that means there is a grave danger to your life, hence we will not talk about that today. Do keep this in mind that Meeramani will never do anything without any reason and you mean to her more than her life, hence she will not do any injustice to you. She is a very devoted and dutiful person and can do anything to save her kingdom and can sacrifice her life in order to save yours. If you are alive today, it's because of Meeramani. Doubting her means doubting God, so never let your trust fade for her."

"Uncle," Samar Dev took a deep breath and said, "I always obey my mother. Her wish is my command and I fulfill it with all my heart. Even if she would ask me to cut my throat, I would not doubt her."

"Dear child," Rameshwar said with love, "Now tell me how do you know so much about us? Initially I thought that this Aghori sage is psychic." Rameshwar laughed and further said, "But now I know that this is not the case."

Samar Dev smiled and told Rameshawar, "When your son Gopaleshwar was leaving the house, I was standing behind your house to stay away from the heavy rain. Your son took some medicines from the clinic and as he was stepping out, the rain started to pour heavily. I ran towards the clinic boundary to save myself from the heavy rains. Your son saw me and offered me to stay in his clinic till the rain stops and then eat food. In this way, his clinic would be secure too. I was standing near the window that opened inside your house when I heard Shiveshwar's stubbornness to go out in the rain. I knew that his father was not in the house and thought to follow you both as your son had given me a shelter, so I would return the favor and take care of those who helped me. Hence, I followed you and the rest of the story you know."

Rameshwar Nath said, "Till the time your mother does not call you back or I get to know the entire story you stay with us and first thing in the morning we will change your look to that of a saint." He further said, "Rather get up with the first ray of the sun and reach the holy river Ganges and I will meet you there. We will change your look entirely and then you can enter my house with a new identity as my cousin sister's son. In this way no one will doubt you and you can live peacefully. You need not wander here and there and I will take full care of your security. One more thing, from now on your name is Dev Kumar Shashtri. You are one of my extended family relative and have come here to learn medicine from me. Your mother's name is Shyaamla and your father's name is Govardhandas Shastri and you have come from Bithoor. Your real identity will be known only to my son Gopaleshwar, also he is very excited to meet you and your family. He would be very happy to see that you are here, hence it makes no point to hide anything from him. Also, he is elder to you. Both of you can live like friends or brothers. Also, you start living with Gopaleshwar and start learning medicine from him. Study never goes in waste. Also, this will keep you busy and rest I will talk to Gopaleshwar."

"Ok uncle, I will do as you say. I will meet you in the morning at the holy river Ganges. I will take your leave now,"he bowed down before Rameshwar Nath and left quickly.

Once Samar Dev left, Rameshwar started thinking deeply.

Next morning, according to the plan Samar Dev entered the Shiromani palace disguised as Dev Kumar Shastri. Rameshwar had already confided his truth with Gopaleshwar Nath and had instructed him to teach medicine to Samar Dev.

Gradually time passed on and Rameshwar Nath sent one of his main Shiva-Jan soldiers to King Neelkant and told him that Samar Dev is protected by him and is currently disguised as Dev Kumar Shastri-his cousin sister's son. He sent the message not to worry for him. He is learning medicine and till the danger goes away or they send him any message, Samar Dev would live securely like his own son. Maharani Meeramani in Jairajgharh, King Neelkant and Queen Ambika in Ballabhgadh, were satisfied with this arrangement.

Chapter 29:
The Atonement of Maharana Ranjeet Dev Pratap Singh

In the great empire Jairajgharh, Maharana Ranjeet Singh started suffering from illness and he would sit quietly in his room while looking out through one of the windows. He would not visit the royal court and would not participate in any of the royal duties. He was visited by the royal doctor a few hours ago, who told Maharana Ranjeet Singh and Maharani Meeramani that his illness is not physical, rather it's mental. If Maharana divert his mind to something else, his health would become better.

Maharani Meeramani asked her commander-in-chief, Akroor Singh, to join her in a private meeting room. As she entered the room the chief stood up and greeted her.

Maharani Meeramani requested the chief to sit down and told him that he was called in the room as a member of the family and not as the commander-in-chief.

Commander-in-chief, Akroor Singh was astonished, and said in surprise, "Family member?"

"Yes brother, you are one of the dearest friends of Maharana *ji* and so you are a family member. Friends are also a part of the family, rather more than that. You and the Maharana *Ji* know each other since your childhood. You have always protected him from all the problems and have sheltered him from any concerns. It would be right to say that you have never let Maharana *ji* face any problem, rather you have taken the problem onto yourself and saved him."

Akroor Singh said, "Now that you have considered me as a part of your family you need not go into any formalities to praise my relationship with Maharana *ji*. By calling me as your brother, you have made this relationship more strong. Please say whatever you have in your mind and without any hesitation, I promise you that I will respect all your wishes."

"So whatever I am going to say, I will be very frank and honest with you. Now that we all are a part of the family, please do not feel bad about anything. Akroor *ji*, though you have always been the best friend to Maharana *Ji*, but this relationship looks more like that of an employer-employee. I don't see any kind of friendship in this relation,"said Meeramani.

Listening to this Akroor Singh looked serious.

Looking at his serious face, Maharani Meeramani continued the talk and said, "You have always protected Maharana *ji*, but has there been any time when you felt that he was at a fault and you could correct him. Have you ever tried making him understand that he was at a fault? If you think that whatever the King has done till date is correct then there is no point to discuss all of this, but for once also do you feel that he has committed some mistakes and do you have the liberty to confront him about that."

"Yes, I do feel this," Akroor Singh said.

"I have felt the same once when Samar Dev's death was being plotted and you came and told me everything rather going to your trusted friend, Maharana Ranjeet Singh. But you had no courage to go and talk to him directly. If you would have wanted, you could have gone up to him and made him understand. But if one is afraid to talk or discuss or confront the other person that relationship is no more than a formal relationship of an employer-employee. If a King behaves like this with everyone around him then for him no relationship is greater than himself be it husband-wife, parent-child or friend. He sees every relation like that of an employer and employee. Neither Maharana Ranjeet Singh has respected any of his relationships nor has he given any importance to any relationship, hence his relations have also no respect for him today. I ask you Akroor Singh *ji*, do you really don't care that in today's time Maharana *ji* has secluded himself from everything and has lost himself in the darkness. If you have felt so, you would have gone to him and would have tried talking to him and help him bring out of this darkness. But you are not at fault here, you are also tired of such a friend who only acts as a dictator and does not respect his relationships. You have stopped thinking about him. Whenever he gives you a command, you follow it just like an employee. You don't think about your friendship with him."

"But in all of this Maharana Ranjeet Singh is himself at fault. Whoever tried to be a friend to him tried to suggest him something or tried making him understand anything, he took all of those as his enemies. He felt that all those people only wanted to act superior in front of him and he would not allow anyone to surpass him, as according to him he is the greatest of all. A person who cannot take constructive criticism from his relations or friends, he does not deserve to be in any relation. Such a person cannot become a good human being, father, son or husband. He can never have a successful relationship because a successful relation can have criticism and praise together. Such people only want to listen to sugar-coated talks of others and consider that as eternal truth," she added.

"Do you agree with my thoughts Akroor Singh *ji*," asked Maharani Meeramani.

"Yes, I completely agree with what all you have just said," Akroor Singh replied with tears in his eyes.

"So go to his room and talk to him and bring him out of this loneliness and darkness that has surrounded him completely. Show him some light. Doing this will also help you understand that does the Maharana *ji* really consider you as his best friend. If you do not get this feeling then do not ever talk to him about your friendship. Just act as his commander-in-chief," said Meeramani.

"I have understood what you are trying to say. You have opened my eyes Maharani Meeramani. You have made me realize that a friendship does not mean helping your friend in tough times only. I thank you enough and now I will go and try to talk to my friend," Akroor Singh said.

"You have my permission Akroor Singh *ji*, may God give

you success. If Maharana *ji* understands your thoughts he will once again come on the right path, whereas, if he fails to understand you and acts with arrogance he will be responsible for his own good-bad deeds. The person who does not understand his well-wishers, even God cannot help such a person," said Meeramani.

Commander-in-chief Akroor Singh got up with determination. He greeted Meeramani and walked towards Maharana Ranjeet Singh's room.

A servant entered maharana Ranjeet Singh's room and announced that his best-friend Akroor Singh wanted to see him.

"Is he not a commander-in-chief now, how are you introducing him to me," said Maharana Ranjeet Singh with anger.

The servant got petrified. He said Akroor Singh had asked him to say all of this to you. He had also said that he had not come for any work as he wanted to meet you as his best friend and.......

"Why have you stopped, continue and tell me what he said further?" asked Maharana Ranjeet Singh.

"He further instructed the servants to go and let the cook know that Maharana *ji*'s best friend was here, so he should prepare some delicious recipes and send them directly to Maharana *ji*'s bedroom,"servant said.

"Both the friends will sit together and eat the food," said Akroor Singh with a smile as he entered his room.

"Come, come Akroor,"said Maharana Ranjeet Singh with joy. "How come you are in my room today and what new role are you talking about to my servants. They are confused."

"You are right, this is a new role," said Akroor Singh with a smile. "I never thought that we are best friends and friends do not need permission to see each other. I am your commander-in-chief only in the royal palace; outside the palace I am your childhood friend. What startles me is that I never gave a thought on this."

"So, how come after so many years this thought crossed your mind," Ranjeet Singh smiled and asked.

"Today I went to Mahishasurmardini's temple and I got this thought from there," Akroor Singh replied with a smile. Akroor Singh looked at servant and instructed him to let the cook know that he has to prepare delicious food for the two friends.

The servant looked at Maharana *ji* for his permission, Maharana smiled, and said him to go out and the servant greeted him and left the room.

"It feels great to see you Akroor Singh, that too as a friend. I was waiting for someone to come to me and pull me out of this loneliness,"said Maharana.

"Friend please get ready and groom yourself because we will go out after dinner and we will talk while we walk in the night,"said Akroor Singh.

"Ok, will you take revenge for the entire life in today's night only," said Maharana Ranjeet Singh with a smile.

Akroor Singh thought to himself that if Maharani Meeramani didn't speak to him about this, he would have never come to meet Maharana as a friend and he would have been in the state of loneliness.

Both the friends had the delicious food and then Akroor Singh gave Maharana a warm shawl and said, "It's cold outside, take this or else you will feel cold."

Both the friends, while talking, reached to Sapt-Sangma lake and then Akroor Singh said, "Do you remember how we used to climb the rocks in the water and slip on them and how we used to hide and sneak into the jungles."

"Can't those days come back again?" said Maharana Ranjeet Singh in a sad tone. "They were such great days of childhood, full of happiness and today nothing is left in life apart from loneliness."

"This life is very ruthless," said Akroor Singh with a serious face. "The time that is gone never comes back. Whatever good and bad deeds we have committed, we have to wait for the repercussions and we both will face it together. Whatever we have done in life we have done it together, so why only you will sit in a lonely room and punish yourself. We are in this together,"said Akroor Singh.

"What are you trying to say Akroor Singh? Kindly explain in detail," asked Maharana Ranjeet Singh.

"Do you remember when I had killed Jagjeet Singh? I knew it beforehand that he had not killed your mother, brother or sister. I purposely did not tell you the truth because you were so deeply immersed in the sadness. I did not want to increase your pain and disclose that you were responsible for your family's death. That would have broken you down. They all were killed because of the poisonous snakes that we had brought. Also, you were always looking forward to get away with your stepbrother, hence I did not tell you the truth. I always thought by doing this I am fulfilling my duty as a friend. It was only after a few years that I realized that by lying to you I have not done any good rather I have spoiled this friendship. I knew that you are going to commit a mistake or a crime, but I never tried to correct you, rather I let you walk down that path and supported you,"said Akroor Singh.

He further said, "When you did not want any of your queens to conceive, then too I supported you and showed you a wrong path and in-turn took the curse of the entire womankind. Queen Vaishali committed suicide because of this and Queen Ambika was so close to committing suicide. If you were cursed by them so was I and, more than you I have got the curse. Queen Ambika gave birth to a homosexual child. This wasn't her fault. She had no clue what politics we had played. I went to Shiromani and asked him about the medication that we were giving to the queens. He told me that the medication completely stops functioning after 6 months of stopping it. Queen Ambika might have stopped the medication due to some reason and in the meanwhile she got pregnant and gave birth to a sexually incapable child. The child could have got any other problems, but God purposely punished us by giving us a physically challenged child. Queen Ambika was not at all her fault, she had no idea of our wrongdoings, neither did the poor child Samar Dev knew anything about this. Sometimes, I think people trusted us so much and we took them for granted and cheated on them. We could not even take care of our own relations. Your third Queen Meeramani is such a well-cultured and truly devoted wife. She fulfills all her duties and then too we are cheating her with our evil plans."

Akroor Singh could not control himself and started crying. When he looked up he saw Maharana Ranjeet Singh was crying too. Both cried on each other's shoulders for long.

Maharana Ranjeet Singh said, "I have not slept since many nights. I cannot see myself in the mirror. I hate myself when I see my reflection in the mirror. Our bad deeds have started taking an ugly shape. I am afraid to go to sleep. As I close my eyes, I sometimes see my step mother Manorama Devi, sometimes I see my stepbrother Jagjeet, his cousin brother Khushaal Singh. Sometimes I see Queen Vaishali, my father Surya Dev Pratap Singh and sometimes my son…my only son Samar Dev Pratap Singh. All of them cry, howl and ask me that why I killed them. I could have thrown them out of the kingdom, but why did I took their life from them. Its true Akroor Singh, people who commit wrong deeds can never sleep properly. Their own soul keeps on cursing them. In today's time, I am afraid of my shadow and myself. What should we do now Akroor? What should we do now?"

Maharana Ranjeet Singh kept crying with his hands on his face.

"Let's go to Mahishasurmardini temple. We will ask for forgiveness by lying in the feet of God," said Akroor Singh while wiping off his tears. "Let's go there."

"I went to the temple of Mahishasurmardini, and when I was inside the temple, I saw that Queen Vaishali was sitting in the lap and the goddess was looking at me with anger and it seemed that she tried to kill me with a sword. I ran from there and came back. I then went to the temple of Lord Shiva thinking that I would get forgiveness from him, but there also I saw that Lord Shiva picked up his trident to kill me as I have committed so many crimes on innocent people," said Maharana Ranjeet Singh.

Akroor Singh said that even if God was not willing to forgive us then there was only one way left.

"We should seek forgiveness from all those against whom we committed crime. If they are alive we should go in front of them and ask for their mercy and if they are dead then we should look up in the sky and plead them to forgive us. Maybe in this way God can also hear us and forgive us. Then we might be able to reduce the burden of our bad deeds," said Akroor Singh.

"You are absolutely right Akroor. First thing in the morning tomorrow let's go to Ballabhgarh because I have done wrong with Queen Ambika. She loved me so much and I cheated on her. I snatched away her child from her. Once we are back I will then go to

Meeramani and ask her to forgive me. You know Akroor, Maharani Meeramani is the one whom I loved the most. But I was always afraid of her qualities, personality and beauty. I always thought that she might overtake my throne with her competent nature. I made her Maharani only to control her. I gave her all the worldly pleasures so that she always felt indebted of me. I never appreciated her qualities. I could not recognize her true capabilities. I always played politics in my relationships and according to my father, Maharaja, Maharana Surya Dev Pratap Singh, this is the reason I am all alone today," said Maharana.

"You go with your true heart and ask for forgiveness and I am sure that Maharani Meeramani will forgive you. She is a very wise woman and loves you a lot. I am also sure that Queen Ambika will also forgive you as she loves you a lot too," said Akroor Singh, while consoling Maharana.

Maharana Ranjeet Singh said, "You please make all preparations for our travel to Ballabhgarh tomorrow. I don't want to delay anymore."

Next morning, Maharana Ranjeet Singh along with his commander-in-chief Akroor Singh and a few soldiers left for Balabhgarh to seek forgiveness from Queen Ambika and to bring her back to the palace.

Adverse to their thoughts, Queen Ambika refused to see him. Even after attempts made by King Neelkant, the queen did not agree and said, the day Maharana Ranjeet Singh plotted against her son and killed him, the queen also considered herself dead for Maharana. She said if anyone tried to pressurize her to see Maharana, she would drink poison and kill herself, but under no circumstances she would see the face of her son's murderer.

Maharana Ranjeet Singh tried to make a last attempt and knelt down in front of Queen Ambika's bedroom. He joined both his hands and started crying and pleaded the queen to forgive him and come back to the palace with him.

Queen Ambika did not open the door. She started crying and said, "You are asking for forgiveness today. You always said that this word is not in your vocabulary. You never forgave anyone in your life. Then why do you expect people to forgive you? You will get punished. God will punish you. Not only punish, he will destroy you. Just like Queen Vaishali's curse, now my curse is also added to your life. Till now you never respected anyone, but today no woman think that you are worthy of her. You are a selfish, cruel and hypocrite."

"Next if you say that you are a changed man now. So just like you, I am a changed woman too. I have no more feeling of love for you. There is only one feeling left, that of hate. Do you hear what I say. I have become mature now, no one can fool me now. I have become intelligent and people, who become extremely intelligent, have only the feeling of hate in their heart and they do politics in the relationships. Now this is all what is left in me too. I hate you enough to even see your face."

Maharana Ranjeet Singh walked away from her room. He had understood by now that he would only get punished for his bad deeds. One of the losses he suffered was in the form of Queen Ambika. The lady who loved him with all her heart and who trusted him blindly, now hated him. He had lost her love forever.

When Maharana Ranjeet Singh reached Jairajgarh, it was already dark. Maharani Meeramani was not in the palace. She had gone to the Lord Shiva temple to offer her evening prayers. Maharana's soul was in deep pain. He too went to the temple to take blessings. Maharani Meeramani was sitting in front of Lord Shiva's idol and had lit a lamp. The light of the lamp was reflecting the jewel that was enthroned in the forehead of Lord Shiva and it's reflection was glorifying the face of Meeramani, who was deeply into her prayers. Her eyes were closed. She was looking like a goddess. Maharana knelt before her with his hands joined and as she opened her eyes, she saw Maharana Ranjeet Singh.

"Maharana *ji* you are back? Did you get Ambika *Jiji* with you as well?," she asked.

"No, she did not come. She even refused to see my face. She did not want to see an evil soul like me," said Maharana. He further told the the entire story to Meeramani that what happened at Queen Ambika's maternal palace.

He said, "Meera, I am a broken man and feel extremely lonely. Please help me. I join hands and plead you to please offer me support. I don't feel like eating, drinking, going out. I cannot sleep also. Please help me in getting forgiveness. I ask you today to please help me. Please explain me how to atone for my sins."

Maharana Ranjeet Singh started crying like a baby and in his sorrow he hugged Maharani Meeramani. He cried for a long time. Once he calmed down, Meeramani offered him panchaamitra (holy water mix with milk) that she had offered to Lord Shiva. In the dim light of the temple, Meeramani saw Maharana and realized that he had become weak. She thought of telling him the truth. But just then she stopped herself and realized that he had not fully atoned to his bad deeds. Maharana still needed to speak about his deeds in front of the God, then only his atonement would be complete.

"Maharana *ji* one can atone once he accepts all his wrong doings. You should ask for forgiveness to all those, whose soul you have hurted with your wrong doings. If they are not alive then ask God to forgive you. God loves all of his beings. He will surely forgive you,"said Meeramani.

Meeramani explained to Maharaana Ranjeet Singh. She said, "This is Lord Shiva. He is the God of the Gods. Though, he already knows all your deeds, not only from this life, but also from your previous lives. He is well aware of all your good and bad deeds. When a person commits a crime, he thinks that the God is not watching him. Also, the man thinks that once you got to the temple all your wrong doings will be automatically cancelled. But this is not the case. Everyone gets what they truly deserve according to their good or bad deeds. When something good happens in his life, the man forgets to thank God. But when something bad happens, the man blames God for it. The man never looks within himself. When he gets hurt, that is the time he realizes what others must have felt when he hurted them."

"Maharana *ji* you please say whatever is in your heart. Speak the truth and accept all your wrong doings. We are all children in front of God. No one is rich, poor, good or bad. Everyone is equal in his eyes. Your royalty, expensive jewellery, and throne, nothing will please him. Ask for forgiveness with all honesty and he will surely forgive you. I don't know if God will forgive you, but one thing is for sure that you will feel light hearted once you say whatever is in your heart."

Maharaana Ranjeet Singh was heart-broken after hearing what Meeramani said. He started crying and said, "I am an offender. I am an offender of Queen Vaishali. I never loved her like a husband and gave her some medication due to which she could not conceive. I then blamed her to be incapable of childbirth. I left her to die minute-by-minute. I always considered women a thing for pleasure. I never respected them or their feelings. In the same manner, I am an offender to Queen Ambika. My marriage with her was that of love. But I still never loved her. Ambika loved me with all her heart. She respected me like a God. But, I didn't do the same to her. I gave her wrong medication, so that she also could not give birth. I never thought she deserved me. Though, now I know the truth that I don't deserve the selfless love that she gave me."

Maharana Ranjeet Singh was in a very sad state of mind. He cried and said that I killed my cousin brother and his cousin brother, and I killed many innocent people. I killed my own son. I did all of this just to satisfy my ego. My ego was so big that it made me blind. I married you because I wanted you to give birth to my child. But before you, Ambika conceived and gave birth to a eunuch child. When I heard this news, I could not control my anger and killed the child. I killed the child whom you loved so much, Ambika also loved him so much, and I loved him too. But in front of an egoistic and arrogant Maharana, a father lost the battle.

"Also, I am an offender to you Meeramani. I loved you a lot, but I could not give you the respect you deserved. I always considered woman as a thing for pleasure. Please forgive me Meera...Forgive me from your heart....Accept me...Meera, please forgive me. I am very lonely and I am in desperate need of love today. Please pity on me and show me some love. You are such a great devotee of Lord Shiva, if you want God will also forgive me.... Happiness will be back in our lives. Everything will come back in our lives," he said while cried.

"What did you say? Everything will come back to you. Happiness will come back to your life," Meeramani said with disregard. "Who will come back to you? Will your cousin brother come back to you? Will Queen Vaishali come back to you or will

Queen Ambika come back to you and love you the way she loved you before? Will your son Samar Dev Pratap Singh come back to you, will your step mother come back to you? Please tell me what all do you think would come back to you?"asked Meeramani with anger.

"What do you think Maharana *ji*," Meeramani said in a harsh tone that, "Prince Samar Dev did not deserve your throne? He was a very skilled warrior, he had the knowledge of politics and cultural traditions. What was he missing? Whatever qualities were needed for this throne he had them. The only thing he missed out was that he could never enjoy a married life. And that is too personal. Pick up old cases and read them. So many bachelor kings have ruled their kingdoms successfully. If only a man is incapable of marriage and starting a family, can he not do anything in his life? Does a eunuch have no brain or heart or blood? Does he have no skin? All of these social stigmas are not made by God. Toxic people, who have dirty and corrupt minds, make such social cultures. These people abuse human life and also abuse the values that are given by God. Just like people behave with a eunuch person, can they behave the same with a celibate? Try and kill the all celibates for they too abstain from marriage and its pleasure, Meeramani said sarcastically. It will be a disaster if one tries to kill them. You cannot even touch a celibate or a saint. Physical weakness is not a crime. We should at least give them a chance to prove themselves. What sorrow you're facing to be away from your child, can be clearly seen on your face today? Every parent cries when they are away from their children be it a eunuch or a normal child. For a parent, child is a child. Nothing more matters to them. Taking away a child from his or her parents is a grave crime. Such crimes are not even forgiven by God."

Meeramani took a deep breath and said, "I had made Samar Dev Pratap Singh such a confident man that he could have taken care of this throne and kingdom in the best possible manner. I made him realize that it is not wrong to be a eunuch. If you are given great education and correct guidance then nothing can stop you in achieving success. You tell me Maharana *ji*, don't you think he was capable enough to take care of this throne. Till the time you had no clue about his physical weakness, you always praised him and once you got to know the truth, he became a loser in your eyes. If you did not want him to be a King, you could have let him know this, why did you kill him? Being a father, how could you kill your own son," Meeramani shouted in distress.

"Why did you take away a son from his mother? Who gave you this right? And now after all this, you expect me to forgive you and give you the love you need. How can you get love when you never loved anyone in your life? I never loved you. We only had one relationship and that was only physical. My true love is only for Lord Shiva. Love is connected to the soul only. My body only has these expensive clothes on it. My soul is that of a monk. My entire love is only for Lord Shiva. This is what human religion is. You should be a doer of good deeds and your soul should be like that of a monk. This entire planet is like a war land where the only purpose of your soul should be to try to do good deeds. In this entire universe all souls are connected to Lord Shiva. Once the body is destroyed, the soul amalgamates into Lord Shiva. This is the eternal truth."

Meeramani took a deep breath and said, "Just because if someone loves me, I cannot give up my love for Lord Shiva. I don't need your love in my life. Your love is full of selfish motives, cruel intentions, politics and now even Ambika *jiji* understood this. Hence, she rejected your love for her."

"You always thought that this woman does not deserve you or another woman does not deserve you. But did you ever looked inside yourself and realized that do you deserve any woman in your life? Thinking of woman as only a sex object is such a horrible and degraded thinking. And you think such a person can get respect anywhere. Love is a sacrifice. Love should not be demanding rather it should be giving. If you feel so, then join me and become a monk. You will have to raise your mental and physical standards to come to my level. I cannot degrade to your level."

Maharaana Ranjeet Singh was stunned. He was on the ground dumbfounded. All these years, he never respected these women in his life. Thought of them only for his physical pleasures and today all these women made him realize his true worth. They all rejected him and made him believe that he never deserved any of them.

Maharani Meeramani left him is this state and walked out of the temple. Maharana Ranjeet Singh kept his hands on his face and started hitting his head on the Shivalinga. He kept on repeating that God please punish me...I don't want forgiveness...I don't want love...I just want punishment.... grave punishment!!!

Maharaana Ranjeet Singh fainted on the Shivalinga. Akroor Singh was watching and listening all of this from outside the temple. He ran inside and took Maharana Ranjeet in his arms and prayed to God that you forgive so many poisonous and dangerous snakes and tie them to your neck. Please forgive us also. He begged to God to give them one change to show their remorse. He stood up and took a nearby vessel and poured all the water from the vessel onto Maharana Ranjeet Singh. Maharaana came back to his senses and saw Akroor Singh chanting and praying- Om Namah Shivaya... Om Namah Shivaya... Om Namah Shivaya. Seeing him chanting the mantra, Maharaana also started chanting the same.

The entire temple was filled with their chanting- Om Namah Shivaya... Om Namah Shivaya... Om Namah Shivaya.... This was their way of showing that they were guilty.

God had crushed their egos and arrogance once again. He (Lord Shiva) made them realize that he (Lord Shiva) was the only supreme power of the entire universe. The cruel intentions of their souls had washed out by their tears and only one chant was echoing there-

Om Namah Shivaya...
Om Namah Shivaya...
Om Namah Shivaya...

Chapter 30: The Divine Throne of Maharani Meeramani

The royal priest suggested an auspicious time for the coronation of Prince Rudra Dev Pratap Singh. The occasion was after fifteen days. Maharani Meeramani had sought permission from Maharana Ranjeet Singh to go to Ballabhgarh because she wanted to convince Queen Ambika and bring her along to Jairajgarh so that she could bless her son on his coronation.

Upon reaching Ballabhgarh, Queen Meeramani familiarised King Neelkant and Queen Ambika of the entire situation. King Neelkant was overwhelmed hearing the condition of Maharana Ranjeet Singh. Maharani Meeramani told them that the exile of Samar Dev Pratap Singh was now over and that's why his uncle, Neelkant, and mother, Queen Ambika, should get him from Kashi themselves and reach the palace at the auspicious time along with Samar Dev. Besides, she also invited Shiromani Pandit Rameshwar Nath Shastri. Meeramani had written a letter to Pandit Rameshwar at that time.

The entire grand empire Jairajgarh was decorated on the occasion of the coronation of the prince. The day of the coronation had arrived, but Queen Ambika hadn't arrived as yet. Maharana Ranjeet Singh asked why Queen Ambika had not come and Meeramani assured him that Ambika *jiji* had promised her that she would reach at the auspicious time to bless her son. Maharana Ranjeet Singh was reassured upon hearing her reply.

Maharana Ranjeet Singh was missing Queen Ambika on that auspicious day and was unable to defocus from the face of his son, Samar Dev Pratap Singh, who was asking him, "Father Maharaja, what was my fault? Answer me, Father Maharaja, why was I not worth the throne of Maharana?" Maharana Ranjeet Singh was getting emotional now.

The curse of his stepmother, Manorama Devi, was echoing in his mind, "Even you would face the pain of separation from your child." And the teaching of his father that, "We cannot run away from our deeds; we all have to face the consequences of it. I have told you the mistakes I have committed in my life, so that you don't repeat them. When you would have children, you would understand that all children are equal before his father. This is a horrendous face of politics. Here, virtue and sin walk together, and most of the times, it is the sin which wins in pride. The politics in relationships is the most dangerous of all as here, even if you win, you lose. Relations are formed and nurtured with only love. The relations made out of politics only leave you alone. Time will tell what and which politics this throne of Maharana will teach you"

Then, Meeramani entered his room and snapped him out of his deep thoughts. She greeted upon entering and this surprised Maharana.

"What is the matter, Maharana *ji*, that you didn't even notice me entering the room?" Meeramani asked.

Maharana said with a grieving heart, "Today, I was remembering the preaching, which I have never respected in my life, given by my father, Surya Dev Pratap Singh. I wish I had paid attention to what he said. My throne could also have been the Brahma-sinhaasan (Divine Throne) today.

"Brahma-sinhaasan (Divine Throne)???... Can you tell me more about this?" Meeramani asked in surprise.

Maharana told Meeramani about the entire life story of his father, Maharana Surya Dev, and all his teachings. Maharani Meeramani listened to it carefully and made a promise to herself. Then, she asked Maharana to proceed towards the royal court palace.

Maharana Ranjeet reached the royal court palace along with Meeramani, his daughter, Amritamani and prince, Rudra Dev Pratap Singh. Meeramani had got the entire palace and the empire decorated under her supervision. Maharani Meeramani and Maharana Ranjeet Singh claimed their thrones. The throne of Queen Ambika was lying vacant; Princess Amritamani claimed her throne.

The royal priests asked Maharana Ranjeet, “Maharana *ji*, allow us to begin with the prayers. The auspicious time has begun.”

“But Queen Ambika hasn’t arrived yet. Could we wait for a little more time?” Maharana Ranjeet was getting restless.

The chief minister, Shambhoo Singh, said, “Maharana *ji*, it is not good to let go the auspicious time; we have received the message that Queen Ambika has entered the boundary of Jairajgarh along with her brother, King Neelkant. Commander Akroor Singh has gone himself to receive them; they would be here any moment.”

Maharana Ranjeet was now content and he gestured the priests to start the prayers.

Maharana Ranjeet vacated his throne and kept his ancestors sword in a tray. Then, he kept his crown in another tray. He did this as the priests would purify the things before the new Maharana would claim them. All these things were a legacy of the ancestors and every new Maharana bows before them and pledges before claiming them.

Firstly, the proceedings to purify the crown began. The royal priests continued to recite mantras, while Maharana Ranjeet Singh sprinkled holy Ganges water on it and applied sandalwood *tilak* on it. Then, he blessed it by sprinkling rice and flowers over it. Simialrly, the sword of Maharana was purified and later his throne.

Then, the priests invited the new Maharana to claim the throne.

Prince Rudra Dev Pratap Singh got up from his Prince seat and progressed towards the throne. At the same time, the chariot of Queen Ambika stopped at the entrance of the palace and she started to progress towards the palace.

Rudra Dev had bowed before the throne and was almost

about to sit on it when Meeramani loudly roared, "Stop, Prince Rudra Dev Pratap Singh, stop right there!" Rudra Dev stopped as his mother's instructions were his command. Everybody was staring at Meeramani in surprise.

The priest said, "Maharani sa, the auspicious time is passing; why are you stopping him from sitting on the throne?"

Meeramani answered, "Only a worthy person can claim the throne."

"So, is Prince Rudra Dev not worthy enough, Maharani sa?" the priest asked in surprise.

"No!" Everybody was shocked listening to Meeramani when she continued, "Prince Rudra Dev is yet to complete his studies to be able to claim the throne. He hasn't received Brahma-*gyaan* (Divine knowledge) yet and he cannot do justice with the throne as yet. He cannot make the throne into Brahma-sinhaasan (Divine Throne) without Brahma-*gyaan* (Divine knowledge)!"

"Brahma-*gyaan* (Divine knowledge) and Brahma-sinhaasan, what are these, Maharani sa?" all the senior officials asked.

Maharani Meeramani continued, "I would impart Brahma-*gyaan* (Divine knowledge) to the new Maharana before he claims the royal throne of the Maharana and this Brahma-*gyaan* was given by ex-Maharana of the grand empire Jairajgarh, Maharana Surya Dev Pratap Singh."

"So, you want to impart Bramha-*gyaan* to Prince Rudra Dev first?" the chief minister, Shambhoo Dev, asked.

"Rudra Dev would get this knowledge when he would be worthy to claim the throne," Meeramani answered.

Maharana Ranjeet was looking at everything in a state of shock. He asked, "Then who is worthy to sit on the throne if not him? Who would claim the throne after me? Answer me, Meeramani."

"The person, who is worthy of claiming the throne, and it is the prince of the grand empire Jairajgarh, and our first son Samar Dev Pratap Singh," Meeramani announced.

Meeramani pointed and everyone turned their faces where she pointed.

Maharana Ranjeet was left astonished when he saw Queen

Ambika walking proudly and she was followed by her son, Samar Dev Pratap Singh. He was accompined by his uncles, King Neelkant on the right, and Shiromani Pandit Rameshwar on the left. They were all led by Commander Akroor Singh.

Prince Samar Dev was walking with proud and Maharana Ranjeet Singh was being pulled towards the ground with embarrassment. Maharani Meeramani gestured him and he touched his father's feet and asked him, "Are you alright, father Maharaja? I have given you so much grief, but nothing was in my hands." All the courtiers were happy thinking Samar Dev would be telling about his fake death, but the venomous remark behind it had now created a space in the mind of Maharana Ranjeet Singh. Then, Samar progresses at the back to bow before his mother. Meeramani hugs him in return.

Everybody was surprised, but happy also and started cheering for Samar Dev. Maharani Meeramani calls Maharana Ranjeet Singh behind the curtains where Queen Ambika was present. Maharana Ranjeet was very happy, but was also carrying the weight of embarrassment. He walks to the back of the curtains exhaustedly.

Maharani Meeramani told Maharana Ranjeet that the time to tell everyone the truth has come. "You have two options – either keep the crown and give the throne to Samar Dev because he is worthy of it and has also proved himself or tell the world about the truth of him being a eunuch as he has proved to the world that in order to be successful in any task, being a eunuch is never a hindrance."

Maharana could never agree to the second option as all his sins would come out in the open and thus he decided to make Samar Dev sit on the throne.

Before Prince Samar claimed the throne, Meeramani asked him, "Stop, Samar Dev, I would give the new Maharana Brahma-*gyaan* before you claim the throne and this Brahma-*gyaan* was given by ex-Maharana of the grand empire Jairajgarh, Maharana Surya Dev Pratap Singh."

"I am ready, mother. All your commands would be followed," Samar Dev bowed before her.

"Brahma-*gyaan* (Divine knowledge)" and "Brahma-sinhaasan(Divine Throne)"

"Brahma-*gyaan* (Divine knowledge)": Maharani Meeramani explained, "Whatever rules, guidelines or laws are made by the king are never followed by him. Pride takes birth in him the moment he claims the throne. He puts all the laws made by him on his progeny and starts to exploit them, but now, this wouldn't happen.

Now, the throne of Jairajgarh would become Brahma-sinhaasan (Divine Throne) and would be ruled as per the ethics.

"Brahma-sinhaasan is a throne ruled by God Brahma himself. The rules of the God goes like, "All the rules and laws made by the person, who claims the throne, should be in the favor of the progeny because the king is a representative of God. The progeny believes that whatever law he would make, would be in the favor of them and would follow all those rules himself first. A king represents God and the progeny expects pure justice from him.

"Brahma-sinhaasan (Divine Throne)": The most intoxicating substance is power; the desire to own the throne is intoxicating; the power to rule over everyone is intoxicating. When the whole world starts bowing before you, you start forgetting yourself. The intoxication of power rides on a man's head that he forgets that he is challenging the power of God. He starts crushing and trampling over everyone and starts imposing his decisions on others; this is the time when he doesn't realize that he has made his pride his God. When a person makes his pride as his God, it should understand that he has challenged God for a war. Now, if the war is with God, humans can never win. Gradually, he starts losing all his relations in the mania of pride and, in the end, is left empty-handed. This is the day of not his physical death but the death of his soul. So, in order to make sure that you never have a war with God, it is important to keep your pride under control. Otherwise, everything will be destroyed and you'd be left all alone.

The throne of Maharana is a symbol of superpower, and if you won't use this power ethically, then it will overpower you to lead to some devastating misuse. Make the royal throne as the "divine throne" and rule it as per the ethics. If you live according to the ethics, your acts will be pure and when your acts will be pure, God's blessings will always be with you.

"From this day, a Maharana would claim the throne only after pledging on Brahma -sinhaasan and Brahma-*gyaan* and he would have to prove his credibilities in order to claim the throne," Meeramani announced.

Prince Samar dev bowed before her and said, "I am making two pledge while claiming the throne of the grand empire Jairajgarh."

My first pledge is that I would not marry in my entire life and the education of the coming princes would be according to principles of Maharani Meeramani, so that he would claim the "Brahma-sinhaasan" of Maharana only after claiming the entire "Brahma-*gyaan.*

My second pledge is that there would introduce another army in the already existing great army called as "Shiva-Jan sena". This would be an expert unit and I would supervise this myself. In our empire, all the officials would be hired according to their capabilities. They would not be discriminated on the basis of caste, creed, color or looks, etc. One more announcement is that the building behind the Shiva temple would be made into a medical centre supervised by my uncle's son, Shiromani Pandit Gangeshwar Nath Shastri and he would live in Jairajgarh with his family. The important soldiers in our Shiva sena, who have acquired important knowledge in medicine, would assist Gopaleshwar Nath in this task. This building would be called as "Shiromani Medical Building.

Bless me, all of you, so that I could run the Brahma-sinhaasan ethically and would guard all the good deeds.

Jai Shiva Shankar! Jai Shiva Jan!"

All the priests started blowing the conch shells and the old Maharana, Ranjeet Dev Pratap Singh, did the coronation of the new Maharana, Samar Dev, and made him sit on the throne. He also made him wear the crown and gifted him the sword. He tearfully sprinkled rice and flowers over him and said, "Congratulations to the grand empire Jairajgarh on getting its new "Maharana". Long live the new Maharana!"

The conch shells were blown and flowers were being sprinkled on him from all over, while everyone cheered, "Long live Maharana Samar Dev Pratap Singh! Long live Maharana Samar Dev Pratap Singh!"

Maharana Samar Dev stood up to make an important announcement, "My respected and progeny, the great ideals of my mother and Maharani Meeramani have made me claim the throne of Maharana and I accept this position in their honor. When I have kept the respect of the promise of my one mother Meeramani, then it is my duty to keep the respect of the promise to my mother, Queen Ambika. The arms of my father, Ranjeet Dev Pratap Singh, are still powerful enough to do justice with all of you. He has been the Maharana of the royal throne, but now he would be called as the Maharana of the Brahma-sinhaasan and having pledged on the Brahma-*gyaan*, he would once again take the empire to new heights. He would be the Maharana of this Brahma-sinhaasan till his last breath; this is the wish of my mother, Queen Ambika.

I would impart training to my younger brother, Prince Rudra Dev Pratap Singh, so that the grand empire Jairajgarh and the Brahma-sinhaasan could get a worthy Maharana after my father. The names of my father and my grandfather would be written in golden letters in the history. However, this *gyaan*(knowledge) has been brought to practice by my mother and the Maharani of Jairajgarh, Meeramani. Her great thoughts and sacrifice would be given as example by the generations to come. That's why this *gyaan* would be mentioned as "The Brahma-*gyaan* of Meeramani" in golden letters in the pages of history and this throne of Maharana would also be called as "The Brahma-sinhaasan of Maharani Meeramani".

I, Samar Dev Pratap Singh, by the blessings of my mothers would spread the knowledge on equality of human rights through my Shiva-Jan Sena so that its benefit is not limited to Jairajgarh and its nearby states, but to all the corners of the world. My sword would be raised to only destroy sinners and unethicals. I would always be ready to protect everyone's rights and build a healthy society. I pledge to serve you all and not rule you. Jai Shiva Shankar! Jai Shiva Jan!"

Then, Samar Dev invited his father to claim the throne

with all the due respect and also requested his mother, Maharani Meeramani, to make him pledge on the "Brahma-*gyaan*."

With the Brahma-*gyaan* of Meeramani, Maharana Ranjeet Singh had once again claimed the Brahma-sinhaasan of Meeramani. With this began a new era in Jairajgarh where the king was not full of pride, but credibilities. He was there to serve to the progeny; he wanted to not rule the heads, but hearts of everyone. Here, a person got his rights not on the basis of his caste or creed, but on humanity, the humanity which has been created by God. Here, the right to live with pride wasn't snatched away because of his shortcomings. Society didn't ostracise him for his deformities. Society do not have any right to separate a child from his parents because of his deformities and force him to become what he didn't want to become. Nobody has any control over the child to be born, neither his parents nor of the child if he will be a boy, a girl or eunuch. We would have change the mentality of society that if a part of a human being is deformed, he is not entirely incapable. Thoughts like these taint the thoughts of humanity. Every religion teaches man to love other human beings; even God doesn't allow hatred. Making the deformity of a person a source of entertainment is a cheap and unethical task.

Maharani Meeramani and her son, Samar dev, had taken the first step in the creation of a healthy society. The Maharana throne of Jairajgarh had been converted into Brahma-sinhaasan (The Divine Throne), which was ruled by the current king, Maharana Ranjeet Singh, ethically and while guarding all the good-deeds as he had attained Bramha-*gyaan* through his wife, Meeramani.

Maharana Ranjeet Singh kissed on the forehead of his son, Samar Dev, and blessed him to achieve his aims and asked for apology with folded hands.

He then kissed the forehead of Prince Rudra Dev and blessed him. He later blessed his daughter Amritamani and told her, "Daughter, follow the ideals of your mother and always try to make the empire prosperous no matter where you go after marriage. A woman is never weak and can never be. She is Mahishasurmardini and I bow before her."

Maharana Ranjeet then progressed towards the Lord Shiva temple with his family as the new Maharana. He lit a lamp along with his two wives and three children. He kept the first lamp in front of Lord Shiva. The reflection from the lamp fell on Lord Shiva and the precious stone on his third eye shined. Its entire reflection fell on the face of Maharana Ranjeet Singh and he got bathed in light. He said, "Wow, Lord Shiva! You have bathed a sinner like me in your light. Now, I am also a Shiva jan, I am also a Shiva Jan!

Jai Shiva Shankar! Jai Shiva Jan!

The dawn of a new era had set in the grand empire Jairajgarh and this was an auspicious beginning.

Om Namah Shivaya!
Om Namah Shivaya!
Om Namah Shivaya!

About the Author

Meenakshi was born on December 27, 1972, in New Delhi. She now lives in Gurugram, Haryana, with her husband and a daughter. Graduated from Jesus and Mary College (Delhi University) in 1994, she got married in 1997. Despite being an Interior designer, she preferred to be a house wife, and invests her lone time in reading (literature, history, spiritual) and writing (poetry and novels). She is a supporter of Indian culture and has a great faith in God and Karma

"The Divine Throne of Maharani Meeramani" is the first fictional social novel of Meenakshi Verma, in which she has raised the question of respect and rights of the 'Eunuchs' along with equal rights of all. She has not only raised the questions, but also tried to suggest solutions to society.